Dark
Vengeance

VOL. 2

READ HOW KERRY'S STORY BEGAN IN:

Dark
Vengeance
VOL. 1

Dark Vengeance

VOL. 2

WINTER · SPRING

JEFF MARIOTTE

SIMON PULSE

New York London Toronto Sydney New Delhi

This book is a work of fiction. Any references to historical events, real people, or real locales are used fictitiously. Other names, characters, places, and incidents are the product of the author's imagination, and any resemblance to actual events or locales or persons, living or dead, is entirely coincidental.

SIMON PULSE

An imprint of Simon & Schuster Children's Publishing Division

1230 Avenue of the Americas, New York, NY 10020

This Simon Pulse paperback edition May 2012

Winter copyright © 2005 by Jeff Mariotte

Spring copyright © 2005 by Jeff Mariotte

SIMON PULSE and colophon are registered trademarks of Simon & Schuster, Inc.

For information about special discounts for bulk purchases, please contact Simon & Schuster Special Sales at 1-866-506-1949 or business@simonandschuster.com.

The Simon & Schuster Speakers Bureau can bring authors to your live event. For more information or to book an event contact the Simon & Schuster Speakers Bureau at 1-866-248-3049 or visit our website at www.simonspeakers.com.

Designed by Mike Rosamilia

The text of this book was set in Adobe Garamond Pro.

Manufactured in the United States of America

2 4 6 8 10 9 7 5 3 1

Library of Congress Control Number 2011921810

ISBN 978-1-4424-2976-5

ISBN 978-1-4424-3626-8 (eBook)

These titles were previously published individually by Simon Pulse.

FOR MARYELIZABETH . . . START TO FINISH

Huge thanks go out to many people for their help, friendship, and support during the life of these books. Some were mentioned in Volume 1, but the author would also like to mention Amy Black, Faith Hochhalter, Alice Speilburg, Rebecca Lovatt, and Alex Bennett.

Contents

WINTER

Kerry Profitt's diary, November 24

I am ready to run.

Not that I brought much with me to Mother Blessing's that I need to take away, but there are a few things—my old red-checked tennies, a couple of sweatshirts and some jeans I've grown attached to, my stash of cash, this laptop, BoBo the clown doll, and some of Daniel's journals—that I don't want to leave behind.

By now I know my way through the Swamp, so I'm not that concerned about provisions for the trip—no need to weigh myself down with energy bars or anything. But when I leave here this time, I'm never coming back. I don't want to forget anything that I might want later.

And, truth? I don't want to leave anything that Mother Blessing might be able to use to track me down.

But by the time I threw the few things I want to take into a duffel bag, Mother Blessing came out of her room and started wheeling around the house, slamming doors and cursing and shouting out—certainly for my benefit—things like "I can't believe what a liar that Season Howe is!"

I was hoping to get out of the house before she emerged from seclusion, so I'd be gone well before she knew I was missing. Because, let's face it, Thanksgiving hadn't exactly turned out like I'd planned. The groceries I had bought were still in my van—the turkey no doubt well thawed by now—at Edgar Brandvold's place, but Edgar had been murdered. I thought by Season Howe, since she seems to make a habit of killing people I know, including Daniel Blessing, Mother Blessing's son and the man I loved. But now everything I thought I knew about Mother Blessing and Season has been turned upside down, with the new information that Season is apparently Mother's mother. And, according to Season, there are other things Mother Blessing hasn't told me as well, which feed into certain questions I have run up against. Such as, which one was really the mega-destructo queen who trashed Slocumb, Virginia, three hundred years ago?

Confusion reigns. All I know for sure is that nothing is for sure. Maybe Mother Blessing killed Edgar to make me think Season had done it. Maybe Mother Blessing destroyed Slocumb and then sent her sons—Abraham and Daniel, both now deceased at Season's hands—after Season, to hide her own guilt.

Almost certainly Mother Blessing has been less than honest with me. And also almost certainly, she knows that since our confrontation with Season I am suspicious of her. The combination, it seems to me, is a dangerous one, which is why I really want to get gone.

But now she's banging around the house, and if I leave my room she'll see me. I'm trying to wait her out, hoping she'll give up and go to bed, and then I can scram.

The Great Dismal Swamp at night isn't exactly my favorite place. Dark, full of bugs and gators and snakes and the occasional bear. But right now, it beats the heck out of staying in this house an instant longer than I absolutely have to.

More later.
K.

1

Mother Blessing's door slammed again.

She'd been doing this for an hour—coming out of her room, rolling around the halls, the rubber wheels of her scooter squeaking on hardwood floors, then going back in. Slamming doors like an eight-year-old throwing a tantrum.

Except most eight-year-olds weren't potentially lethal.

Is she in for the night this time? Kerry wondered. *Or just for a couple of minutes?*

The answer could, literally, be that proverbial matter of life and death.

Gotta get out of here gotta get out of here gotta get out ...

The door opened. Wheels squeaked. Barely breathing,

Kerry closed her laptop and listened. Mother Blessing had stopped shouting so much, but she was muttering something under her breath that Kerry couldn't make out. Panic gripped Kerry for a moment—the scooter was coming all the way down the hall to the guest room, the room in which Kerry had spent much of the autumn, learning magic at Mother Blessing's side. Given what had transpired earlier—Season Howe informing Kerry, in front of Mother Blessing, that most of what she had been told about the mutual history of the two witches was wrong—Kerry couldn't help feeling that Mother Blessing would not be in a jovial mood when next they met.

Kerry had power. She knew that now. She had learned well, and magic seemed to come naturally to her.

But she was nowhere near Mother Blessing's level. If the old witch decided that it would be advantageous now to just take Kerry out, there would be little Kerry could do to dissuade her.

She held her breath for several seconds, but then the scooter's wheels squeaked again as Mother Blessing turned away from her door. Kerry heard the door to Mother Blessing's room open, and then slam shut again.

Is she working up her courage? Kerry thought. *Why? What kind of threat could I be to her?*

Sounds from Mother Blessing's room filtered down the hallway to her. They could have been the sounds of Mother Blessing preparing for bed—it was past ten now, her typical bedtime—but rain still hammered the roof, and it was hard to be sure.

Kerry waited another half hour. The minutes dragged by like days, weeks. Finally the noises from Mother Blessing's room died out.

Kerry was convinced that if she stayed, tomorrow would bring a confrontation with the old witch that she would probably not survive. She had successfully dodged it for tonight, probably because Mother Blessing herself was so weakened from the afternoon's magical battle with Season that she hadn't wanted to force the issue.

By morning Mother Blessing would have regained her strength. She would want to discuss the things Season had said—a discussion that would lead inexorably to Kerry's concerns that she had been lied to since arriving at the cabin in the Swamp earlier in the fall. If Kerry lived long enough, she would most likely accuse Mother Blessing of having lied to her own sons as well—of sending them off to kill a witch they didn't even know was their grandmother.

If Kerry was to get another day older, she had to leave tonight.

She had been ready for hours now, but she waited still longer. She wanted Mother Blessing to be deeply asleep. The old house's floors could creak when she walked across them, and the last thing she wanted was for Mother Blessing to wake up and find her on her way out. That would precipitate the very confrontation Kerry was trying to avoid.

Every minute was torture, every tick of the guest room wall clock agonizing. She almost took out her laptop to write some more in her journal, but then stopped herself. She wanted to be alert, aware, in case Mother Blessing woke up. Losing herself in her diaries was a distraction she couldn't afford. She couldn't even pace, for fear that her steps would wake the witch whose house she shared.

Midnight passed. *The witching hour,* she thought. Except for Mother Blessing, who, witch or no, almost always slept right through it.

But then, I guess I'm a witch too, now. Not as skilled and practiced as Mother Blessing or Season Howe. But if being a witch is defined by doing witchcraft, then I am one. So I can observe the witching hour all by my lonesome.

She waited, and let Mother Blessing sleep.

When the clock ticked over to twelve thirty, Kerry decided she had waited long enough. Her bag was already packed. She tied her long black hair back with a leather thong, pulled a coat from the closet, wrapped it around herself against the cold and rain she knew were waiting outside in the dark, and opened her door. Her room was at the end of a hallway, and she had to go past Mother Blessing's room to get out of the house. She stepped as lightly as she could manage, holding the duffel away from her body so it didn't rub against her jeans. In her other hand she carried boots, which she would only pull on when she was at the door.

She had almost made it when Mother Blessing's bedroom door opened, spilling light, and her scooter nosed out into the hall. Kerry's heart leapt into her throat as she spun around to see Mother Blessing glaring at her over her oxygen mask. The woman's breathing was labored, her voice muffled when she spoke.

"Where are y'all goin'?"

This was precisely what Kerry had hoped to avoid. She hadn't wanted a confrontation or a scene. She simply wanted to vanish, as she had from Northwestern University when she had decided that she wanted to come here, to the Swamp, to have Mother Blessing teach her magic so she could take revenge on Season Howe.

That worked out great, huh? she thought.

Now, facing Mother Blessing's glare, Kerry delivered the line she'd been practicing. "I'm . . . uh . . . going after Season," she said. "She can't be too far away yet."

Mother Blessing just stared, her breathing Darth Vader–esque through the mask.

"You've taught me a lot," Kerry went on. Her mind screamed at her to *shut up, already!* but her mouth didn't comply. "I think it's time to move on, though. Got to stay on Season's trail until I can kill her."

Mother Blessing stared. Finally she spoke again. "I don't think that's a good idea."

"Yeah, well, I kind of do," Kerry returned, defiance starting to rise in her. "So, thanks a lot and all, but I've got to get going."

"No."

Obviously conversation wasn't a good idea. Kerry dropped the duffel, tugged on her boots, picked it up again. Another glance at Mother Blessing, who was rolling in her direction now, her mouth scowling behind the oxygen mask, and Kerry stepped out the door.

"No!" she heard Mother Blessing cry behind her.

Kerry slammed the door and ran through driving rain to the shallow-bottomed skiff Mother Blessing kept for traveling out of the Swamp. She hurled the duffel in, pushed it off the bank, climbed in, and shoved the oars into the oarlocks. As she started to row, she glanced back toward the house—which always looked like a tumbledown old trapper's cabin from the outside—and saw Mother Blessing silhouetted in the doorway, her arms raised in the air.

That, she thought, terrified, *is not good.*

But with strength that came from working hard around the Swamp for weeks, she dipped the oars into the murky water and pulled.

It was impossible to tell where the water ended and the trees began, and just as hard to know where the tops of the trees merged with the sky. Moonlight filtered through only in rare spots. Trees were a wall of black against black. The toads, crickets, night birds, the rare and piercing howl of a bobcat, were all but drowned out by the pounding rain and the occasional crack of thunder, adding to Kerry's confusion and disorientation.

At this moment, however, she was more concerned with steering the shallow boat between the trees and not grounding it than with direction. She needed to find her way through the honeycomb of canals and creeks to someplace where she could catch a ride far away from here, but it wouldn't do her any good to get away from Mother Blessing if she killed herself trying. Since she wasn't sure who had killed Edgar Brandvold, or why—and since she had told Mother Blessing that she'd left the minivan at his place when she arrived and found Edgar murdered—she didn't want to risk going back there. Mother Blessing had not been happy about her leaving, and if she were going to try to stop Kerry—or to send her simulacra to do that—the van would be the obvious place to start.

A flash of lightning momentarily illuminated a barricade of tree trunks right before her. Kerry put her oars to water and pulled backward, trying to brake herself, to lessen the impact of imminent collision. At what she figured was the last moment, she raised an oar and thrust it out before her to stave off the bank. She felt the oar hit the bank, felt the boat stop in the water just before it rammed.

But when she tried to lower the oar to the water again, something held it fast. She yanked at it, but to no avail. Whatever had her oar wasn't letting go—and, she realized, it was drawing her in toward the bank.

Simulacra? Kerry wondered. If she'd just snagged it on something, she would be able to free it, she was certain. She had a flashlight with her but hadn't bothered to use it, since it would have meant taking a hand off the oars. Now, though, she released the stuck oar and grabbed for the flashlight at the top of her duffel bag. She drew it out and flicked it on.

Something had her oar, all right, but it wasn't one of Mother Blessing's manufactured men. It was a bald cypress root sticking out from the bank. It had wound itself three times around the end of the oar and was waving it like a magician with a wand.

Kerry knew the root could not have grabbed the oar like that without help. Mother Blessing was trying to stop her—and using the Swamp to do it!

While she watched, another root snaked toward her. She ducked away from its grasp. It came again, and she bashed it with the flashlight.

That wouldn't hold it for long. She clicked off the light and jammed it back into the duffel, zipping the bag closed to keep out the rain. With her remaining oar—no way would she be able to fight the tree for the other one, not while it had dozens of roots that might attack her—she pulled hard against the water, alternating sides of the skiff to keep on an even course.

She was only a few yards away from where she'd lost her oar when she felt something damp brush her face. *A spiderweb,* she thought, *or some low-hanging Spanish moss.* Either was possible here. She swiped at it with one hand—and it snaked around her wrist, pulling tighter as she tried to tug away.

Kerry screamed and yanked her arm. Whatever it was—she thought she felt leaves on it, like a vine of some kind—wouldn't let go. She swung at it with the oar but couldn't break its grip. It started to lift her up out of the boat.

Panic threatened to overtake her as she struggled against the vine. Another one wrapped around her waist and tightened there, like a belt cinching up. Her free right hand dropped to her own belt, but the knife she wore sometimes in the Swamp wasn't there, and she remembered tossing it into the duffel when she'd packed.

When the next vine looped around her throat, she thought it was all over. It closed tightly on her, cutting off her airway. By now she was mostly out of the skiff, could feel with her feet that it was drifting away from her.

Which was when she remembered that she was a witch too.

A kind of calm settled over Kerry's racing mind. Mother Blessing was turning the Swamp against her through magic. But she wasn't the only magic-user around. She had taught Kerry quite a few tricks—but more important, she had taught her philosophies and systems. She may not have known a specific spell to free herself from living vines, but that didn't mean she was defenseless.

With her throat closed off and one hand out of commission, speaking the Old Tongue and making the correct gestures was tricky. But she managed to croak out the word *"Kalaksit!"* and curl the fingers of her free hand toward her palm while splaying the thumb out. White flame crackled at her fingertips. She felt herself relaxing even more, letting the now-familiar sensation wash over her—the thrill of power, the rush of magic. Raindrops sizzled against her fire. Aiming by the light the flickering flames provided, she pointed at the vine that encircled her throat and willed the fire into a narrow, straight blast. It cut the vine as keenly as a laser.

Next came the one around her waist, and then her arm. Kerry dropped back down to the skiff, but unbalanced, she went over backward, landing faceup in the shallow water. She allowed herself a bitter smile. It hardly mattered; she was already drenched from the rain. The flames at her fingertips died in the creek, but that was okay. She could always make more.

She climbed back into the skiff, found the remaining oar, and started to row.

Okay, then, she thought as she churned the water, driving the boat quickly up the creek.

Mother Blessing is definitely opposed to me leaving. Don't know yet if she's homicidal about it, but she's obviously serious.

Kerry rowed and rowed. Her arms started to ache, her shoulders and back protesting from the effort. The rain gave up, and by the time light started to show itself, patches of silver and pink visible through the leafy ceiling to the east, she knew something was wrong. She had been making for the old Slocumb site—the blasted, cursed township Season and Mother Blessing had once shared—and she should have reached it within a few hours. Navigation had been difficult in the dark, but even so. . . .

More light filtered in through the trees and Kerry saw a bank that she recognized, with roots reaching through the bluff of clay and diving into the water, a big, pale mushroom sticking out of one like a dinner plate wedged halfway in. She had seen that bank at least an hour or two before, on one of the occasions when she'd taken out her flashlight to gauge her path. She was positive she hadn't been rowing in circles—the Swamp wasn't so well organized that one could even do that intentionally. Which could only mean that the Swamp itself was shifting, changing itself around in an effort to keep her here.

What if it isn't Mother Blessing? Kerry wondered as the icy hands of fear gripped her again. *What if it's Season—or the Swamp itself? What if it doesn't want me to leave? Will I ever get out then?*

But Kerry Profitt was the Bulldog, she reminded herself. It didn't matter who—or what—was trying to keep her here. The only thing that mattered was that she was determined to get out, and so she would. She drifted past the familiar bank. Now that the sun had come up, she knew which direction east was. Slocumb was to the east, and a highway ran alongside the Great Dismal in that direction. She would find an exit, at one spot or another.

Kerry had traveled maybe another half mile when the water started moving faster under her boat. It took her in the direction she wanted to go, so she let the current carry her, using the oar only to keep herself away from the banks. A family of feral pigs watched her race by from a bluff; crows and three snowy egrets took flight at her rapid approach.

Then the creek widened, and ahead she could see where it joined with a broader canal. By now she was completely lost—she was nowhere she had ever been before, or, more likely, the Swamp had never been configured in just this way before. She put the oar to water to help ease herself into the canal, but when her smaller tributary hit the larger one, the water there rushed faster than she had ever seen water move here. It was like a river's rapids, not like the near-stagnant swamp water she was used to. Her heart raced as she tried to steady the shallow skiff, but the little boat was no match for the sudden flow.

Water roared in her ears and splashed ahead of the skiff, and Kerry found herself spinning around and around, the oar useless to stop her. Then the tiny craft was hurled against a jagged bank, where it splintered. Kerry snatched up her duffel bag as the water rushed in, and hurled it up onto the bank. The water in the Swamp was rarely deep, but things lived in it that she didn't want to encounter if she could help it—water moccasins and alligators foremost among them. Grabbing exposed roots, she pulled herself onto dry land, where she sat down hard and watched the boards that had once been the skiff separate and float away.

The waterways were the highways of the Swamp, Kerry knew. There were trails on land, but they were mostly animal paths, unsuited for anything as big and ungainly as a human being. Kerry was slender enough for most trails, but when they wound underneath spreading ferns and fallen trunks, they could be impassable even for her.

Still, it didn't look like she had much choice now. She headed vaguely east until she found a faint track and then followed it.

And still Mother Blessing wasn't done with her, she discovered. After maybe a mile or so, Kerry discovered that she was being followed. She heard the chuffing sound of a big cat first and froze in place. Slowly, carefully, she turned and looked back down her trail, and after a few minutes a bobcat showed itself, its strange golden eyes fixed on her. But the bobcat wasn't alone—a black bear parted the brush and stood beside the feline. Kerry knew that would never happen in nature—only Mother Blessing's intercession could have made those two creatures into allies.

Knowing that didn't make Kerry feel any better about it. Either one, bear or bobcat, could do a lot of damage if it attacked her. Both acting together, impossible as it was to imagine, could easily tear her to shreds.

She could defend herself, of course. But the idea of hurting either of those animals, forced against their own natures to cooperate in her destruction, was repellent to Kerry.

Fighting the tremor in her knees, the urge to run, she turned away slowly, showing them her back. She then continued down the trail she had found, heading into the morning sun, moving at a steady clip—not running, but not slow.

Behind her, she heard the animals keeping pace.

To panic, to run, would certainly bring them both charging down on her. This way they remained at bay, tracking without charging, while she tried to think of a way to reverse the spell that had enchanted them.

No such reversal came to mind. Kerry was exhausted. She hadn't slept since yesterday morning, Thanksgiving, which seemed a lifetime ago, and then the battle with Season, the effort of rowing all night—it was no wonder answers weren't coming to her as quickly as they might have.

Finally an idea occurred to her. The animals had been set on her trail by Mother Blessing, no doubt with malicious intent. They hadn't attacked her yet, but Kerry was convinced that they would when their instincts told them she was a threat or when she tried to run. She didn't know how she could alter the programming, but she was pretty sure she could change their target. She stopped, then spun around, facing them again. Speaking a couple of the magic words she had learned, gesturing with both hands, she pointed toward a nearby puddle and raised the water from it. With the water that now hovered in the air between herself and the animals, she sculpted the image of Mother Blessing—all three hundred pounds or more of her, complete with scooter, oxygen tanks, and beehive hairdo. She tried to look into the eyes of each animal, and she drove into their minds the concept that this person was their enemy, their mutual target. Finally she hurled the water sculpture at them. Bear and cat both flinched away, but it splashed against them, harmless but soaking.

When it was over, both creatures regarded Kerry almost casually, and then looked this way and that, up and down the path. They were no longer fixed on her, she believed. She waved her arms at them, and they backed away, turning and going back the way they had come.

Kerry didn't know how long Mother Blessing's spell would last—or how long her own would, for that matter. But if it held, and if these two unlikely companions found their way to Mother Blessing's cabin, the old witch was in for an unpleasant surprise.

The path twisted and turned, widening here, narrowing to almost nothingness there. Always it led east, which was where Kerry had decided salvation lay anyway. So she stayed with it as best she could.

In another hour or so, she could hear the rush of cars on the highway. She struggled to place her weary feet. The duffel was so heavy she was regretting having brought it. The world no longer seemed to conspire against her—when vines snatched at her ankles or thorns tore at her sleeves, they were simply doing what vines and thorns naturally did. But she was almost ready to admit defeat anyway, not sure how long she could continue the hike. The sound of cars perked her up a little. But they were still at some distance, with plenty of thick swamp between her and them.

She drove herself on. When her mind started to wander, when she began to lose her focus, to fall asleep on her feet, she reminded herself of Mace Winston, whom Season had killed back in San Diego during the summer. That summer had changed everything for her—had taken a life that was moving in one direction, as surely as the creek that had carried her skiff, and spun it around just like the canal had done the little boat. Summer had introduced her to Daniel Blessing, three hundred years old and, as it turned out, the love of her life. She allowed the memory of his smile, kind and genuine, to fill her for a moment. It brought her a few seconds of peace, reminded her why she was doing all this. He was the handsomest man she'd ever seen—centuries old, sure, but witchcraft, she had learned, was the original Botox and didn't even involve needles or deadly germs.

But the summer had also brought Season Howe into her life, and Season had killed Mace, and later Daniel. Then, during the fall, when Kerry was in the Swamp learning from Daniel's mother, Season had apparently tracked down Rebecca in Santa Cruz, and Josh in Las Vegas. Josh hadn't survived the encounter. The only ones remaining from the summer house in La Jolla were herself, Rebecca, Brandy, and Scott.

Finally Season had shown up here, in the Great Dismal. Where it had all started, so many years before. Here she hadn't been able to defeat Mother Blessing and Kerry, but neither had they been able to triumph over her. It almost didn't matter— the things Season had said were enough to make Kerry rethink everything that had happened since August. She had been motivated by thoughts of revenge against Season ever since Daniel had died.

Now it wasn't so much revenge that spurred her on, although that was still a factor. Now—just since yesterday afternoon—what Kerry discovered she wanted most in the world was the truth. She wanted to know who had destroyed Slocumb. She wanted to understand the relationship between Season and Mother Blessing, wanted to know what Daniel and his brother Abraham had known about it.

That quest, instead of just simple revenge, kept her putting one foot before the other, ducking branches, dodging thorns. She tried to remain alert, worried that Mother Blessing would have turned the Swamp against her in ways she hadn't encountered yet. But her eyes grew bleary and her concentration flagged.

Until finally she topped a low rise and saw, at the bottom of a weed-choked slope, the highway she sought. Highway 17 ran north-south here, along the edge of the Great Dismal Swamp. It would take her away—away from Mother Blessing, away from Season Howe.

It was so beautiful, that strip of lined asphalt, that Kerry thought she would cry.

2

Kerry didn't know exactly what she looked like, but she was pretty sure she was a horrific mess. A full night and all morning in the Swamp, in the rain, falling out of the boat—all after an epic battle—would do it to anyone, she decided. She hadn't spent time on her appearance since yesterday morning, when she'd cleaned up and brushed her hair and even put on a little makeup because she was going into Deep Creek to do the holiday feast shopping.

If she were driving and spotted herself hitchhiking, she would lock her doors and speed up.

She couldn't do much about her physical appearance—not without a shower and a hairbrush and maybe a new wardrobe. But that didn't mean she had to let passing motorists know what she really looked like. Casting a glamour was one of the first tricks Mother Blessing had taught her. It was basic, and while it didn't necessarily have anything to do with the more common definition of "glamour," there was no reason it couldn't apply. She decided she would look like a clean-cut, friendly student, in the Swamp to study its biology or something. She visualized what she wanted people to see, changing as little of herself as possible. The muddy, torn coat became a clean sweatshirt with a UVA logo on it, the shredded jeans were crisp and new, the fouled, mud-caked boots were shiny green duck boots. She imagined her hair as she liked it best, loose and flowing in the breeze, raven-dark and fine. She visualized herself only lightly made up, her natural porcelain complexion undisguised, her green eyes almost luminous. As a finishing touch she imagined a faint scent of lilac, instead of the swamp mud and sweat she really smelled like.

Once that was accomplished, she ventured out to the edge of the roadway and stuck out her thumb when the next batch of vehicles raced up the highway. She wanted to go north, toward Portsmouth and Norfolk, and points beyond. But either of those nearby cities would do for a start.

Six months before, Kerry would have been petrified to even consider hitchhiking anywhere. She still understood that it was not the safest mode of transport, particularly for a young woman. But compared with what she had survived in the past twenty-four hours alone, it was a piece of cake.

The third car that came along stopped for her. A man in

his early thirties drove, a pretty woman by his side. In the back was an array of photography equipment—camera bags, tripods, backpacks, and the like. The woman rolled down her window as Kerry jogged up to the car.

"Where are you heading?" she asked.

"Portsmouth, I guess," Kerry told her.

"We're going to Newport News," the woman said, "so that's on the way. If you can find a place to sit with all that junk in the back, you're welcome to ride."

"I don't take up much space," Kerry promised. She climbed into the back. The driver pulled back out into the lane, and the woman started to say something else. But the motion of the car on the highway lulled Kerry, and though she tried to listen, within minutes she had slipped into a deep sleep.

The Friday after Thanksgiving is, retail legend has it, the busiest shopping day of the year. Brandy Pearson saw no reason to doubt the conventional wisdom. Her parents lived in Needham, a Boston suburb, and she had foolishly tried to go to one of the town's independent bookstores to find something to read during the Thanksgiving break that wasn't required for one class or other. She didn't have anything particular in mind—she enjoyed chick-lit, legal thrillers, suspense, and the occasional romance, as well as popular biographies, and she figured she could easily find something in one of those categories that caught her eye.

So she fought the bundled-up throngs, trying to peer past

anxious shoppers at the covers and spines of the books on the store's shelves. She browsed new hardcover fiction first, picking up and putting back at least a dozen books. She had experienced a lot in the past several months, since San Diego and the discovery that witches were real—and deadly. She had mourned Mace and Josh and even Daniel, who had drawn them all into it. She had broken up with Scott, who had been, for a time, the guy she thought was forever. Now she found that fiction that took some matters too lightly—the existence of the supernatural, life and death, love and hate—didn't appeal to her anymore. She picked up a book with a knife on the cover—she had heard somewhere that knives on book covers were guaranteed sellers—flipped it open, read the cover flap. Then she put it back where she'd found it.

"Do you taste them too?" a voice asked from behind her. "Or just squeeze them to see if they're ripe?"

Half-expecting to see someone she knew, Brandy turned around. But the young man who had spoken was a stranger— *a handsome stranger,* she corrected herself, but a stranger just the same. He was about her age or a little older, early twenties, maybe. His friendly smile revealed even, white teeth. His hair was short, neatly cropped, his eyes were wide and cheerful. His skin was several shades darker than her own, set off nicely by a cream-colored dress shirt underneath his heavy winter coat. Clean blue jeans and expensive leather shoes made up the rest of the ensemble. Brandy had to approve.

"If you take them home too early they just spoil," she

replied. "Vine-ripened is always best, at least for hardcovers. Paperbacks you can keep in a bag for a few days if you need to, and they'll usually turn out just fine."

"I see you know a lot about the care and feeding," the man said. "Maybe you can give me a lesson sometime."

Is he asking me out? Brandy wondered. *We just met, like, seconds ago. We* haven't *met, really. Well, one way to fix that.*

She extended her hand. "I'm Brandy Pearson," she said with a smile. "World-famous expert on book botany."

"Adam Castle," he said, taking her hand in his. His hand was large and warm, and he shook hers with a firm grip and then released it. "Not world famous at all."

"Give it time," she said. "I'm sure you'll find your niche."

"I'm afraid my specialty is a little more mundane. Urban planning."

A browser reaching for a new Dean Koontz novel jostled Brandy. "Nothing wrong with that," she said, sidestepping so as not to take another elbow to the ribs, and glad she wore a heavy woolen pea coat over her lavender turtleneck and black yoga pants. "Especially if you can urbanly plan a shopping experience where there's some kind of consideration for personal space."

The shopper put the Koontz book down, shot Brandy a glare, and said, "Excuse me," as he moved down to the next shelf unit.

Adam laughed. "Ouch. You don't pull any punches, do you, Brandy?"

"Only when there's a good reason to," Brandy replied. "Which, it seems, is pretty rare."

"Yeah, you're right about that, I think," he said. "And to answer your question, yes, I think I do have some interesting ideas about retail spaces. Of course, this is an example of what I like—smaller independent stores, as opposed to big-box chains. But there are ways to situate them, and to organize the insides, that create a more efficient and user-friendly shopping experience, and . . . you were just saying that, right? You didn't really want to hear my theories."

"Not that they're not fascinating," Brandy assured him. "Because I'm sure they are, in the right setting. I just don't think this is it."

Adam laughed again. Brandy found herself responding to his laughter—it was honest, with a lack of self-consciousness that she found refreshing. She knew virtually nothing about this man except that he was strangely appealing. She wasn't in the market for a relationship, especially so soon after breaking up with Scott. But there was some kind of instant connection going on here, it seemed. This guy was cute, he made her laugh, and he seemed to have a few brains in his head, all of which were qualities that Brandy appreciated.

She wasn't the kind of person who could just fall into a romance, anyway, even if she had been looking for one. She was too analytical for that. She tried to look at every aspect of a person or situation and make up her mind based on the facts as she found them. The fact that she was even thinking in romantic terms, just minutes after seeing Adam's face for the first time in her life, was unusual for her, and she figured that when she took the time to analyze her own reaction she might find that it was meaningful in that context. Her immediate response to him indicated to her that there might be something there worth responding to.

But on a friendship basis only, she decided. *I am not looking for a new boyfriend already.*

Adam seemed to be thinking along similar lines. He ticked his head toward the bookshop's coffee bar, where a few empty tables stood among people reading through magazines, chatting, or working on laptop computers. "Would you like to get something to drink?" he asked her. "And then we can talk about what the right setting might be."

Brandy had to think about the invitation for almost three whole seconds before she accepted.

The Charles River separated Cambridge, home of Harvard University, from Boston. The river wasn't visible from Scott Banner's family home on Marlborough Street in the Back Bay, but one knew it was nearby just the same—its edges choked with ice at this time of year, hardy runners blowing out clouds of steam as they jogged its footpaths.

The house was ridiculously large, Scott had always thought, five stories of red brick on the outside, its roof turreted and dotted with four chimneys. Snow webbed the trees in front of it. Old New England money had paid for the house, and Scott Banner's father—now known as Judge Banner, though he'd spent most of his professional life as a partner at a downtown law firm—was perfectly happy to take full advantage of the privileges life had cast his way.

Scott knew that his gut response might be written off as typical teen rebellion. But even as he relaxed on a leather couch in the media room, watching old movies on the plasma TV, he couldn't help thinking about the millions of hungry people who could be fed for the cost of this one house. His father was a philanthropist who gave heavily to dozens of worthy causes, but Scott had decided that someday when he inherited all of this, he'd sell the house, live a more reasonable lifestyle, and share with the needy the wealth that had been passed down to him.

For now it was a nice place to relax after the Thanksgiving feast of the day before. The grand dining room had been full, with family friends and relatives spilling off the main table, which seated twenty-four, and using two additional tables that had been set up for the overflow. The meal had been huge—again, bringing Scott a rush of guilt over those who got their only Thanksgiving turkey from a shelter, if they even had that option. After dinner the party had split into different rooms: Scott and his older brother Steve had gone into the game room and taken all comers on at the pool table, while others had gone to the media room for football, or onto the patio in back, heated with standing propane warmers, for cigars and brandy.

Last year, he kept remembering, he and Brandy had been

together on Thanksgiving, spending part of the day here and part at her family's home in Needham. The contrast had been marked—her parents were well-off, but they had earned it themselves, and their lifestyle was comfortable but not ostentatious. Her family seemed to like him, and his family definitely enjoyed her company. He must have explained thirty times yesterday why she wasn't with him for the meal.

The truth was, he had a hard time figuring it out for himself.

She accused him of secretly longing for Kerry Profitt. And when he was honest with himself, he couldn't really deny that charge. Kerry was a remarkable young woman—beautiful, brave, and resourceful. Of the group of them who had been thrown together in a house during the summer, she had been through the worst of it. Scott's heart had gone out to her, and that, plus the undeniable physical attraction he felt, created the situation that bugged Brandy so.

His brother Steve came into the room, glancing at the movie playing on the big screen. "Can't go wrong with Indy," he said. "Well, maybe except for that middle one."

"That's why I'm on number three," Scott agreed.

Steve sat in a club chair next to Scott's couch. Like Scott, his eyesight was terrible, but unlike Scott he'd been willing to have lasers beamed into his eyes to correct it. He was a little taller than Scott, sandy-haired and tennis-fit. "You've been pretty down last couple of days, little bro," Steve said. "What's up?"

Scott shrugged. There was so much he couldn't tell Steve— about Season Howe, and the friends who had died. "I guess a little class consciousness," he said. "Feeling bad that we're the haves in a world of have-nots."

"Feel free to join the Peace Corps, dude," Steve suggested. They'd had this discussion before.

"Maybe I will," Scott said. With a grin, he added, "You tell Mom."

Steve was six years older than Scott, and they had been close since childhood. In the last couple of years they'd grown apart, largely because they hardly ever saw each other—Scott was busy with Harvard, while Steve was busy climbing the tenure track at Amherst. Even so, it wasn't hard for one brother to tell when the other was hedging something. "Is it Brandy?" Steve asked. "Must've hurt yesterday when people kept asking where she was."

Scott nodded. "Yeah, that's part of it. A big part, I guess. I just miss her a lot, you know?"

"Understood," Steve said. He was married to a girl he'd known since his senior year of high school, so Scott was pretty sure he had no recent experience with break-ups. "Life goes on, right?" Steve added.

"That's what they say."

"She was a good lady," Steve said. "I know you'll miss her a lot. But you know what? There are plenty of good ladies out there. You'll find another before you know it."

The problem was, Scott had already found another. Kerry. Only he'd found her too soon, when neither of them had been ready for each other. Now that maybe they were—now that he was ready, at least—she was MIA, somewhere down in the swamps with Mother Blessing. Out of touch, but not out of mind.

He hoped she would contact him over the holidays, because he was turning over an idea in his mind, persuading himself to commit to it, and it would involve her. At least, after the fact.

He couldn't say anything about that to Steve, however, or tell his brother how much he hoped she was okay. He hated the fact that he was unable to reach her—he could send e-mails to her address, which she could sometimes log on and receive through some magical Internet access Mother Blessing had arranged. But there were no guarantees that she'd get them, and he couldn't call her, and he had no way of knowing for certain that she was safe down there.

"You're right," he said after a while. "Brandy's great, but there'll be others. Like Linda, right?"

"Exactly," Steve agreed. "Just like that. Give it some time, that's all I'm saying."

"I hear you." Scott nodded and glanced toward the screen, where Indiana Jones was in mortal danger yet again. Somehow he always pulled out of it. Like Kerry, he was gutsy and resourceful. Like Indy, Kerry had always managed to survive.

So far.

Scott only hoped that if there ever came a time when she needed him to help her do so, he would be there for her.

New York at Thanksgiving was a magical city. The usual bustle went on, but people's moods seemed improved somehow—

strangers smiled at one another on the sidewalks instead of growling. Horns still honked, but the blasts were shorter, not as angry. Rebecca Levine was willing to admit that it might simply have been her imagination, that because she loved the holiday season she projected that feeling on those she saw.

But she had grown accustomed to the Santa Cruz lifestyle; the small California beach town felt like home to her now. She had grown up in the city, in her family's Upper West Side apartment. Her room was still there, and it was still home in a way, but the city felt alien now, crowded and impersonal. It was only at this time of year, between Thanksgiving and New Year's Eve, that she really enjoyed being back.

She had stayed in yesterday, watching the Macy's parade on TV but unwilling to brave the crowds to see it in person. Today she ventured out into the wind and cold, partly just to see the city in her favorite dressing, and partly to get away from her family. Her father had taken a few days off from his insurance company job to spend time with her, since she was out from California. Her mother only worked part-time, and little sister Miriam was off from high school for a week. So privacy was hard to come by in the apartment, and after sharing a comparatively large house with just Erin, Rebecca had become accustomed to plenty of privacy.

Plus, people kept trying to cheer her up.

That was probably okay, probably what families were supposed to do. Miriam, especially, was relentless, regaling Rebecca nonstop with stories about who was going out with whom, and who had said what, and what did people think about this, until Rebecca thought she was about to explode.

Because the world wasn't about which girl liked what boy who didn't like her back. At least Rebecca's wasn't.

In Rebecca's world, Season Howe existed. Witchcraft was real—and terrifyingly deadly. Friends died. Witches could use stupid college kid séances to hunt people down.

There was a lot in life to be thankful for, but having the blinders ripped off, being exposed to the truth about the supernatural world that paralleled the one most people thought of as real, wasn't part of that.

Rebecca would rather have lived in blissful ignorance of the whole thing. But that ignorance had been torn away from her, and there was no going back. It meant building walls between herself and her family, because there were so many things she couldn't talk to them about. Every conversation had to be parsed to make sure she didn't accidentally say something about Mother Blessing, or Josh's brutal murder, or Season.

So getting away from the apartment, losing herself in the happy holiday crowds, was her answer. At least short-term.

Rebecca had a few more weeks of school before the long winter break, which meant she'd have to go back to Santa Cruz. She found that the prospect pleased her.

In Santa Cruz she'd be alone. But at least she wouldn't be alone in the midst of her whole family.

She thought maybe that was better.

Kerry Profitt's diary, November 26

Never let it be said that a night's sleep can't do a world of good.

Okay, to be completely accurate, more than a night. I crashed almost as soon as I got into the Hendersons' car—and a good thing for me they were basically honest folks, right?—and didn't wake up until we were in Portsmouth. Then once they shook me into consciousness, they drove around until they found a hotel that they were comfortable letting me stay in. Never mind that they still didn't know the first thing about me, except maybe that I snored and drooled a little (okay, maybe not, but who knows? It's not like I was awake and watching). Never mind, too, that I'd have been satisfied at that point with a cot and a soft rock for a pillow.

But the place they found was clean and tidy, with locks on the doors and starched sheets and everything. I checked in, paid in advance with cash, went up to my ninth-floor room. Once I got there, I realized that I was ravenous.

So guess what: room service!

No greens or pork chops or Scooter Pies or any of that stuff that Mother Blessing lives on, either. I ordered a steak, medium-rare, with fries, a salad, and a slice of cheesecake. Ate every bite. Then I took a bath that lasted more than an hour, running more hot water every time it turned too cool. When I started to get so sleepy I worried about drowning, I got out, toweled off, and climbed in between the crisp white sheets.

That must have been about six. In the p.m.

When I woke up again it was past noon. Princess Aurora, much?

Now I'm sitting on the queen-size bed, the big TV with cable channels and everything running to give me some company, typing this on the trusty laptop that, miraculously, survived my escape from the Swamp. Outside the floor-to-ceiling windows, the sun is setting, the sky over the Atlantic is purple and indigo with a few streaks of salmon. There's a sandwich on the way up, courtesy of room service again— well, I guess it's not courtesy if you pay for it, right? But still . . .

Still, the point is that now I'm awake and fed and there's a laundry room in the building, so soon I'll have clean clothes, and downstairs there's one of those little overpriced hotel shops, so I have makeup—real makeup, for the first time in months! So . . .

. . . it's time to figure out what's next.

And that, dear diary, is the hard part.

I got away from Mother Blessing. For now, at least, which is not to say that she won't send someone—or something— after me still. She's kind of run out of sons, but she still can manufacture simulacra to hunt for her.

Not that I'm as big a problem for her as Season is. But I get the feeling she was a little ticked off that I ran out on her like that. And I get the additional—and related—feeling that she is a sore loser. So I've got to watch my step, Mother Blessing-wise.

And the other thing is that Season is still out there in the great wide world someplace. She is still, whatever the real story between her and Mother Blessing, the person who killed Daniel. And Mace and Josh. She's got a lot to answer for.

I've got a few new tricks up my metaphorical sleeve that I didn't have before, thanks to Mother Blessing (I keep wanting to write Mama B., but somehow, even though I know she'll never read this diary, I can't quite bring myself to do it). I know enough to get myself out of a swamp that wants to keep me there. What I don't know, I'm pretty certain, is enough to be much more than a momentary headache for Season Howe. I definitely am not skilled enough to defeat her in one-on-one combat, unless maybe she was comatose. And tied up.

Even then it wouldn't be a given.

So my quandary—and isn't that a great word, quandary?— is, how do I hone my skills now? How do I learn more, so that I can go after Season with some hope of winning? Who is there to teach me all the things I don't know?

I can't beat Season. But I can't really rest until Season is beaten. I can't beat Mother Blessing, but I can't give up until I know what really happened in Slocumb, and whether Mother Blessing, as I'm coming to believe, bears a lot more responsibility for what happened to Daniel than I originally thought.

Hence, quandary. Dilemma. Perplexity, even.

Hark—a knock at the door. Room service.

More later.

K.

3

Kerry stayed in the Portsmouth hotel for two more nights, watching the world from the ninth floor, behind the protection of a dead bolt. The TV stayed on most of that time as Kerry caught up on the various news items, reality shows, sitcoms, and personal hygiene commercials she had missed during her time in the Swamp. All in all, she decided, she really hadn't missed much of any importance at all.

But on the last night she started to feel uneasy. This was far too close to Mother Blessing for any kind of real comfort. And she didn't have any fake ID, so she had checked in under her own name. It wouldn't take much effort to find her here.

If anyone was looking. That was the big question mark, the great unknown. She had every reason to suspect that Season might be—she had, after all, shown up at Rebecca's séance and then found Josh in Las Vegas.

Or was it Josh who found her? That part was never completely clear. If that was the case, then maybe the séance sighting was the optical illusion Rebecca had first thought it was. Maybe Season wasn't hunting them after all.

Which would be good, because it would take some of the heat off Kerry while she figured out how to go about hunting Season herself.

Her first priority had to be getting out of this neighborhood. Where to go, she hadn't yet determined. She didn't think she had to cover her tracks as much as she had when she had run away from Northwestern to come down here. Then, she had worried that her aunt Betty and uncle Marsh would call the cops when they learned she was missing, and she needed to make sure she couldn't be easily found. She knew Mother Blessing would have her own methods of searching for her, but she highly doubted that involving the authorities would be one of them.

When she woke up the next morning, she had the answer.

Hide in plain sight, she thought. She would go home— back to Illinois, back to Aunt Betty and Uncle Marsh. Then even if there was any kind of search effort going on, it would be called off. Mother Blessing would never think she would go back there, so it would be the last place she'd look. The other alternative was going back to Northwestern, but she was pretty sure she'd have been expelled by now, what with the not going to class or making her tuition payments.

She called for room service one last time, showered, ate breakfast. When she was done with that, she packed her duffel again and caught a hotel shuttle to the airport. There was a flight to Chicago that afternoon that she could get on, and then a commuter plane down to Cairo. Still weary, she dozed on the longer flight, but on the commuter she stayed awake, drinking bottled water and paging through a magazine.

From the airport she took a taxi. At nine thirty, she knocked on the door of her aunt and uncle's home, a single-story ranch house with snow on the front lawn and the blue glow of a TV showing in a window.

Uncle Marsh opened the door with a half-empty highball glass in his hand and a questioning look in his eyes. He stood unsteadily in the doorway for a moment, as if unsure of what he was seeing.

"Hi, Uncle Marsh," Kerry said meekly.

He put an arm around her shoulders and drew her into the house. His breath reeked of alcohol. "Call off the Coast Guard, Betty!" he called. "Look what the cat dragged in!"

Aunt Betty emerged from the kitchen carrying a dishtowel and a china plate, which dropped from her hand the instant she saw Kerry standing in the entryway. It hit the ground and smashed into a hundred pieces. "Kerry!" she cried, and ran toward her niece.

Standing there, enveloped by her closest living relatives,

Kerry had a moment of wondering why she had ever left this house. But that only lasted for a few moments. Aunt Betty was weeping openly and clinging to her, repeating, "We were so worried about you," over and over. Uncle Marsh knuckled Kerry lightly on the chin and said, "I was just joking about the Coast Guard. We figured if you'd wanted us to know where you were, you'd have told us."

And then it all came flooding back. Uncle Marsh was a drunk, a harsh man who had taken every tenderness ever offered him and turned it away, using a crude sense of humor like a shield against the blades of kindness. Aunt Betty gave new meaning to the term codependent, and the worse Uncle Marsh behaved toward her—or anyone else, for that matter, within earshot of her—the more she decided he needed to be protected. From what, Kerry was never really sure. But she became his one-woman security squad, running interference, keeping him safe from his own worst instincts. She wept openly and often, which drove him mad. The madder he got, the more she decided that he was being persecuted, and the more she wept.

Kerry hadn't been inside for ten minutes before she realized that coming back here was one of the biggest mistakes she had ever made. She would have been better off letting them think she was dead. At least then they could have continued driving each other crazy without dragging her back into it.

The next morning she sat at the table having breakfast with Aunt Betty. Uncle Marsh was still asleep—sleeping off the effects of the previous night's alcohol intake, Kerry guessed, although Aunt Betty insisted that he had been "working awfully hard lately." Kerry had managed to forestall the inquisition last night by claiming exhaustion, but she knew it couldn't be dodged forever.

"I called the police last night and told them to stop looking for you, Kerry," Aunt Betty said over the rim of a bone china teacup. She was a birdlike woman, thin and frail, with bad eyes for which she wore glasses whose lenses were nearly as big as her entire head, a pointed beak of a nose protruding from between them. Her hair was brown, but from a bottle, because it should have been gray years before. She held her cup in two bony hands. "We really were terribly worried about you when you just disappeared. The college called, and that girl you shared a room with, Sophia—"

"Sonya," Kerry corrected. She pushed runny scrambled eggs around on her plate with her fork. There were many ways to describe Aunt Betty, but "skilled chef" would never be one of them.

"Right, Sonya. She was no help at all. She said you were antisocial—which Marsh and I, of course, knew wasn't true—and that you had probably gone to live in a cave somewhere. Well, I said that was just the most ridiculous thing I had ever heard, that my niece wasn't the kind of girl who would live in a cave, and that you were perfectly nice and very reliable, and if you were gone, then obviously something had happened to you. You were kidnapped, or murdered, or something like that."

"Well, I'm fine," Kerry said. She bit into some rubbery bacon.

"I can see that, and I'm so glad to hear it. I told the police that, of course, after I saw you. The detective who's had your case, a young man, Pembroke or something like that, he called back first thing this morning while you were sleeping, and said that he'll be by this afternoon to talk to you. He'd like to know where you've been, of course, and he'd like to know whatever happened to you.

"We all would like to know that, of course. I'm sure it was something just dreadful."

She continued yammering on, speaking words that Kerry was no longer listening to, without seeming to notice that Kerry hadn't replied. What could she tell the police? "Sorry, detective, but I was off learning magic so I can kill the witch who killed my boyfriend. Next time, I'll call more often."

Yeah, that'll fly.

She had managed to convince herself that Uncle Marsh and Aunt Betty would be glad she had disappeared. They no longer bore any financial burden on her behalf, if they ever had—an insurance settlement, after her mother's death, had paid for Kerry's college, and even though there wasn't much of an estate left after all her mom's medical bills, the sale of the house they had lived in had netted some money for her aunt and uncle.

And Uncle Marsh had wasted no time—as soon as she left for school, not even waiting for her to vanish completely—in turning "her" room back into the den it had been before she had come to live in their house. She had spent the night on a foldaway couch in there, with Marsh's big-screen TV and wet bar. She always thought their house looked like something decorated from a thrift store, except that the reverse was true: Their furnishings were the kind that ended up at thrift stores, but they were the original owners. There were lots of items that looked like carefully tooled wood, except that they were really molded wood-grain plastic, lots of veneers, lots of composition board. Everything except real wood, it seemed.

Given her uncle's speed at eliminating every trace of Kerry from the house, the fact that they'd called the police at all was a little staggering. The idea that she would have to explain her whereabouts to the authorities was terrifying. How thoroughly would they check her story out, if at all? If she claimed to have run away to San Francisco, or Sweden, would they ask for addresses? Known associates? Would they expect some kind of verification of her statement? If she turned out to simply be a runaway, instead of a kidnap victim, would they want to be repaid for the expense of their investigation?

She doubted that, but on the rest of it she was completely in the dark. She hadn't anticipated anything like this when she came back here.

"Aunt Betty," she said, interrupting whatever her aunt was going on about now. "I'm not sure I'm really . . . you know, up to talking to the police today. Can't we just tell them that I'm fine, and let it go at that? I mean, don't they have better things to do than investigate people who aren't missing anymore?"

"Well, but they'll want to try to find whoever took you," Aunt Betty said.

"No one took me, Aunt Betty. I . . . had something I needed to do. I went to where I could do it. I . . . well, I didn't do it all, not really. Not yet. But I did some of it, and then I came back."

Aunt Betty regarded her, the teacup cradled in both hands again like something rare and precious. "You just . . . left?"

"I'm almost eighteen, Aunt Betty. I'm capable of making my own decisions. It was something very important."

"It must have been," the older woman said. "Aren't you going to tell me what it was?"

Kerry looked at her plate. "I can't."

"I see." A long pause, and then the teacup clattered in its saucer. Aunt Betty's hands were trembling, and when Kerry looked up, she saw tears welling in her aunt's eyes. "Noreen trusted us," she said. She almost never used her sister's name, it was always "your mother." "I'm sorry you can't."

"It isn't that, Aunt Betty," Kerry said, already knowing the conversation had veered from difficult to hopeless. "It's just . . . it's hard to explain. I can't explain. Not without telling you . . . telling you everything. And I can't do that. I guess I'm asking you to trust me, this time."

"I see." Again with that. She always said that when, of course, she didn't see—when she couldn't see at all. Soon the tears would be flowing, and the sacrifices they had made would be drawn into the discussion—sacrifices which were real, Kerry had no doubt about that. She appreciated completely the fact that they had opened their house to a child who was not their daughter, whom they had never asked for.

"I'm so sorry, Aunt Betty," Kerry said, hoping to head all that off at the pass. "I really . . . I wish it hadn't happened the way it did. I wish I could tell you the whole story. I honestly do. But . . . it's something you're better off not knowing, you've got to believe that."

"Yes, well . . ." Tears ran down Aunt Betty's cheeks now, and she dabbed at them with a paper napkin. At least she hadn't started sobbing. That was the worst.

"Haven't you ever known something you wish you didn't, Aunt Betty?" Kerry pressed. She blinked, feeling tears of her own coming on now. "Something that you couldn't tell another soul about, something that was just too huge and too terrible to share? That's what I have, what I know. I can't tell you what it is, and you wouldn't believe me, probably, if I did. And if by some miracle I could convince you, it still wouldn't do you any good to know it. It would only make you miserable, in fact. So why share it? Why work so hard to persuade you of something that you can't do anything about and that will only make you hurt? I can't do it to you and Uncle Marsh. I'm sorry that it's this way, but it is. There's nothing I can do about that now. No way I can undo it. The best I can do is try to make it right, and even if I do that, you'll never know about it. . . . But I will.

"So that's what I have to try to do. And you—you'll just have to try to understand that I love you, and you'll have to either trust me, or—or not trust me, I guess. I hope it's trust, but it really doesn't make much difference, either way, in the long run."

Kerry snatched her napkin from her lap and blew her nose. Aunt Betty was sobbing now, long looping sobs that Kerry had always thought must have been a real hit at funerals. And Kerry was crying too, tears falling from her cheeks and splashing into the watery eggs and rubbery bacon she hadn't eaten. Tears that came from knowing that she had somehow stepped off the path her life was supposed to have taken onto a different one, a road that was dark and frightening, for which there was no map and no guide. Tears for her mother, who couldn't be around to try to deal with this new and sinister aspect of her life, and tears for her aunt, who was but could never understand it. Tears, too, for Daniel, whom she had known for so short a span and loved so hard, who had both set her on this path and tried to protect her from it.

Both women cried now, sitting at the breakfast table, each consumed by her own private grief that Kerry suspected had little, if anything, to do with the other's.

Which was when Uncle Marsh wandered in, unshaven, his white hair askew, in a sleeveless white T-shirt and flannel pajama bottoms, scratching his belly under the shirt.

"Who died?" he asked.

And Kerry started to laugh through her tears.

4

Kerry hadn't unpacked her bag yet, so it didn't take her long to get ready to move on again. Aunt Betty called the police detective she had been talking to and told him that the whole affair had been a misunderstanding, that Kerry had left school of her own free will and now was back. The detective peppered her with questions for a few minutes, but agreed to close the books on the case. Kerry was still a little surprised that there had been a case with open books in the first place.

She found herself oddly touched by it, and by Aunt Betty's willingness to help. Uncle Marsh remained his typical grumpy self, and Kerry tried to limit her interaction with him to just the right amount so that she might actually miss him when she left.

Even though she had barely arrived, there was still a lot to get done. Aunt Betty drove her downtown to a branch of her bank, where she withdrew a few thousand more dollars from her insurance money to cover expenses wherever her new course took her. When they got back home, Aunt Betty suggested that Kerry take a look inside some boxes she had stored in the attic—things that had belonged to Kerry's parents, as well as some of Kerry's childhood items—while she made lunch.

The attic was close and musty, and even though the air outside was near freezing, Kerry found it uncomfortably warm up there. Aunt Betty had separated out the boxes that had come from Kerry's parents' house, so Kerry knew just which ones to look at. Each box was taped across the top. Kerry took a knife up with her and sliced through the tape carefully so she wouldn't damage any of the contents.

She had no memory of this stuff being packed up, even though she must have been around. Her mother's death had been hard on her, but in a way—after nursing her through illness for more than a year, alone because her father had died a couple of years before that—it had been both a heartbreak and a relief. Her mother's long suffering had finally come to an end, and Kerry, having been pressed into service at too young an age, could have what was left of her teen years.

Well, we know how that worked out, Kerry thought grimly. Her first summer out of high school had been spent in San Diego for a summer resort job. That had ended when Daniel

Blessing had stumbled, injured, into her life, and she and her housemates had been swept up into his world—a world of dangerous witchcraft and intrigue.

Not so much the teenage dream, she knew. It was okay, though. She had learned long ago that adaptability was one of her strong points—a key to survival, really. *Go where the river takes you.*

But during that period, right after her mother's death, she had been an emotional basket case, she remembered. Aunt Betty and Uncle Marsh had packed up the house and sold most of the furnishings and the property. They had been named Kerry's guardians and the executors of her mom's will. Which made it not especially shocking that she would have been unaware of precisely what had been saved and stored up here.

Some of the things she found were expected, but they still brought a lump to her throat. Her parents' wedding album and a couple of additional albums of family photos, including shots of Kerry as a little girl, dark haired, wide eyed, and skinny. Her dad had called her string bean until she was twelve, when she declared that he was never to use that term around her again. Old documents: tax information, birth and death certificates, medical records. A few objects that probably could have been sold or that Aunt Betty herself could have used—some jewelry, an antique music box with intricate gold filigree, a set of fine silverware that had been a wedding present from Kerry's grandmother and that had always remained inside its cherry-wood box, "for company."

Then there were the boxes that had come from Kerry's room, where less stuff had been disposed of. Kerry found old school papers, mostly forgotten, including some that made her smile with fond memories of certain teachers and friends. Books she'd liked over the years, going back to *Where the Wild Things Are* and Dr. Seuss, all the way up through her poetry phase in high school, including such diverse poets as Sylvia Plath, Robert Frost, Walt Whitman, and Pablo Neruda. A small selection of mysteries, including Nancy Drews and Agatha Christies. Mostly, after about the sixth grade, she had read books from school libraries or Cairo's public library system and from her parents' library, so her own collection was limited. But she found herself glad that Aunt Betty had saved these, and she hoped that one of these days she'd be able to settle in one place so that she could have them again.

She found old toys, locked diaries, drawings she had made, yearbooks friends had signed for her. Nothing earth-shattering, but looking through the boxes somehow crystallized things for her. Her life had been one thing, now it was another. The past was part of her; there was no denying its influence. But it didn't define her by itself, and it didn't control her direction from here. She found that she could remember it with a sense of pleasant nostalgia without feeling that she had to be dragged back into the life she had left behind.

Her life, Kerry decided, was like these boxes. The part of it that was her childhood, that included her parents, could be wrapped up in paper and sealed inside one box. It would never change; it was what it was. The precious part spent with Daniel could go into a second box. The third box had to remain open—it included everything since Daniel's death, and it was an unfinished project. There would come a time, she believed, when it could be wrapped and stored as well, but she didn't know what the shape of it would be at that time.

Whether she'd be alive to do the wrapping was anybody's guess.

Kerry spent one more night under Aunt Betty and Uncle Marsh's roof. The next day they drove her to the airport. Aunt Betty welled up again; Uncle Marsh was gruff and offhand about the whole thing. Kerry figured he was just glad to get his house back, while Aunt Betty had seen her as a kind of reinforcement in her ongoing struggle with his drinking, his temper, and his generally unpleasant attitude. But she would never leave him, Kerry knew, never even force the issue of him changing his ways, because the worse he got the more she protected him from himself and others.

As she walked through the terminal, past the point where only ticketed passengers could go, she found herself glad for the short time she had spent with them—happy she had been able to spend it, but also happy that it had been so brief. She had an hour to wait for her flight, so she sat in the waiting area and studied every blond head she saw, just in case one might be Season. Not seeing her, she took one of Daniel's journals from her duffel and started to flip through it, looking for a section she hadn't read yet.

There comes a time in the life of every young man when he must leave the home of his parents and make his own way in the world, for good or ill. In my case, this time was doubly complicated. First, I have a twin, Abraham, so there are two of us, not one, striking out to find our fortunes. And second, our father has been gone for our entire life, so when we left, that meant Mother Blessing would truly be alone for the first time in a very long while.

Perhaps triply complicated would be more apt, for there was yet another matter to consider. We were not leaving simply to start families and households of our own. We were leaving with a very particular purpose in mind—one that has been instilled in us from our earliest days.

Mother Blessing had trained us and instructed us. We were ready, we were equipped, and we were anxious to go forth into the world to find and destroy Season Howe. As we have learned since infancy, she killed our father, demolished our town, and drove our mother into hiding in the Swamp. Mother Blessing alone knows the truth of that day, so long ago in Slocumb, and Season will likely not rest until she has

murdered the last surviving witness of her crime. Abe
and I are to locate her and make sure she can never
accomplish that sordid goal.

Though Season has had years to hide herself away,
we are not without clues. There is, in the community
of witchcraft, some small amount of communication.
Season has been seen, and spoken to, here and there.
Reports of her whereabouts occasionally reach Mother
Blessing. A pattern has been observed.

Season Howe, unlike Mother Blessing, does not
confine herself to a specific location. She moves from
place to place, occupying new homes like a hermit
crab inhabiting the shell of some other creature. She
seems to make few alliances, and those temporary and
short-lived. She wants for little, and seems always to
have means at her disposal. Though it is unusual for a
woman to travel alone, she does so often, and not just
within the colonies but also to foreign lands.

Our most recent report, although it was several
months old by the time word reached Mother Blessing
in the Swamp, had her in the city of Providence, in
Rhode Island. Abe and I packed a trunk, loaded it into
a wagon, and set off, striving for manly composure in
the face of Mother Blessing's weeping. She had known
that we must depart, of course, for it was she who set
us on our path, she who taught us from childhood what
our task in life must be. Even so, the actual doing of it,

setting out on that journey, was a sorrowful event for us all, as it must always be.

And yet our circumstance is not like that of others, as Abe and I discussed on the road today. Other men of our age are indeed setting out to build their own lives. But we are different, we know. We have every expectation of living far longer than they. In a very few years they will be twenty, their lives likely half over already. When we reach twenty our lives will still be in the beginning stages, still in relative infancy. We will likely still not have achieved the full measure of our powers, but at some point thereafter our aging will cease, or at least slow considerably. Time, which has passed for us at much the same pace as it has for other boys, will, from this point forward, mean something very different. The days will pass, but each one will be the merest moment in time for us, each year as an hour or less.

Abraham and I know this to be true, and yet we struggle with the idea. We are not immortal, but we are witch born and witch bred, and so as close to that exalted state as mortal man can be.

Our journey is just begun. We may find Season at its end, and we may not. But if she eludes us now, we will have time enough to seek her out again.

We will, in fact, have all the time in the world.

I remain,

Daniel Blessing, Ninth of August, 1720

Her flight called, Kerry wrapped the leather thong around the book and tied it. He had been just sixteen when he wrote that, she realized. Younger than she was now—a boy, by contemporary standards. But that was a different world—she would have been considered an old maid, unmarried a week before her eighteenth birthday. If all this had been revealed to her at sixteen, she was sure she would have fallen apart, completely unable to handle it. She supposed she had been relatively mature for her age, since she was effectively running a household and helping to care for a mother who could barely get out of bed. But there was a big difference between that and being willing to accept evidence of witchcraft, of magical feuds that had been raging for longer than there had been a United States.

All in all she thought she had handled it pretty well. And continued to do so. Like Daniel in his journal entry, she was leaving home—or the place that had once been her home, if only briefly—with no certainty of when, or if, she would return. The last time she had gone away she had done it in secret, but this time her aunt and uncle knew where she was going, if not why. Last time she had been consumed with a specific desire: to find Mother Blessing and learn magic. This time her goal was more vague. She wanted to find Season, but didn't know where to look. She did know, however, that she didn't want to make Cairo her base of operations—she couldn't bring herself to live in Aunt Betty and Uncle Marsh's home again and didn't want to expose them to possible danger even if she could.

A few minutes later, Kerry was buckled into her seat and a flight attendant was demonstrating how oxygen masks would fall from above in the event of a sudden loss of cabin pressure. As the plane headed down the runway, a sense of ease fell over her. With no specific urgency before her, no crisis under way, she was more relaxed and comfortable than she had been in a long time.

She hoped the feeling would last a while.

5

Kerry flew into San Jose, and Rebecca Levine met her at the airport. She hadn't seen Rebecca since Las Vegas, when Josh had died. They had talked a couple of times since then, most recently when she had called from Aunt Betty's to tell Rebecca she was headed for California. But they hadn't spent any real time together since summer, in San Diego, before the group had split up to go their separate ways.

When she came out of the gate, Rebecca ran to her with a squeal, embracing her like a long-lost sister. "Kerry!" she shrieked. "Oh my God, it's so good to see you!"

"Hey, Beck," Kerry replied, a little more subdued. "It's great to see you too."

"We have so much to talk about," Rebecca gushed. Kerry

thought her enthusiasm sounded a little forced, and when she pulled away from the hug she realized that Rebecca had lost weight, probably twenty pounds or so. Her typically loose clothing—in blues and golds today, a pleated long skirt with striped tights under it and a voluminous fuzzy sweater—hung on her, and there were dark circles under her eyes. A red paisley bandanna covered copper hair that looked like it could use some attention. Rebecca hadn't complained of any problems on the phone, but it was obvious at a glance that something was very wrong.

"I guess we do," Kerry agreed. She had carried on her one bag, so they walked straight outside to Rebecca's parked car. It was dark out, and cool, but not nearly as cold as Illinois had been. As they walked, Rebecca babbled casually about classes, her roommate Erin, and life in Santa Cruz.

It wasn't until they were on the freeway, heading south over the coastal hills, that she stopped her constant, upbeat chatter. She glanced over at Kerry. "I'm . . . uh . . . I'm not doing so well," she admitted.

"I kinda guessed that," Kerry said.

"Yeah, I know. I'm a mess."

"That's overstating it," Kerry answered. "But I've seen you looking better."

"Yeah," Rebecca said again. She returned her attention to the freeway, driving with both hands firmly on the wheel. "I don't know exactly what it is. I went home for Thanksgiving, but I just couldn't wait to get back here, you know? I wanted to be here. Dad said I was becoming a hermit and I needed to snap out of it. He's probably right, but he let me come anyway."

"You said you had only been back for a day when I called," Kerry remembered. "How was New York?"

"I don't know. I love New York at this time of year. I thought it would snap me out of this . . . this funk that I've been in. But instead it just got worse. It's like, when there are that many people on the streets, and a significant percentage of them have their heads covered, you can't even tell which ones are blond. Any of them could be Season. I thought I saw her a few days ago when I went down to Ground Zero, and I screamed. People looked at me like I was freaking insane. I guess maybe I am."

Kerry had known it wouldn't be long until Season's name came up. She was the great uniter, the common bond that held their summer group together long after they would ordinarily have lost touch. "I don't think you're crazy, Beck," she said, stroking Rebecca's arm. "Season is a scary person. You saw her, or thought you did, and then she killed Josh. And then—you don't know this yet, so don't let it freak you out more, because I'm here and okay—she came to the Swamp. Mother Blessing and I fought her."

Rebecca almost lost control of the car, swerving into another lane, and a horn blasted behind them. "Oh, jeez, I'm sorry!" she said after she had corrected her course. "Kerry, are you okay? What happened?"

Kerry told her about the assault on Mother Blessing's

cabin, and about the things Season had said—and implied. She explained her suspicions—that Mother Blessing seemed to know an awful lot about the destruction of Slocumb for someone who claimed to have run away to hide in the Swamp; that she had apparently kept from her sons, and from everyone else, the fact that Season was her own mother; that she had tried to keep Kerry in the Swamp by force when she'd started to run away.

"I don't know anything for certain, really," she admitted after she had detailed the whole story. "And I'm sure if we asked her, Mother Blessing would have all kinds of excuses and explanations. But I just get a bad vibe from her—and I've come to trust feelings like that, intuitions, vibrations, a lot more since I started learning witchcraft. There's more to them than we sometimes think."

"Seems like there's more to lots of things," Rebecca agreed. She paid attention to the road as they came down a long slope, with the lights of Santa Cruz spreading before them. "There's home," she announced.

"It looks nice," Kerry said. The town hugged the shore—she could see moonlight sparkling on the water. The city was not big, but a small, comfortable size.

"It's great," Rebecca said. "When it's daylight I'll show you the boardwalk and the beach and all that good stuff. It still feels like an old-time California beach town."

"That's cool." But Kerry couldn't help thinking that an old-time California beach town would be full of blondes. She was worried about Rebecca, concerned that her friend was letting her fear of Season develop into full-blown paranoia. While she was here, she'd have to focus on helping Rebecca get better—sleeping and eating on a regular schedule, going to school, and not worrying too much about things she couldn't control.

She glanced at Rebecca, driving with one hand now while she nibbled on the fingernails of the other.

This might be a lot of work, she thought.

Kerry Profitt's diary, December 16

Beethoven's birthday. At least, according to the old Peanuts cartoons. I haven't run across any specific references in Daniel's journals, but Beethoven lived and died during his lifetime, so I suppose it's possible they crossed paths at some point. It always strikes me as weird that someone I knew was alive at the same time as people who I think of as practically prehistoric.

Santa Cruz is a pretty awesome little town. It doesn't have the natural beauty that La Jolla did, but it's more laid-back, less glitzily commercial than La Jolla. Rebecca was right, now that I have spent some time here—it does have a kind of old-fashioned charm to it. The boardwalk has carnival games and a roller coaster (that you'll never catch me on), and the beach is full of surfers in wet suits. Of course, it's winter—probably in summer it's also full of sun worshippers and families.

Near the beach is a railroad trestle that looks sort of like the one in *Stand By Me*, except for the lack of adolescents about to get run over by a train. Plenty of adolescents hanging around it, though, and jumping from it for kicks.

Not me. I'm sitting on the rocks nearby, watching them as I write in my too-long-neglected journal. The day is cold, with a brisk wind coming in off the water, making me glad I'm not trying to write the old-fashioned way. The laptop screen doesn't blow around like notebook paper would. I'm bundled up in a watch cap and coat and jeans and my red-checked tennies with thick white socks, and anyway, as a Midwestern girl, I'm still used to real winters, not this kind, so I am not overly concerned.

Except, of course, about Rebecca.

I don't think she sleeps for more than three hours at a stretch, ever. I've been staying at her house for a while now, crashing on the living room sofa, and I hear her at all hours. She says she's going to sleep, but then I wake up and she's reading, or she's online, or she's sipping hot chocolate by her window, looking out at an empty street.

As if she's afraid someone will be out there.

Which, duh. She is.

I have tried to tell her she's safe with me here. I've done a couple of little demonstrations, some handy tricks I picked up back in the Swamp. But she knows I still am not nearly powerful enough to beat Season, if she decided to come around.

And maybe it's worse with me here. Maybe, since I've seen Season more recently than she has—and since Mother Blessing is a little miffed at me too—she's afraid that my presence here makes this place even more likely to be visited sometime. She could be right. That's the thing. None of us know Season's mind, or Mother Blessing's for that matter.

For the first week or so I thought she was doing better. I got her eating regular meals, even though it meant getting up early enough to cook her some breakfast before her first class. I woke her up, walked her to campus, hung out there or went downtown while she was in class. Met her in the afternoon and came back here with her. She had a job earlier in the fall, but apparently she just stopped going. Usually a good way to become "formerly employed."

Then it was my eighteenth birthday, and she wanted to have a big celebration. Planned it out. She would invite a bunch of people, have snacks, drinks, music. She talked about it for days. December 9 came, and hey, I'm legally an adult for most purposes. I can vote, I can join the army, I can do lots of things.

What I couldn't do was get Rebecca out of bed.

Missed her first class. Halfway through what would have been her second, she finally emerged. Puffy-eyed, teary. "I'm canceling the party," she said. "I can't do it. I haven't been able to go to a party since that night."

Now, the party? Not really that big a deal to me. Turning 18 is cool and I'm glad I made it this far—and, as an aside, I totally loved the pen she bought me, silver and chunky, with purple trim and a clip so I can hang it on my backpack or whatever, so happy birthday to me—but I don't need a bunch of strangers to validate that. What bothered me was, she wanted to cancel it because months ago she went to a party at which there was a séance, and at that séance she thought maybe this blond chick turned into Season Howe for a second.

And okay, it freaked her out. Can't blame her for that.

But is she going to let that one incident rule her life? I mean, we all watched Season kill Daniel in front of a house, but that hasn't kept her out of houses. We know Mace was killed by his car, or in it, and ditto for cars.

Me? Never so much the party girl to begin with. But I wouldn't let one Season sighting keep me away from them forever, especially if they were something I liked in the first place.

I've spent the week since then trying to keep her steady, but it seems like she's getting worse, not better. Sleeping less. Eating when I sit down with her and watch her, but I don't think she eats a bite if I'm not right there. I hear her at night sometimes, crying, when she thinks I'm asleep.

Paging Doc Brandy. Rebecca has a serious problem here, and it's something I am not equipped to deal with, I guess. I mean, shaking her a lot and shouting, "Snap out of it, girl!" probably won't help, right?

Beyond that, I'm fresh out of ideas. And she's not going to have a very happy Hanukkah if I can't figure something out fast.

More later.

K.

In the run-up to the holidays, the ski resorts were full of people. New England was loaded with resorts, of course—winter sports were practically a religion here. But Scott guessed that New Hampshire's were the most prized, particularly those centered in the White Mountains. He seemed to spend most of his day in traffic, jammed between SUVs with skis and snowboards on their roof racks, loaded with folks in bright-colored outfits and dark tans.

These were his people, but they were not. He was of their social class and background, and had he chosen to be a ski bum or a 'boarder, he could have. But the whole thing just seemed too elite for his tastes—he couldn't enjoy an expensive hobby knowing that there were millions of people who couldn't afford a square meal, much less lift tickets and Rossignols. He knew it was a foolish attitude that marked him as a buzzkill to many people. He certainly wasn't opposed to fun, but there it was.

Still, he could afford the clothes and he had the car—okay, his SUV was just a RAV4, not a Hummer or anything, but it would pass. So he could move among his tribe as if he were a native. If only he could get through the traffic and find a parking space.

And the other problem was that there were so many resorts to choose from. His theory was that if, as Daniel had said, Season Howe liked to hide by moving from resort area to resort area, staying where populations were transient and most people didn't delve into the affairs of strangers, then in winter she'd be most likely to hang out at winter sports resorts.

There was, of course, another alternative—that she might go to Florida or someplace warm for the winter, but he was just one guy and he couldn't be everywhere. The other alternative, worse yet, was that she would leave the country altogether.

That would just stink. Because Scott was determined to find her. School was out for a while, he had no girlfriend, no job, nothing to tie him to Cambridge or Boston. Sure, it'd be great if he could be home in time to spend Christmas with the family. But they'd just load him down with pricey gifts he couldn't really use and didn't want.

What he wanted was Season.

He thought he had developed something that resembled a plan. Nothing concrete, more of a feeling that might be worked into a real plan if he toyed with it. His idea was that Season's guard was probably up when there were other witches around, other magic users. Even in Las Vegas, when Josh was killed, Kerry had said she saw evidence of some of Mother Blessing's simulacra around.

So Scott reasoned that if there were no witches, no simulacra, no magic, maybe she would be more relaxed. If he could catch her with her defenses down, maybe a simple human-style killing would suffice.

So here he was, cruising the ski resorts of New Hampshire, with murder on his mind.

In Boston's combat zone, a guy with the money to spend could put his hands on just about anything he wanted to acquire. In this case what he had acquired, during one truly terrifying evening at some of the seediest bars he had ever imagined, was a Kel-Tec P11. It was a few years old, the guy said, a nine-mil with a ten-shot magazine and polymer grips. He barely knew what all that meant, just knew that the gun and a box of ammunition set him back a thousand bucks—and maybe ten years of his life, which he was pretty sure had run out of him in horrific sweat while he was making the buy. He was not a gun guy, and the idea of buying one and using it went against everything he had thought he stood for.

But he had seen Season. She might be a witch, but she was still a human being. A bullet could kill her.

All he had to do was find her.

He started at the aptly named Gunstock and worked his way north, through King Pine and Cranmore and then east into the White Mountains. Black Mountain, Attitash Bear Peak, the Waterville Valley. Which was where he was now, in the parking lot at the beautiful Golden Eagle Lodge, trying to angle into a parking spot that a full-size Ford Expedition had just given up on. Scott was pretty sure he could slide the RAV4 into the space, though, if he could just get the right approach.

He waited for a couple of other vehicles to go past, and then he backed and filled until he made it in. He killed the ignition with a little flush of triumph and stepped outside into the blinding sun and snow.

Walking toward the lodge, he was once again reminded that ski areas were crawling with blondes. He had to hope he

could recognize Season if he saw her, and that she didn't recognize him. He didn't want to get into a confrontation with
her—Brandy had always said he was an all-time champion at
conflict avoidance, and she was usually right about that sort of
thing. He just wanted to sneak up on her and drop her.

Surviving was another big part of his almost-plan, because
the deal was, once Season was down, he would call Kerry at
Rebecca's place, where, according to her latest e-mails, she had
gone to stay. Part of the whole conflict-avoidance thing also
meant that he was not exactly the big heroic type. But that
didn't mean he never wanted to be, and if he could single-
handedly off the big bad witch, that would be about as heroic
as it got. Kerry could not fail to be impressed by that.

Even Brandy would take notice. But at this point Kerry's
attention was more important to him. Brandy had hurt
him, while Kerry had never really noticed him, romantically
speaking—she was so hung up on Daniel she hadn't had eyes
for anyone else. Now he could change that.

6

It was funny how one could see familiar places through fresh eyes, just by spending time with a new person. Adam Castle was a relative newcomer to Boston, having moved to the area just over a year before from Washington, D.C., to work on his master's degree at Harvard. But cities were his element, his passion, and he had delved into this one, quickly digging past its tourist facade and learning it like a native. He had taken Brandy to lunch at the Locke-Ober Café, an old-time, formal dining establishment where the waiters wore tuxedoes, even for lunch, and male guests were expected to wear jackets, and to one of the best dinners she'd ever had at Rialto, in the Charles Hotel in Harvard Square—a building she had seen a thousand times but had never thought to eat in.

Now he and Brandy walked hand in hand through the Quincy Market. In summer she liked to sit at the outdoor cafés and watch all the people, but this time of year, the indoors was much more comfortable. It was still crowded with tourists and locals alike, buying food at the market stalls or eating and drinking at the cafés. Musicians roamed the cobblestone promenade aisles and a juggler commanded a small crowd in one spot. A mime worked the masses too, but Brandy and Adam managed to dodge him.

People-watching had always been one of Brandy's favorite leisure-time pursuits. It fed her interest in psychology, her curiosity about the factors that make people act the way they do. Now everything had changed slightly. There was a new awareness that not everyone she saw was what they appeared to be from the outside—that some of them might, in fact, be more conversant with the supernatural than she'd have guessed. One couldn't go through experiences like she had, she theorized, without having those experiences color one's perceptions. People were still people, but her impressions of them had changed, as if she were eyeing them through a window glazed with ice, so reality shifted a fraction of an inch to the side.

"How did you like San Diego?" Adam asked her, once he had filled her with more information about Quincy Market than she had ever known.

"It was beautiful," she answered without even thinking about it. "The weather was just gorgeous. You know what they say, America's Finest City."

"That's what they say," Adam agreed. "But that's in terms of climate only. There are plenty of cities that beat it on almost every other score. For charm and natural beauty, San Francisco has it all over San Diego. For architectural beauty, Chicago. For sheer scale, of course, New York is the champ. San Diego has no history, especially if you compare it with Philadelphia or right here in Boston. In terms of being livable, its infrastructure is nothing compared to D.C., or New York, or Boston—there's no worthwhile public transportation there, and it's hard to get from one spot to another."

"Sounds like you've spent some time there," Brandy observed.

"Just a weekend," Adam admitted. "But I pack a lot into a weekend, and I've studied it."

"Maybe you should give it another try, and just spend a few days relaxing on the beach."

Adam shrugged. They stopped to look at a market stall selling oysters and every kind of lobster imaginable, from live ones to magnets, postcards, stuffed animals, and ceramic figures. "I will one of these days, I'm sure," he said. "But there are plenty of other places I'd like to see first."

"I hope you get to them all," she said. She was starting to hope she'd see some of them with him. This was their ninth date in two weeks, and she had already started thinking of him as her boyfriend. He made her laugh, he taught her things, and he had an easy self-confidence that made her comfortable right from the beginning. It had been a long time since she'd dated a black man, not for any special reason except that she wanted to live a color-blind life, in which the shade of one's skin was less important than the hue of the heart. His color made no difference to her now, either—it was his personality that was important, and the fact that, unlike Scott, he seemed to be with her because he wanted to be, not because the person he really wanted was unavailable.

Perhaps most important, she realized, was that when she was with him she didn't think about Season all the time. She began to see a possibility of life beyond Season, a life in which she didn't startle every time she saw a blond head on a slender female body. She would never forget the horror of that summer and fall, but someday it might just be a distant memory—something that had happened, instead of something that might happen again. She pressed herself up against Adam's arm.

That would be something worth fighting for.

Rebecca wasn't a very strict observer of the Jewish faith, but Kerry had bought her a Hanukkah present anyway: a digital camera. Kerry figured it was something that would take Rebecca outside herself, would force her to interact with the rest of the world, even if from behind a barrier of metal and glass. Of course, she didn't detail her reasoning for Rebecca, who loved the gift.

They had taken it to the boardwalk on a bright, sunny early morning at the end of the semester, the day before Rebecca was to leave for New York to be with her family. Rebecca was framing a shot of the roller coaster when her cell phone broke into song. She handed the camera to Kerry and tugged the phone from her coat pocket. "Hello?"

Kerry watched Rebecca's face change. Her mood had been good today, cheerful, and she'd answered the phone with a smile. But as she listened to the voice on the other end, her smile crumpled into something else. Her lower lip started to quiver, her eyes widened, her forehead creased like a freshly plowed field. After listening for a minute, she handed the phone to Kerry and walked away.

"Hello?" Kerry asked, inadvertently echoing Rebecca's response.

"Hey, Kerry." It was Scott Banner's voice, but he sounded anxious, upset.

"What's wrong, Scott?"

"I—I found her, Kerry. I found Season. She's in New Hampshire. But—well, can you come out here? Fast? She hasn't seen me yet, but I'm afraid she will."

"Sure, of course," Kerry said. "Soon as I can get a flight. Be sure you stay safe, okay?"

"I'm trying," Scott promised. "But I don't want to lose her either."

"I know, but staying out of her way is the most important thing. How did you find her?"

"A wild guess," Scott said. "I figured, you know, winter, ski resorts. I've been making the rounds up here and finally spotted her."

"That's amazing," Kerry said. The familiar and terrifying notion that maybe Season wanted to be found came to her—the idea that Season wanted to pick them off, one by one. "But listen, you keep a low profile. She's dangerous." *To say the least.*

"I know, Kerry."

Yeah, he knows, she thought. *But he went there anyway, by himself, looking for her. What was he thinking?*

It wouldn't help to harangue him. She just needed to keep him safe somehow. "Have you told Brandy?"

"I was going to call her next," he said. "I figure we need all hands on deck."

"No," Kerry said sharply. "If you haven't told her, don't." She looked at Rebecca, who stood fifty yards away on the beach, her red coat and yellow cargos standing out in sharp contrast to the blue-gray sea and blue sky. A stiff wind whipped her hair, and she looked very small against the wide background. "I'm not going to bring Rebecca, either. I don't want to put them in any danger if I don't have to."

"But . . . Kerry . . . ," he began.

"I know what I'm doing, Scott." *Which is a lie, of course, but maybe he'll buy it.* "You're just going to have to trust me."

"Okay," he said. "The nearest airport is a tiny one in Laconia, so get a flight into there and then call me. I'll keep tabs on her until then."

"I'll let you know when to expect me. Good job tracking her down."

"Thanks, Kerr." He sounded a little more relaxed than when she had first taken the phone.

"And you be careful!"

"You don't have to worry about that," he assured her.

I already am, she thought.

Kerry said good-bye and ended the call. Rebecca was still down on the beach, looking out at the sea with her arms wrapped around herself. Kerry walked down toward her, but the thunder of the surf and rush of the wind covered the sound of her approach. When she touched Rebecca's shoulder, the girl almost screamed.

"Jeez, Kerry, you scared the crap out of me!" When she turned around, Kerry saw that she had been crying. Mascara streaked her face.

"I'm sorry," Kerry said, spreading her arms. Rebecca moved into them and they shared a hug. Kerry's long black hair flew around them, mixing with Rebecca's, shorter and red. Kerry couldn't help remembering her first kiss with Daniel, also on a beach, several hundred miles to the south. "I didn't mean to startle you, Beck."

"It's okay," Rebecca said into Kerry's shoulder. She pulled away and looked into Kerry's eyes, her own brown ones still moist. "So, should I pack for New Hampshire?"

"No."

Rebecca's face brightened immediately, like the sun breaking through clouds. "You mean it? We're not going after her this time?"

"You're not," Kerry explained. "You've got to go to New York. I'm going alone."

The clouds returned. "Kerry, no!"

"I have to, Rebecca. Scott can't handle her by himself, and the longer he stays there the more danger he's in."

"Then why doesn't he just clear out of there?" Rebecca insisted, tears beginning to flow again. "Who says she has to be our problem?"

Kerry dug her sneaker in the sand. "She's our problem because we inherited her. She's our problem because she killed Mace and Daniel and Josh. And because it looks like maybe she's tracking us down, one at a time. Which means that Scott could be in a lot of trouble if I don't get there soon."

Rebecca's mouth hardened. "And what can you do about her, Kerry? You said you and Mother Blessing together couldn't take her."

"Yeah, well, that's just something I'll have to figure out when I get there," Kerry said.

"There's no way I can talk you out of this?"

"No, Rebecca. I don't really know how to explain—it's like, my destiny is linked with Season's now. As long as she's out there, my life isn't completely my own. I have to go."

Rebecca sniffled and wiped her eyes with her hand. "Doesn't mean I'm not going to try," she vowed.

"All the way to the airport if you want," Kerry agreed.

They stopped by Rebecca's house on the way out. Kerry said good-bye to Erin, Rebecca's housemate, whom she had only seen a handful of times since arriving, and packed up her few belongings. Once again she would get on an airplane that would take her toward Season Howe. She knew Rebecca's arguments made sense—if she just told Scott to get out of there, if they never went after Season again, she might just forget about them, right? Let them live out their lives in peace?

Maybe. And then again, maybe she really was hunting them. Maybe it wasn't happenstance that Scott found her, and Josh before that. If that was the case, then leaving her alone didn't help any of them.

Besides, Kerry wanted answers almost as much as she wanted revenge. She had been killing time in Santa Cruz, cooling her heels and getting stale, without even realizing it. Now she had a direction again, a purpose.

Scott had spent days cruising ski resorts before he spotted her. Countless blondes, many with stocking caps covering their hair, had passed before his eyes. He was growing frustrated, starting to think the whole plan was just crazy. *There's an entire world to choose from,* he thought. *Why would she pick New England just because it's convenient for me?*

At the same time, the longer his hunt stretched out, the more relaxed he became. He forgot, for brief periods of time, about the gun in his jacket pocket, though the memory of it always crashed back over him like a tidal wave of anxiety. He enjoyed the fit, attractive bodies around him, in more colors of spandex and nylon than he had known existed. The sun, the clean mountain air, the pure white snow, and the physical beauty, both of the natural region and the resort buildings themselves, all lulled him into a kind of contented languor. He was sipping a Coke in a huge, soft chair near a roaring fire in a lodge, its walls log and stone, when he saw an attractive blonde walking past the window with a pair of skis balanced on her shoulder, clad in a snug black ski outfit.

For a quarter of a second Scott forgot why he was even here. He appreciated her beauty and had a moment's sense of familiarity. Abruptly, though, he realized *why* she was familiar, and more urgently, why it mattered. He slammed the Coke down on the closest table, left a few bucks for the waitress, and wove around skiers until he found a door.

Outside, of course, the air was frigid and the walkway jammed with people, many, like the blonde he'd seen, carrying their skis. Scott looked around frantically. He had only caught a glimpse of her, and it had been months since that day in San Diego. He could easily have been wrong.

But at the moment that he had thought that the woman was Season, his whole body went cold. It was, in the words of the old cliché, as if someone had walked over his grave. Which always seemed a little strange, since why would that be a problem to someone who wasn't dead yet?

Still, it seemed suddenly, disturbingly appropriate. Scott put his hand inside his jacket pocket, closed it on the little nine-mil he carried there. Its cold steel brought him scant comfort.

He dodged and ducked, and finally he spotted the familiar form. Her clothes were skintight spandex, but she had taken off her cap and tucked it into a pocket. She stood at a coffee cart with her back to him. Scott slowed his pace and walked past the cart, then, trying to appear far more casual than he felt, he stopped and turned, looking past the cart at the blonde.

There could be no mistaking that face—the cheekbones, the vivid, almost cobalt blue eyes, like infinite sky, framed by short golden hair that curled toward a strong jaw.

It was the face of Season Howe.

He spun away quickly, before she could spot him. She was a dozen feet away. The gun was suddenly hot in his hand. He could walk up to her before she left the cart, or with her hands full of hot coffee and skis. A couple of shots in the head, close range. Sure, he'd go to prison, and it would kind of mess up the whole plan of ending up with Kerry.

But he would also be putting an end to a monster. Preventing a killer from killing again. There was something to be said for that.

Even if Kerry had to visit him in jail.

The gun was loaded, the safety off—he double-checked that with his thumb, inside his pocket. He'd never actually fired the thing, but he had practiced inside his Plymouth motel room for the last few nights. He understood it in theory, if not in practice.

Besides, how hard can it be?

In spite of the cold air, Scott felt sweat pouring from him. His hand slipped on the gun's grip. The world seemed like it was spinning too fast, colors whirling around him. He was light-headed and nothing sounded right, his ears rang as if he was deep underwater. He took a few steps toward Season but his knees felt like jelly, his feet wouldn't connect firmly with the ground.

It wasn't going to work. Before he reached Season—before, he hoped, Season saw him—Scott turned away, walked in the other direction until he found a vacant seat on a bench. *Who am I trying to kid?* he wondered. *I'm no gunman.* With shaking hands he drew his cell phone from its inside pocket, glad he had Rebecca's number programmed in. No way he'd be able to dial right now.

He punched send and waited.

Kerry would know what to do.

7

Kerry Profitt's diary, December 23

I'm almost getting used to writing in this journal on airplanes going to or from an encounter with Season Howe. I say almost because it's always an adventure seeing how far the person sitting in front of me is going to push his seat back, and whether I can actually see the screen as I type. This particular one is really pushing his luck—just about asking for someone to flick the bald spot on his head with her finger. I guess that someone would be me. Lucky for him I'm not the violent sort.

Or am I? It occurs to me (a little late, maybe? Am I not examining my life enough or something?) that I have spent most of the last five months, going on half a year, on an effort—unsuccessful so far—to commit a violent act against a person. A person I have plenty of reason to be mad at, but whom I really don't know.

That's not like me—at least, not like the me I used to be. I don't know if "meek" would be the word I'd have used to describe me. "Mild"? Maybe. I have always had a stubborn streak, and if something got in the way of getting what I thought was important, I was willing to do whatever it took, steamroller anyone. (Poor Ms. Tomkins, back in eighth grade, who really didn't understand how important my friends and I thought it was to have an anime club in school. A short-lived fad, at least where I was concerned. But man, did we hound her.) But actual violence? One of the reasons I lost interest in anime was the amount of violence in it.

So I guess there's a new me in town. I'll try to decide if I like her or not.

Glancing at the business type sitting in the seat next to me, also laptopping. Only on his there are, like, spreadsheets and numbers and stuff that looks suspiciously like work. I haven't done any of that since the Seaside Resort, and I can hardly remember what it feels like to cash a paycheck.

That's okay—I bet Mr. Business Type doesn't know what it feels like to cast a spell. He probably doesn't even believe in magic, which is so ingrained in me now I can hardly remember NOT believing in magic. Seems so . . . naïve, now. People don't believe because they don't want to believe. Because the world is simpler, they think, without it.

Well, tell you what, people. The world is a freaking complicated place. Magic doesn't make that more or less true. But with magic, if I need to, I can make you think I've had a shower and changed my clothes in the last twenty-four, even if I haven't. Let's see you top that with technology.

Ha!

More later.

K.

It turned out to be not so easy to fly from San Jose to Laconia, as Scott had recommended. Instead Kerry flew into Chicago's O'Hare, from which she phoned Aunt Betty to tell her she was fine. From Chicago she flew into Manchester, New Hampshire, and then hung around for several hours until she could catch a puddle jumper into Laconia.

There were only ten seats on the plane, of which four were occupied. The single flight attendant made Kerry and her three fellow passengers spread out on the little plane to make sure it was balanced, an idea that filled Kerry with dread, and then it took off, lurching and bouncing all the way into Laconia. The town turned out to be relatively flat, though surrounded by lakes, including Lake Winnipesaukee, which was large but maybe, Kerry thought, not quite as big as its name.

It was almost midnight when she arrived, and she was both exhausted and anxious. The closer they came to landing in Laconia, the more frightened she became. She remembered

Las Vegas, when everyone but Josh had hung around the airport waiting for her. She would probably never know just how late they had been, but she guessed it was only minutes—minutes that had cost Josh Quinn his life.

Now, with Scott's life potentially in the balance, Kerry couldn't dial his phone number fast enough. He answered on the second ring.

"Kerry?"

"Hi, Scott. I'm here. Where are you?"

"You're in Laconia?"

"Right. At the airport here."

"Okay, you're going to have to get a car," he said. "You're still almost an hour away."

An hour? Anything can happen in an hour, Kerry thought. "Are you safe?" she asked. "Do you know where she is?"

"I think so," Scott said. "She's in a hotel room here at Loon Mountain. I couldn't get a room in the same place, but I've been hanging around as much as I can. Haven't been kicked out yet."

"And she doesn't know you're there?"

"I'm pretty sure not. She seems to be enjoying herself and not paying any attention to me."

Kerry felt a flash of anger at that idea. *Enjoying herself While we run around like mad, just trying to stay sane and alive, she's up in the mountains having fun.*

"Okay," she said. "Tell me how to get there."

She wasn't sure how she would get a car—no one was

likely to rent to her, even if there had been any rental places open at this hour. She looked frantically around the terminal building, and finally a dour-looking man—central casting New England, she thought—ambled toward her with a broom in his hands. He wore a janitor's uniform with a name patch that said MITCH. "You look like you're lost, miss," he said. "Somethin' I can do?"

"I'm trying to get to a place called Loon Mountain," she said.

He spoke slowly, and there was something on his face that might have been a smile. *Or maybe gas,* she thought. "Well, you could wait till mornin'. Be a bus then."

"That's great," she replied sarcastically. "But I really have to get there tonight. As fast as possible."

Moving just as slowly as he spoke, Mitch glanced at a clock. "Well, I get off at twelve," he said. "I could give you a ride up there, you want."

"It's after twelve," Kerry pointed out. The clock read 12:06.

"Ayup, that it is. Just workin' late," Mitch said. "I don't sleep too good these nights."

He apparently doesn't tell time too good, either, Kerry noted, but she didn't want to mention that if he was going to do her a favor. She recognized the danger inherent in accepting a ride from a stranger, on a dark night, into unfamiliar mountains. But then, the hitchhiking thing had gone okay. And she figured she could handle Mitch if he got out of hand. If he drove like he did everything else, she could probably get out and run at any point and still make better time than he could.

"Okay, I guess," she said. "Are you going that way?"

"Nobody's goin' that way. That's your whole problem, isn't it?"

"Well, yes, I suppose it is."

He carried the broom over to a janitor's closet. "Wait right there, miss," he said. "I'll be back directly."

Kerry spent the few moments that he was gone running through self-defense spells in her head. She felt comfortable with them. Unless old Mitch turned out to be a witch, there was nothing he could do to hurt her. And if he tried anything, then she'd wind up driving after all, and he'd have a long walk home.

A minute later he came back from the closet wearing an anorak and tugging on furry gloves. He made that expression again, like someone trying on a new smile to see if it fit. "You ready to go?"

"I've been ready," she said.

"Kind of impatient, aren't you?" he asked.

"You could say that."

"I just did."

Kerry tried to walk fast, but Mitch just kind of shuffled along at his own pace, and she knew she couldn't get too far ahead since she didn't know where they were going. Once they were in the parking lot, it became clear—there were only a scattered handful of vehicles there, and Mitch plodded toward the oldest one, a truck that might have been state-of-the-art in the 1950s, but not since. He opened the passenger door for Kerry and then climbed in behind the wheel.

"You say you're in a hurry?" he asked her, although he knew full well, she was sure, what the answer would be.

"You know, that old life and death thing," she answered.

He put the ancient truck into gear and stomped on the accelerator. The truck left rubber behind in the parking lot and roared onto the street. "Well, then I reckon we ought to get a move on," he said. He kept both hands on the wheel in a death grip, as if afraid it would get away from him if he relaxed. But dark, sleepy Laconia zipped past outside the windows much faster than Kerry would have believed possible. Within fifteen minutes they were climbing up into the White Mountains. Snow gleamed silver, reflecting the moon overhead, trees strobed past, and Mitch drove silently, his eyes forward, his lips pressed together. Kerry figured that his picture would be in the dictionary under "taciturn," maybe cross-referenced with "crusty."

But she wasn't going to complain. The guy was going more than an hour out of his way just to get her where she needed to go. He hadn't mentioned money, or any other reward, and he hadn't asked her any questions. She was grateful for his help and delighted that a human being would make the effort to assist another in this cynical age.

About forty minutes after they had left the airport, Mitch pointed out the windshield at an array of buildings glowing in the darkness. "Loon Mountain Lodge," he said.

"Wow, that was fast."

"What you wanted, right?"

"That's right," Kerry agreed. She dug her phone out. "I've got to find out where my friend is."

"Asleep, if he knows what's good for him," Mitch commented.

"Well, if he knew that he wouldn't be here at all," Kerry said. "That's never been his strong point."

"People don't know how important sleep is," Mitch said. "Take it from me."

"I've had plenty the last couple of weeks," Kerry told him. "But I don't always. I know what you mean." She dialed Scott and he picked up immediately.

"Where are you?" he asked.

"We're here, basically," she said. "Where are you?"

"Come to the parking lot closest to the lodge," Scott replied. "I'm in the RAV4. Look in the second row."

Kerry relayed the directions to Mitch. "Okay, we're just about there." She disconnected and scanned the snow-laden cars, trucks, and SUVs. Near the end of the row, she saw his black Toyota. "There it is!" she shouted. As they pulled up, Scott got out of the vehicle. He wore a dark blue down coat with the hood pulled up, a knit cap on his head beneath the hood, jeans, and snow boots. His breath steamed as he stood by the SUV, waiting.

"That's him?" Mitch asked. "Looks cold."

"That's him," Kerry agreed happily. "Thank you so much for the ride. Can I pay for gas or something?"

"Nope," Mitch answered. "I'd stayed at the airport I'd've been makin' messes just to have somethin' to clean up. You just have sense enough to get in out of the cold, that's all I ask."

"It's a deal." She shook Mitch's big hand—slowly—and then climbed down from the truck. As soon as her feet hit icy pavement, Scott enveloped her in a hug.

"Kerry," he breathed. "I'm so glad you're here."

Kerry couldn't help laughing. "You must be freezing," she declared. "Haven't you been running the heat?"

"Off and on," Scott admitted. "But I haven't wanted to sit there with the engine running because I figured that would attract attention."

"Can we go inside?" Kerry asked. She was an Illinois girl, used to harsh plains winters, but time in California and southern Virginia seemed to have thinned her blood. She rubbed her arms vigorously through her heavy coat. "It is really cold out here."

"We could," Scott said. "But there are various doors out of the building. Unless Season's planning to leave on skis, she'll have to take the road. We can see it from here, but if we're inside we could miss her."

"Maybe. But if we turn into a couple of corpsesicles out here, she could waltz right past us anyway."

Scott nodded. "Good point."

"Do you have any reason to think she's going to skip out tonight?" Kerry wondered.

He contemplated a moment before answering. "She put in a pretty full day on the slopes," he said. "Ate a big dinner, couple glasses of wine."

"Sounds like you kept a close eye on her," Kerry commented.

"I did what I could without being too obvious. Anyway, I figure once she hits the sack, she's there to stay. At least, that's what a human would do."

"She's a witch, but she's still human. Just . . . differently abled, as they say."

"Well, whatever she is, I bet she's sound asleep. Like we should be."

"Will we be too obvious if we go in now?"

"It's, what, a little after one? The bars are still open in there. We'll fit in."

He locked up the RAV4 and they started the trudge up to the lodge. "By the way," he said as they walked. "Merry Christmas Eve."

"Oh, yeah." She had forgotten, in her weariness and worry, that when midnight hit it had become Christmas Eve. "Heck of a way to spend a holiday, huh?"

Scott put a gloved hand on her shoulder. "I'm not complaining."

8

The Loon Mountain Lodge was all peaked roofs and large windows. Some faced onto the parking lot, but the best looked out toward the slopes. When they got inside, Kerry saw that Scott had been correct—in spite of the late hour, there were still plenty of merrymakers inside wishing one another happy holidays. It wouldn't last; they wouldn't be able to stay inside all night, she knew, without getting a room. And Scott had said the hotel was full. So they'd be heading back to the RAV4 in a while. But at least until then they could warm their bones a little.

Neither one was old enough to get into the bar, but there was enough spillover into the lobby that they felt comfortable just taking a seat there. A fire crackled in a big stone fireplace with a wooden mantel, scenting the air with the tang of wood smoke. On the mantel, pine branches decorated with glass Christmas balls crowded a couple of antique duck decoys. In a corner away from the fire stood a Christmas tree, at least ten feet tall, fully decorated, with giant boxes strewn underneath it as if waiting for the next morning.

Scott sat close to Kerry, his knees touching hers. His cheeks were flushed with the cold, his eyes glittering. Something about him seemed different than when she had last seen him, in Las Vegas after Josh's death. He seemed more . . . alive, maybe. Like his internal batteries had been running low, but were now recharged.

Kerry had only had a few short conversations with him since then, too involved in her own life, she guessed, to delve into his. She felt uncomfortable bringing up Brandy, but didn't see any way around it. "I'm sorry," she began. "About, you know, Brandy."

Scott nodded, then shrugged. "Life happens," he said. "She was ready to try something different, I guess. I'm doing okay, though. I think maybe I was ready for it too, but just didn't know it yet."

"Are you . . . seeing anyone?" she asked.

"No." His answer was immediate and emphatic. "No, not at all. She is, I guess. I don't know him, but she's mentioned a guy named Adam a couple of times."

"Are you okay with that?"

"Like I have a choice? Sure, I'm okay. Just time to move on, right? I guess you haven't had time for any . . ." He let the question trail off, but she knew what he meant.

The truth was, since Daniel had died she had hardly thought about romance at all. He was the man she had wanted to be with, the only one she had ever met with whom she could imagine a future. "Nope. No time at all."

"You'll . . . you'll find the right guy," Scott assured her. "You'll probably find out he was right there the whole time, and you just didn't know it. You've just had a lot on your plate."

"That's for sure," she agreed.

"Listen, I should tell you," he said, changing the subject abruptly. "When I came here, I brought a gun. I was going to kill her."

"Season?" She couldn't keep the surprise from her voice.

"Of course, Season. What, you don't think a gun could kill her?"

"I know it can't," Kerry stated firmly. "Mother Blessing shot her four times with a rifle, close-up. She just spat the bullets out into her hand."

It was Scott's turn to be surprised. His color had already started to pale from being inside, out of the cold, but now he blanched. "You're kidding me."

"Not at all." She sat back in the seat—he moved to stay close to her, she noticed—and told him the whole story of the battle outside Mother Blessing's cabin in the Swamp.

When she was finished, his hand was on her knee, squeezing it. "I don't see how you could have done all that, Kerry," he said. "I'd have been absolutely terrified."

"What makes you think I wasn't?"

Late-night had turned to middle-of-the night while they talked, and the bar crowd had started to thin. "We should get out of here," Kerry observed. "They're going to charge us for a room pretty soon. Can we stay warm enough in your car?"

"I've got a blanket," he answered. "I think if we huddle we'll be all right."

"Okay, then. Huddle it is." She rose and led him out of the building. It bothered her that Season was inside sleeping—she wanted to go back in and bring things to a head right now, but she knew that wasn't the way to go. Instead, they went to Scott's RAV4, put the seats back as far as they'd go, and snuggled close to one another underneath his blanket. He ran the heater for a few minutes until the car warmed up a bit, and soon they were toasty.

Scott had never been Kerry's idea of gorgeous. But it had been a long time since she'd had a man's body pressed against her. Feeling his warmth and solid bulk, she found the idea of kissing him swimming to the forefront of her thoughts. By the time it occurred to her, though, his breathing was regular and deep. He was out. Kerry tried to stay awake, to keep watch, but the day had been long and she was worn out. Within minutes, they were both sound asleep.

Kerry assumed that the skiers getting the earliest starts were not the ones who had been up drinking all night, but there were plenty of them. She woke up feeling pretty well rested despite the difficult conditions and late night, but famished and needing some grooming time. She was dying to take a shower and wash her hair, which had been tied back into a ponytail since she'd left California the day before. *Shampoo would be great,* she thought. *And conditioner. And an exfoliating scrub . . .*

Thinking like that wouldn't help. She shook Scott awake.

"Hey," she said brightly. "It's Christmas Eve. I'm starving, and if I don't brush my teeth my breath is going to kill somebody. Let's go inside."

Scott blinked a few times and found his glasses on the dash. "Okay," he said. "I could go for food. And dental hygiene."

They went back inside and found a restaurant where they could eat and watch the lobby, just in case Season woke early too. They still hadn't seen her when they were done. Over the last of their coffee, Kerry brought up what she knew would be a difficult subject.

"It's time for you to head out, Scott."

"What do you mean, head out?"

"I mean . . . when I confront Season this time, it's got to be alone. I need to do this by myself."

He looked at her like he couldn't believe what he had heard. "By yourself? You can't!"

"I have to. There's no other way for it to work." She didn't describe exactly what her plan was, but he'd never go along with it anyway. That was why she needed him gone.

"Kerry, no."

"Scott. It's not a request. I'm sorry, but you've got to go."

He was still shaking his head, still not going along with it. She was going to have to be harsh, she feared. It was for his own good. There was no telling what fireworks might happen when she confronted Season.

"I can—whatever you need me to do, Kerry, I'll do it," he insisted. "Just let me stay with you."

"You can't, Scott. It won't work. I'm glad you found her, that was great. And I appreciate you keeping me warm all night and everything. But your part is done now, and it's my turn."

"Your turn? Kerry, it's always you. Why not let me help?"

"You've done the part you can do." Kerry was firm. "Now the best thing you can do to help is to go away, before she comes out."

Scott frowned angrily. "Okay," he said, getting up in a huff. "If that's how you want it, that's what you get. I thought we were partners here, but I guess not."

"That's right," Kerry said. "No partners this time out. It's a solo deal."

"Whatever," he said. He grabbed his backpack off the restaurant floor. "I hope you're not making a big mistake," he said as he stormed away.

Oh, you and me both, Kerry thought. She hated to make him angry, but he'd never have left otherwise. And as much as it hurt her to see him so upset, he really was better off.

Now, of course, came the really hard part. It had been one thing to make a big show of courage and resolve in order to drive Scott away. But she had to follow through—she had to confront Season, all by herself, and not let the resolve she had faked so convincingly turn into outright terror.

Hands trembling, she left the restaurant and went back into the lobby to wait for Season.

Fortunately the wait wasn't too long—otherwise, Kerry believed, she might have lost her nerve altogether. But less than twenty minutes after paying the breakfast bill and finding a chair in the lobby, she saw Season's sleek form, clad in tight royal blue ski attire, heading for the back door.

Swallowing hard, steeling herself for anything, Kerry followed Season outside. She wanted to catch the witch before she got too far, and definitely before she realized Kerry was here. Catching her off-guard seemed like the only way this had even a chance of working.

"Season!" she said sharply once they were both outside. She thought Season tensed for a moment—a sudden lifting of shoulder blades, straightening of spine—but then she kept walking. *Not going by that name here, then,* Kerry reasoned. *But she'll answer to it anyway.* She moved closer to Season, who had increased her pace.

"Season Howe," she said again. This time her voice was lower. She knew Season would be listening for it.

And this time Season turned—casually, as if just looking around to admire the beautiful morning—and faced her. Her expression didn't reveal any surprise or consternation—she had a pleasant smile fixed on her pretty face, and it stayed there while she regarded Kerry. Still casual, she moved some of her neatly trimmed honey-blond hair off her face. "I'm surprised to see you," she said. Her voice was soft, almost friendly.

She's good, Kerry thought. *Anyone watching us would think we were old pals.*

"I want to talk," Kerry assured her. "That's all, just talk."

"I don't think we really have anything to say to each other."

"Oh, you're wrong, Season. We have plenty of things to discuss, trust me."

Season laughed. "Have you ever given me a reason to trust you?"

"I've never given you any reason not to."

"You've tried to kill me."

Kerry's turn to laugh. "Point taken. And vice versa, I have to say."

"Maybe I should do it again now," Season said. "I could, you know."

"I know that," Kerry said. "I know you could try, at least. But I know a few tricks now too." Which was almost a lie—she knew nothing now that she hadn't that last day in the Swamp. She hadn't quite exhausted her repertoire that time, because Mother Blessing had been calling the shots. But she hadn't picked up anything new since then.

Season smiled again. "Enough to stop me? Show me."

They were talking on a busy walkway, with skiers bustling past them on their way to the lifts. So far no one had paid them any attention, because their poses and attitudes were nonchalant. Kerry wanted to keep it that way, but it was looking like Season would need some convincing if she were not to blast Kerry on the spot.

She needed to demonstrate her skills, but in a way that would not draw any notice. Beside her was a wooden railing, with a snowy expanse beyond that led to the base of the slopes. Not far away, cable lifts ferried skiers up to the runs, which were already strewn with colorful specks, like sprinkles on a frosted doughnut, except that these sprinkles were moving swiftly downhill. Close to the lodge, the snow was dotted with trees and rocks. She ticked her head toward it, and Season's gaze followed. Kerry concentrated, gesturing toward the ground, and said, *"Ashashalika,"* one of the old words of magic.

Rocks shifted, shaking off their dusting of snow. Big ones rolled quickly to the points Kerry had visualized, and smaller ones filled in the spaces between. When they had settled, they spelled out SH in the snow.

Season laughed again, a sound that Kerry realized was a pleasant one. Season was pretty, she was cultured, she had good manners. It was just too bad she was an evil killer.

"Cute," she said. "But how does it keep me from killing you?"

"It doesn't," Kerry admitted. "But I can't show you that kind of thing without drawing a lot of eyeballs this way. I don't think either of us wants that."

"You're probably right," Season said. "But I could cloak us, and kill you just the same."

"Oh, cloaking," Kerry said, feigning surprise. She had pulled it off, drawn Season right where she wanted her. "If you want cloaking, look." She brought her hands together, touched her thumbs, and then spread them wide, which dissipated one of the cloaking spells that had kept her real stunt from Season's eyes. As far as any other onlookers were concerned, she and Season were just standing and talking—Mother Blessing had taught her that the real test of a witch's cloaking skills was the ability to reveal something to one person or group while keeping it hidden from others.

But what Season saw was a cartoon-style weight labeled 16 TONS hanging in the air, inches above her head.

"Oh, bravo," Season said, clapping her hands. "Misdirection *and* a genuine threat, cloaked. You're better than I thought."

Coming from Season Howe, that was real praise, and Kerry felt a flush of pride. "Thanks," she said. Another word of the Old Tongue, another gesture, and the weight had vanished, the rocks returned to their original positions.

Season regarded her closely for a moment, her head shaking slowly from side to side. "You really have a lot of guts to do this," she said. "Or you're stupider than you look. And I don't think that's the case."

"No, it would be a bad idea to count on that."

"We should get out of here, then," Season suggested. "If we're going to talk, I mean."

"I kind of like it public," Kerry countered, still trying to sound bolder than she felt. "How do I know you wouldn't take me someplace just to kill me?"

"I guess you don't," Season replied, turning the tables. "You'll just have to trust me."

9

Scott couldn't believe what Kerry had said to him. Everything he had done was for her. Hunting Season, finding her, keeping her in sight all day—even risking his life by buying that stupid gun. All for Kerry . . . and then she just dumped him from the whole thing. *Get lost, basically. Go away, little boy, you've done your chore for the day. Merry Christmas Eve, but I'm done with you.*

As if that wasn't bad enough, she had completely ignored the subtext of his remarks, blown it off as if she hadn't understood. He was offering himself to her, and she either didn't notice or wasn't interested. She had a lot on her mind, so it was possible, even probable that she might have missed some cues. And it probably came out of left field—he didn't know if she had ever been aware of his attraction to her.

Still, he didn't think he'd been overly subtle. Especially with the whole snuggling through the night thing. He thought it was one of the best nights of his life—fraught with the terror of possible discovery by Season, and on the cold side, but still . . . amazing just to be near to Kerry.

And then she just turned it all away. Sent him packing.

Well, she might not think he had anything to contribute, but he knew better.

He walked all the way out to the RAV4, furious at her. He tossed his backpack into the cargo area and was about to get in behind the driver's seat when he thought better of it. *Who says she gets to make the rules?* Scott wondered. He stuffed his keys back into his pocket and returned to the hotel. Much as he had done with Season, he stayed out of Kerry's view but kept an eye on her. It was only a few minutes until Season showed up and Kerry chased her outside.

He hadn't been able to get close enough to hear, but he could see just fine. They feigned a perfectly friendly conversation, but from Kerry's body language and some of her movements, he knew there was more to it than met the eye. Then Season led Kerry away—straight toward the parking lot. Scott had to spin away and insert himself between a couple of skiers to make sure they didn't spot him, but after their backs were turned he followed.

Outside, Season led Kerry to a black Jeep 4X4. Scott ran to the RAV4, jumped in, and cranked the engine. By the time

Season was leaving the parking lot, he was three cars behind. He opened his cell phone and dialed.

"Hello?" she answered a moment later. "Scott?"

"Brandy, listen, I know you don't want me calling you, but this is important. Season Howe just kidnapped Kerry."

"Kidnapped? What are you talking about, Scott? Where are you?"

"I'm at Loon Mountain, in New Hampshire," he said, the words spilling out of him in a torrent. "I came up here looking for Season, and I found her. So I called Kerry. She came out, and then she wanted to confront Season by herself. But I watched. I think they did some magic stuff, and then Season took her away in a Jeep. I'm following them."

"Scott," Brandy said, and her concern sounded genuine. "You be really careful. I know you like Kerry, but she's different than we are now. She has powers that we don't. She can take care of herself."

"She can't take Season by herself."

"You don't know that."

"Yes, I do," Scott protested. He had to make a hard left turn, so he held the phone between his cheek and shoulder while he did. "She told me this story—she and Mother Blessing together couldn't beat Season, and that was only a few weeks ago. Before she went to stay with Rebecca."

Brandy was quiet for a second, taking that in. "Okay. So where are you, exactly?"

"I'm driving. I'm following them. North on I-93."

"But they don't know you're behind them?"

"I sure hope not."

"Make sure you keep it that way. If Kerry sees you back there, Season will figure it out."

Scott eyed the horizon ahead. Storm clouds glowered; the sky was a ferocious leaden gray. "It looks like the weather is turning, too," he reported.

"Scott, I'm coming up there. It'll take me a while from here, but I'll leave as soon as I can."

"If you're going to come up, Brandy," Scott replied, "maybe you should call Rebecca. Kerry said she's in New York visiting her folks. Maybe she can come too. The more the better."

"Okay, I'll try her," Brandy promised. "And I'll have my phone, so keep me posted. And be careful!"

He ended the call. People kept telling him to be careful, like he was some kind of simpleton. Kerry had warned him to be careful, and look where it got her. Snatched by Season and driven up into the mountains.

It occurred to him to try Kerry's phone. He punched her number, and it rang three times before she answered it.

"Kerry, is everything okay?" he asked.

"Yes, Scott. Everything is fine."

"Can you talk freely?"

"Sure, why not?" She sounded normal, relaxed. Not like Season was holding a mystical gun to her head.

"I was just wondering. If you need me for anything, you can call me. You know that, right?"

"I know, Scott. Thanks."

"Okay. Talk to you later." He ended the call, feeling like an idiot. Either she was being kidnapped or she wasn't. Would a kidnapper let her keep her cell phone? Maybe, if she knew it couldn't help her.

He hung back, at least a half mile behind—just far enough to keep them in sight from time to time, but not so close that they'd realize they were being followed. The radio brought in a mixture of reggae, ska, and punk from a college station in Manchester, keeping him alert. After an hour or so, the station began to fade, and snowflakes started to slap against his windshield. They didn't stick, but before long he had to turn on his headlights and wipers. He started to feel hungry. He could use a bathroom. And his shoulders were getting sore from the driving. But they kept going, so he did. Season had left the interstate but continued on what seemed to be a fairly major two-lane highway.

His mind whirled with conflicting thoughts of Kerry. He was sick with worry about her. Had Season hypnotized her, or enchanted her somehow? Why else would she get in a car with a known killer—one she had battled just weeks before?

And then those thoughts mixed with his memories of earlier—of the joy he had felt when he'd seen her step down from that old truck. Even in the dim light of the parking lot, her big green eyes had seemed to glow, her smile radiating like a small sun. His heart had swelled at the sight of her and at the sensation of holding her in his arms—and of her returning the hug—when they'd embraced. Her scent filled him with a happiness he could barely believe.

He wasn't sure if other people felt things with the intensity he did, but he had often suspected not. For others, emotion sometimes seemed secondary to the regular grind of life. Brandy, for instance, prioritized feelings after intellect, after psychology, or her interpretation of it. And his own parents loved each other, or said they did, and had been married for more than a quarter of a century. But while they tried to have dinner together a couple of nights a week, one or the other always seemed to be off at a meeting or function that the other wasn't part of. Work or obligations got the best of people, he believed, forcing them to put off their emotional lives and well-being for later, which couldn't be healthy.

But not Scott. He found himself trying sometimes—making an effort to, as Brandy said, sublimate his feelings. But they wouldn't be put in a box. They *were* him—surface, inside, everything. The rest of him was just the clothes they were dressed in.

And right now his emotions were a stew of love and terror—but they were rapidly being mixed with anxiety about driving in the worsening storm.

When Season and Kerry pulled off the highway he almost missed them. He had spaced out, the snow creating a field of pure white ahead of him, and his focus was all on not losing the road. So when he realized that he couldn't see their taillights anymore, it was almost too late. At the last moment he spotted the small side road leading off to the right, higher up into the White Mountains. He yanked the wheel hard, and the SUV's rear wheels started to fishtail out from under him. He corrected by turning into the skid, and brought the vehicle under control in time to avoid going off the road or flipping over. If anyone had been coming up fast behind him, it would have been trouble. And there was precious little traffic—if he'd gone off the road, it could have been a long time before someone found him. He let go of the wheel long enough to wipe the sweat from his eyes, then nosed the RAV4 toward the side road.

The wind was really blowing now, coating everything with snow. Tracks showed on this little road, but there was already snow sticking to the blacktop, beginning to cover them up. Trees and bushes and hillsides were frosted as thickly as a wedding cake.

At least there was just one way they could have gone. The road only led up.

Scott pressed down on the accelerator. His wheels slid on the snow and ice, but then they caught and carried him forward. He realized, too late, that he hadn't even noticed if this road had a name, or a sign—if he had to tell Brandy how to find him up here, he'd be out of luck.

Wipers flailing, he drove on through a nearly impenetrable curtain of snow. He was getting genuinely worried now—this was starting to look like a blizzard, or a whiteout. If he was stranded up here, without food or water or shelter, he could be in some serious trouble.

But Kerry already was, he was convinced. He couldn't back off.

The road wound up a mountain, becoming narrower. Trees hemmed it in on both sides, looming dark and menacing in the dim light. The roadway was completely covered by snow now, and his tracks seemed to fill as soon as he passed.

So when he reached a fork in the road, he had no idea which way to go.

Both directions looked equally unappealing. Both seemed to lead deeper into thickly forested mountains. Neither had so much as a signpost or marker. He realized that he couldn't remember when he'd seen the last human, the last car other than Season's Jeep. He might as well have been in a primeval wilderness. He picked the right fork, because that seemed more of a continuation of the road he was already on, while the left would require actually turning off that road. But after driving that way for about ten minutes, he still hadn't caught sight of the Jeep, and the snow was, if anything, falling faster than before. The road was practically obliterated by it. Even with four-wheel drive, it was treacherously slippery. And if he had picked wrong, then with every passing minute they were getting farther and farther away on the other road, their tracks wiped away by the blizzard.

At a loss for any other options, Scott stopped his vehicle and killed the engine. He stepped out into the snow, listening. The air smelled like pine; falling snowflakes kissed his cheeks and eyelids. He had hoped to hear the roar of Season's Jeep, but there was only utter silence—not a bird, not a distant airplane, not the chirp of a cricket.

He tried Kerry's phone again. No service.

He ducked back inside, got the gun from his backpack. He hated the thing. Aiming for a faraway tree, he threw it as far as he could. It hit some branches and fell through them, crashing to the ground beneath. Snow shaken loose by its passage dropped over it. Then the silence returned, made somehow more absolute than before.

He could have been the last person on Earth.

This was just *perfect.*

Christmas Eve. Taking the new honey to meet the folks for Christmas dinner. And the ex calls and says drop everything, never mind your life, the girl I have the hots for now is in danger.

Ninety percent of the world's females, Brandy figured, would have offered a two-word response. But then, ninety percent of the world's population—more like ninety-nine point nine, probably, with a few more nines thrown in for good measure—were blissfully unaware that beings like Season Howe existed. That knowledge, combined with the belief that Season had targeted their little summer group for extinction, meant that Brandy's reaction would have to be somewhat different than the vast majority's.

Instead of telling him to get lost—or any of the other combinations of two words that came to mind—her answer had to be "I'm coming." It wasn't fair. But then, no one had ordained that life had to be fair. In fact, it often seemed that the better it was going in one area or another, balance decreed that it had to get worse somewhere else.

So: Adam good, Season bad. And as good as Adam was, on the scale Season's badness was far, far worse.

Which meant her response wasn't in doubt. The only question remaining was, how did she tell her parents and Adam that she was going to New Hampshire for Christmas, instead of their house?

Her mom would want her head. Her dad would sulk unpleasantly. DJ, her little brother, would probably threaten bodily harm. The various relatives—aunts, uncles, cousins—who were expected would be overly concerned and offer bits of helpful advice to the family. Of course, she wouldn't be around so she wouldn't have to listen to that part, but she'd get plenty of complaints about it when she got back.

Bright side, she thought, *maybe I'll get killed and won't have to face them at all.*

Not funny, she amended. *Ask Josh and Mace if it's funny.*

Still, there were times when one needed black humor to fend off the real horrors of life, and this was looking like one of those times. If she couldn't make unpleasant jokes about it, she probably couldn't face it at all.

Brandy realized that sitting in her apartment stewing wasn't going to do any good—this was one of those occasions where the sooner she acted, the better. She picked the phone out of her lap and dialed Rebecca's cell.

While she drove through the gathering storm, Season chatted casually about a wide variety of subjects, from clothes to cars, environmental issues to restaurants and resorts all around the world. She was well informed and erudite, and Kerry couldn't help enjoying the conversation.

The only thing Season refused to discuss was what Kerry had wanted to talk about in the first place. "We can talk about all of that, but not here, not in the car," Season had said when Kerry pressed the issue. "When we get where we're going." But she wouldn't tell Kerry where it was they were going, only that it was someplace safe, someplace they wouldn't be disturbed.

Kerry was terrified by the whole idea of going anywhere with Season.

But curiosity outweighed her terror. Season had made some explosive charges at Mother Blessing's place, and Kerry was determined to get to the truth about them. Was Season Mother Blessing's mother and Daniel's grandmother? Who was really responsible for the tragedy at Slocumb, Virginia, in 1704, which had kicked off this whole multicentury war of witches? These were the issues that Kerry was really concerned with, not which European chef made the best chocolate desserts— although chocolate still ranked pretty high on the priority scale.

She rode along beside Season, commenting or asking a question on occasion and answering some about her own earlier life—before San Diego—and found herself surprised at the witch's geniality. The radio played holiday music that made a strange counterpoint to the ride. She didn't relax— that was a leap of faith she wasn't ready to take, not when the woman behind the wheel had the power to end her life with a word or two. But she became somewhat less tense as the drive wore on, at least until the storm blew in and erased visibility down to a few yards. Season expressed full confidence in her Jeep's ability to handle the snowy roads, and Kerry could see that she was a capable driver. *But then,* she thought, *she's had a century of practice, so why not? Probably started out driving a Model T.*

They drove deeper into the wilderness, and Season became less chatty as she had to struggle more with just keeping her wheels on the road—or seeing the road at all. It was still only early afternoon, but the sky was twilight-dark, the world reduced to nothing but snowflakes flickering in the head-lights. Looming over everything were the mountains, rounded and stolid, like hunched-over elders quietly disapproving of everything they observed. Kerry knew these mountains were older than the Rockies she had flown over twice, earlier in the year. Those had knife-edged peaks that looked like they could slice open the airplane. But these, while less imposing, were still higher than anything back home in Illinois, or down in the flat mid-Atlantic region.

Finally, when Kerry was starting to worry that they really would become trapped by the ever-thicker downfall, Season pulled off the road onto a barely-there driveway and stopped with her headlights shining on a small wooden cabin nestled in a stand of tall pines. Snow had drifted in front of the cabin's door and piled on its rooftop, but the structure seemed sound enough.

"Here we are," Season announced.

"*Where* we are?"

"Where we're going. Kind of a little hideaway I have."

"I thought you liked being where there were lots of people around," Kerry mentioned. "The whole safety in numbers thing, like with the resorts?"

"I do," Season confirmed. "But I also know that, strategically, sometimes it's important to be able to change the way I do things. Can't be predictable all the time. So I have a few of these kinds of places scattered around the country, for emergency use."

"Are we still in New Hampshire?"

"Yes," Season replied. "I like to keep my hideaways within an hour or so of the resorts I frequent. Weather permitting, of course."

Kerry looked at the weather. "Think we'll be snowed in?"

"Almost definitely," Season said. "We'll be fine, though. There are plenty of supplies and firewood inside."

"Okay, then. Might as well get to it." She opened the Jeep door and grabbed her duffel from the backseat. "Guess it's going to be a white Christmas for us."

10

The cabin was, in fact, much more impressive inside than out. That seemed to be a habit with witches, Kerry thought, remembering the way Mother Blessing's place in the Swamp had looked like a falling-down old trapper's cabin from the outside, but a modern suburban home on the inside.

Witches had other advantages, too. Starting a fire was no problem for Season, who simply laid some logs into a gigantic stone fireplace and ignited them magically. Within minutes the place had already started to warm up, and Kerry was able to shed her coat and look around a little.

The interior reflected the cabin theme from outside, but in a much more luxurious way than Kerry would have guessed from the primitive facade. The walls were knotty pine, but highly polished, warm, and rich-looking. The hardwood floor was dotted with beautiful rugs. Season's furniture was rustic but comfortable, all wood, well crafted and padded. A counter or breakfast bar separated the huge main room from a kitchen area with cabinets in the same golden pine as the floors. The place had two bedrooms, and Season showed Kerry which one would be hers—a cozy space with a big wooden bed covered by a lush comforter. The room was tucked under the eaves at the back of the house, timbered ceiling slanting away toward what looked, through the one small window, like unlimited, infinite pine forest.

We really are alone up here, Kerry thought, with a sensation of dread. *Anything could happen. They'd never find my body.*

But if Season had intended to kill her, she could have done so at any time. Why bother bringing her up here, showing her a bedroom, getting towels from a linen closet for her?

No reason that Kerry could determine. Which could only mean that Season hadn't brought her here to kill her, but to talk, as she had insisted.

Well, that was fine. That's what Kerry wanted too. She had hoped to do it nearer civilization, where she could get away if she needed to. But she wasn't the one calling the shots. Since they'd climbed into the Jeep, Season had been, literally as well as figuratively, in the driver's seat.

Season had suggested that Kerry take a shower, and given how nasty she felt, Kerry had happily agreed. She took her towels into the hall bathroom—her own master suite, Season said, had another—and was delighted to find that it was just as deluxe as the rest of the place. The fixtures were gleaming brass, the tub enclosed in sparkling glass. When Kerry undressed and turned on the shower, the water rushed forth steaming hot. Bottles of shampoo, conditioner, and cleanser were lined up on a shelf inside the tub enclosure. Twenty minutes later, showered, having found a brand-new toothbrush and a tube of toothpaste lying next to the sink, she felt like a new person. She wrapped her long black hair up in one of the towels, wrapped the other one around herself, and went back across the hall to the bedroom. When she opened the bathroom door, she realized that Season had been busy too—cooking aromas competed with the wood burning in the fireplace, and the smell instantly reminded Kerry of how long it had been since breakfast.

Back in her room she dug a clean pair of sweatpants, a thick green cableknit sweater, and fuzzy white socks from her duffel. After rubbing lotion into her hands, arms, and legs, she dressed quickly. She carried the towels back into the bathroom to hang, tied her hair back, applied a little eyeliner. She could have done more, but she felt more presentable than she had in days, and the smells from the kitchen were making her crazy.

"I hope pasta's okay," Season said when Kerry found her. She had a big pot boiling on the stove. She'd changed into a soft tan turtleneck and faded jeans and wore her hair loose. "It was fast and easy. There's garlic bread, too, and some salad."

"Pasta's fine," Kerry said. She was afraid that she might actually start to drool. "Smells wonderful."

"Thanks," Season said with a smile. "I like to cook, but I don't really get much chance to."

"How did you get fresh salad vegetables here if you haven't been here lately?" Kerry wondered.

Season just laughed.

"Oh," Kerry said, realizing the foolishness of her question. There wasn't much Season couldn't do, apparently—conjuring some fresh lettuce, tomatoes, and cucumbers wouldn't be much of a trick for her.

There was a rough-hewn pine dining table beside the breakfast bar, on which Season had put out thick white linen place mats and heavy pewter tableware. "Can I do anything?" Kerry asked.

"It's just about ready," Season said by way of reply. She picked up the pot with two massive potholders and carried it to the sink, where she dumped it into a colander. "Meat sauce all right with you?"

"Yeah, that's fine," Kerry said. "Thanks for this, by the way. I am just starving."

"Me too." She put the pasta back into the pot and put it back on its burner. On another burner a pot of red sauce simmered noisily. Season poured the red sauce over the pasta, stirring the two together, and let it cook for a couple of minutes. "This makes it so the sauce doesn't just slide off the pasta," she explained. "Holds the heat in, too, so it stays warm longer."

"Works for me," Kerry said. She appreciated the effort,

although right at this moment she was less concerned with
technique and more with actually eating.

"Can you grab the bread?" Season asked. She was busy
stirring the pasta and sauce, so Kerry picked up the potholders
and went to the oven. Inside, the crusty garlic bread was just
the right shade of golden brown. She drew it out and put it on
the cutting board that Season indicated, carrying that to the
table and setting it down.

"I think we're ready," Season announced. "What do you
want to drink?"

"What is there?" Kerry asked. But at Season's smile, she
answered for herself. "Oh, right—everything. I'll have a peach
Snapple, I guess."

"It's in the fridge," Season said, putting the pasta into a
serving dish. "Help yourself."

Kerry opened the refrigerator. There was indeed a peach
Snapple there, on the top shelf.

And nothing else. Kerry took the bottle, leaving the refrigerator empty. She suspected it had not been empty a minute
earlier, and probably wasn't now.

So Season had a sense of humor, on top of everything
else. That was unexpected, but the kind of surprise—like this
lunch—that Kerry could use more of.

After they had eaten—both largely silent, more interested in
consuming than conversing—Kerry cleared the dishes and
they retired to the living room to sit by the fire. Outside, night

had fallen, but snowflakes continued to drop past the light from the cabin's windows. Season took a glass of red wine in and sat on the rug in front of the fireplace, setting her glass down on the hearth. She carried in a bowl of mixed nuts and a plate of cookies and put them on a coffee table. Kerry brewed some orange pekoe tea and joined her, taking a seat on a cushy couch. Season watched her get comfortable, a serious expression on her lovely face. She chewed a little on her lower lip, which Kerry found surprisingly girlish for someone as old as Season was.

Then again, if you get right down to it, walking and breathing are pretty girlish for someone as old as her. Especially if she's really Daniel's grandmother.

After a minute Season broke the silence. "You've got some questions, Kerry," she said. "Not all at once, please. And I reserve the right not to answer everything right away. I'm tired, and I don't want to talk all evening."

This presented Kerry with a quandary. How would she know which questions to ask and which to avoid? There was so much she wanted to know—not just about the areas in which Season and Mother Blessing contradicted each other, but about Season's long war with Daniel, and about her powers and abilities. She was still furious at Season, but the long day with her had exposed a human side that she had never expected to find, and that tempered her rage somewhat. Season may have been a monster, but she wasn't all monster, all the time.

"Start at the beginning, then," she said finally. "What happened that day in Slocumb?"

Season shook her head. "Not tonight," she replied. "That story's too long for now. Next?"

Most of Kerry's questions were going to involve long, complex answers, she figured. She hoped Season wouldn't try to dodge them all. "Okay," she said after coming up with a different approach. "The way I see it, you killed three of my friends: Daniel Blessing, Mace Winston, and Josh Quinn. And poor old Edgar Brandvold. How can you justify murder?"

Season took a sip of wine and studied Kerry with her deep blue eyes. "Murder has been justified in human society since the first caveman clobbered another one over the head with a stick," she said. "But you're not here for a civics lesson, so I'll take them one at a time.

"Yes, I killed Daniel. From your reaction at the time, and some things you've said and done since then, I take it he meant something to you."

"We were in love," Kerry said quietly. She didn't want to start talking about that, didn't want to shed any tears for him in front of his murderer.

"I thought it was something like that. For your sake, I'm sorry. For my own, though—he had been chasing me for centuries, Kerry. We've battled many times, done some damage, but there was never anything final. Never a conclusion. I was tired of running, tired of having to look over my shoulder, of never sitting still or trusting anyone. And he was never going to let up."

"That's true."

"And I shouldn't need to remind you, Kerry, that when it happened, he attacked me. You were there. You saw it all. He hit me with everything he had, thought he had killed me. And I was hurt, bad. Just not as hurt as he believed."

Kerry remembered the day vividly, especially in her nightmares. It had happened just as Season described. They had trapped Season in her rented house—Daniel, Kerry, Brandy, Scott, Rebecca, and Josh—and lured her outside, where Daniel had unleashed a barrage of magical attacks against her. As Season said, she had gone down. Even Kerry thought she was finished. But from somewhere, she had summoned an unexpected reserve of strength. With Daniel's guard down she had been able to claim the advantage, and she had bested him, while Kerry and her friends looked on in horror.

"Okay, yeah," Kerry admitted. "That's true. But—"

"There are no buts, Kerry," Season said. "He would not have just given up. There was no talking to him, no rational discussion. He wanted me dead, and he wanted it to happen before the next Witches' Convocation. You know what that is?"

Mother Blessing had told Kerry about the Convocation, a gathering of witches held every five hundred years to discuss problems and techniques and to try witches accused of crimes. "Yes."

"If I thought he would let up, if he would have let me live until the Convocation, where I could have taken some legal action, that would have been fine. Obviously, I've spent the last few hundred years running and hiding, trying to avoid violence, instead of seeking him out and just finishing it off. But the closer we got to the Convocation, the more he came after me. Finally, I'd had enough. At that moment, with all of you there, he almost got me, and I did what I had to do."

Kerry didn't want to admit there was any truth at all in what Season was saying. She wanted to hold on to her anger, to wave it like a flag. Whatever the circumstances, Season had been the one who struck a fatal blow, not Daniel.

She knew, however, that Daniel would have if he'd been able. His intention had been to kill Season or die trying. She had simply held the better hand, or played her cards more skillfully. Either way, Season's version of things rang true.

"It happened more or less like that with Abraham, too— Daniel's brother. Have you heard about him?"

"Daniel said they ambushed you in your room," Kerry told her.

"That's right. And killed my lover. I fought back hard. I killed Abraham, and thought I had killed Daniel then too." She took another sip of wine and looked away from Kerry. "My life would have been a lot simpler if I'd made sure."

"What about Mace?" Kerry asked. "What threat was he to you?"

Season glanced up again. "I don't know the name. He was the one with the big blue car?"

"That was Suzie," Kerry replied. She was still stuffed from the meal, but she took a couple of nuts and nibbled on them.

"The car, I mean. Yes, Mace had a big blue Lincoln."

"Yes. That one might have been avoidable," Season admitted. "I knew I had injured Daniel, but he'd escaped before I could finish him. I thought if I could track him down quickly enough, before he had healed . . . I could end things that much sooner. But he had come into contact with you and your friends, somehow, and he was screening you all from me. When that one—Mace, you said?"

"Right, Mace Winston. Kind of a hick, but sweet, you know?"

Season nodded, biting a cookie. "When he left your group, he suddenly came onto my radar. That's a metaphor, by the way—not real radar. So I interrupted his escape to question him about where Daniel might be found. He tried to resist. I admit that I overreacted. I didn't mean to kill him, but I did. I'm terribly sorry for that."

"Not so sorry that you didn't kill Josh, too."

Season looked confused. "I'm sorry? You mentioned that name before, too. I don't know who you mean."

"Oh, come on," Kerry said, anger simmering to the surface again. "Josh. Pale-faced Goth boy, Las Vegas. Do you kill so many people you can't remember them all?"

Season put her wineglass down and pointed a finger at Kerry. "Oh, now I know who you're talking about. I was there when he died, but I didn't kill him."

"He wrote your name in his own blood on the side of a slot machine," Kerry said.

"I didn't know that," Season admitted. "But it doesn't change anything. Maybe he wrote it because he recognized me, or because I was the last person to speak to him."

"Because you killed him."

"I didn't, Kerry," Season insisted. "I've admitted to the ones I did, even Mace, which was accidental. Why would I lie about this one?"

"Why did you talk to him, then?" Kerry pressed.

"He helped me, or tried to. A couple of Mother Blessing's simulacra were attacking me in the casino. He stepped in front of them, slowed them down. It was like—like he was trying to reason with them. You know simulacra?"

"I've met a few."

"Reasoning isn't their forte," Season understated. "If he was one of your friends, I would have thought he'd have been egging them on."

"He knew we were coming. We were in the parking structure, I think, when it happened. Or almost there. Maybe he wanted them to hold off until we arrived so we could all attack you together."

Season shrugged. "Perhaps. All I know is that the simulacra didn't react well to being thwarted. They removed your friend from their path the only way they knew how. After I dispatched them, I checked on him—on Josh—but it was too late. He was already fading. And casino security was on the way. I made him comfortable in his last moments, so at least he wouldn't be in pain, and I left."

Kerry found herself wanting to believe that, even though she didn't know if she should. But she liked the idea that Josh's death had been without pain.

"You said one other name, earlier," Season reminded her.

Daniel, Mace, Josh, Kerry thought. Those were the deaths she had carried around inside her for so long, the reasons she had wanted Season Howe dead. Then it came back to her. "Oh, yeah. Edgar Brandvold. Down in Wallaceton, Virginia. Outside the Swamp."

"Oh, right," Season said. "A longtime ally of Mother Blessing's."

"He did her favors from time to time," Kerry countered. "Brought her groceries, that kind of thing."

"More than that," Season said. "He was a kind of early warning system for her. She'd taught him a few tricks, and he patrolled the eastern border of the Swamp to make sure her privacy wasn't compromised. When I found him, he cast a spell, tried to tear my head off. But I've got pretty good reflexes. I dodged and counterattacked. His reflexes weren't so good."

"His walking stick was driven through his heart."

"A girl's gotta do what a girl's gotta do. It was a walking stick when you saw it. It was a serpent before that, with a mouth the size of a car door, trying to chomp on me."

The story sounded just ridiculous enough to be true. And Kerry had seen equally bizarre things. She had wondered why Season had killed Edgar—the man seemed ancient and frail, like he couldn't possibly have been a threat. It seemed clearer now.

"Okay, I guess I can buy that. So then, what—"

Season held up a hand to stop her. "That's enough for one night," she said. "I'm beat. Driving through that snow really took a lot out of me. And it's early enough that I can shower and get a good night's sleep. Let's turn in now, and we can talk more tomorrow."

"But—"

"If we don't go to sleep," Season cautioned, "then Santa Claus won't come."

"There isn't even a tree," Kerry pointed out. "Somehow, I doubt that Santa is going to visit this place. There aren't any good little girls here anyway."

"You might be surprised," Season said. "Never count the old guy out." She stood up and took the dirty dishes to the kitchen. "Tomorrow!" she called back over her shoulder.

"Okay," Kerry said. "But tomorrow everything's fair game."

"I promise."

And I'm going to hold you to that, Season, Kerry thought. *That's a promise you won't get out of.*

11

Kerry Profitt's diary, December 24

All righty, then.

It wouldn't be fair, I guess, to say that twenty-four hours ago I had been ready to kill Season Howe on sight. I had already decided at that point that I wanted to talk to her first, to try to get some things straight in my own mind. I wanted a clearer picture of what it was I had become involved in.

Then I would kill her.

And now . . .

Is it called the Stockholm Syndrome? Something like that. Wherein kidnap victims begin to identify with their captors, sometimes even helping protect them from the police. Although it's not fair, probably, to say that someone going,

"Hey, let's take a ride so we can talk," and the other some-one going, "Okay," is the same as being kidnapped.

She's not exactly holding me here against my will. Except it's not like I could leave, at least not easily, given that we are a million miles from civilization and I have no actual idea of where.

But I came willingly, and I don't feel like I'm in real danger from her. That could change. I'm not sure I'll sleep all that soundly tonight, and it has nothing to do with listening for reindeer hooves on the roof. But I don't think she'd have fed me and talked to me about having killed Daniel, and Mace, and Edgar, but not Josh, if she was just going to turn around and kill me.

I'm not sure, in fact, why she brought me here, why she agreed to tell me all this. Maybe that's something she'll reveal tomorrow.

That would be good, because I could sure use a clue here. Once again I'm feeling kind of out in the wilderness without a map, which is not only literally true but metaphori-cally as well. I still don't know what happened in Slocumb, but if Season is to be believed, then Mother Blessing, not Season, is really responsible for Josh's death. And Mother Blessing knew, when I got back to her place from Las Vegas, that I was devastated by what had happened there.

So why would she continue to let me think Season was responsible, if she knew full well that she wasn't? That would be . . .

Hello! Clue much? If she wanted some proxy stand-in to take over the hunt for Season when Daniel was gone, what better way to keep that person interested than throwing the body of a friend or two down and letting her think Season had done it?

And, once again, Kerry the slow-witted comes to realize there's much more to Mother Blessing than meets the eye. And none of it good.

So tonight. Kind of strange, sitting around with the killer of the man I loved, sharing cookies and nuts, drinking and talking. And underneath it all—also kind of strange—feeling like, hey, I'm glad I haven't killed her, because she's kind of neat.

"Kind of neat." Too old-fashioned? Kind of rad, maybe. Kind of phat. Whatever, it's Christmas Eve, and if there is ever a time when old-fashioned is apropos, this is it. "Apropos," also old-fashioned, methinks.

And "methinks," again also.

Methinks I'm dodging the central issue here, which has to do with not killing Season after all. But she makes a kind of sense that I am having a hard time disregarding. Yes, she killed Daniel, and I hate her for that. But she's right: He was trying to kill her. I really thought he had killed her. She was so brutalized, so still—I thought she was dead, and so did he. But she wasn't, and then he was, and it was just about that fast.

And tonight, when she was talking about the necessity

of killing him and Abraham, she was looking right at me, flat
and level, letting me see that she was telling me the truth.
But then she turned away. Not like someone who was lying
might, but . . . when she turned back, it looked like there
might have been a tear in her eye.

A trick? Too much wine? Anything's possible, right? But
the fact is, it looked like talking about their deaths choked
her up.

Like, maybe, a grandmother would cry when talking
about the deaths of her grandsons.

Sleep on that, Kerry Profitt.

It's almost midnight. Merry Christmas.

K.

"Merry Christmas!"

After coming down off the mountain, Scott had paid
higher-than-premium fare for a short-term condo rental near
Berlin, New Hampshire, offering enough to make the people
who had really rented it happy to go bunk with friends, knowing that their ski holiday had netted them a significant profit.
But he had figured they'd need a base of operations if they
were going to have any hope of finding Kerry.

"They" came at seven o'clock on Christmas morning.
Scott woke to their insistent ringing. Bleary-eyed, he pawed
for his glasses. He had slept poorly, worrying about Kerry,
but a couple of hours ago had finally drifted off. Then the

doorbell started in. On the way out of the bedroom he caught a glimpse of himself in the mirror—bed-head sent his brown hair shooting off in every direction at once. He had slept in a T-shirt and boxers, so he tugged on yesterday's jeans, then opened the door for Brandy and Rebecca, who, in spite of having been on the road for hours and hours, both looked at least ten times more awake than he felt. They entered with holiday greetings at least twenty times more cheerful than he could return, given the circumstances.

"Hey, you guys," he said. Brandy accepted a quick hug, even returning it with a couple of friendly pats on the back. Her familiar, slightly fruity scent brought a rush of emotion flooding into him, even more than the sight and feel of her did.

"Did we wake you?"

"Well, it's either that or I always look this bad," Scott said. "I'll hope for the former."

Brandy shook off her vintage fake-fur-lined coat and handed it to Scott. Fortunately, the place had come with a standing coatrack, so he didn't have to try to figure out someplace to put it. "You don't look—well, okay, yes you do. You look awful. You want to get some more sleep?"

He turned to Rebecca, who squeezed him tighter than Brandy had. "Don't listen to her," Rebecca said. "Anyone has a right to look like they spent the night under a bus if they want to."

"Gee, thanks, Beck," Scott said, stifling a yawn. "I'll make coffee. You want some?"

Brandy shook her head. Underneath her coat she wore a red wool turtleneck and brown denim pants. Her hair was tightly braided and lay close to her scalp. "Caffeine is what got us here. I think we sampled every energy drink on the market. If I have any more, I'll start bouncing off your walls. Which, by the way, nice place. How'd you score it?"

"Found someone willing to accept a wheelbarrow full of cash. Don't tell the landlord, because he doesn't know."

Brandy smiled. "You're becoming very resourceful, Scott," she said. "Good job."

"Definitely," Rebecca added. She doffed her puffy blue ski coat, revealing a gray UC Santa Cruz sweatshirt with pink corduroy pants and black lace-up pleather boots.

"You don't know the half of it." He was thinking of the gun he'd acquired. That had been resourceful. *And stupid,* he added.

"I'm sure not." Brandy went into the living room, furnished in Modern Rental oaks and earth tones, and took a seat on a sofa.

"Have a seat," he said, after the fact.

"Thanks," Rebecca replied. *Other people are always more polite than exes,* Scott observed. He crossed through the living room into the condo's kitchenette to start the coffee. He needed a jolt, even if no one else did.

"What do we do now?" Brandy asked. "Is there a plan?"

Scott was suddenly, unreasonably infuriated by her. "I don't know, Brandy! I don't have a plan. All I know is that

Kerry is out there somewhere, that Season's got her, and we have to find them!"

Brandy got up off the sofa, putting her hands out. "Whoa, Scott. I know you're frantic over this. I am too, believe me. But let's keep our eye on the real problem, okay? Don't take your frustrations out on me."

"Yeah, I'm sorry, Brandy," he said, deflated just as quickly as he had blown up. She was right, he wasn't mad at her. He was just mad.

"I was looking at a New Hampshire map on the way here," Brandy pointed out. "And there must be, like, thousands of square miles of wilderness up here."

"Probably," he agreed glumly. He stared at the coffee, willing it to brew faster. He was either going to have to go back to bed or down the whole pot, and Brandy seemed intent on talking.

"So how are we going to—"

"Brandy!" he interrupted, unable to keep his emotions in check. "I just said I don't have a plan, okay? I don't know how we're going to find her! I just know that we have to—that if we don't, Season's going to kill her! That's what she does."

"Okay, you guys," Rebecca said, obviously uneasy with their arguing. "We'll figure something out. Or she'll get in touch with us. Have you tried her phone lately?"

"I tried it all day and night yesterday. She's out of range, or else she has it turned off."

"That'll make things tougher," Brandy pointed out. "But

there's got to be a way. You know where you lost them, right?"

"Yeah, basically," Scott replied. "But it was snowing like crazy. I'm pretty sure I can find it again, but there are no tracks or anything."

"But maybe we can come up with some kind of organized search pattern," Rebecca suggested. "Mark off a grid and take it section by section."

"We'd have to have snowmobiles for that," Scott countered. "It's really wilderness up there—not many roads, lots of open country and forest."

"But they were in a car of some kind," Brandy said. "So there must be a way to get to where they are on roads."

"They were in a Jeep," Scott answered. "They were sticking to roads as far as I saw, but it's possible that they didn't have to. They could have taken some little dirt road, or even left the roads altogether."

"You still have the RAV4, right?" Rebecca asked him.

"Yeah," he said. "It's got four-wheel drive, but it's not the off-roader the Jeep is. They could definitely get to places I can't."

"Okay," Brandy said. "But at least it gives us a place to start. And if we get going soon, we'll have a full day of light. The longer we sit around here the less time we'll have to search."

That was true, Scott knew. But the coffeemaker was just beginning to fill the pot. He had not had enough sleep to function at his best all day. While he knew that caffeine was no substitute for sleep, it looked like it was the best he was going to get.

Rebecca had gone almost immediately to Grand Central Station upon receiving the anxious call from Brandy. She had been expecting it ever since Kerry had taken off for New Hampshire. Kerry was brave and smart, but she wouldn't be able to cope with Season all by herself. It had been stupid of Rebecca to let her go off and try. She had hoped that Kerry could keep Scott out of trouble, but now it seemed she was in danger herself. That knowledge was the only reason Rebecca had been willing to come, to risk facing Season again. Kerry should have gathered them all from the beginning—not that there was much the rest of them could have done that Kerry couldn't, but at least they'd have been together. Taking them one by one seemed to be Season's standard procedure, and they couldn't let her continue to do that.

Her parents had been upset, but not outrageously so. Their holiday was over anyway. She had been on a train within an hour. Four hours after that—four hours of increasing anxiety, mingled with some outright terror—she was in Boston.

Brandy met her at the train station looking terrible—her eyes bloodshot and puffy, the skin under her nose raw. She had obviously been crying.

Once they were settled in the car, heading out of town, she had asked Brandy what was wrong.

"It's just . . . this whole thing stinks," Brandy answered. "I'm seeing this great new guy—his name is Adam, you'd love him, Rebecca. Really, you would. Anyway, things have been moving kind of fast, and it seems like we're pretty serious about each other. He was going to go with me to my folks' house for Christmas dinner. We were both super nervous about it, but I was looking forward to it too, because Adam is really mature and charming and everything. He would have blown Mom away.

"But then, you know, Scott had to go all *America's Most Wanted* on us."

Rebecca was shocked. "Brandy! It's not like he made Season take her."

"No, I know," Brandy admitted. "I don't mean to make light of it. Kerry's in trouble and we've got to be there for her, just like she would be for us. It's just—the timing was incredibly sucky. I told Adam I had to cancel, and he was all pouty and sad. I think it would have been better if he'd been mad, but he wasn't. He was just, 'Okay, if that's what you really want to do.' Which, of course, it's not. But it's what I have to do, and he didn't seem to get that."

"What did your parents say?" Rebecca asked.

Brandy concentrated on her driving for a minute. Rebecca figured she was probably trying to compose a response. "Let's just say they weren't happy," she said finally. "Mom just about blew a gasket. 'I've been cooking for three days! Everyone's expecting to see you, and to meet Adam! What do you mean, you have to go?' That kind of thing. DJ thought it was Adam's fault somehow and offered to break his legs."

"You tell him to break Season's instead?"

"If I dared to tell him about Season, he'd try it. And of course she'd fry him."

"Like she'll do to us if she gets a chance."

"Well, yeah," Brandy agreed. "Anyway, there was a scene. Mom shrieking, Dad kind of humphing, DJ storming around hitting things. It wasn't pretty."

"Doesn't sound like it."

Rebecca was glad to be with Brandy, happy to see her friend in spite of the unpleasant reason for the reunion. Conversation drifted to less emotionally charged topics as the miles melted away behind them. The farther north they went, the worse the weather grew, until what should have been a four-hour drive turned into eight. Christmas carols and caffeine helped them stay alert and on the road, but even those things couldn't help stave off the very real horror Rebecca felt as they got closer to where Season had last been seen. Rebecca worried about Kerry, but she worried about herself and the others, too.

And now they were here, in Scott's emergency rental. And Kerry, the reason for their hurried trip, was somewhere out there.

12

Kerry slept better than she'd expected—*better than I had a right to, under the circumstances*, she thought—and when she got up in the morning, donning the fuzzy terry cloth robe that hung on the back of her bedroom door, Season was already busy in the kitchen. The cabin smelled like bacon and garlic, which were both happy aromas as far as she was concerned.

"Merry Christmas," Season said when she saw her. She wore a white sweater with a red reindeer shape on it and black pants.

"Merry Christmas," Kerry echoed. "That smells great."

"I hope you're hungry," Season said. "There are omelets, garlic home fries, bacon, and juice. And I made a pot of Earl Grey."

"Mmm," Kerry said. "Sounds wonderful."

"Well, you were right. Santa didn't find us. So I figured we could eat our sorrows away."

"I'm in favor of that idea." Kerry still felt strange, socializing like this with Season. But she had slept all night under the witch's roof, and she had not been attacked. She was still here, still in one piece. The more she got to know Season, the more she believed that they had all been wrong about her. Not completely wrong, since she had admitted to killing Mace and Daniel. But wrong in some very significant ways nonetheless.

A few minutes later Season had dished up breakfast, and Kerry sat across from her at the table. The food tasted delicious— Season could become a chef, if she ever decided to give up the witch gig.

They ate in relative silence, Kerry realizing with the first few mouthfuls how truly ravenous she was. After they were done and Kerry was washing dishes, Season made her an offer.

"For your Christmas present," she said, "I'll answer ten questions for you."

"Just ten?" Kerry replied.

"Choose carefully," Season admonished with a smile. "Now you're down to nine."

"Oh, jeez," Kerry said. "It's going to be like that? That wasn't a question, so don't count it."

"Whenever you're ready," Season said. "Have you looked outside? We're not going anywhere today, so I'm not in any hurry."

Kerry hadn't, but she wasn't surprised. The way the snow had still been coming down when she'd gone to bed, she would have been amazed if any of the roads they took here had still been passable.

Nine questions, though. And she had to be careful how she phrased them, obviously. It wouldn't do to waste another one.

She finished washing out the last pan and pulled a towel from its hook to begin drying. "Okay," she said. "Here goes. Is Mother Blessing your real daughter?"

Season looked directly at her. "Yes," she said simply.

"I hope that's not all the elaboration I get," Kerry said, careful to phrase it as a statement.

"I'm not trying to be difficult, Kerry," Season said. "But there are rules about this kind of thing. And before you spend a question asking what kind of thing I mean, I'll just tell you: Witches aren't supposed to give non-witches unnecessary information about our kind."

"But I am—I mean, I'm becoming a witch. Mother Blessing was teaching me. She said you didn't have to be born a witch, but you could be trained."

"And she was right. That's the only reason I'm giving you this chance now. If you were completely non-witch, you wouldn't even get this much. Daniel broke more rules than you'll ever know when he told you everything he did. Had he survived until the Convocation, he'd have been severely disciplined."

"Well, I think that sucks," Kerry said. "He loved me, and he wanted to protect me."

"I didn't say that I thought he did anything wrong," Season said. "Only that he broke the rules. I'm trying to be more careful. But I won't leave you with just yes or no answers. Yes, she is my daughter. She wasn't always, as you might guess, called Mother Blessing. When she was born, her father and I called her Myrtle. It was traditional in those days for the children of witches to have names from nature."

She stopped, and Kerry guessed that meant the answer was complete. She was going to have to be very careful, with just eight questions remaining. She could jump around, asking the first things that came to mind. But that would probably be a good way of ensuring that when they were done, big holes in her understanding remained. She had to play it smarter to make sure she got the whole story.

With the last of the dishes dried, she came out from behind the kitchen counter. She still hadn't dressed, but it was a lazy Christmas Day and she didn't care. The fuzzy robe kept her warm and comfortable. "Let's sit down," she suggested.

Season followed her to the living room. As on the night before, a fire crackled in the fireplace, giving the room a homey, pleasant feel. Kerry sat in a soft chair while Season stretched out on the couch.

"Who was Mother Blessing's father, then?" she asked.

"His name was Forest. We married young—but then, everyone did in those days. That was in 1649, in England.

Charles I was beheaded, Charles II crowned, and I was married, all in the same year. It was an eventful time."

"Sounds like it."

"Anyway, Forest and I had many good years together. We moved to the colonies, where it seemed there was more freedom, and we were less likely to be hanged for witchcraft. I was pregnant before I learned that Forest was, in fact, evil—he had been hiding it well, but not well enough, as it turned out. I left him and moved to Slocumb with young Myrtle, my only child. We were happy there, for a while, and the people came to accept my skills, seeking my help when they needed something I could provide.

"But Myrtle, as it happened, inherited her father's nature, not mine. Evil can only be repressed for so long; eventually it reveals itself. The same happened, sadly, with Myrtle. I think having a child herself set it off."

A child? Kerry wondered. She had only ever heard about Daniel and Abraham—twins, and born after Slocumb's demise. She had to ask.

"What happened to that child?"

"I think I want more tea," Season said instead of answering. "How about you?"

"No, I'm fine," Kerry replied.

Season went into the kitchen, and came back a moment later with a steaming mug. "Sorry," she said. "All this talking makes my throat dry."

"That's okay," Kerry assured her.

"You wanted to know what became of my first grandson. That's part of a longer story. The easy answer is, he died, but you want more than that. I won't count that one, but find another way to ask."

Kerry thought that over. That question had almost been wasted, because she had been suckered into rushing it. She didn't want to do that again. After a minute, she had figured out how to phrase it. "What was the progression of events that led to the destruction of Slocumb?"

Season smiled, and Kerry felt like a student who has come up with the correct answer to a tough problem. "Are you comfortable, Kerry?" she asked. "Don't have to go to the bathroom or anything? Because this one might need a long answer."

Kerry performed a quick mental diagnosis. "I'm fine," she said. "Go ahead."

"All right." Season sipped her tea and smiled again. "Well done, by the way."

"Thanks."

"As I said, Myrtle and I lived in Slocumb. She grew to adulthood there, married a man named Winthrop Blessing— a useless man, I'm afraid, of small mind and scant courage— and had a child of her own. Again, I think it was that event that somehow brought out her dark side. I had been well liked in Slocumb, and Myrtle had been too, until then.

"But she was her father's daughter, after all. Things began to happen in Slocumb, sinister things. Children disappearing, or dying young. Crops failing. Lights appearing in the Swamp, leading hunters to their deaths. Animals going rogue, terrorizing the townsfolk.

"I should have known it was her, should have been able to stop it. But I was blinded, I guess. She was my daughter, and even though we had been estranged by that time, I still couldn't bring myself to suspect anything like that. Besides, it had been a long time since I had known Forest, so I guess I had forgotten just how horrible some witches could be.

"What I didn't know was that Forest had come to town. Somehow he heard that he had a grandson—Darius, she had called him, having already abandoned the tradition of naming children from nature and begun to express her perverse irony by choosing biblical names—and he wanted to see the boy. So he sought Myrtle out—or Mother Blessing, as she called herself by then. He didn't tell me he was there, gave me no indication that he had come to visit. But when he and Myrtle got together, they fed one another's madness."

Season paused for a minute. She was staring into space as she talked, with a complete lack of self-consciousness. Kerry thought Season was remembering too deeply, the pain of long-ago events drawing itself clearly on her face.

"If you want to finish this later . . . ," Kerry offered.

But Season shook her head. "No, I'm sorry. I'll keep going. There was an—an incident. A widow with three young children woke one morning to find all three children dead, horribly, brutally slaughtered in their beds. Wolf tracks were seen outside in a light snow that had fallen, although no one believed that a wolf had climbed in through a window and silently murdered three children.

"The whole town was up in arms. Some blamed me, some blamed Mother Blessing. I knew it must have been her, of course. But by that point, nobody wanted to listen to reason. They wanted all witches gone, or better yet, dead, and they set out to make that happen.

"Cornered, Mother Blessing and Forest fought back, hard. I did too—fighting for my own life. The town, not that big to begin with, became a magical battleground where no one was safe. Before it was all over, the townspeople had killed Forest and Darius. Mother Blessing's response to that—to two deaths she had prompted in the first place—was to go mad, to level the whole town.

"I tried to stop her, but she was beyond control at that point, her fury having made her a wild woman. And then, to top it off, when the town was a smoking ruin and people from other towns nearby came to offer help, she blamed me. I had been injured in the battle, could barely defend myself, and suddenly they were raising a virtual army against me, going town to town to recruit able-bodied men willing to chase me into the Swamp.

"So I did the only thing I could do. I ran. My grandson, my former husband, my daughter's husband, had all died, and I was made to run like a coward. I found out later that not only did my daughter tell the locals that I was responsible for the devastation in Slocumb, but she went to every witch she could find and spread the same story. Her version of things has become the accepted wisdom, while I've never had a chance to tell mine. Not in any official way, at least."

Kerry sat silently when Season was done, taking it all in. It was much like the story that Mother Blessing had told Daniel, which Kerry had read in his journal. But it was unlike it in other ways, important ways. Ways that rang true to her. In Daniel's version, Mother Blessing had escaped the town before the worst of the destruction began, but still somehow managed to know what had happened, point by point. Season admitted to having stayed through the worst of it, only to leave after the fact when she was blamed for her daughter's crimes.

"I guess I'll have some of that tea now," Kerry said after a little while.

"Do you believe me?" Season asked her.

"I still don't know what to believe," Kerry admitted. She went into the kitchen for some of Season's Earl Grey. In a small microwave oven, she heated a cup. "But what you say makes sense, I think. I'm surprised Daniel never said anything about there being another brother."

"I doubt if she ever told him," Season said. "By the time he was born, she had cemented her story. I was responsible. If she brought Forest and Darius into it, that might have muddied the waters."

"I guess that's true," Kerry said, sitting back down with her tea. "We can take a break if you want."

"I'm okay," Season said. "Thanks for offering, but let's just keep going."

"All right," Kerry said. *Glutton for punishment,* she thought. If this had been her playing true confessions—not that she had much to confess—she'd have been ready for a time-out. But she had thought of her next question, one to which she already had Mother Blessing's answer. "What happens next, in terms of Slocumb? I understand the Witches' Convocation is coming up."

"That's correct," Season said. "Next spring. There I'll finally get a chance to tell my side of the story, and Mother Blessing will tell hers. It'll be a fair hearing, the first one there's been. One of us will be acquitted and the other will have to pay some penalty.

"But there are more important things at stake here. I doubt that Mother Blessing talks about this much, because she's on the wrong side of it. There is a balance of power in the world, an eternal struggle between order and chaos. Mostly these are natural forces at play. Nature has a tendency toward entropy, but at the same time, its designs are magnificently detailed and precise. Think of a forest left completely on its own—trees grow, trees fall, the underbrush goes wild, until the whole place is completely chaotic—you could never find your way through it. But at the same time, think about the complicated inter-relationship between species that allows the forest to grow. Think about the precision with which you can measure the age of the tree by counting its rings. The struggle never ends.

"But witches can help push it toward their preferred way. I try to battle for order. Even my garden, when I had the time and opportunity to grow one, was structured, arranged formally, weeded and tended on a daily basis. No overgrown forest for me.

"Mother Blessing and her sons have kept me on the run so much, though, that I haven't had much time to pull my weight. The scales are tipping—slowly at first, but now faster and faster—toward chaos. If she keeps me from making my contribution—or worse, if she can go to the Convocation and have my powers stripped—then it'll be very hard to stop her from getting her way. Every witch must play his or her part in the balance, and without me in the mix, our side is losing.

"So the Convocation is terribly important, for a number of reasons. But just as important, Mother Blessing can't be allowed to keep me out of action. Things have become too unstable, too desperate."

Kerry wasn't quite sure how to respond to that. It was a whole new and unexpected level. Season was right—Mother Blessing had never given the slightest indication that the stakes were so high. Kerry had been led to believe that, while there might be lives at stake, they were primarily those of witches and of people who had accidentally been drawn into their battles. But now Season's talk of order and chaos made it seem like those few lives were just the tip of the proverbial iceberg, and many, many more might hang in the balance.

"Now I need a break," Kerry said. "That's a lot to take in."

"I know," Season agreed. "I would have broken it to you in an easier way if I could have, but you have to have all the data if you're going to understand it."

"Well, I'm feeling pretty data-rich at this point. I'd like to knock off for a while. Maybe a soak in the tub would help me absorb some of this."

"Sure, no problem," Season said. "You've still got five questions to go."

13

Scott drove Rebecca and Brandy back up to the point where he'd lost Season and Kerry. Snow had covered the little side road, as he had thought, but it had stopped falling, at least for a while, and a heavy gray sky sat atop the peaks as if tethered to them. In four-wheel drive he was able to get up the road to where it forked. From there both roads were buried under drifts—a formless expanse of white spreading in every direction, with trees and snow-topped mountains as background.

"This is where I don't know which way they went," he explained. "I tried one direction for a while, but the snow was falling so heavily I was afraid I'd get stuck. I worked my way back down the hill, and that's when I went into town."

"But that was late yesterday," Brandy observed. "So we

don't know if they're still in this area. Or if this was just a back road they took up into Canada or something."

"That's true," Scott admitted.

"Which means we could drive around up here for days, looking for all kinds of side tracks off into the mountains," Rebecca said, "and still never get close to them."

"That's what I'm thinking," Brandy said. "Maybe if we had a helicopter or, I don't know, a spy satellite or something, then this would be a reasonable way to search for them. But without that, this is really a wild goose chase."

Scott stopped the SUV and gripped the wheel, looking glumly at Brandy in the passenger seat. "I told you I didn't have a plan."

"I know," Brandy said mockingly. "And I fully expected that from you."

He made a face at her. "Don't start, Brandy . . ."

"Don't either of you start," Rebecca wailed. "I hate it that you're not together, and if you guys argue I'm just going to cry."

"Crying's not going to help," Scott said. "I should know. I thought I was going to bawl like an infant yesterday when I lost them."

"Because that would have been so manly?"

"Brandy!" Rebecca poked her in the shoulder. Scott caught the motion, and Brandy's wince, out of the corner of his eye and felt secretly glad. Rebecca may not have been on his side, but she wasn't going to sit idly by and let Brandy torment him either.

"So, Mrs. Einstein, do you have any better ideas?" he asked.

If Brandy felt insulted by the nickname, she didn't show it. "We're here now," she replied. "We might as well make the effort. If you couldn't travel much farther, maybe they couldn't either—or maybe they didn't have to. They might be just around the corner."

Scott looked at the snow, the trees. "If there were any corners."

"It's a figurative corner," Brandy shot back. "Like the figurative corners on your blockhead."

"If you guys don't quit it, I'm going to get out and walk," Rebecca threatened.

"That'd probably be a better way to find them," Brandy opined. "More likely to see their tracks than from a car."

"But also cold," Scott added.

"There is that," Rebecca agreed. "And with my delicate constitution, not to mention thin blood from all that time in California, maybe I'd better not. So you guys just chill out."

"I'm sorry, Rebecca," Brandy said, turning in her seat to regard their friend. "I guess there's a little leftover tension here, and we're trying to defuse it in a, sort of, you know, good-natured way."

Scott couldn't restrain a bitter laugh. "A *little* tension?"

Brandy turned back to him. "We're riding in a car together and we haven't pulled out any sharp objects," she said. "I'd call that pretty minor."

"Could we, maybe, start looking for Kerry?" Rebecca

pleaded. "This is worse than being with you both when all you wanted to do was make out."

Scott remembered those days fondly. He still cared about Brandy—probably still loved her, if he let himself accept the truth. But he knew now that he loved Kerry more. If anything happened to her—if, by his reluctance to interfere yesterday when he'd seen Season leading her away, she was injured or killed—he didn't know how he would live with himself. He guessed that he would be like Kerry had been when Season killed Daniel—driven by lust for revenge. And next time, when he had Season in his sights, he wouldn't back down, wouldn't allow himself to be afraid. He was already regretting having thrown that gun away. No way to find it, not before the spring thaw, and by then, he guessed, the moisture would have ruined it.

But he couldn't let himself think like that for more than a couple of moments, or he'd be drawn into a spiral of despondency. Kerry was safe, she was alive, and he would find her before anything bad happened. He *had* to.

He put the RAV4 into low gear and felt its tires slip a little before they bit through the snow to grip the road. This time he took the left fork that he had ignored before. "We're going this way," he announced, hoping to change the subject away from the uncomfortable topic of him and Brandy. "Keep your eyes peeled for any sign of them."

"I always wondered about that phrase," Rebecca said. "Is that peeling your eyes like they were grapes? Peeling grapes is hard, and I'm not sure it would actually help you see better."

"I think the implication is that your eyelids are the peel," Brandy told her. "So by peeling your eyes, you're opening them."

"Why not just say 'Keep your eyes open,' then? Makes a lot more sense than peeled."

"If old sayings made sense," Scott ventured, "they probably wouldn't be so memorable. 'A stitch in time saves nine'? It'd be just as easy to say something like, 'Hey, better fix that before it gets worse.' I mean, why nine? Because it sort of rhymes with time, only not really?"

"Yeah," Brandy put in. "Or 'One bad apple ruins the whole bunch.' Does it really? And if it does, how long do you have to leave it in there before they're all ruined? If you leave it long enough, is it really that apple ruining it, or just the fact that you've ignored your apples too long?"

"I thought it was 'One bad apple doesn't ruin the whole bunch,'" Rebecca said.

"Well, then," Brandy said, suitably chastened. "I guess that's different."

The road was hard to follow, and Scott let the conversation continue on without him while he gave all his focus to crawling forward, cutting through the drifted snow without losing the packed earth underneath. This direction led into a meadow scooped from the mountains as if with a shallow spoon. In spring it would probably be a riot of color as wildflower blooms filled its grassy expanse, but now it was just more white in a landscape of it. At the other side of the meadow, Scott could see where the roadway carved a notch through a stand of pines. The SUV growled as he pushed on and up, and a few minutes later they passed into the shade of the trees. There hadn't been much sun to begin with, and now that it was gone, a chill enveloped the vehicle. Scott shivered and cranked the heater up another notch.

He hoped his sudden chill was just from the temperature outside and not from anything else—not from any sense of foreboding that came from heading into the deep woods.

But he wouldn't have put money on it.

Somehow Christmas Day often seemed like the longest day of the year, although Kerry knew it wasn't. She supposed it must be the lack of pressing commitments. People didn't expect much of others on Christmas, most businesses were closed so there wasn't much reason to leave home, and relaxing was the order of the day.

In Season's New Hampshire refuge, the same rule applied. The witch had indicated that leaving would be almost impossible, so deep was the snow outside. After their morning talk, Kerry had taken a long bath, letting the hot water soak her completely. Then she had dressed, checked in on Season, and gone back to her room for a nap.

But sleep wasn't in the cards for her. She sprawled on the bed for a while, tossed and turned, tried to get comfy. But her mind was racing, everything Season had told her roiling around in it trying to find purchase. It seemed every time she believed she had a handle on how the world was really laid out, she discovered new information that completely redrew the map. *Christopher Columbus must have felt this way,* she thought. *Only, sometimes I think I really am sailing right off the edge.*

When she needed grounding, needed to reconnect to those things in her crazy life that seemed to truly make sense, she turned to Daniel Blessing. All she had left of him now were memories and his journals, so she took one of those heavy leather volumes from her duffel bag and slipped off the thong that held it closed. Turning a few pages, she found a passage she had never read.

The town wasn't much more than a flat spot where someone had scraped away the desert and built a couple of saloons, a church or three, a stable, a jail, and a random scattering of houses. I hadn't come for the scenery, however, or for the fine cuisine. I had come in search of a man named Stearns, who, I was told, had a score to settle with Season Howe and maybe reason to know where she was. Seeing as I had a score or two of my own, I reckoned maybe we could be friends.

When I rode in this afternoon, it was through brutal, punishing sun and heat. My horse was stumbling for the last half mile or so, even though I imagined he could smell the water waiting at the stable. I imagined that I could smell it too, and gave some thought to leaving the horse there if he fell and finishing the trip on foot.

Luckily, the horse held out. We covered that last stretch and made it to the relatively cool shade of the livery stable, where he dunked his muzzle into the trough and drank deep. It was all I could do not to join him, but I left him there and headed to the nearest saloon. A sign painted on the wall above the door said it was the Lucky Sack, but there wasn't much about it that looked lucky to me.

I had never let that stop me in the past, and wasn't about to now. I walked in out of the dusty late afternoon sunlight. A barkeep stood behind a plank balanced across two barrels, with a row of bottles and some glasses on a shelf behind him. Eight other men, mostly crowded around two tables but for a couple of lone drinkers, looked up when I entered. I suppose I must have looked like a threat—a stranger, rare in these parts to begin with, and one who carried a Colt strapped to his side. I almost never used the gun, of course. I had other, more effective weapons at my disposal. But I carried it to forestall any questions about why I wasn't armed, which had come up with depressing regularity until I'd bought this one.

I ordered a whiskey and a water from the barkeep, a portly fellow in a stained shirt and fraying suspenders holding up his britches. He put two glasses down in front of me without a smile. I did smile as I put my coins on his plank, overpaying by a wide margin.

"That's too much," he said.

"Not necessarily," I said. "You have rooms to let here?"

"Couple, upstairs. You might have to share."

"That's okay," I told him. I drank the water down, asked for another one. He brought it. This time he smiled a little, or at least his bushy mustache twitched.

"Anything else?" he asked.

Parched, I drained the second water. "Yeah," I said when I was done. "I'm looking for a man named Stearns. Know him?"

The barkeep blanched visibly. "Never heard of him."

"You always turn white when you hear a name for the first time?" I asked him.

"I didn't," he said. He turned away and started to wipe out glasses with a filthy rag.

"You did," I said. "And I hope you didn't dry these glasses with that thing."

"Look, mister, you don't like the way I do business, you can just move along."

"I got nothing against your business practices," I said, which wasn't entirely true. "I just don't like being lied to."

When he came back over to me his voice was low and the look on his face was surly. "I don't need the trouble, okay?" he said with a snarl. "Sayin' that name out loud around here is like askin' for a fight to start."

"One starts, I'll finish it," I said softly. "Just tell me where I can find this Stearns."

He looked around like he was afraid someone would jump him if he talked to me, and then he leaned closer, still wiping out a glass with that rag. "I couldn't tell you if I wanted to," he whispered. "People don't find Stearns. He finds them."

"What does that mean?" I asked. "Either he lives somewhere around here or he doesn't."

"That's what you'd think," the barkeep said. "But it ain't always the truth."

I couldn't figure out what he was talking about, but I knew better than to push too hard. Surely few knew better than I that things weren't always what they seemed, and that sometimes asking questions only revealed answers that you didn't really want to know.

"So just by asking you about him, he'll come to me?"

"If he wants to," the barkeep answered. "He don't do things he don't want to do, way I hear it."

"A man of mystery."

"Don't laugh about him," the barkeep warned me. "Way I hear it, he don't like that."

"Well, give me a room, then," I said. "I'll have some dinner and then see if old Mr. Stearns pays me a visit."

And I did just what I said I would. I wandered

around the town, what there was of it, for a little while. Ate some stringy steak and biscuits for dinner, and then went up to the room, which in fact I didn't have to share. And I waited. Eventually, I slept.

I didn't even hear him come into the room, which is rare for me. I woke up when I heard the click of his revolver. When I opened my eyes he was pointing it at me.

"You must be Stearns."

"What makes you think so?"

"I was told if I looked for you, you'd find me."

He smiled. The room was dark but there was some moonlight leaking in through a window, and I could see that he was lean and rangy, with a droopy mustache and some gold in his teeth. His eyes were narrow and dark, and I had the feeling they didn't miss much. The pistol in his hand looked like it had seen plenty of use. There was no shake there, either, like there usually would have been when someone snuck into another man's room and pointed a gun at him. Mr. Stearns was just as calm as he could be.

"Why were you looking?" he asked.

"We have a mutual acquaintance," I said. I sat up a little in the bed now, my hands spread on the blanket in front of me so he could see I wasn't making a play for the Colt. "Name of Season Howe."

"Not sure I know that name," he said.

"No one around here seems to know anyone else,"

I said. "You don't have to worry that I'm a friend of hers or anything. I aim to kill her."

Stearns smiled at that, uncocked his gun, and slid it into his holster. "Well, why didn't you say so?" he asked. "What do you call yourself?"

I told him my name. He nodded slowly, as if he had to think on it for a while. "What's your gripe with Season Howe?" he asked after a bit.

"Let's just say she owes a price that's bigger than she can pay in this lifetime," I said. Not knowing Stearns, I didn't want to go into detail.

"That's true," he said. "You don't know the half of it."

"I know enough."

"Sounds like you've really got it in for her," Stearns said. "I like the sound of that. And I can see you're a man who can handle her."

This man Stearns was full of surprises. "What makes you say that?"

"Well, being a witch and all, I mean. Same as her, that's all."

Which was what I thought he was getting at, but I didn't expect he'd come right out and say. He said it without hesitation, like he just knew it was true. So I didn't see any reason to deny it. I just sat there on that uncomfortable slab of a bed staring at him.

"You're wondering how I know," Stearns said.

"Can't blame you." He moved closer to me, tilting his head up toward the ceiling. Beneath the edge of his whiskers I could clearly see the raw, choppy line where his throat had been cut. "I got a score to settle too, but I can't do it by myself," he said. To demonstrate further, he reached toward my bed, but his hand passed right through it with no resistance.

"I can see how that might be a problem for you," I admitted.

"Reckon you'll have to set things right for both of us," he said. "I can tell you where to find her— information is easy to come by on this side of the divide. She's in Durango. I don't know for how long, so I'd be on my way in the morning if I was you."

I was going to say something else, but didn't. Next thing I knew, I was waking up at first light. The whole thing might have been a dream—there's no sign that Stearns was ever here at all. So I'm putting this down just as it happened, in case I forget any of the details later.

After I get some breakfast in me, I'm lighting out for Durango. I have a feeling it wasn't a dream.

And I have a feeling that if I pass the town cemetery on the way out and look at the markers there, I'll see one with the name "Stearns" on it.

I remain,

Daniel Blessing, Twentieth of July, 1871

Kerry closed up the book and put it back in her bag. She knew there was a long tradition of ghost stories at Christmas—even the old chestnut "A Christmas Carol" was a ghost story, after all. This one she would once have read as a ghost story and felt a little shiver at, but knowing that Daniel had put it down—and that, at least when he wrote it, he believed every word he wrote—gave her a serious case of the creeps. Sure she had seen plenty of strange and spooky things over these past few months, but this little tale struck her as especially frightening.

Still, somehow she couldn't help feeling a little encouraged by what she had read too. There were times when she felt like she was the only person who was constantly surprised by others—like she just didn't have a handle on who people were and how they acted. She was glad to know that Daniel could be fooled too.

Maybe she hadn't been wrong to trust Mother Blessing. At least until she showed her true colors. Lacking evidence that someone presented themselves as something other than what they were, a person could go crazy not trusting anyone. *And where,* she wondered, *would that get you? That's probably why people become hermits—living in caves because they just don't know who they can believe and who they can't.*

Kerry preferred to trust first, and doubt, if there was a reason to, later. She had doubted Season—with perfectly good reason—but now that seemed to be turning around. Would it turn into trust? No telling yet. But that possibility was open now, where it wouldn't have been even a few days before.

She thought that, in some way, Daniel might approve.

14

Scott kept cranking the heat higher and higher, but the air outside grew colder as the afternoon dragged on. Brandy zipped up her coat and shoved her hands into her fleece gloves. But she didn't get really nervous until Scott said, "You know what would really stink? Running out of gas up here."

"Yeah, that would stink, all right," Rebecca agreed. "Does running your heat use extra gas?"

"I know running the air-conditioning does," Scott said. "I guess heat probably does too."

"Turn it off, then, if you're getting low," Brandy urged.

"But we'll freeze," Scott protested.

"We'll freeze if we run out of gas," Brandy countered. "Or

have you seen a service station that I missed somewhere in the last hundred miles or so?"

"We haven't gone anywhere near that far," Scott said.

"I'm talking square miles."

"Okay," Scott said, beginning the complicated process of turning around on a narrow, snowbound road. "It's getting late anyway, and we don't want to be caught up here after dark."

"I sure don't," Rebecca said.

Brandy didn't answer. She was trying not to give Scott a hard time, but she felt like the day had been mostly wasted. They had cruised through the woods, up and down whatever little dirt roads they could find beneath the snow. But there was no rhyme or reason to it, no actual plan beyond just looking and keeping their fingers crossed. They hadn't seen any buildings or stray Jeeps, but New Hampshire was a big place, and not far from here was the Canadian border.

She had gone along with the day's agenda—or lack thereof—so she couldn't blame anyone but herself. Now it would be night soon, and their search would be ended until tomorrow. Who knew what could happen in that time?

Merry Christmas, Kerry, she thought bitterly. *Sorry we failed you.*

But tomorrow, she swore, would be different. Tomorrow they would use their heads, would approach the problem logically. "No more of this driving aimlessly," she said. "Soon as it's light, we've got to get smart about finding Kerry."

"You have any ideas, Brandy?" Scott asked. "Because you didn't when I was looking for some earlier."

"Maybe I do," Brandy replied. "I was thinking: If we were the police, we wouldn't look for a missing person by driving around the neighborhood, would we?"

"I guess not," Scott said.

"Of course not. We'd ask questions. We'd investigate. That's what we'll do tomorrow—we'll hit the little towns around here and see if anyone knows Season, or if anyone's seen her. If she's hiding out in this area, then she must buy food from someone. If she has a place to live, she must have bought or rented it from an agency or somebody like that. So we ask around."

"I like it, Brandy," Rebecca said. "It makes sense to me."

"Can I just remind you both that she's a witch?" Scott shot back. "We don't know if she needs a grocery store, or if she can just conjure up a meal from thin air."

"Well, she'd have to buy gas, then. Something. At least it's a chance," Brandy insisted. "It's better than trying to cover a million square miles of wilderness."

"Do you think we should call in the real authorities?" Rebecca suggested. "I mean, if Kerry's been kidnapped for real, maybe we should be getting the FBI or the National Guard or something after her."

Brandy snorted. "You want to try to explain Season to the New Hampshire state police? You're gutsier than me."

"Yeah, okay, maybe that wouldn't work," Rebecca admitted.

"But it just seems like we need some, I don't know, reinforcements or something."

"Reinforcements would be great, but I wouldn't hold my breath," Scott said. "I think we're it."

"What about Mother Blessing?" Brandy asked. "Could we ask her for help somehow?"

"I don't think we'd want to do that," Rebecca cautioned. "It sounded like she and Kerry had kind of a falling-out."

"But she still hates Season, right?" Brandy pressed. "We were talking about stupid old sayings earlier, and 'The enemy of my enemy is my friend' fits into that."

"You were wrong about the apple one," Scott reminded her. "What if you're wrong about this one too? What if it's something like, 'The friend of my enemy is my enemy'?"

Brandy shrugged. They were on their way back down the hill, coming out of the trees, but still a long way from civilization. The sun was a pale copper ball perched at the crest of the mountains. "Same idea," she said. "Mother Blessing and Season are enemies. Season has Kerry. Anyone who could help, I think we ought to consider."

"Yeah, but Beck and I have had more time than you have with Kerry recently," Scott argued. "She didn't give me the whole scoop—you know how she's been, always holding stuff back—but I got the same sense that Rebecca did. Kerry and Mother Blessing didn't part on the greatest terms."

"Whatever," Brandy said, throwing up her hands. Here she was intentionally trying not to ignite some kind of great debate, but she was in the middle of one anyway. All she wanted was to make sure Kerry was safe. Then she would make the argument that what they really needed was to leave Season alone, to stop this crazy hunt for her. Sure, there was a chance that Season was after them. They continued to get mixed up with her because they were worried about that possibility. But realistically, if they just went about their own business, ignored Season, wouldn't she do the same to them? They weren't really a threat—that had been proven time and again.

She didn't know how the others would feel about it. She wasn't even really sure if she cared anymore. She missed Adam, she missed her family. It was Christmas! And instead of celebrating her favorite holiday of the year with loved ones, she was traipsing all over the White Mountains with her ex-boyfriend and someone she had known for one summer.

That was messed up.

"Okay," Scott said as he urged the SUV onto yet another ribbon of trail. "Tomorrow we do it your way, Brandy. We'll hit the towns, question the local yokels. Anybody have a picture of Kerry? It'd be easier if we had one of Season, but anything is better than nothing, right?"

"No picture here," Brandy said.

"I have one on my website," Rebecca offered.

"You have a website?"

"I've just been working on it the last couple of weeks," she said. "Kerry bought me a digital camera, and I've been putting up some pictures."

"That's just peachy," Brandy said. "So all we have to do is go into the grocery stores and gas stations and ask people to browse the Net for a while."

"No, silly," Rebecca answered. "We just need to find a computer that we can print from. Maybe one of the hotels around here has a business center, or there's an Internet café or something around."

"At the risk of starting another bizarre digression," Scott said, "we'll be going through a few towns on the way back to the condo. Everybody keep your eyes peeled."

Kerry and Season bundled up and went for a walk in the woods. The bitingly cold air smelled freshly scrubbed, the snow crunched loudly underfoot, and a few of the hardier birds whistled and fluttered from branch to branch overhead. The sun hung in the sky like a decoration, with no discernible purpose, since Kerry couldn't tell any difference in temperature between shade and bright sunlight.

"This is what winter should be like, to me," Season said. "I've spent plenty of them in warmer climes, but I can never get used to listening to Christmas music while the palm trees sway, or going out in January in shorts and sleeveless tops. It just seems wrong to me."

"I wouldn't mind the chance to find out," Kerry said. "I kind of liked the couple of weeks I spent in Santa Cruz. And

Rebecca said it's relatively cool there because it's right on the water and everything—back down in San Diego, she said, it'd be a lot warmer."

"That's true. And down in Baja, or the Florida Keys, it's warmer still. But it's just not winter to me. I guess I'm old-fashioned or something. I think winter should be the time you put on a lot of clothes, drink hot chocolate or eggnog, and complain about the cold."

"And go sledding," Kerry added. "Sledding's good. I haven't done it since I was a kid, but . . ." She waved a hand toward a slope that faced them through the trees. "That'd be a great spot for it."

"You're right," Season agreed, a broad smile on her face. "Shall we?"

Kerry looked at her for a moment, confused. "But . . . with what sleds?"

"Kerry," Season said, shaking her head sadly. "Witches, remember?" She spoke one of the old words and gestured toward the slope. Kerry saw a faraway flash of light, and then two colorful objects appeared against the white snow.

"Sleds?"

"Flexible Flyers," Season confirmed.

"I am so there." Kerry broke into a run, and Season started in right behind her. When she was a kid, back in Cairo, there had been a street near her house that was steep and straight. On winter weekends the residents there closed the street off and ran hoses down it, icing it up, making a sled run out of it. There was always the unhelpful neighbor who left a car or truck parked at the curb, but most pulled into driveways or garages to clear the path. Someone would build a bonfire at the top of the hill at night, and the adults would gather around it for drinks and conversation while the kids sledded. Kerry had spent many happy winter hours streaking down that hill, and the few frightening moments, when her sled was caught on the ice and seemed determined to plow her into one of the parked cars or a fellow sledder, just made the whole experience that much more memorable.

A few minutes later Kerry huffed her way up to the top of the slope, leaving a trail of deep bootprints in her wake. The sled she found looked brand new, but at the same time it looked like one that had hung high up in her parents' garage when she'd been little—supposedly it had been her dad's when he was a kid. It was made of blond wood slats with red metal rails, and it had the familiar arrow logo in the middle.

"This is great!" she shouted when Season caught up.

"Take her out for a spin," Season suggested.

Kerry hesitated for just a second, part of her still looking for the trap, the angle. She had been at war with Season. Could this be for real? But then she felt the combination of sun warm on her face and snow cold at her feet. That was real. The sled felt real, too. She grabbed its edges, ran a few steps, and then hurled herself on top of it as it rocketed down the slope. The sled gained speed as the hill grew steeper. Wind pummeled Kerry's face, snow flew as she sliced through it.

A shriek behind her told her that Season was on her way down too.

At the bottom of the slope, she had to turn away from a couple of large rocks jutting up through the snow, and then from a creek that carved through the valley. She ended her ride in a spray of snow and a fit of laughter.

Season rolled her sled at the hill's end, and she came up laughing hysterically. "That was so fun!" she shouted. "This was such a good idea, Kerry!"

"I know!" Kerry called back. She was already using the attached length of rope to drag her sled back up the hill for another ride, her earlier moment of paranoia almost—but not completely—shoved away. Season caught up to her on the climb.

"I'm so glad you thought of this, Kerry. It's been a long time since I've done something just for fun."

"If I was a witch I'd do fun stuff all the time," Kerry replied.

Season grabbed her arm. "If?"

Kerry realized what she meant. She did not yet always think of herself as a witch, even though she'd been trained by Mother Blessing and could do things far beyond the abilities of most other people. To hear Season confirm her status somehow carried a lot of weight with her. "Yeah, okay," she said. "I guess I am a witch. But I've been kind of, you know, preoccupied." *With killing you,* she thought but didn't say. She was sure Season understood that anyway.

"Me too," Season said. "Having to be on edge all the time,

literally for centuries . . . it interferes with my enjoyment of things."

Kerry nodded. "Even before—before I met Daniel and got all mixed up in this, I had kind of given up on fun," she admitted. "I was too busy taking care of Mom, and then going to school, working . . . I kind of let fun go by the wayside."

They had just reached the top of the slope. Season threw her sled down to the snow. "So let's go again!" she cried, pushing off and starting her trip.

Kerry spun and started hers as well, shooting down the hill behind Season.

Later they sat in Season's living room, nursing cups of hot chocolate. Kerry's cheeks were chapped, and they hurt from smiling so much and laughing so hard, but the fire and the warm beverage helped. They had sledded until the sun started to slide behind the hills, staining the snow as surely as if someone had spilled a bucket of red ink on it, and the air turned so cold that both were shivering almost uncontrollably. Kerry noticed near the end that her sled was literally breaking down—its hard edges softening, becoming less distinct, bits of it just disappearing from view. Season explained that most magically created items couldn't last very long—they were made by repurposing other materials, which needed to return to their original state before too long. Food was an exception to that rule—it was composed of tiny bits of organic material from so many different sources that they weren't missed.

At a quiet moment in the conversation, Season offered Kerry a gentle reminder. "You have five questions left. Do you still want to use them?"

Kerry had been turning things over in her mind, trying to narrow down what she wanted to ask about. But her major questions had already been answered, and the rest of it seemed small-time compared with the things she'd asked earlier.

"Okay," Kerry said after contemplating awhile. "We were talking about having fun earlier, and I know you have tended to hide out in resort-type areas. Daniel said it's because the population in those places changes a lot, swelling during their main seasons, so you can come and go without really being noticed. And I know you were in Las Vegas in the fall, because that's where Josh saw you. I also know you were in a casino on Samhain, which, I've got to tell you, really ticked off Mother Blessing. So what I want to know is, what is a witch doing in a casino on the holiest night of the year?"

Season considered her answer only briefly. "I'm not surprised that Mother Blessing was perturbed by that," she said. "She likes to make a big issue of being all traditional. When, of course, if she was truly that traditional she would never have done the things she did, back in Slocumb or since."

"Like what?" Kerry asked, before realizing what she was saying. *Another one down.*

"Witches aren't evil by nature," Season replied. She had changed into a soft cream-colored sweater and brown pants, but in honor of Christmas her socks were red and green striped. Once again she sat on a rug on the floor, leaning on the hearth, where her mug rested. "Or at least we're not supposed to be. Most of us are not, but there is a minority that are—that's why the natural slide toward entropy, or chaos, is so hard to resist. It was not traditional of her to allow the deaths of children that she could have prevented. It was not traditional of her to put me in the awful position of having to kill my own grandsons. But let me go out for an evening's entertainment, and she's offended?

"Samhain is, in fact, a holy night to most witches," Season went on. "And it's perfectly appropriate to celebrate it with ritual and solemn observance. But it's also fine to celebrate it with a party, or by having a good time in some other way. There is no single way that Samhain must be observed, regardless of what Mother Blessing might say. I paid attention to Samhain in my own way, and part of that was going to a casino—the closest thing there is to a truly holy place in money-worshipping Las Vegas—to enjoy myself. And was attacked by her simulacra. Surely she knew I was there because your friend called you."

Which means, Kerry extrapolated, *that I got Josh killed. If it hadn't been for me, Mother Blessing would never have known where to send the artificial men who killed him.* The realization hit her like a truck. *Good thing she doesn't know where Season is now, or I'd be in real trouble.*

"Can I—I mean, I'd like to save the rest of my questions for another time," Kerry said. Her sudden insight depressed her, and she felt very tired. "If that's okay. I think I'm ready to call it a night."

"If that's what you want, Kerry."

"Yeah, I think so. But thanks for a great Christmas, Season."

Season appeared to be unexpectedly touched by Kerry's sentiment. She swallowed, and her hand went to her chest. "Thank you," she said. "I hope I've cleared some things up for you."

"A lot," Kerry assured her. "Doesn't mean I don't still have a long way to go. But you've helped."

"Good night, then, Kerry. I'll see you in the morning."

Kerry wished Season a good night, and then retired to her room.

Kerry Profitt's diary, December 25

Well, that was certainly one of the strangest Christmases ever.

A fantastic one, for the most part. If you don't count the lack of a tree with presents underneath it. Which I kind of do, but I'm trying to look beyond that.

Anyway, there's more to life than presents and material things. Back when I was mall-happy I'd never have believed I would ever think that. And the truth is, even though I'm snowed into this cabin with no one around but Season, I still put on clean underwear today, and socks, and did my makeup, and brushed my hair. Not that good grooming is necessarily the same as being materialistic, but I guess what I'm saying is that I'm not going all Flintstones or anything.

More like Gilligan's Island, I guess, where the women had plenty of clothing and makeup even though they were only going on a three-hour tour.

And what would life be without old TV references to keep us sane? Thank the Goddess for TV Land, I say.

Well, enough of that. And enough digressing, keeping me from the main point of this little diatribe, which is . . .

. . . is . . .

First of all, I really can't remember the last time I just let loose and laughed like that. I guess some of those nights at home with the La Jolla gang, when Mace would start complaining about modern life and our strange back-east ways, and then Scott would go off on him—all in fun, of course, but fun with an edge to it.

So the walk in the snow, and the sledding, and the fact that we didn't have to drag our sleds home because they never really existed somehow . . . I don't quite get that, but at least no trees had to die for our enjoyment—that was all great.

So was the other part, in a different way. Just relaxing with Season, getting some questions answered. I am horrified—just wrenched apart—by the idea that I got Josh killed. I couldn't have known, of course. I trusted Daniel's mother. My mistake.

And now, it seems, I am starting to trust Season. Another mistake? I already know she's a murderer, so the answer should be a resounding "Duh!" But maybe it's my own naïveté. . . . I can't bring myself to doubt her when she speaks so frankly. She could be telling me one lie after another. Without evidence to the contrary, I just don't know. I'm reminded of those first days with Daniel, when I trusted him instinctively, or so I thought, but I found out later that, in fact, he had enchanted us.

We always say we are "enchanted" by people to whom we feel an instant, inexplicable attraction. Maybe we are, but that kind of enchantment is different from this kind— less manipulative, I guess. A matter of chemistry and phero- mones and personal taste.

I don't know that Season has intentionally enchanted me. But I don't know that she hasn't.

Is trusting her some kind of betrayal of Daniel? Or of my vow to avenge his death? Should I go in there right now and just kill Season? I'm sure she trusts me enough now to let me get close. One of those carving knives, from the kitchen. It would be over in a second, except for cleaning up.

But would it be the right thing to do? Not just because she killed Daniel, but in the greater scheme. And listen to me (well, okay, read me), thinking about the greater scheme. Like my actions can affect the whole world.

Except, to hear her tell it, maybe they can. Which means I have to think before I act.

I hate that.

I also hate not knowing who to trust.

I guess I've got to stay on my guard. If I catch Season

in a lie, or turn up something that proves she isn't telling the truth, then I call her on it. Or I make like a tree and "leaf." Except around here, most of the trees are pines and so the bad pun doesn't even work. Unless needles are leaves, in which case . . . oh, never mind.

It would be so much easier if . . . if it was easier. Same could be said for the rest of life, right? Think it ever is?

Me neither.

More later.

K.

15

Berlin had a copy shop with Internet connections, but it didn't open until ten, so they got a late start on their day. Rebecca brought up her website and saved the photo of Kerry—really of the two of them together, taken by Erin on one of the few occasions she had been around while Kerry had been visiting. Erin had a new boyfriend, and she'd been spending most of her time at his place, leaving Rebecca in the house alone. She had loved having Kerry visit, because she didn't like being home by herself—didn't like being anywhere by herself, she had realized. Being by herself just gave her too much time to think.

Once the photo was downloaded, it was an easy matter to crop herself out. She wanted the picture to show just

Kerry, to keep any confusion to a minimum when they started spreading it around. It was a small file, fine for online viewing, but it printed blurry and grainy. Still, Kerry's pale skin, long dark hair, and huge green eyes were visible. They had been in Rebecca's kitchen, and there was a yellow wall behind Kerry that set her off nicely.

The first person they showed it to was named Frank, according to the tag on his shirt. He worked in the copy shop, and Rebecca slid it across the counter while Scott paid for the computer time. "Have you seen this girl?" she asked. "She might be with an older woman, a very pretty blonde."

Frank looked at the picture for a long time—maybe taking some time to admire as well as checking to see if he recognized her. "Nope," he said after a while. "Think I'd remember her."

"Okay, thanks," Brandy said, snatching the picture away.

They went outside onto Berlin's main drag—mostly brick buildings, very traditionally New England-styled. Here and there a cupola or clock tower broke the rooflines. Many businesses were closed, their storefronts boarded over or shuttered up. Signs for commercial real estate agencies hung on most of them, but they looked like they'd been there a long time. Rebecca remembered a mill they had seen on the river the day before—empty and abandoned, like a ghost town. For a minute she had thought it looked that way because of Christmas; no one would be working the mill on Christmas. But a closer look proved that to be false: The parking lots were blanketed in untouched snow, the buildings had broken-out windows and caved-in walls.

They tried a restaurant, a coffee shop, a drugstore, a gas station, but in each place they had the same response. No one remembered having seen Kerry or recognized the description of Season.

Finally, after searching for more than an hour, they reached the office of Bald Cap Realty and pushed through the heavy glass door. An old heater made the air smell stale. There were two people inside sitting at desks behind a long wooden counter. The woman looked up first—fiftyish, lean and bespectacled, with brown curls framing her pinched face. "Can I help you?" she asked, her tone suspicious. *No way do we look like we're shopping for a house,* Rebecca realized.

"We're wondering if you've seen someone," Brandy began.

Rebecca put the photo down on the counter. "This person," she said. "Or another one. They might be together."

Scott took over. "The other one is a pretty blonde, older than the girl in the picture. Mid-thirties, maybe. Striking blue eyes, the kind you don't forget. They're not from around here, so you'd have noticed their accents, maybe."

"That sounds familiar," the man said, rising from his own desk. He was younger than the woman, but not by much. Round and balding, but with a gray beard hugging his chin. He buttoned his red blazer as he approached the counter, seemingly out of long habit. "An attractive blonde, you say?"

"What is this about?" the suspicious woman asked.

"We're afraid they might be in trouble," Brandy said, repeating the line they had agreed on in case anyone asked. "We haven't heard from them in several days, but we know they had a place around here."

The man looked at Kerry's picture. "Haven't seen her," he said.

"The older one was here first," Scott interjected. "This one just came a couple of days ago."

"You remember, Margaret," the man said. "Couple years ago, that property up by Mount Cabot?"

"Hush, Steven," the woman called Margaret said sharply. "Why don't you young people go to the police if you think there's something wrong?"

"We don't really know if it's as bad as all that, ma'am," Rebecca said. "We'd hate to get everybody stirred up if it turns out to be nothing."

"But if you know where on Mount Cabot," Brandy added, "we'd sure appreciate a tip."

"We have nothing more to tell you," Margaret said.

"Okay, then, thanks for all your help," Scott said sarcastically.

As they left the office, Rebecca tried to remember where Mount Cabot was on their map. It wasn't much to go on, but it was better than they'd had before.

"Are you crazy?" Margaret fumed after they had left. "Don't you remember what she said?"

"Not exactly," Steven admitted. "What was it?"

"She paid us both an extra ten percent if we'd promise to keep quiet about her buying that place."

Steven sighed. "That was two years ago," he said. "I'm sure she just meant for a while, not forever."

"It was three," Margaret said. "And she didn't put any time limitations on it. Maybe you don't take your commitments seriously, but I do."

"Look, I'm sorry, Margaret. I didn't think it was a big deal, and I forgot." Of course it *was* a big deal to Margaret—it was always a big deal when anyone let her down in any way, or revealed that they were merely human. Margaret liked to think of herself as godlike, while everyone around her failed in their attempts to achieve her exalted level. Steven thought it was probably difficult to go through life surrounded by abject failures and the willfully unkempt, but Margaret seemed to thrive on her demonstrated superiority over all beings.

"Well, I just think you would keep the desires of our customers in mind," Margaret huffed.

Before Steven could answer, the door opened again. *Probably those same kids coming back for something they forgot,* he figured. He hadn't expected much business the morning after Christmas. He was surprised they were willing to brave Margaret again, but if they were he had to give them credit.

But when he turned back toward the door, it wasn't the kids at all, or anyone else that he had ever seen. It was two men—*well, things that are like men, anyway,* he corrected. They were mostly brown, the brown of the mud by the banks of the Androscoggin River, and slick like that mud, but there were other components as well. He thought he recognized the spokes of a bicycle wheel, a crushed aluminum soft drink can, and a plastic bag from a supermarket mixed in with the river mud. They wore no clothing, just mud from head to foot.

Then he blinked, because he couldn't really be recognizing those things, that made no sense at all. It was just because the men were coming in from outside and the light was behind them, that was it. He was about to rub his eyes and say something when Margaret screamed.

"It's—it's all right, Margaret," Steven said. When he addressed the . . . the *things*, he tried to sound forceful, but his voice caught and it came out squeaky and uncertain. "Look here, what do you want?"

One of them came forward and leaned its fists down on the wooden counter. Steven was sure he could see mud squish out from between its fingers, but then suck back in somehow. He felt a chill that went to the core of his being.

The thing spoke then, and its voice was surprising. Not in its inhumanity, he expected that. But this was at once inhuman and yet feminine, in some way, like this creature was only a speaker box for a female talking through it remotely. "Season Howe," the strange voice said. "Where is she?"

"I don't—I don't know who you mean," Steven said. He knew full well, but how could these bizarre man-shaped concoctions know that?

"Season Howe," the thing said again.

Margaret had begun to sob as soon as her initial scream died, and she was still sobbing now, sitting in her desk chair with her face buried in her hands. Through the sobs, she said, "She's the one those kids were looking for, you fool. On Mount Cabot. Just tell them what they want to know, get them out of here."

The thing leaning on the counter, the mud-man, looked into Steven's eyes with an eye that was nothing more than a thumb-size space in his crudely sculpted head. There seemed to be some kind of intelligence there just the same, Steven thought. He would go to his grave believing that the thing read him like a book. "I—I didn't recognize the name," he sputtered. "But she—she's right. Mount Cabot. That's where she is. Where her cabin is, anyway."

"Mount Cabot," it repeated, in that same semi-feminine voice.

"That's right," Steven said. He was terrified, afraid that he would lose control of himself at any moment, that these horrible creatures would drive him completely mad. He was a hairsbreadth away from becoming a gibbering idiot, rolling into a ball and hiding in the footwell of his desk. "Mount Cabot. Now please, just go—"

Before he could finish the thought, the thing came across the counter at him, moving fast and . . . and fluidly, not like a man but like a liquid, splashing itself at him. Margaret screamed again, and Steven saw that the other one was on her, arms swinging, fists pumping. Then Margaret was silent, and Steven felt a wet, slick hand contract on his own throat, felt muddy fingers clamp over his mouth and nose. He couldn't breathe, and when he tried he sucked mud in, inhaled it; it filled him up, and then it was over his eyes too, or the world had gone mercifully dark.

Six dead people. That was more than the town had seen in— well, ever, as far as Will Blossom knew.

Ordinarily there wasn't much a constable had to do to keep order in Berlin, New Hampshire. Not much crime. Most people didn't have much to steal, anyway, except the tourists and skiers who came during the season. They found themselves victimized from time to time, but Will didn't feel too bad about that. They left their car doors unlocked and their fancy stereos disappeared, that was too bad. He would rather it didn't happen, but the end result was that they usually bought new car stereos, sometimes before they even left town, and that was good for the local economy.

The town's only gang was a pack of punk kids who couldn't make the high school football team, smoked cigarettes, and pushed around smaller kids for their lunch money sometimes. At least that's what Chief Blossom liked to think. The truth, which he seldom allowed himself to contemplate, was that there were other things going on under the surface of the town that he didn't like or understand. Sometimes there were kids who wound up in the river, or on a hospital slab. Someone was responsible for that. He didn't know if it was a gang or simply random circumstance. But as long as it didn't affect most of the townspeople, he didn't push too hard on it.

He was understaffed, of course. Every law enforcement agency was these days. And there had been a little more crime since the last big mill on the river had closed. Someone stealing a few cans of food, a loaf of bread, those things he could overlook. Life was hard all around, and he didn't leave himself out of that equation. The less he had to do to claim his bimonthly paycheck, the better he liked it.

So this morning he was a very unhappy man. The phone in his office was ringing off the hook, and every time it did it brought more bad news. He had already been out of the office more than he'd been in it today. Carla, his dispatcher, had a stack of pink message slips in her hand when he came in this time, and she shoved them into Will's fist.

"More calls," she said. "I'd have called you on your wireless but I knew you were just about here. You're going out again, though."

He had been dreaming about the chocolate bar in his desk drawer and a Coke to wash it down with. "I don't want to go out," he protested, knowing it was pointless. This was going to be one of those days that didn't let up, and then it would lead into a week or more of the same—funerals and distraught family members and demands for answers. He would find those answers, one way or another.

"You got a big staff of investigators going to do it for you?"

"I'm going out again," he relented. "Where am I going?"

"Depends," Carla said. "You want to work them in order of when they called in? Or maybe alphabetically?"

"In order," Will said.

"Then you're going to the Tas-T-Scoop, Virgil's Café, Notions 'n' Things, and Bald Cap Realty."

"I know that's the name of the mountain," Will said. "But doesn't it sound like something an actor would wear if he needed to be bald?"

"You're wasting time, Will."

"I'm delaying the inevitable, Carla," he protested. "That's different."

"In what way?"

He couldn't think of any. "Okay, maybe not. Anyone else needs me, call me."

He left the office to go back into his town. The town he was supposed to keep safe, and in which half a dozen people had already died today. Maybe starting last night, he amended, since he didn't know precisely what time the murders had started to occur.

The scary thing was, nobody had put it all together yet. Some people knew a victim or two, but no one outside of his department knew how many there were. When they did, it would be trouble. Panic. He didn't want that.

He just wasn't sure how to avoid it.

He drove down to the Tas-T-Scoop. Kitty Russell was there in her colorful uniform, with the little striped cap and everything. But her eyes were red and her nose was running, and she was shaking like a leaf in a nor'easter. Will got out of his car and walked over to where she sat on a bench in the dining area, pointedly not looking toward the counter.

"What's wrong, Kitty?" he asked, afraid he already knew the answer. "What happened?"

She tried to point to the Formica counter, but her muscles failed her and her arm fell limply to her side. "It's—it's Mr. Penrose," she said through her tears. "He—he—he's back there."

Will massaged her back for a moment. "I'll just take a look, Kitty. You stay right here. Everything's going to be okay. You're safe, I promise you that. Okay?"

"O—okay . . . ," she said, without apparent conviction.

He left her and let himself through the opening into the kitchen area of the ice-cream parlor. *Who'd buy ice cream on a day like today, anyway?* he wondered. *Penrose should have just stayed home, and let Kitty stay home too. They'd both have been better off.*

On the floor behind the counter he saw just what he expected to see—what he'd seen at every other stop this morning. Same as Hoot Buffington, and Sandra Cliff, and Nat Landers. Penrose was dead. His clothes were foul, muddy, and they stank like the Androscoggin on a hot day. Mud caked his chin and neck, dribbled from his slack mouth. His eyes were open.

He looked terrified, even in death.

Will Blossom shuddered. He was a little terrified himself.

16

Writing about TV shows in her journal the night before had made Kerry realize how much she missed television. That, and the fact that TV had been part of her family's Christmas tradition: Charlie Brown, the Grinch, Rudolph, *Miracle on 34th Street* and *Holiday Inn* and *A Christmas Story*. It had been just ages since she had sat down and watched TV. A couple of days at the hotel in Portsmouth, and not for months before that. Maybe she'd been too busy living her life to simply observe, but on some level she felt removed from the rest of the country because they had gone on watching while she had been doing other things. TV might be overrated, but it helped define America in a very real way, and she missed that attachment to her fellow citizens.

Besides, being stuck up on this mountain with Season was starting to wear on her. She liked the sledding and the fireplace and the conversation, but she craved communication, connection. She wondered if there was some sort of plan. When would the roads open—or had they already? When would they come down from the mountain? And, maybe most important, how did her new perception of Season fit into her life? What came next?

In the morning, while Season slept in, Kerry tugged on sweats, tied her hair back, and scouted around the cabin. No telephone—and her own cell, she had determined long ago, had no signal up here—no radio, no TV. Even Mother Blessing had owned a TV.

But, Kerry remembered, *witch.*

She racked her brain for a long while, but couldn't come up with a spell that would make a TV appear where there was none.

While she dwelled on it, sitting on the living room couch with her ankles crossed, knees up, hands resting on knees and chin on hands, Season came in.

"Good morning, Kerry," she said. She looked warm and comfy in a man's loose-fitting corduroy shirt and soft, flared gray pants.

"Do you have a TV? Wait—does that count—no, strike that. I'm hoping that doesn't count as one of my remaining questions. I'm still not sure how these stupid rules are supposed to work."

"Rules can be stupid," Season agreed. "But often you'll

find that the stupidest ones aren't so bad once you realize why they're there."

"That doesn't answer my . . . my not a question."

"I won't count it, okay? And the other answer is no, no TV. But if you'd like to watch some today, you can."

"I was just feeling a little, you know, cut off from the world. This hermit deal isn't so much me, I guess. I'd kind of like to talk to my friends, too."

"I think we can arrange both," Season said. "Let's have some breakfast first, and then we'll get on that." She went into the kitchen and Kerry got off the couch to follow her. She had come to like watching Season cook, although not as much as she liked the eating part.

Season cracked a few brown eggs into a bowl. "I think an omelet would be good today. Sound all right to you? Maybe with biscuits and some fresh fruit."

"Sounds yummy," Kerry said. "Why—and I guess this one can count—why do witches like to cook so much? Mother Blessing did too, and even Daniel was a good cook. I mean, you could just kind of *poof!* and there's an entire meal, right?"

"I could, yes," Season agreed. "I think part of it may be that we enjoy the process, though. Most witches I've met are good cooks. It's not unlike witchcraft, when you get down to it. We take natural ingredients, combine them in a specified manner, and the end result is something that isn't what it was, something that's new and different and functional. A lot of spells work the same way."

"That makes sense, I guess."

Season's hands flew with practiced assuredness. Kerry was a pretty fair cook herself—she had taken over the culinary duties at home once her mom got too sick—but her repertoire was basic. Breakfast was far more likely to be cereal and toast than Belgian waffles, sausages, and strawberries cut into the shape of roses. Anyway, there were lots of choices of breakfast cereal. She hadn't counted them all, of course, but in her local supermarket if you stood at one end of the cereal aisle you could almost see the curvature of the Earth in the shelves. She figured you could easily eat cereal every day for the rest of your life, a different box at a time, and never have to repeat yourself because they'd just keep coming up with new ones. Soon the cabin was filled with wonderful aromas that pushed any thoughts of such basic foods from her head.

"So . . . what comes next?" Kerry asked as they ate Season's delicious food. She felt awkward about it, but knew the subject had to be broached sometime. "I mean . . . you know. With . . . all this? I guess I don't want to kill you as much as I used to."

"Well, that's a relief," Season said with a warm smile. "I don't want to kill you either. I really am not a killer by nature."

"I think I've figured that out," Kerry admitted. "It was hard, though. Took me a long time to accept."

"Understandable. You've been through a lot, and you've seen a lot of awful things. And we've been on the opposite sides of most of it. I guess the only way to answer your question is to ask you one. What do you want? There's probably no reason you have to stay involved in any of this. You can go back to school, go on with your own life, and leave our little intrigues behind. At least that's what I'd do if it was my choice."

Kerry dwelled on that for a moment. Back to Northwestern? Back to live with Aunt Betty and Uncle Marsh? Neither of those choices had very much appeal. She was eighteen—not a little girl, barely an adult by society's standards—but without the hunt for Season, without Daniel, she was completely adrift.

"I've been thinking about it a lot," she said. "But I haven't come to any firm decisions. Part of me would like to keep studying witchcraft, I think. That's the only thing that has really interested me lately."

Season looked a little surprised by Kerry's comment. "I would think you'd want to leave it as far behind you as possible, as fast as you could. I don't want you to jump into anything without giving it a lot of thought. It's not so easy to do, and there are a lot of sacrifices that have to be made, especially if you're not born into the community."

"I get what you're saying," Kerry said. "But I don't know. It seems like something I'm good at. Maybe I could make some kind of contribution."

"You probably could," Season agreed. "More omelet?"

After Kerry had done the dishes, she came into the living room to see Season looking at a TV set that stood on the hearth. It wasn't plugged into anything, Kerry noted, but there was a picture on its screen just the same.

"Cable or satellite?" she joked.

"Astral plane," Season answered with a grin. "Much clearer reception."

She held a remote control that looked perfectly authentic to Kerry. Pointing it at the TV, she started clicking through the channels. "Anything in particular you want to watch?"

"I've been so out of touch I don't even know what's on anymore," Kerry moaned. "And a million new songs are probably out, by a thousand new bands I've never even heard of. And movies? Is Josh Hartnett even a star anymore?"

Before Season could answer, something on the TV screen caught her eye. ". . . gruesome murders in Berlin this morning have authorities baffled. The early morning killing spree has left seven dead. Berlin police chief William Blossom has asked all residents to stay inside with their doors locked as much as possible, until more is known about who has committed these savage crimes . . ."

"Look," Season said in a hushed voice. The screen showed a reporter standing outside a café in what must have been Berlin. There were muddy handprints on the doorjamb behind him, and more tracks of mud on the ground. Season pushed a button on the remote and the screen froze, as if they were watching a DVD or TiVo, and not a broadcast with the word "Live" in the corner. She pushed another button—*That's some remote*, Kerry couldn't help thinking—and the picture zoomed in on the muddy footprints.

Mixed in with the mud, Kerry could see cigarette butts, stray leaves, bits of paper, and other detritus. "Is that—?" she began.

"Simulacra," Season said anxiously.

"But they're—they're killing people! Why would they do that?"

Season's voice was solemn, her brow furrowed with concern. "That's what they're best at." She eyed Kerry for a moment, then shook her head. "Sorry," she added. "That was flip. This is serious, and you deserve a real answer. Here's what I think: Mother Blessing is using them to look for me. She has tracked me to this area somehow. Instead of coming herself, she's sent the simulacra to find me. But she doesn't want anyone who sees them to be able to tell anyone else about them."

"Usually when she's with one," Kerry remembered, "she uses a glamour to make sure no one really sees them."

"That's right," Season agreed. "From this distance, though, it would be all she could do to keep them animated. So she would command them to kill any witnesses after they got whatever information they could."

Kerry shuddered. Sometimes she forgot just how brutal Mother Blessing could be. "Can we stop them?"

"We have to try," Season said. "But we have to get down there, fast."

Scott, Rebecca, and Brandy had just reached the RAV4, parked at a curb a few blocks from the real estate office, when they saw the police car race down the street past them, siren blaring, roof lights flashing. Scott realized that they'd been hearing sirens around town for the last twenty or thirty minutes, but they had been so busy trying to track down any information about Season that they had barely paid any attention.

"I wonder what's going on," he said. He wasn't curious enough to want to backtrack and find out—he was more concerned with getting on to Mount Cabot and finding Kerry. So much time had gone by since she had disappeared; he had a horrible feeling, sitting in his gut like a lead weight, that they would be too late to help her. It had taken only seconds for Season to kill Daniel, and Daniel had been a much more formidable opponent than Kerry would be. The only saving grace was that Season had taken Kerry away, instead of just finishing her off on the spot—to Scott, that suggested that the witch had some use for Kerry. If so, Kerry might still be alive.

But every minute might count.

"Looks serious," Rebecca added. She nodded toward a nearby intersection, which an ambulance screamed through at top speed.

"None of our business," Scott said. He fished his keys from his pocket to open the SUV. But before he reached the door, a dark shape separated from the nearby building and lumbered toward them. It took Scott a moment to realize that the figure was dark not because of shadows—as soon as it peeled away from the building's face, it moved into bright sunlight—but because it was, top to bottom, rich brown mud, not flesh or clothes.

"Umm . . . Scott . . . ?" Rebecca's voice quavered with fear, and he knew she had seen it too. His own voice seemed to fail him, as if it were out of his reach somehow.

But Brandy stepped up, the only indication of her own emotions a barely noticeable shaking of her legs, like her knees wouldn't quite lock under her. "It must be a . . . what do you call them? Simulacra? One of Daniel's mother's . . . things."

The man-shaped creature continued toward them with its odd gait, and Scott found his voice. "What do you want?" he asked. The thing's arms were at its sides, and there was nothing sinister or threatening in its demeanor. But when it stopped a few feet from them, its head cocked as if listening for something, it didn't speak, didn't answer in any way. "Tell us what you want," Scott insisted.

Finally, the simulacrum uttered one word, in a raspy, high-pitched voice that didn't seem to match up with its large, bulky body. "Season."

The three of them stood in place, stunned by the being's statement. Scott realized they shouldn't be—Brandy was almost certainly right, this thing was a simulacrum, and they were Mother Blessing's creations. It was only natural that the creature would be looking for Season.

"Mother Blessing must have . . . I don't know, tapped our phones or something," he speculated. "Or she's keeping tabs on us somehow, anyway. So when we found out where Season is, she sent her simulacrum. I don't think he wants to hurt us, or he already would have."

"Are you—do you want to go with us? To find Season?" Brandy asked the thing.

"But remember," Rebecca put in, "Kerry said Mother Blessing was kind of crazy or something when she left. I'm not sure she's actually on Kerry's side."

"She's against Season," Scott reminded them. "That means she's okay with me right now. If we find them—when we find them—we're going to need whatever help we can get to fight Season."

"Season," the simulacrum repeated in the same strange voice.

"How did you find us?" Brandy asked.

"Season."

"Kind of a one-track mind."

"If Mother Blessing can 'see' through its eyes, then she might have recognized us," Rebecca guessed. "She probably knows what we look like."

"We're going to find Season," Scott told the creature. "Do you want to go with us?"

The simulacrum shambled toward the SUV, which Scott took as an affirmative. "I guess we have company."

"It—he can ride in back with me," Rebecca offered. Turning to it, she added, "You don't mind if I open the window a little, do you?"

Scott understood—the closer it came, the more odiferous he realized it was, with a smell like rancid fish. He wondered if he'd ever be able to clean his vehicle sufficiently after this.

It left mud tracks on the ground with every step, and he was afraid that after sitting on his backseat for the hour or so it would take to get up to Mount Cabot and find Season, there would be a permanent stain.

But cars were replaceable. Kerry wasn't. They all piled in, the simulacrum scrunching itself in next to Rebecca. As soon as it was seated its head drooped to its chest, as if it had gone to sleep. *That's fine,* Scott thought as he started the vehicle and pulled away from the curb. *It won't be needed again until we find Season. And then we're going to want it to have all the strength it can manage.*

As they drove out of town, more sirens split the morning air.

17

Season's Jeep roared easily through the half-melted snow of Christmas Eve's storm. Season had warned Kerry that if the simulacra were so close they might not be able to return to the cabin, so they had taken a few minutes to pack up necessary belongings and thrown their bags into the back of the vehicle.

"How do you think she could have found us?" Kerry asked as they bounced down the snow-packed road away from the cabin.

"I don't know," Season said. Her knuckles were white on the steering wheel. "You didn't tell those friends of yours where we've been, did you?"

"I hate to shatter any illusions," Kerry replied, "but I don't even know where we've been. With the snow and everything, I was lost as soon as you left I-93. Anyway, at the cabin my phone didn't have any signal, so I couldn't have told them even if I wanted to."

"Well, somehow she figured it out," Season stated.

The "she," Kerry knew, was Mother Blessing. And Season was right—she might well have been looking for either of them, or both. The news report on the TV had been brief, but terrifying—if Mother Blessing was willing to let her simulacra kill half a dozen innocent people in one morning, she had stepped things up considerably. Maybe she knew that Season and Kerry were together, and she believed they might be forming an alliance. That would be something, Kerry was sure, that Mother Blessing would go to almost any lengths to stop.

And it intensified her sense that teaming up with Season was the right thing to do—that Mother Blessing, not Season, was the real enemy. The long struggle between them had taken too many lives, but it was Mother Blessing who pressed the issue, who wouldn't let up. Season's responses, Kerry had come to accept, had been mostly defensive. Running and hiding weren't the actions of an aggressor.

Season would be aggressive now, Kerry was sure. The set of her jaw, the determined way she muscled the Jeep around turns and over the unpaved road—everything Kerry saw pointed to a Season who was outraged and ready for anything. Finally, their wheels hit pavement, and Season stomped on the gas, hurtling the Jeep toward Berlin and the ultimate confrontation.

* * *

The beast in the backseat made Brandy nervous, but she knew that it would be an important ally in the confrontation to come. She, Scott, and Rebecca had no magic, no special powers. They could find Season and Kerry, and then . . . they could yell and scream at the witch, maybe throw rocks at her. That was about the extent of their ability to cause her harm.

With the simulacrum in tow, maybe they could succeed in freeing Kerry from Season's grasp. She knew Season had beat simulacra before, but at least it was *something. Which,* she reasoned, *is better than nothing.*

Scott raced toward Mount Cabot with a seriousness of expression that Brandy at once admired and despised. Clearly the danger to Kerry was foremost in his mind, and it may not even have occurred to him that by trying to rescue her, all he was doing was putting the rest of them into equal jeopardy. She hadn't tried to dissuade him—besides understanding that the effort would have been pointless, she wanted to force a showdown too. She hated the idea that Season was taking them one by one, like a fox picking off sheep who wandered too far from the flock. They needed to present a united front, to let Season know once and for all that she had to face them together or leave them alone.

Stinky mud-man would help make their case. They didn't have much power, but they had powerful friends. Maybe that would be enough.

As they sped up the road, she noticed a vehicle coming toward them. Scott spotted it too, and, glancing at him, Brandy saw his eyes widen in surprise. "It's the Jeep!" he said, almost breathless.

"Season's Jeep?" Rebecca asked from the back.

"Looks like it," Scott said.

Brandy narrowed her eyes, trying to sharpen her focus. There were at least two people in the oncoming Jeep, but that was all she could make out at this distance. Scott didn't wait for confirmation. He pulled the RAV4 over to the side of the road, off the pavement, and jumped out. Standing at the edge of the roadway, he flapped his arms like a crazed penguin trying to fly.

Twenty yards away, the Jeep pulled over. Its doors opened and Season and Kerry got out.

Kerry didn't look like a prisoner.

The two women started toward them. Kerry, Brandy saw, had a wide smile on her face. *She's all right, then,* Brandy thought happily. She realized how tense she'd been only when her tension started to dissipate at the sight.

But a dozen yards away, Season put a hand against Kerry's chest, holding her back, and pointed toward them. Both women's faces changed, expressions of joy becoming looks of concern. They stopped their advance and took what could only be defensive positions.

"Scott . . . ," Brandy warned. He had already started toward them, but he read the body language and halted in his tracks.

"What—," he started to say, but he let the rest of it die in his throat.

Season's posture—and Kerry's—were unmistakable. They were ready for war.

* * *

The sight of Scott's RAV4 pulling off the road had made Kerry's heart leap. "There they are!" she shouted gleefully. "We have to stop!"

"Okay," Season said. "For a minute. Just long enough to bring them up to speed. Then we have to get into Berlin to find those simulacra before they hurt anyone else."

"Deal," Kerry agreed. Season halted the Jeep and they both tumbled out, heading down the slope toward Scott, Brandy, and Rebecca. *They all came,* Kerry thought, her heart swelling. *Those guys are the best.*

Then Season's hand was on her, and they both came to a dead stop. "Look," Season cautioned. "Simulacra."

At first glance, Kerry saw only one, unfolding itself from the backseat of Scott's ride. But it was alone only for a moment. As Kerry watched, more shaped themselves from the packed snow and dirt beside the road, from pine needles and stray leaves, from litter and the tread of a shredded tire and a hubcap someone had lost. They formed from the ground up, a head first, then, as more matter clung together, growing taller and broader until they each stood on two strong legs. There were two, then four, then ten, and finally an even dozen, standing around Kerry's friends.

No, she corrected herself, *standing* with *my friends. Allied with them.*

"They—," she began.

Season confirmed her unfinished statement. "They're with Mother Blessing now."

"But—they can't be."

"No one else uses simulacra like she does."

"But someone could," Kerry suggested.

"Could, maybe. They don't. That's just the way it is."

"That doesn't mean—"

"Kerry, we don't have time to argue. They are there with the simulacra. One came in their car. Don't deny what's right in front of you."

Kerry felt her voice catch in her throat. "What—what are we going to do?"

"We're going to fight," Season answered. Kerry recognized that she had already taken a defensive posture, ready for the simulacra to attack. "The only alternative is to die, and I'm not keen on that one."

"Don't hurt my friends," Kerry pleaded. "We have to talk to them, make them explain what's going on."

"I'll try," Season agreed. But then she didn't speak anymore, because the army of snowmen rushed toward them, a massive wave of human-shaped debris.

Season spoke a few words of the Old Tongue, and a sudden, violet glow formed around her hands, which crackled with power. Kerry caught on and echoed her. She felt the energy tingle as her own hands sparked and the glow surrounded them also. A scent like fresh watermelon in the summer filled the air. Neither witch waited for the simulacra to get any closer, but both blasted at them—Season first, Kerry close behind—with energy pulses that radiated from splayed fingers. Where the pulses hit, simulacra burst apart, snow and earth and other ingredients flying apart, returning to their pre-enchanted states.

But they moved fast, and before Kerry and Season could dispatch all of them, Kerry felt a hard-packed fist slam into her ribs. The simulacrum had charged in so quickly she hadn't even seen it come, focused as she was on a more distant target. She doubled over and it swung again, its heavy hand smashing into her face and driving her down into the snow. She tried to blast it but the distraction had dissipated her energy field. She started to say the old words again. The thing gave her no opportunity, though—it came at her again, this time kicking at her. She dodged the foot, barely, and tried to grab its leg, hoping to pull it off balance. It was too fast, and she too weak from the brutal beating. She missed. It launched another kick that looked like it would take her head off.

Then the simulacrum blew apart, and Kerry, shielding her face from the sudden shower of snow and dirt, saw Season toss her a smile. "You owe me one!" Season shouted. "Now get back into the game!"

Season was surrounded by them, Kerry realized. The dozen that had initially formed had been joined by many more, a virtual army of the pseudo-men. Even Season was in danger of being overrun by them, and yet she had taken the time to save Kerry from one.

Kerry forced herself back to her feet, wincing at the pain in her ribs, the throbbing of her face. The determination that had earned her the nickname Bulldog filled her with a sense of purpose. *"Malificant!"* she shouted to the skies, raising her arms as if to grab a cloud. *"Konatifat benilias!"*

This time the glow wasn't confined to her hands, and the electrical sensation rippled through her whole body. Kerry had made herself a living weapon. She didn't hesitate, but unleashed her power on the simulacra, throwing off blast after blast. Each one found its target, blowing another simulacrum back to its component materials. She began with the ones closing in on her, and then turned to the ones surrounding Season. As she destroyed one after another, she felt herself reveling in the power she wielded, taking a kind of joy from the destruction of her unliving enemies.

When it was over, when no more simulacra rose from the ground, she felt almost let down. She relaxed, shook herself, let the power slip back into the universe from which she had called it, and saw Season doing the same. They went to one another and shared a quick embrace, and Season's whispered "You were great" brought Kerry a swell of pride she hadn't felt in a long time.

Then Kerry turned toward her friends, toward Scott, Brandy, and Rebecca, who still stood beside Scott's SUV.

She expected to see happiness written on those familiar faces, pleasure that their foes had been defeated, that she and Season had prevailed. The happiness of a reunion with old comrades. She hadn't seen any of them since she had sent Scott away, and she had known she was hurting him terribly when she did. She wanted to hug him, to let him know she hadn't meant any of it, was only concerned for his safety. She wanted to hug all of them, to enjoy the reunion, to get past the adrenaline rush of the battle in the company of friends.

That was what she expected.

What she saw instead was absolute terror. Rebecca shrank visibly under her gaze, crossing her arms over her chest and taking a step toward the vehicle. Brandy and Scott stood their ground. None of them spoke, but their faces said it all.

They were afraid of Kerry. After all they had been through, all she had done for them . . . now she horrified them. They had seen her power—and her capacity for violence—and instead of being impressed, or pleased, or heartened, all it had done was scare them.

She had been one of them. Now she was something else. Something . . . other.

Kerry had become a witch, and her friends were frightened of witches. Who could blame them, really, considering what they had seen, what they knew?

But reasoning through it, understanding their reactions, didn't make any of it any easier to take.

Kerry thought that her wounded heart, which had so recently begun to heal, would finally break.

SPRING

Kerry Profitt's diary, December 26

It's hard to describe exactly what I was feeling, standing there beside the road that led down to Berlin, New Hampshire, looking at the expressions on the faces of my friends and realizing that they were afraid of me.

Because we're talking about *me*. Not only am I the kind of person who wouldn't, as they say, hurt a fly, I'm the kind who the fly could probably beat up. Old stringbean Profitt, that's me. Arms more like Minnie Mouse than Popeye.

Lately, however, I've learned that one doesn't have to be all buff and weight-liftery to be powerful. And it's that kind of power—the kind that comes from understanding one's relationship to the ebb and flow of natural forces—that made Brandy, Rebecca, and Scott so afraid of me. They saw me with Season Howe—whom they had known only as a hated enemy—battling Mother Blessing's simulacra.

And since one of those simulacra had come up from Berlin in the car with my buds, while I was coming down the selfsame mountainside in a car with Season, they unsurprisingly assumed that I had gone over to Season's side.

Which, to be fair, I had.

But also to be fair, Season isn't the monster they thought she was. And Mother Blessing, whom they still believed was trustworthy, is a monster.

All in all, a confusing situation. Which didn't make it any easier to look at their faces and know they feared me.

I did what I had to do at that minute. Mentally and

physically drained as I was from the fight, I made like a cross between an auctioneer and Dr. Phil and fast-talked them out of panicking and running away. Then I persuaded them to follow us, in Scott's car, back up the hill to Season's cabin. Once we got there, Season made us some hot spiced apple cider while I laid the whole story out for them—starting at the beginning, which was 1704 and the destruction of Slocumb, Virginia. I told them how Daniel Blessing had always been told by his mother that it was Season who destroyed Slocumb, and how when Daniel and his twin brother Abraham were old enough, Mother Blessing sent them out on their quest for revenge. Or *her* quest, to be more precise. But it turns out that Mother Blessing is a stinking liar, and she's spent all these years blaming Season for something she did herself. In the process, she cost both of her sons their lives, and got our friends Mace and Josh killed too.

Okay, technically, Season is the one who killed Mace. She doesn't get off the hook for that one so easily. But the winds of war, I think somebody once said, can shift in an instant. When she killed Mace, he had been hooked up with us, and we were hooked up with Daniel, and Daniel was trying to kill Season. So self-defense? Kind of hard to argue with.

In the end, I must have been persuasive. Scott and Rebecca were easy, of course—Scott because he majorly crushes on me, and Rebecca because she always wants to believe the best of anybody. Brandy was tougher, as I had known she would be. But finally she came over to my side as well. Season helped—she speaks well for herself, articulate and bright and convincing. By the end of it they had all agreed to spend the night there, in the cabin, with the understanding that we'd move out by first light. It isn't safe here anymore, Season told us. Mother Blessing had been able to track us this far, had even been able to get one of her magically constructed pseudo-men to join up with them. She was getting too close, and we had to abandon this hidey-hole and go somewhere else.

The hugs and kisses and tears that should have accompanied our reunion—the first time we had all been together since Josh's death in Las Vegas—came then, at the end of the evening instead of the beginning. We were all wrung out emotionally by then, all exhausted. With the prospect of a very early morning facing us, we went to our assigned sleeping areas—I'm still in the bed I've been in since Christmas Eve—to get some shut-eye.

Except of course, me being me, a day like this requires some journaling time as well. But sunup is going to feel awfully early, so I should probably fold up the trusty laptop and actually shut that aforementioned eye.

Both of them, even.

More later.

K.

1

In the morning Season pounded on the door to her room, and Kerry started, as surprised as if someone had lit a fire-cracker under her feet. She sat up in bed, took stock quickly of where she was, rubbed her bleary eyes. Another four hours of unconsciousness would have been good, another six even better. Christmas Day had been relaxing, but it was bookended by days that were anything but, and she was feeling the strain.

She heard the sounds of her friends being similarly roused, though, so she climbed out of bed and dressed hurriedly. She'd showered the night before, knowing from hard experience that any time she could grab a shower she had better avail herself of it, because it might be the last for a while. It meant sleeping with wet hair—and lots of it, given the length of Kerry's dark tresses. But that was a small price to pay for the pleasure of being able to stand her own company all day.

Even moving as quickly as she could, by the time she made it out, Season had put together one of her signature breakfast feasts. Kerry was a little too sleepy to take full advantage, but she managed an English muffin, a couple of cups of strong black tea, and a slice of bacon. Scott Banner filled his plate with a little of everything—scrambled eggs, hash browns, fruit, two kinds of toast, and bacon.

Brandy Pearson looked at his plate and snorted. "You have eaten before, right?" she prodded.

"Let him indulge," Season said. "We're not taking it with us, and I won't be coming back here again for a good long time, if ever. Might as well not waste it."

Scott simply nodded at Season's defense and shoveled another forkful of eggs into his mouth. He'd put on a bulky wool sweater with black jeans and the all-weather hiking boots he had been wearing the day before. Kerry thought he had put on a few pounds since summer, when they had all shared a house together in La Jolla, California. The weight looked good on him, filling out his gaunt cheeks a bit.

Rebecca Levine had taken too many off, and Kerry was still worried about her. She had hoped the redheaded free spirit would stay down in New York—or better yet, back in school at Santa Cruz—and far away from Season and the whole long-unresolved conflict. But here she was, too bighearted to let her friends face danger without being there too.

Brandy was the one Kerry had gone the longest without seeing. Her thick black hair was tied down with a red scarf, and her off-white sweater beautifully complemented her cocoa skin. Brandy had always been a girl who could put herself together, even when trouble was brewing. She shrugged off Season's defense of Scott and took another bite of the honeydew that, along with a cup of coffee, seemed to comprise her entire breakfast.

"You said before that we have to leave here," Brandy observed. "I get that. But where are we going? If Mother Blessing could track you guys down here, where will we be safe?"

Season set down her own coffee mug and regarded Brandy calmly. "I wish I had an answer for that," she said. "The truth is, I don't know. I can only strategize, but I have no guarantees."

"Okay, what's your strategy?" Rebecca asked.

"Here's what I've been thinking," Season replied. "We need to split up. Together, we'll be far too easy to find now that she has a line on all of us. Without you, Kerry, or her sons, she has no champions left, but she still has power, and even though we can beat her simulacra, there's still the chance that they could catch us by surprise. Or she could join the fight herself. I can beat Mother Blessing in a fair fight on neutral ground, I'm sure. But I don't think a fair fight is what she has in mind."

"So we all have to go different places?" Rebecca asked.

The idea obviously caused her concern, and she didn't get her hands into her lap quickly enough to hide their quaking from Kerry.

"For the most part," Season said, "I think you should all go back home. You back to Santa Cruz, Scott and Brandy back to Boston. Resume your normal lives and activities, as much as possible. That way even if she does locate you again, there won't be any advantage to her to harass you, because you'll be out of it."

"Will we?" Scott asked. "Because I'm getting the distinct impression that this whole deal is kind of like the mob, or the CIA. Once you're in you can never really get out."

Season's nod was barely perceptible, but it was there. "There's some truth to that, Scott. I won't lie and say that you'll be completely safe. It depends partly on Mother Blessing. But if she observes you and understands that you're not in contact with me, that you're just going about your lives, then your chances are that much better. If we all stayed together, then you'd always be in jeopardy."

"Who is this 'we,' then?" Brandy wanted to know. "I notice you didn't say anything about Kerry going home."

"Maybe that's because I don't have one anymore," Kerry pointed out.

"Kerry is in this much more deeply than the rest of you," Season said. "She's a witch, Mother Blessing knows her well, and she's a target. She's probably in more danger because, skilled as she is, she still has a long way to go. If Mother

Blessing really came at her, Kerry couldn't win. She needs to stay with me, for her own protection and training." Season paused, making eye contact with Kerry. "Does that sound okay to you, Kerry?"

If she had been asked even twelve hours earlier, Kerry would have hesitated. She hadn't decided quite how she felt about Season. The witch had, after all, killed Daniel, who was the only man Kerry had ever loved. And she had no real proof of her contention that it was Mother Blessing, and not herself, who was behind the slaughter in Slocumb. Her story rang truer than Mother Blessing's did, but Kerry was no expert lie detector. It was one witch's word against another's.

So she couldn't have said exactly why, but she agreed almost immediately. "Sure," she said. "I've got nowhere better to go, right?"

"That's one way to look at it."

Kerry knew there were several other ways to look at it too, but they all added up to the same response. She really was running out of other options. She had made a powerful enemy in Mother Blessing. She had left her Aunt Betty and Uncle Marsh behind too many times, and wasn't so sure she'd be welcome back there. Her parents were dead, and her best friends in the world were the people in this room with her—the only people who could ever really know what she had been through since August.

And she figured Season was right in her evaluation of Kerry's abilities. She could do more witchy stuff than she'd been able to a few months before, but that probably meant she was just powerful enough to harm herself and others. She still needed tutelage, a mentor, and if Season wanted to be that, Kerry was happy to avail herself of the opportunity.

"Okay, then," she said cheerily. "I guess you're stuck with me."

Brandy eyed them both suspiciously. "But where are you guys going?" she inquired.

"I think it's best not to tell you," Season replied. "Not because we don't trust you—clearly, Kerry trusts you with her life, and that's good enough for me. But the fewer people who know, the safer everyone is."

"I don't like it at all," Brandy said. "But I guess I see your point."

"I'll be in touch as often as I can," Kerry promised. "So you guys don't have to worry about me."

"I'll still worry," Scott said.

Brandy nodded. "Don't take away Scott's favorite leisure-time activity. He's a gold medalist when it comes to worrying about you."

"I'm fine," Kerry stated flatly. "I've been in a couple of tight spots, but I've always come out okay. You don't need to worry about me, Scott. Especially if I'm with Season."

"I know," Scott said, blinking behind his glasses. "I mean, I understand that, intellectually. But it's not so easy when I don't know where you are or what you're doing. I always find myself thinking about the worst thing that could be happening, and assuming that *is* what's happening."

Rebecca laughed, covering her mouth with one hand. "But the truth is that whatever is really happening is usually even *worse* than Scott's imagination."

"Look, you guys." Kerry really hoped that she could persuade them of her safety, just as she had convinced them last night that she hadn't turned traitor or fallen under some kind of evil mind-control power of Season's. She knew what she was doing—okay, maybe that was a stretch. But she had some sense that she was doing the best thing for herself. These days—since the night she had met Daniel Blessing, really, changing her life forever—that was the most she could ask for. "I know I've said this before, but I really need you all to support me in this. And that means not worrying too much about me. You've all got your own lives to live, and I have mine. Mine is taking me in some directions that I didn't expect—but I think everyone probably finds out that's true, at some point or other. I mean, did your parents grow up thinking that they'd be pharmacists or lawyers or whatever? So I'm not taking the usual path. But I'm taking my own path, and you're taking yours, and we all just have to have some faith in one another's decision making."

Brandy snorted. "She's talking to you, Scott."

Kerry couldn't suppress a grin. "Thanks for not taking me seriously, Brandy," she said. "I could hardly believe that was me talking."

"It was a little drippy," Rebecca agreed. "But still—it made sense."

"Rebecca's right," Scott put in. "I don't mean to freak you out or anything, Kerry. I guess I'm just a worrywart by nature. But I do respect your decisions. If you and Season think you'll be safer, then Brandy and I will just go home and let you guys go wherever."

Season had been silent for a long time, just listening and letting the four friends work out their issues. Now she broke her silence. "I do think that's for the best," she said.

Kerry was glad the conversation had gone her way. "Sounds like it to me, too."

Scott looked at Brandy. "You need a ride, lady?"

"I guess I'm going your way," Brandy said. "If you think you have room for me."

"There's always room for you, Brandy," Scott said. "If you don't mind the stink of that mud-man we had in the backseat."

Brandy looked as if she was thinking it over. "I guess I can put up with it as far as Boston," she admitted. "If we can stop at a car wash on the way. But we should probably be hitting the road—I'll have a lot of explaining to do when we get there."

Kerry was sorry their reunion had been so brief. One of these days, she wanted time to really catch up with her friends, to find out what was going on in their lives instead of just telling them what was up in hers. This wasn't going to be that time, though. Season was right—the sooner they vacated this cabin, the safer they'd all be.

2

I've been doing some thinking," Rebecca said on the way to the airport in Burlington, Vermont, the nearest city with what passed for a "major" airport. "You guys should fly to California with me."

"That doesn't really help with the splitting up thing," Kerry answered. She guessed that Rebecca just really didn't want to be left alone again—even with her hardly-there roommate Erin. "Anyway, aren't you going back to New York, to spend the rest of the holidays with your folks?"

"I don't want to put them in any danger," Rebecca explained. "And anyway, I don't think I'd ever really feel safe there. California is about as far away from Mother Blessing as I can get, and Manhattan is so crowded that I'd never know who was real and who was one of her simulacra. In Santa Cruz you see the same familiar faces every day, and I'm more comfortable there.

"Anyway," she went on, "I wasn't thinking that you'd go to Santa Cruz with me. California is a huge state. I have these friends who own property up in Bolinas, on the coast up above San Francisco. They get tourists, but mostly it's this really out-of-the-way place where people value their privacy. Half the people up there are old-time hippies, and the rest are artists or hermits of one kind or another. There are a lot of marijuana farmers, too. They tend to be a suspicious bunch and don't like outsiders nosing around much. If you were there, I think you'd be pretty safe from Mother Blessing's minions."

"But we'd be outsiders too," Kerry said. She rode shotgun, and Rebecca sat in the back of Season's Jeep, which they would abandon at the airport. Kerry wondered momentarily how many vehicles Season had left behind in her life. Enough to fill a stadium parking lot, probably.

"Yeah, but you'd have someplace to be, so it would be okay."

"If we had the permission of your friends to use their place," Season added. "But getting that permission might endanger them."

"I'm sure I could swing that without telling them what it's for," Rebecca said. "That privacy thing cuts both ways. People who don't want others knowing their business are usually happy not to know yours."

"Sounds like it's worth checking out," Kerry suggested. "Unless you already have someplace in mind, Season."

Season glanced over at her and smiled, then faced the road once more. "I like it precisely because it's something I wouldn't have thought of," she said. "It's good to break out of old patterns if you're hiding from someone who knows you well. I'm pretty sure Mother Blessing is aware of most of my tricks by now."

"I'll call them," Rebecca said. "And when we get to the airport we can all fly together to San Francisco. From there I can get a shuttle to Santa Cruz, and you guys can rent a car or something to head up to Bolinas." Kerry heard a rustling as Rebecca dug out her cell phone and then dialed it. Kerry only half paid attention as Rebecca worked on persuading her friends, the Morgans, to let Season and Kerry use their place.

She realized she was happy to be on the move again. Since August she had spent a fair bit of time on the road, running toward or away from one witch or another. Rootless, her only permanent home now had a white line running down its middle—either that or two wings and jet engines that lifted her far above the Earth. Motion was the only constant, staying in one place too long the greatest danger. This had been Season's reality for centuries, and now it was also Kerry's. She wasn't sure if she truly liked it, but she was getting used to it.

If nothing else, she had learned the virtue of flexibility.

Scott pulled his RAV4 away from the curb after dropping Brandy at her parents' home in Needham, where she had wanted to go instead of back to her own apartment. He had wanted to be invited in. Even though he was a little nervous about seeing her brothers, afraid they blamed him for their breakup and maybe for her missing Christmas, he liked her family and missed spending time with them. She didn't extend that invitation, though. They had chatted amicably enough on the drive down from New Hampshire, with Brandy slipping in the occasional stinging barb, as she had a habit of doing. But she had grown quieter as they closed on the Boston area, her mood almost visibly darkening. He knew she was worried about Adam Castle, her new boyfriend, and about facing her family after skipping out on them at Christmas. At the end of the trip, she quietly thanked him for the ride and gave him a perfunctory hug.

Scott was still not thrilled with the idea that Brandy had a new boyfriend, but he was trying to adjust. He and Brandy had been a good thing for a long time, but that was over. He and Kerry could be a good thing too, he was sure, but it was looking like that would never happen. He glanced in his rearview mirror as he drove away from her block, watching it recede behind him like some kind of suburban metaphor for the longest romantic relationship of his life.

He knew he would still see Brandy from time to time, no matter what. Kerry too—or at least he devoutly hoped so. She would be farther away, however, and he would continue to worry about her, no matter what she wanted. Season would be a better ally for her than he could ever be, but he nonetheless felt better when she was someplace where he could keep an eye on her. Now she was no doubt winging or riding some-where halfway across the continent, and he was back in the position of having to wait for her to get in touch with him whenever the mood struck her.

As he turned the corner he stole one last glance at Brandy's house. But in his mind's eye he could see Kerry's slow but genuine smile, her green eyes flashing like twin emeralds catching the sun, her long black hair falling over her face and then being swept away, and he knew that such a beautiful vision would never leave him, no matter what else happened in his life.

The San Francisco airport was a terrible place for good-byes. It was crowded and busy, with travelers bustling in every direc-tion, all pulling wheeled suitcases as if they were oversized, blocky dogs, with security people, flight attendants, pilots and staff, and families waiting for or dropping off their loved ones. It meant there was no real privacy, no place for the kind of conver-sation Rebecca, Season, and Kerry really needed to have.

Instead of trying to talk in detail, they resorted to a kind of code. "So," Rebecca said. "You have my number. If you need anything, just call. Otherwise, my friends are expecting you to be at their place. If it goes more than a couple of months, it wouldn't hurt to call up, but I don't think they're planning on being back up there until early summer. I told you where the key is, right?"

"Yes," Season said. "We know where to look for it."

"And you have my cell, right?" Kerry asked redundantly, knowing full well that Rebecca did. What she didn't know was whether she'd have coverage in Bolinas—it sounded pretty rural, the way Rebecca described it. But she had also said it was a tourist destination, so maybe her phone would work fine. At the very worst, she could always augment it magically, as Mother Blessing had done with her laptop in the Great Dismal Swamp. "If you see or hear any signs of her, you let us know, okay? Don't take any chances with her." Obviously, everyone knew who the "her" referred to.

"Hello," Rebecca said. "Do you know me? Do you remember me being someone who takes chances?"

"You've taken a lot of them, Beck," Kerry said. "I just want you to be safe, okay?"

"That's what I want too," Rebecca assured her. "Well, for both of us—all of us—to be safe."

"The sooner we split up the safer we'll be," Season said. She scanned the crowds like a wary hawk. "I'm sorry, I'm not trying to rush you, Rebecca, but we really need to get going."

"I know," Rebecca said. "It'll be late by the time I get home too. I just . . . I don't want you guys to go."

"I don't either, Beck," Kerry said, suddenly sorry for her friend. Of all her summer friends, Rebecca might have been the least capable of dealing with the kinds of things they had learned—the existence of real witches, the magic, the constant danger. Kerry knew that going back to college in Santa Cruz, living in that big, ramshackle house with Erin, and being so far from the others was going to be tougher on her than on anyone else. She wished there was something she could do to make it easier.

But there wasn't. Inviting Rebecca to stay with them up in Bolinas would just expose her to even more potential danger. Season was right—Rebecca was safest living her own normal life, far away from them. She wouldn't like it, at least at first, but it was for the best.

Kerry wrapped her arms around her friend and gave her a firm squeeze. Rebecca returned it, sniffling a little as she did. *No tears,* Kerry mentally pleaded. *I don't know if I can take it.*

When she pulled away, there was moisture in Rebecca's eyes, but none escaped. Kerry blinked back a little of her own, and then Rebecca turned away and headed for the shuttles. Kerry and Season stood there for a few minutes, until Rebecca was out of sight. Then Kerry turned to the older woman.

"What now? We can't take a cab to Bolinas, right?"

"For tonight?" Season asked, almost incredulous. "We're in San Francisco, girl. Let's get a hotel room and do it right."

Kerry Profitt's diary, December 27

As it happens, Season's idea of doing it right was not precisely the same as mine would have been. Not that I'm club-girl or anything. But a little shopping might have been fun. It was pretty late at night by the time we were checked in at the Mark Hopkins, but still, big city, right? Something must have been open.

Instead, Season got us a cab and went into North Beach, where she took me to a hole-in-the-wall Italian restaurant that I never would have looked twice at. Once I was inside, though, it was like Pavlov's dog all over again— the aroma was heavenly and I was suddenly so famished it was like I had never eaten the cardboard baguette sand-wich they served on the plane. Which, in fact, I hadn't, because, you know, cardboard.

I just let her order, because the whole menu was in Italian and I was too hungry to even read English. I won't try to re-create the dinner here—let's just say that every-thing I ate was so good that my mouth thought it had died and gone to heaven, leaving the rest of me earthbound. The staff treated us both like old friends, although Season swore that's just the way they are, and she had never seen any of them before.

After dinner we walked around North Beach for a while, just watching the people, tourists and locals alike. It's quite a show. We chatted about the people we saw and the weather—cool, but nothing like Chicago or New Hampshire, with a fog that eventually rolled in off the bay like someone pulling a blanket over a bed. Basically, we covered every-thing except Mother Blessing and what lay ahead of us.

Which was fine. I dwell on that stuff enough as it is. It was good to have my attention distracted by something else for a bit.

I almost typed "for a spell" but decided that would be

just too witchy of me. Witchy and old-fashioned, which kind of go together, considering that other than me, the youngest witch I know is, like, three hundred and some years older than I am.

Now we're back in the room—*très luxe!*—and Season's getting ready for bed while I do the dear diary thing. But she'll come out soon and then it's my turn, and then another early start in the morning. I'm a little trepidatious, I admit, about what tomorrow holds, and the day after that, and so on. Me and Season Howe, teamed up? Who'd have ever thought?

More later.

K.

"I'll be Margaret Thurston," Season said. "And you're my niece, Melissa King."

They were in the back of a taxi, bouncing over San Francisco's famous hills on the way to a used car lot Season had found listed in the hotel room's phone book.

"But you'll have to show some identification to buy a car, right?" Kerry asked. "I did, when I bought that van to go down to the Great Dismal."

Season just looked at her, smiling. It took Kerry a few seconds to realize her mistake.

"Oh," she said when she caught on.

To demonstrate, Season opened her wallet and handed

it over. Inside it, every identifying item showed the name Margaret Thurston: a valid California driver's license with a Bay Area address, several credit cards, a Social Security card, even a library card. A checkbook had the same name, with a local address imprinted on the checks. "And mine all say Melissa King, right?"

"That's right."

Kerry double-checked the window between the front and back seats. It was mostly closed, but there was a narrow gap through which passengers could speak to the driver. The driver had her radio on, though, playing loud reggae music, so Kerry figured as long as they spoke in low tones they wouldn't be overheard.

"So on top of everything else, you could be a world-class counterfeiter," Kerry said. "Do you manufacture your own money, too?"

"I don't," Season answered. Under a tan leather jacket, she wore a snug blue turtleneck that was almost as vibrant as her piercing blue eyes, with faded brown jeans and black boots, and her blond hair hung loose, framing her face. "I know I wouldn't ever make so much of it that I'd have a real impact on the national economy, but the possibility exists—a witch could manufacture so much cash, and flood the markets with it, that it could devalue our currency. Because I want to make sure that never happens, I only spend money that I earn."

"But you don't have a job," Kerry pointed out.

"Maybe 'earn' isn't the right word," Season admitted. "I

have investments, under various names. I gamble sometimes, although I try to resist the temptation to push the odds in my favor. I have a bank account in most cities, collecting interest. Every few years I move them around, because an account in constant use for a hundred years might raise some eyebrows. One of those accounts is here in the Bay Area, under the name Margaret Thurston. I have as much as I need, especially since I make a lot of my own clothing and food."

Kerry thought of her own bank account, established with money from an insurance settlement after her mother's death. She had tapped it a few times since summer, never putting anything back in. There were still several thousand dollars in it, but if she continued on as she had been it wouldn't last a whole lot longer. Would she follow in Season's footsteps, constantly on the move and making witchery her lifelong career? Or was this just another phase in her life that she'd pass through in a little while? She had a hard time picturing herself doing anything more mundane after this experience. Working a food service job or being stuck inside an office seemed like they'd be claustrophobic at best. And her experience with higher education—vanishing from Northwestern a few weeks into her first term—was not promising so far.

She wanted to talk to Season about it, to find out more about her early life and how she had made the decision to be a witch—if there were even any other options open to her—but the cab pulled to the curb beside a sprawling car lot, decorated with multicolored pennants on ropes and sporting dozens of gleaming, polished vehicles. "Here you go, ladies," the driver said through the window. Season pushed a twenty through the window at her, and the two witches stepped out onto the sidewalk.

"Let me do the talking," Season said. "The van you bought was okay for you, but I think we're going to want four-wheel drive up in the country. And you never pay sticker at a place like this."

Another vital life lesson from Season Howe, Kerry thought as a salesman approached. He grinned like a hungry shark, and Kerry realized she was happy to let Season handle the negotiation.

3

An hour later they were crossing the rust-red span of the Golden Gate Bridge, heading north out of the city. Bolinas wasn't far up the coast, but it sat on the end of a little spur of land, separated from the rest of the state by the Point Reyes National Seashore. That isolated it enough that the locals felt they had their much-sought-after privacy.

Through a spattering rain, Season drove the old silver Dodge Raider they'd settled on, up Highway One through affluent Marin County. They made one stop, at a supermarket where they laid in some provisions—"real food," Kerry called it, as opposed to the magically created kind.

As they neared Point Reyes the rain picked up, a solid

curtain of it through which visibility was almost nonexistent. Heading into the park, sheets of water filled the narrow roadways. Kerry noticed that Season's knuckles were white on the wheel, and her easy chatter of earlier in the drive had died. All her focus was on the task of negotiating the road. The beauty of Point Reyes was unmistakable, but Kerry could barely see it, and she knew that Season was missing it altogether. She hoped they'd have a chance to come back sometime, to explore the oddly twisted pines and the wind-and-water-sculpted cliffs.

Instead of letting up as they progressed, the storm just dumped ever more rain on them—glimpses of the ocean were redundant, as there seemed to be as much water falling from the sky as in the Pacific. A few cars passed them, their occupants looking like tourists distressed that their trip to Stinson Beach had been ruined by the downpour. But they soon turned off the main road onto an old country lane that led away from Bolinas's minimal "downtown" and through rolling, grassy hills.

The storm let up a little, and Kerry noticed that Season visibly relaxed now that she was off the main road. So she decided to bring up a question that had been on her mind for a long time—one of those that she thought of, then forgot to ask, on a regular basis, usually remembering again at only the most inopportune moments.

"Season, that storm, when you attacked Mother Blessing's place in the Swamp—did you cause that? Or was it one of her defenses? Or just a natural occurrence?"

Season glanced at her. "I guess this is as good a time as

any to bring up something I wanted to talk about," she said, apparently ignoring Kerry's question altogether.

"What?"

"I've offered to teach you, to help you develop your obviously significant gifts. And for the last few days, I've pretty much been willing to answer any question you threw my way. But once we get settled into our new place, we'll be going back to a routine like we had at Christmas."

"The no-more-than-ten-questions thing? Why?"

"We might change the number—maybe fifteen per day, or something like that, since we'll be working closely together. But the reason we'll be working together is so you can learn. To do that, you have to be focused. Asking a million questions about any trivial matter that pops into your head is a scatter-shot way of learning, and it's not that effective. If you have to think your questions through, really narrow down what you need to know and sift out those things you can figure out on your own, then you'll learn much more quickly, and you'll retain more."

"I guess that makes sense," Kerry admitted. She felt a little thwarted by the idea, although Season's reasoning seemed sound. "But you said that starts when we get settled?"

"Right."

"Which means I can ask questions now, right?"

"Uh-huh," Season answered. Most of her attention was still on the road, keeping the vehicle in contact with the wet pavement and trying to follow the directions they'd been given.

"So why are you doing this? Why take me under your wing like this? What's in it for you?"

Season hazarded another, longer glance at Kerry before facing front again. "I thought it was obvious," she said. "Like I told you, you are a gifted witch. A kind of diamond in the rough, I suppose. But anyone who learned as much as you in those few weeks with Mother Blessing is a person to be reckoned with."

Kerry thought her heart would burst with pride at that description. She wasn't sure she could live up to it, but she would definitely try.

"Part of being a witch is giving back to the community of witches," Season went on. "One way to do that is to help teach and develop young witches, so that the traditions are carried on. In this case, of course, there's also a much more practical consideration."

"What's that?"

"Mother Blessing and I have been at each other's throats for centuries," Season explained. "We've each won some battles, but the overall war goes on. One of these days, one of us is going to have to prevail. I would much rather have you on my side in the conflict than hers, because frankly, I could use some allies here."

Kerry started to say that she was honored that Season would consider her aid anything to be desired, but as she was composing her thoughts, Season interrupted. "And that storm in the Great Dismal, by the way, was mine. Mother Blessing

knew I was coming, but I was hoping to mask my exact progress to some extent, so she wouldn't know precisely where I
was or when I'd reach her home."

"It worked," Kerry said. "She was trying to prepare, but
you caught her before she was completely ready."

"And still, I couldn't beat her," Season recalled. "Partly
because she is most powerful on her home ground, where she
has lived for so long. And partly because she had your help."

"Did I really make that big a difference?" Kerry asked, surprised.

"Do you really have to ask?"

Before Kerry could answer the question, Season pulled off
the little country lane onto a rutted dirt track, just the width
of two sets of wheels. "Here we are," she said, ticking her head
toward a mailbox with a street number painted on it.

The track wound between spreading oaks, down into a
little incline where a wood-sided house stood. It was a single
story, with a porch across the front. Its blue paint, faded,
blistered, and peeling from the sun and weather, was rain-
darkened, and water dripped from its eaves. The roof had seen
better days, but Kerry figured if it was dry inside, after the
storm that had blown through today, then it would hold up
fine.

Season parked at the end of the drive, in a little dirt circle
right before the front door. "Home again, home again," she said.

They had left New Hampshire with very little. Kerry
brought her usual duffel containing a few changes of clothes,

some of Daniel's journals, and her laptop computer. Season had a leather backpack that seemed to contain anything she would ever need. Kerry was convinced that if she ever looked inside, it would be empty, and that Season just conjured what she wanted from it. They hauled the groceries inside and dumped the bags on a table made from raw oak planks, sanded but not sealed or painted. The kitchen was small, but clean water ran from the tap, the refrigerator was cold, and the gas oven and stove seemed to work. The owners had an interesting sense of color—the kitchen's walls were fire-engine red and bright blue, while the floor was yellow and the appliances white and gold.

The rest of the house echoed the general color chaos. Wooden walls were painted in seemingly whatever color had struck someone's fancy at a given moment, or maybe just in whatever was on sale at the hardware store. Most of the floors were unpainted, but there were exceptions, including a forest green one with red polka dots.

There seemed to be a great deal of wildlife—spiders, ants, flies, and other less immediately identifiable creepy-crawlies—inside the house that Kerry would just as soon have had living outside instead. She figured that it was a function of the house having been unoccupied for a stretch, and that once she and Season had made the place their own, the bugs would move out. Living in the Swamp had given her a greater tolerance for insect life than she'd ever had before, and learning witchcraft had impressed on her the role that all living things played in the world. Mother Blessing had told her it was scientific fact that if all the insects in the world were to suddenly vanish, all other life on the planet would end within two weeks. Mother Blessing had made a lot of outrageous claims, but Kerry couldn't help suspecting there was some truth to that one.

In spite of the colors and the creatures, the house was cozy and plenty comfortable enough for Kerry's liking. The furniture was old, mismatched, and lived in, as if it had grown up organically within the house. A door led from the kitchen into a small grassy backyard with a few rows of herbs and vegetables, overgrown now but offering the promise of fresh food with only a little work and attention. Beyond that were woods that seemed to go on forever. The room Kerry chose as her bedroom was next to the only bathroom, and though it was a little smaller than the other bedroom, it had a built-in window seat where she could already imagine herself reading and writing at night.

In the middle of the afternoon, after Kerry had hung up her clothes in the room's tiny closet and shoved some furniture around so she'd be able to see trees out the window from her bed, Season called her into the kitchen. Two cups of hot tea and a plate of cookies were set out on the table. Season sat in one of the four random chairs that surrounded it, looking expectantly at Kerry. It was clear that she'd been summoned for a particular reason, so Kerry took a chair and drew one of the cups to her. She wasn't going to waste one of her questions by asking what was up.

"I wanted to tell you what is really going on here," Season said after a moment. "Why Mother Blessing has stepped up the pace of attacks against me, and why staying with me puts you in considerable danger."

"Okay." Outside, the rain continued to beat down on the roof, creating a kind of staccato background music for their conversation.

"You know about the Witches' Convocation," Season declared plainly. "It starts on the first day of spring. One of the important functions of the Convocation is to rule on disputes between witches, as well as on crimes against witchcraft and crimes by witches against humanity. We firmly believe in policing ourselves, so that the outside world never decides it has to take action against us."

"Which means that the Convocation will finally address what happened in Slocumb," Kerry said, careful in her phrasing. She was determined to save her questions.

"That's right," Season agreed. "We have a very rigid and highly developed system of justice, which is prepared to deal with all of those issues I just described. The Slocumb incident will definitely have a hearing in Witches' Tribunal. Mother Blessing has been spreading her version of things ever since it happened, and even though her version is a lie, there's a little bit of that 'common knowledge' thing operating in her favor."

"People tend to believe something they've heard over and over, even if there's no truth to it," Kerry stated.

"Exactly. I've tried to get my story out there too, but it's been harder for me. For one thing, I didn't know she was spreading her tales for a long time, until they started filtering back to me. And then, she had me on the run for so long that it was hard to get a fair hearing—I looked guilty simply because I wasn't sitting still and waiting for her to finish me off."

"That's not fair."

"That's true. But then, fairness is what the Convocation is for. I'll be at a disadvantage because so many will have heard Mother Blessing's side of it, but the hearing will be as impartial as possible. Which is why Mother Blessing would love to get rid of me before it happens. She could use the Slocumb incident as a defense when the hearing about my death came up, as it certainly would. But that would be an easier sell for her, since she wouldn't have to worry about my testimony contradicting hers."

"So she'd like to kill you before it starts, but even if she doesn't, she stands a good chance of beating you in court?"

"That about sums it up," Season admitted sadly. "She isn't guaranteed to win. I happen to believe that the truth will sway the Tribunal to my side. And I think there's a way to prove that truth. But I'm going to need your help."

"My help?"

"That's right. I need someone I can trust completely, someone familiar with the facts, and someone who is very powerful and skilled."

"But I have a long way to go before I'm those things."

"And it's not quite January," Season replied. "Which is

why we need to train so hard between now and the Convocation. I'm going to want you by my side, Kerry. More than that. I'm going to need you. Will you be there for me?"

Stunned that she was being asked, being trusted with so much, at first it was all Kerry could do to nod her head. "Of course," she said finally. "I'll do whatever I can."

"That's good," Season said, a warm smile spreading over her face. "That's the best I can ask for."

4

Mother Blessing wheeled angrily around her home in the Great Dismal Swamp, her motorized scooter's rubber tires squeaking on the hardwood floors. Somehow Season Howe had survived her onslaught. It had taken every ounce of strength Mother Blessing could bring to bear to create nearly a hundred simulacra, and still the witch had defeated them. If only she had been able to manifest them all at once instead of one at a time, however quickly. That might have proven too much even for someone of Season's abilities.

But that great an effort, over such a distance, was beyond her. She had lain for days in her bed after the post-Christmas assault, exhausted by her efforts. It was only now, a couple of days after the passing of the year, that she was able to get around again. The immediate aftereffects of her spell had passed, but the fury hadn't.

Allowing Kerry Profitt to receive communications while she was here in this house had been a stroke of genius. Doing so had enabled Mother Blessing to learn who was close to Kerry, who might be keeping tabs on her whereabouts. So when the urgent call had passed from one to the next—*We've found Season!*—Mother Blessing had known approximately where to begin looking. By watching through the eyes of her simulacrum scouts, she had spotted the young interlopers, and they had led her right to Kerry and Season.

It only added to her rage that Kerry and Season seemed to have teamed up. She had groomed Kerry to be an arrow that she could let fly at Season at any time. For that weapon to be turned so quickly against her was nothing short of infuriating.

But there was no one in the house to shout at, no one to complain to or abuse. So she slammed doors and made sharp turns with her scooter, envisioning the faces of her enemies on the floor and wishing she could roll over them as easily.

A new year had begun. The Convocation would be upon her in a matter of weeks. There was a chance that she would prevail in the Witches' Tribunal, but there was also always a chance that she would not. Far better to finally get Season out of the way before then.

And she could do it, she was convinced. Her mistake had always been in sending others to do the job. Her sons had turned out to be weak—not ruthless enough, or possibly not determined enough. She didn't know what the problem was, but they obviously had some failing that she had not recognized before. Kerry Profitt might have been forged into a useful weapon, given time, but she had been young, inexperienced, and Season had come before Mother Blessing had had a chance to finish with her.

So the task fell to her. Had she recognized this fact years ago, perhaps this war would have been long since over. She had always thought there was time, plenty of time. But suddenly the Convocation loomed. If it had been an annual event, or even a centennial one, perhaps she'd have been better prepared for it. Over the course of five hundred years, though—and this being the first and possibly the only one of her lifetime—it had kind of crept up on her.

It would take her a while to be ready for another battle. Weeks, maybe. Months would be better, but she didn't have months. Any moves against Season this close to the Convocation would automatically be suspect.

On the other hand, Season's presence at the Witches' Tribunal would be more perilous still.

She would just have to make sure that Season didn't show up for the Witches' Convocation. No matter what it took.

Dawn hadn't even cracked, if that's what dawn really did, when Kerry rolled out of bed at Season's summons. For the last several weeks, Season had been running her ragged. Up at first light, warming up, performing calisthenics in the cold morning air. Then a long run, at least five miles, before breakfast. Kerry kept thinking she'd get used to it, but so far she hadn't. Every night she went to bed with muscles sore from the day's workout, and every morning she woke up with aches worse than she'd had the night before.

After the run and a big breakfast, she and Season went out into the fields, forests, and beaches of the area for nature lessons. This area wasn't as rich in biological diversity as the Great Dismal Swamp had been, but it was still abundant in its plant species, and only slightly less so in animal life. And as Season explained, variety wasn't an absolute necessity—more important was the practitioner's connection with the natural forces that flowed through those plants and animals. Kerry, Season noted, had an almost innate ability to make that connection.

She could sit in the middle of a meadow with the wind pushing the tall grasses toward her, and the susurrus of the grass seemed to be a private conversation that only Kerry could understand. She could wait patiently with her arms extended in a forest glade, and birds would drop down to her hands. She had to overcome her distaste for insects, but once she had, they would crawl up her arms and legs without stinging, biting, or otherwise molesting her. Even the enormous elephant seals on the beach at Point Reyes responded to her. She made eye contact with one, which then rolled over onto its back, flippers extended out toward her, and uttered three long, deep-throated squeals in her direction.

After time spent communing with nature, the daily schedule called for a reading period. Kerry knew that Season had not brought an entire library's worth of magical texts with her to the Bolinas house, but the books were there, and Season assigned a heavy study regimen. These books reinforced what Mother Blessing and Season had taught her, but went into considerably greater detail about the origins of witchcraft, the theory behind individual spells, and even some of the great witches of the past.

The reading period was followed by lunch, and then by one-on-one instruction from Season, putting some of the things she had read into practical use. This usually took most of the afternoon, but if there was time, Season put her through more physical training.

"Stamina is just as important as knowing the ancient words of power backward and forward," Season explained on one of the many occasions when Kerry complained about the hard workouts. After dinner they sat around together, making small talk or discussing the events of the day. "It does you absolutely no good to know the words you say if you don't have the strength to put behind the spells. And if the first couple of spells knock you on your tail, you won't be around long enough to become an experienced witch."

"Yeah, but if the workout kills me, what good does all the knowledge do?"

"People almost always survive exercise," Season answered with a smile.

"And if I'd wanted to join the Marines, I would have."

"Are you calling me a drill sergeant, Private Profitt?"

"Hey, if the combat boot fits . . ."

The thing was, Kerry believed it was working. She had been in the best shape of her life when she'd been in the Swamp with Mother Blessing, but now, after just a few weeks with Season, she was even stronger. Her stomach was flat, her thighs and calves hard and sinewy, her arms and shoulders rippling with muscle. The old "no pain, no gain" saying seemed to have a lot of truth to it. Kerry definitely had the pain, but the gain was also unmistakable.

And the changes weren't confined to the physical. Kerry realized that she was sleeping more soundly—and falling asleep earlier, thanks to the way too early wake-up call—and her mood was generally positive and upbeat.

In this way the days sped by quickly—days of wind and weather, of frantic activity, of cramming her head so full of information that she was sure it would explode.

One night in late January, Season sat across from Kerry in the house's living room, crowded with a sofa, several chairs, and an assortment of tables that looked like they'd been purchased at flea markets over the years. Outside, yet another winter storm battered the roof. Season looked cozy in a red polar fleece top and black corduroy jeans. Kerry had layered a couple of T-shirts together, and sitting near the fire she was perfectly comfortable in those and blue jeans.

"I've noticed something interesting these last couple of

weeks," Season began. She had poured herself a cup of hot tea, and on the oak coffee table she placed a cardboard box full of herbs she and Kerry had collected early on and hung in the kitchen to dry, and an old stone mortar and pestle. Kerry put down the book she was reading—a thriller from the 1970s that she'd found on a shelf in the house, not one of the magical texts—and looked at Season.

"What is it?" she asked.

Season put some of the herbs into the mortar before she answered. "Teaching you, working with you, has had an unexpected benefit for me as well," she said.

Kerry waited for her to continue. Season had a habit of revealing things at her own pace, no matter what.

"I've been pretty consumed," Season went on finally, grinding away with the pestle, "with either running from, or battling, Mother Blessing and her minions. It's taken so much of my time and energy that there hasn't been much left for anything else. Watching you, trying to see the world—and witchcraft—through your eyes, I've remembered what drew me to witchcraft in the first place."

"You were drawn?" Kerry asked. "You weren't born into it?"

"My father was a witch," Season replied. "Not my mother. She wanted nothing to do with it, and in fact convinced him to renounce his gift. Those were dangerous times for witches in Europe, so it was probably a good decision in terms of prolonging his life. But it meant that I had aunts and one surviving grandmother who could tell me stories about the craft and point me in the right direction when I had made up my mind."

"And when you did, obviously you decided to go the witchy route," Kerry observed.

"Not at first. But there weren't a lot of opportunities for women in those days. I could have worked as a scullery maid, or married, or joined a convent. None of those particularly suited me, even then. My father always tried to impress upon me that I was different, special somehow. I guess I believed him. And then I watched women all around me leading miserable lives but saw that my aunts and grandmother were not only healthy and well kept, but commanded respect in their villages. With those role models, I could hardly turn my back."

"So they fulfilled the mentor role for you . . ."

"That I am trying to do for you, Kerry. That's right. And by doing so, I've reconnected to some of that sense of discovery I felt in those days. Learning how the world really works, how everything is connected. Feeling the excitement of creating a spell and watching it come about. There's a thrill of creativity that happens, which I've kind of lost track of."

"I know what you mean," Kerry said. "I feel the same thing when one works just right."

"Watching you, seeing the spark in your eyes, that's what reminded me of it all. I'm indebted to you, Kerry. Thanks for showing it to me again."

Kerry was nonplussed—not for the first time since meeting Season. "I—I'm the one who should be indebted, Season," she stammered. "You could have killed me, or at least sent me back to Mother Blessing. But you agreed to take me on, just like that—I can still hardly believe my luck."

"I think you're failing to see the big picture, Kerry. It's not just you who needs me. We both need each other." She took the pestle out of the mortar, in which she had crushed the dried herbs to a fine powder. "Think about that, okay?"

Kerry Profitt's diary, January 24

So Season owes me? The first impression test tells me that's crazy. So do the second and third. I owe her, huge. But what I've done *for* her could be measured in a teaspoon, I think. If you had a microscope to find it.

I mean, that whole thing she said earlier this evening about having connected somehow with the reasons she became a witch. A little touchy-feely, maybe, but still really sweet. And maybe there's even a modicum of truth to it— "modicum" being a word I was reacquainted with in one of Season's books, and I like it. It's kind of like forgetting how good popsicles taste on a hot day, and then you take a little kid to the store and buy him one, and you get your own, and when you lick it you remember why you liked them in the first place.

Or something like that. Only probably more profound.

But she told me to think about the fact that we both need each other, so that's what I've been doing. I can come up with plenty of reasons I need her: so I don't get killed, so I don't kill myself, so I can continue my training, so I can become the witch I'd like to be, etc. etc.

As for why she needs me . . . ? To help her battle Mother Blessing, I guess. And for whatever is coming at the Convocation, for which she told me she'll need my help. But I still don't know with what. The Convocation is a couple of months away, but getting closer all the time. Every now and then she drops hints about it, things she's heard over the years, and it sounds *amazing*. I can't wait to see it for myself.

I guess I have to, though. Wait, I mean.

What's it going to be like? Has a girl ever looked forward to something with such delirious anticipation?

Well, it so happens that I didn't go to my prom. I guess this is my consolation prize.

Although if you want the truth, this is about a million times cooler.

More later.

K.

5

Rebecca stood on the boardwalk, quiet this time of day. On a weekend, or later in the evening, it would be bustling with people playing for a chance at cheap prizes, lining up for the roller coaster, eating corn dogs and cotton candy. It was like a county fair or a circus all year long, except even more threadbare than most, with a sense of desperation underlying it, as if anyone who couldn't have fun here was just out of luck altogether.

Rebecca wasn't having any fun.

February had already bled into March. The school year was passing by, and she was attending class (well, most of the time—she should have been in class now, instead of at the beach) and trying to pay attention. Her grades had been passable, though not excellent. Nowhere near what she could have done if she had "applied herself"—a phrase Rebecca had heard many times during her school career—but at least she wasn't flunking out.

But although she got up every morning, ate a meal, went to school, did homework, read a little, the whole thing seemed like an exercise, a rehearsal for real life instead of life itself. She spent every day waiting for something that didn't come.

She knew what the problem was, of course, and it had more than one part. She lived on the edge of fear now, never knowing when Mother Blessing, or Season, or some other witch entirely might re-enter her life. Death followed in the wake of witches, that was her experience. And she couldn't quite believe that witches were gone from her life. Kerry Profitt, after all, seemed well on her way to becoming one. And the last time she had talked to Kerry, a month or so before, they were still up in Bolinas at the Morgans' place, and Kerry seemed to be more excited by her new path than ever.

So that was the first part—one of these days, Kerry or one of the witches associated with her would show up, and her life would be spun topsy-turvy again.

The second part was the fear that the first part wouldn't happen after all.

Because now Rebecca knew what most people never did. She understood that there was another aspect to life. And while that aspect was often terrifying, it was also exciting. Even the terror made her feel more *alive* than anything else she had ever encountered. The whole thing—the thrill of the chase, the shiver of horror when she learned that something she had believed was nonsense, or legend at best, was true— she couldn't shake her hunger for it.

Is that why Kerry threw herself into it? Rebecca wondered as she stared off into the blue distance, looking at the line where sky met sea. *Is she addicted too?*

And can addictions ever be good for you?

It was one of those Boston days when people begin to believe that spring will come around again. The gutters ran with melting snow, which for at least a week had been dirty and blackened by exhaust and grime. Joggers ran along the banks of the Charles in shorts and T-shirts instead of all bundled up in sweats. Light green leaves caught the brilliant sunlight, adding grace notes to branches that had been bare and gray for months.

Ordinarily, Brandy would have loved being out on a day like this.

But not today.

Today Adam Castle had decided to pick a fight.

They had gone for a walk to enjoy the springlike weather. Brandy wore a light leather jacket over a cashmere sweater, with black pants and black flats. Adam had on blue jeans, white athletic shoes, and a navy Cambridge sweatshirt. Both had felt relieved at not having to put on a winter coat.

When they got back to his apartment, Adam stopped just

inside the door and turned to Brandy. "I've been trying to figure out a way to say this for a long time," he said. "And I just
can't think of anything except coming right out with it."

Brandy felt like she'd been sucker punched. She prided
herself on being able to read people, but she hadn't known
there was anything weighing on Adam beyond the usual work
stuff. She closed the door gently behind herself. "With what?
What's wrong, Adam?"

"It's . . . I feel like you don't trust me, Brandy. Like there's
a whole huge part of your life you don't let me see. It's like
you're one of those people who has a second family in a different city."

Now the sucker punch sensation turned into a twisting
of her gut, because Adam had proven to be extraordinarily
perceptive. He was exactly right. She had been keeping something from him—something huge. She felt like she couldn't
explain about Season Howe and Mother Blessing and Kerry.
So she had made up stories about her summer job in San
Diego, and then others to explain things like her sudden trip
to New Hampshire at Christmas. The lies she had fabricated
then demanded other lies to support them, and she had found
herself constructing a whole network of untruth.

Still, she had thought her psychological insight and studies
had allowed her to pull it off. Now, learning that she hadn't,
she felt terrible about the whole thing.

Just not terrible enough to confess, she thought. *Some things
he really is best off not knowing.*

"I don't know what you mean, Adam," she said, after a hesitation that she recognized had stretched a little too long.

"Are you sure?" he pressed. "Do you really want me to run down the laundry list of little lies I've caught you in, or times you've evaded questions? Because I can, Brandy. I've dwelled on it long enough."

"That's not what I'm saying, Adam." She searched his face, dark and scowling, for any sign of the man she had come to care about so deeply. She couldn't yet bring herself to use the word "love," but the very fact that it floated at the edge of her consciousness meant something. At any rate, she enjoyed his company and didn't want to lose him.

"Then what?" he asked. "Either I'm right or I'm wrong."

"You're . . . you're wrong, then."

He flopped down on his couch, his hands folded into tight fists. "You're sure about that. You haven't been hiding anything from me. That trip out of town at Christmas, the one you took with your ex and came back from all exhausted and freaked out—you were visiting a sick friend? Come on, Brandy, that story's always been lame."

"That's not what I said, and you know it," Brandy objected.

"Sorry," Adam said with an angry sneer. "Not a sick friend. A friend in trouble. What kind of trouble you never told me, though."

"Because it was none of your business," Brandy fired back. "If she had wanted strangers to know her personal issues she would have said so. You don't know her, and you don't need to know what she was going through—you just need to know that she needed me, and that should be good enough for you."

"Should be," Adam said. "But it isn't. Not on top of everything else. I'm sorry, Brandy, but I can't be in a relationship with half of someone. If you can't open your whole life to me, then it's just not going to work."

"I . . . I've given you as much of myself as I can, Adam," Brandy said, aware that she was on the verge of sounding like she was pleading. She wouldn't go that far, though. Not for Adam or any other man. He was smart, funny, good-looking, and successful. A real prize. But not prize enough to humiliate herself over.

"That's not all of you, though." His eyes had been burning a hole through her, but now he went to the window and looked away, toward the far side of the river. "It's not enough."

"Adam, hasn't there ever been anything in your life that you just had to keep to yourself? Something that was maybe too private, or too dangerous, for other people to know?"

Adam let out a soft chuckle, but one with no humor in it. "What are you now, Brandy? Some kind of spy?"

"That's not what I'm trying to say, Adam."

"I wish you knew what you were trying to say, then, because it isn't working."

"But . . . Adam," Brandy said, bordering on desperation again. She couldn't tell him the truth, and he would have to live with that. "You've got to just understand on this one. You can't push it."

He spun around to face her again. "I *am* pushing it, Brandy. Consider yourself pushed. You've admitted that you've been lying, hiding things from me. That's what I needed to know. Now you have two options. You can either tell me the truth—all of it, from jump—or you can admit that your secrets are more important to you than I am."

Now anger that had been simmering below the surface pushed itself up. "You know what I'm hearing, Adam?" she asked. "I'm hearing that you don't trust me. I would never ask you questions about parts of your life that are off-limits to me—and I recognize, even if you don't, that everyone has places they don't invite others into. No one's an open book, Adam, so don't pretend that you are."

Adam looked startled by the ferocity of her attack. "Don't turn this around on me, Brandy, I'm warning you . . ."

"You're warning me? Adam, obviously there's a lot you don't know about how human beings work. I don't have time to teach it all to you, though—not if you can't bring yourself to have a little faith in me."

"Brandy . . ." Adam didn't finish the thought. Brandy picked up her purse from the chair where she'd dropped it.

"Think about it. You have my number," she declared. She let herself out and closed the door firmly when she went. Out in the hallway, tears sprang to her eyes. She hadn't meant to storm out—hadn't even meant to spin the whole argument around and make him the bad guy. After all, she *was* keeping secrets.

Secrets of life and death. Secrets she couldn't tell anyone

outside the small circle of her summer friends, no matter what.

Dabbing at her eyes with her right hand, she started for the stairs.

Adam sat on his living room sofa, still amazed at what had just transpired. *Did she break up with me?* he wondered. *Because I thought I was breaking up with her.*

Hadn't worked out quite as he expected, though. He had stewed in his suspicions for long enough to work up a good head of moral indignation. Then somehow she had yanked his footing out from under him and made it seem like he was the one with the problem.

Well, I guess I am, he thought. *And my problem is named Brandy Pearson.*

She had been gone less than five minutes when he heard a heavy footfall in the hallway outside his apartment. Brandy? His heart leaped at the thought that she had returned already—confusing, since until he heard the sound he had wanted her out of his life. *Emotions are like that,* he thought. *Can't expect consistency from them.*

He had his hand on the door before she even knocked, and had started to pull it open when a powerful thrust knocked him off his feet.

"Brandy?" he asked, startled. Even furious, she shouldn't be that strong. And when the dark figure swung into the apartment, slamming the door, he knew it wasn't her at all. It was a man—or something like one, anyway. The guy was enormous,

the size of a linebacker, and dark, and he looked like he'd fallen
into a vat of acid or something. His features were indistinct, as
if his face were melting on the spot. And something else—he
looked as if he'd been put together from mud and dirty snow,
with leaves and branches for skeletal structure. And he stank
like the worst locker room Adam had ever been in, multiplied
by a thousand.

All this flitted through Adam's mind in less than a second, and he realized that something was terribly wrong. He
needed to get out of here, get away from the thing, call for
help. Something. But the impossible creature moved quickly,
crossing the floor space between the door and where Adam
had fallen before Adam could even scramble to his feet. One
second he could see the phone, on a side table next to the sofa,
not seven feet away. The next, a strong and somehow unclean
fist smashed into his face, driving him down again. Intense
pain made him screw up his face and shut his eyes. He was
pretty sure the thing had broken his nose.

He tried to scramble for the phone again, but he couldn't
see through the pain and the tears, and then he felt the creature's hands on him, lifting him into the air and slamming
him down again. Miraculously, this time it had chosen to
throw him down on the sofa, almost as if it didn't actually
want to snap his spine.

Adam forced his eyes to open, just as the thing put its
rudimentary face close to his. One of its knees was pressing
down on his chest, in real danger, Adam thought, of collapsing

his lung. The stench of it was overwhelming, and he nearly gagged. But then the monster spoke in a strangely high and feminine voice, with the most absurd Southern accent.

"Tell me where she is," the voice said. It came from the bizarre man-shaped creature, but Adam could tell it was not *of* him. "Tell me and I won't have to hurt you."

"I—I don't know who you're talking about," Adam managed. "B—Brandy?"

"Season!" the voice answered. Even through the filter of the strange creature, Adam could tell that there was rage behind the response.

"I don't know any Season," he said helplessly.

"Where is she?" the thing demanded again.

"I don't—" The words had barely escaped his lips when the monster swung at him again, its giant fist crashing into his face. It hit him again and again, and he felt blood spray down his shirt, teeth loosen in his mouth, and bones crumble beneath its hammering fists.

6

I've made kind of a point of keeping away from wars, these last many years. Not because I don't love my country, but simply because I have been involved in what amounts to a war of my own, a long, seemingly never-ending campaign against Season Howe. I am both a foot-soldier and an officer in this war, although I grant General status only to Mother Blessing (with whom communication has been sparse of late). And, I suppose, to Season, who is a one-woman army of no small ability.

Kerry held Daniel's journal open on her lap and glanced out the window. Season had said she had an important challenge for her today, and she'd gone to scout conditions. The weather was lovely—clear and crisp, with only a few wispy clouds dotting the blue sky. Kerry didn't know what other conditions might be pertinent, and Season hadn't said.

She liked to read Daniel's diaries, if only as a way to keep his voice in her head and his life connected to hers. For a while they had been an important learning tool, teaching her things about witchcraft—as well as guiding her to Mother Blessing's home in the Swamp—but now she mostly read them for her own emotional well-being rather than for their educational value.

She turned back to the heavy leather volume and kept reading.

But this current conflict, I am sad to say, has become nearly impossible to avoid altogether. It rages across most of the nation, pitting North against South, neighbor against neighbor. As one who takes a somewhat longer view of history than most, I believe there might have been ways to avoid it, but then I am no politician.

Probably it's best that I am not, for I don't have the temperament for it. Endless discussion and compromise are not my strengths, and though there are certainly politicians who are also decisive men of action, I fear they are few and far between. More of them would rather talk about action than act.

These last few days, however, have been hard for me because I find myself in the middle of it, near a place called Chancellorsville, in my home state of Virginia. I had gone home to the Great Dismal to see Mother Blessing, since my leads on Season had more or less run out, and I hoped that Mother Blessing could find some new way of locating her. There was, of course, military troop movement all around me as I journeyed, but I made myself hard to see and was able to travel unmolested.

I spent two days in my mother's house in the Swamp, enjoying her company and her cooking and being back home for a short while. But then she said she thought that Season had been seen in Washington, so I rode out and headed north.

It didn't take long to realize that there was more troop activity than ever. Confederate forces, the troops of Stonewall Jackson, were manning bulwarks, trying to stand against the advance of Union general Hooker. Hooker, I've heard, hoped to crush the armies of Jackson and Robert E. Lee, but he hesitated too long and Jackson's army surrounded his.

I could see the smoke from miles away, like the entire forest was ablaze. And I could hear the thunder of cannon and later, of rifles. But I had chosen my path and had foolishly decided that keeping to my chosen course was more beneficial than delaying my arrival in Washington by picking a new one. I could weave my way unnoticed through the battle, I was convinced.

I was wrong.

By the time I realized my mistake, I was in the middle of it. The fighting was all around me. The forest was, in fact, on fire. Soldiers ran in every direction, from every direction. Minié balls and bullets flew past. I spoke a few words to Augustus, my horse, to calm him, as the fire and the noise and chaos were driving the poor beast to distraction. I shielded him from the worst of it.

But before I thought to extend the shield to myself, I was hit. A fierce blow knocked me from the saddle, and as I fell to the ground I realized my shoulder had been smashed. I tried to regain my feet, then fell again. Augustus, loyal creature that he is, stayed beside me, but I could not use his strength to help me. Moments later I lost consciousness.

I woke up some time later in a field hospital. A nurse, her uniform torn and bloody, smiled so sweetly that for a moment I thought that she must be a heaven-sent angel. But then she wiped a lock of hair off her face and her hands left a trail of blood across her cheek, and I knew that I yet lived. No angel in heaven ever looked quite so ghastly, I am certain. Confirmation came a moment later, in the form of a jagged-toothed saw she held in the other hand.

"I see you're awake," she said to me.

"I seem to be," I replied. I inhaled, and the stench

of spoiled meat and sewage filled my nostrils. I tried not to show my displeasure. The nurse, it seemed, had become immune to it, just as she seemed to be able to disregard the moans and cries of the injured and infirm that sounded all around us.

"Sorry to see that," she said. "Doc says you've got to lose that arm. Be easier to cut, you were still out."

I glanced at my shoulder, a mangled, repugnant mess of blood and raw meat. I could hardly blame the doctor, who I had not seen as of yet, for wanting to remove as much of it as possible.

Of course, I could have healed it myself given some time and a few herbs and unguents. I probably could have found the appropriate items in the forest myself, if the soldiers had not been in the middle of burning it to the ground.

But now I was in the middle of a field hospital, laid out on a table covered only by a filthy blanket, with, when I turned to look, at least a hundred other wounded soldiers all around me—the source of the shouts of pain, and also of the stink that surrounded me.

If I got up and walked into the woods, surely the nurse would raise some kind of alarm. But if I stayed where I was, she would wield that saw against me. Restoring my shoulder and arm, once they had been butchered, would strain my abilities to the utmost.

If I even survived the surgery. I could see by the pile of bodies stacked up against the wall of a nearby tent that many did not.

"You ready for me to do it?" the nurse asked, indicating with the saw what she meant. "Or do you need a slug of something first?"

I would need several slugs, of some concoction stronger than she might have available, before I would let her near me with that instrument of torture.

"I'm sorry," I told her, "but I have no intention of letting you saw into me with that."

"I don't take it off, gangrene'll set in," she told me. "It'll kill you."

"That's a chance I'll take," I said. I knew that I could mend myself before that happened. But only if I could make my escape from this tool-wielding devil, whom I had once seen as an angel.

"Doctor's orders," she insisted.

I sat up on the rickety table, an action which, to judge from her face, surprised her. She probably hadn't thought I had the strength. "Miss, I do not see a doctor at present. Perhaps if you were to turn your back and attend to some other patient, I would be able to spare you the trouble of either cutting off my limb or further debating with me about it."

She gave me a suspicious glare. "You ain't thinking about killing yourself?"

"Quite the contrary," I assured her. "I'm talking about saving myself."

She looked hurt. "Most of my patients survive," she declared.

Somehow I did not feel comforted. She seemed to be growing more anxious by the minute, and I was worried that she would call out to someone. The more time that went by, the greater the danger that she would be joined by a doctor or another soldier. I decided that it was time to act, if I was going to save myself.

I glanced around quickly, to make sure that we were not yet observed, and then performed a hasty immobilization spell. I was still weak from my wound, and it would not have worked had she been braced against it or expecting it. But for the moment she was stunned into paralysis, simply standing with the wicked saw clutched in her hands and her eyes wide open, watching me.

With her incapacitated, I gingerly climbed off the table, making sure not to upend it. Walking as swiftly as I dared, trying not to attract attention to myself, I made my way through the field of injured, dying, and dead, back toward a corral where I hoped to find Augustus.

I had thought that I was successful in not being seen, but it turned out that I was mistaken. Just as I reached the far edge of the field hospital, a young, hollow-eyed soldier who sat against a tent wall smoking a cigar spoke to me. His left arm was in a bloodied sling, and recent cuts spiderwebbed his cheek and jaw. "I seen someone else do that," he said.

"Do what?" I pretended to be utterly innocent.

"What you done there. Freeze that girl like that."

"I did no such . . . where else did you see that?" A sudden thought changed my sentence midway through.

"Not twenty miles up the road," the young man said. He coughed, a deep, unhealthy, racking cough. "She was like a vision, too. Lot prettier'n you, that's for sure."

"A woman, then?"

"A woman, sure enough." He began to cough again, and this time I wasn't sure he would ever stop. Finally he brought it under control and looked at me with liquid eyes. "She stayed at the camp for three days, helping with the wounded. Fixed up many a man I thought would never see another dawn. Finally said she had to move on. But one time, right before she did, one of the boys got a little too friendly with her. She froze him solid, just like you done."

"Do you know where she might have gone?"

He laughed, which triggered another coughing fit. "Wish I did," he managed to rasp.

I thanked him and went to look for Augustus. Was it Season he had seen? From his vague descrip-

tion, it could have been. But the Season Howe I was seeking—spending three days helping the wounded in a filthy Army field hospital? More like her, I should think, to wipe them all out with no second thoughts.

Still, if Season it was, then she is not far ahead of me. I put pen to paper in a public house not a day's ride from Washington. If she is still there, perhaps I'll find her in the next day or two.

I remain,

Daniel Blessing, Fifth of May, 1863

It didn't take long for Brandy to realize that she had done Adam a terrible disservice. He had been right, after all. She was hiding things from him. He had every reason not to trust her, and the fact that he didn't was only an accurate assessment of the situation, not a reflection on him.

Three blocks from his place, she stopped short. Probably he'd been leading up to breaking it off with her. She could live with it, if that was the case—she had broken up, and been broken up with, and though she preferred the former, neither one would kill her. She was too strong, too independent for that.

So she owed it to him to at least let him have his say, owed him the respect he had earned by being so good to her for so long. If at the end of it he still wanted to call it quits, then fine. She would be okay with it, she was sure.

She turned around and headed back to his apartment. With each step it felt as if a great weight were being lifted off her shoulders. She had felt guilty about walking away, about minimizing his concerns with her own smokescreen. What she was doing now was a better thing, and she felt good about it.

When she reached the front door to his building she felt a moment's concern. The door was ajar, and she distinctly remembered having shut it when she left. That had been a few minutes before, though, so someone else could have gone out—even Adam himself, she supposed—and left it open.

But worse, there was a muddy print on the door, almost head-high for her. A putrid smell wafted from it. The first thought that entered Brandy's mind almost made her run screaming from the building.

Simulacrum!

There was no guarantee that was it, however, and any number of other possible explanations presented themselves. The melting snows had left the whole city wet and muddy. Anyone could have gotten some gunk on his hands and touched the door. . . .

Still, her heart was pounding as she slipped through the door and into the lobby.

The smell in here was worse, and there were wet footprints on the stairs that led up to Adam's place. Big footprints. Brandy eyed them, swallowing back her terror but ready to run at the slightest provocation.

She already had her cell in her hand as she followed the huge footprints up. Scott's number was still programmed in, so she scrolled to it and held her finger over the send button. Walking as quickly as she could while still remaining silent, she hurried down the hall toward Adam's door, stepping beside, instead of on top of, those awful prints.

At Adam's door, the worst was confirmed.

A massive mud print marred its finish. Inside she could hear voices—one of them was Adam's, but it sounded garbled, like he was talking with water in his mouth. She couldn't make out any words, but she knew that it was bad.

She also knew she couldn't handle it alone.

She pressed send.

Scott lived only a few miles from Adam's apartment. He hopped in the RAV4 as soon as he got Brandy's panicked call and drove like a madman the whole way. Ten minutes after his phone had rung, he was screeching to a stop outside the building. Brandy waited outside, terror contorting her face.

He left the car in the street and ran to her, gripping her upper arms anxiously. "Are you okay, Brandy?" he asked.

She nodded and wiped away tears. "I couldn't stay up there and listen," she said, her voice breaking. She was bordering on hysterical, he thought, as bad as he had ever seen her. "He's hurting Adam."

"There was nothing you could have done about it," Scott assured her. He put his arms around her, and she moved into his hug in a way she hadn't done for a very long time.

"I—I tried to call Kerry," Brandy said, "but I couldn't get through to her. But I reached Rebecca. She promised to keep trying Kerry."

"That's the best thing you could have done. If it is a simulacrum, there's nothing we can do against it."

"Scott, we have to try. Maybe we can just hit it with clubs or something. Anything. It'll kill Adam!"

He hated to ask the obvious, but it needed to be asked. "How do you know it hasn't already?"

"I was up there a couple of minutes ago," she said. "I stood out in the hallway again, just to check. I could still hear Adam's voice, crying for help."

"And there's nobody else in the building?" Scott asked.

"Most everybody works during the day," Brandy said. "There's no super or on-site manager or anything."

Scott nodded. It was just a small building, a family home that had been converted to apartments a decade or two ago. Eight apartments, he guessed, at the most, spread over two stories.

"Okay, then," he said, hoping he sounded much braver than he felt. "Let's go do this."

He led the way into Adam's building, with Brandy clutching his arm so tightly he thought he would lose circulation. Inside, the place stank to high heaven. Heading up the stairs, his courage almost left him—his knees wobbled so much he wasn't sure he could actually make it up unassisted.

Somehow, though, he did. Brandy pointed out Adam's door, as if the giant mud splat on it didn't give it away. Scott thought the whole exercise was kind of silly—there was no way the two of them could do any damage to one of Mother

Blessing's manufactured men. But Brandy wanted him to try, so he would. He was no hero, but for him the equation was that simple. Brandy wanted him to try.

In her time of need, she had called him.

Adam's door was closed, but not locked. Scott gulped in a deep breath and hurled it open, afraid of what he would see.

The sight that met him couldn't have been much worse.

Blood was everywhere—more than he thought could possibly come from someone who was still alive. Adam's place was cool and modern, with lots of black steel, glass, and chrome. The glass was spattered with red, the chrome was smeared, and only the black didn't show blood. His off-white Berber carpeting looked like a grisly rainstorm had showered it. Windows looked tinted.

But Adam was still alive. He had rolled into a ball on his sofa, broken and battered. The simulacrum towered over him, no longer beating him but instead simply intimidating the poor man with his unnatural presence. Adam whimpered, and his breathing sounded wet and shallow.

"Get away from him!" Scott demanded. His own throat felt very dry, his muscles tense. If the thing attacked him, he'd end up like Adam or worse. Adam was bigger and stronger than he was. The biggest difference between them was that Scott knew precisely what he was facing. *And somehow,* he thought, *I don't think that's necessarily an advantage.*

Slowly the simulacrum turned, as if gradually becoming aware that there was someone else in the room. It straightened as it regarded Scott and Brandy. Then, as if triggered by the realization of their presence, it charged.

"Scott!" Brandy's voice was little more than an exhalation of breath behind him. Scott trembled, keeping his body between the creature and Brandy. He had been allies with one of these beings once, for a short time. It rode in his car with him. But he had been afraid of it even then. Now he was petrified.

The best he could do was to raise his hands defensively as the creature came toward him. His knees locked, seemingly of their own accord.

Then it was upon him, its surface slick and viscous, its stench overwhelming. Scott opened his hands and clamped them down on the simulacrum's arms, trying to break its charge. The creature barreled into him, knocking him backward a few steps, and Scott felt Brandy's hands on his back, bracing him. Still, the thing's momentum shoved them both back against the wall. Its strength was enormous; Scott knew it could easily tear his head off.

Except it didn't.

Instead, where he held it, the monster began to come undone.

Wet glops of mud and snow fell to Adam's carpeted floor. Bits of tree debris and trash followed. The thing seemed to collapse in on itself and then spill down as if melting under Scott's touch.

"Scott," Brandy said from behind him, only this time her tone was much different than the last time she had spoken his name. Something like awe sounded in her voice. "Scott, what's happening to it?"

He held on to the thing, afraid that if he let go the process would reverse and the monster would re-form. "I don't know," he said. "I guess it doesn't like me."

"I guess it doesn't," Brandy echoed.

The disintegration continued until there was nothing left for Scott to grip. Gunk covered his shoes and left a big pile on the floor, but within moments even that started to dissipate, as if it were evaporating.

"I . . . this is just bizarre," Scott said. "I don't get it."

"I don't either," Brandy said. "But I'm not complaining."

Neither am I, Scott thought. *Neither am I.*

His relief was checked by a sudden anxiety, however. "We'd better check on Adam," he pointed out. "He probably needs a doctor."

Brandy shoved past him to do just that. "We'll need some kind of a story," she said. "We can't tell the paramedics what really attacked him. We'd spend the rest of our lives in a mental hospital. Or prison." She knelt beside Adam and started stroking him gently, comfortingly, speaking so softly that Scott couldn't hear what she was saying. Adam just remained curled in his fetal position, crying quietly.

She was right, Scott knew. They had to come up with a story, and fast. He was already on his way to the phone to dial 911. Help would be here soon, and they'd need to be able to tell them *something*.

The simulacrum was almost completely broken down already, with just a few bits of random detritus remaining on the floor amid a big muddy stain.

"Okay," Scott said after considering for a few moments. "Here's what we'll say. . . ." Before he had a chance to finish, the emergency operator came on the line, and Scott gave her Adam's address.

By the time he was done, he had almost started breathing normally again. The immediate danger was past.

But one thing was all too certain. Mother Blessing was on their trail again.

Once again Mother Blessing knew the fury of being thwarted by people for whom she had no respect. Those meddling teenagers should have fallen immediately before the might of her creation. Instead, her simulacrum had been defeated by that boy—the one she thought she had been attacking in the first place. She remembered, from her interception of Kerry's communications, that the boyfriend kept better tabs on her location than the girl did. So now that she was ready to continue the battle—to end it—she had waited until she could catch them apart.

But somehow, it had been the wrong boyfriend. He had looked wrong as soon as she saw him through the eyes of her creation. She was committed by then, so she just kept at it, trying to pry from him information that he no doubt truly didn't have. It wasn't until she saw the girl and the boy enter together that she really understood her mistake. The girl was a tramp, or they had broken up.

And even when she realized what had happened, she hadn't known the power that rested in the boy's hands. He was unnatural. He had died, and yet lived—that was the only thing that could explain the simulacrum's response. A creation like that couldn't cohere in the face of the unnatural. A simulacrum's grip on life, Mother Blessing knew, was too tenuous—meeting anything else whose life was false or wrong would cause its immediate dissipation.

So she was angry with them, these children who had defeated her far too often, considering who and what they were. Insignificant insects who muddled along by accident and who needed to be stamped out. They would pay the price, though—once Season was no longer a problem, these others would taste her revenge too, and they would find it painful indeed.

At the same time, she was heartened. Because the girl had made two other calls—one to Kerry, which had not been answered, so Mother Blessing couldn't discern its destination, but the second to Rebecca Levine. Another of their troublesome pack. Rebecca, though, seemed to know where Kerry was. The implication of their conversation was that Kerry was somewhere not too far away—somewhere Rebecca could drive to in a relatively brief time, if need be.

Rebecca was in California. Which meant that she needed to be in California, too. Mother Blessing would not trust a simulacrum to do the whole job this time. So close to Season, she had to be on the scene in person, just in case.

She would leave immediately. This was a war that needed to be finished, and with the Convocation almost upon them, the end had to come soon.

7

Kerry clambered up the side of the cliff as rapidly as she could. Loose dirt and soft stone gave way beneath her hands, but she pressed herself to the wall and dug in with fingers and feet. Jags of rock scraped her cheek. She allowed herself a couple of quick breaths, a moment to collect her thoughts. *What spell can help me here?* she wondered.

None, she decided. This was one of those moments that required physical strength, agility, and courage, not witchcraft. Short of some kind of antigravity spell—or the traditional flying broomstick, which seemed pretty much in the realm of the absurdly mythical—she was on her own.

She glanced up to see how much farther she had to go, and how far out the overhang extended at the top.

Heights had never been a particular problem for her, but she decided that there was no advantage to looking down. Nothing but a narrow ribbon of sand, big sharp rocks, and churning surf, thirty feet below her where the ocean carved away the coastline.

Above, Kerry saw some likely handholds, so she stretched for the closest one, shoved the fingers of her right hand into a narrow crevice, and pulled herself up. She raised her right foot to the little shelf on which her right hand had rested a few moments earlier, found firm footing there, and then felt above with her left hand. It was a slow process, but she was no practiced climber.

Almost thirty minutes—and as many scrapes and bruises— later, the overhang was within reach. This would be the tricky part. She'd have to work her way out hand over hand, digging in with her toes, until her back was almost parallel to that narrow beach way down below. The overhang was only four or five feet out, so she wouldn't be in that precarious pose for long, but even a minute or two was distressing. She'd have greatly preferred to scale a section of cliff that was straight at the top—but then, she'd have preferred a hunky instructor and one of those spiffy fluorescent-colored nylon ropes, too. All of which, no doubt, were reasons why Season had picked this spot, which contained none of the above. Kerry had only sneakers, track pants, and a T-shirt on—if she fell, it was going to hurt.

Nothing to be gained by waiting, she decided. She began the excruciating process of holding herself as close as she could to the wall while she inched up and out, feeling gravity trying to yank her back to earth at every moment. Her terror at this stage was almost palpable, and she worried that her palms would sweat so much that she'd lose her grip on the rock face.

A few minutes later, however, she had hold of the upper edge. Some loose dirt and pebbles slid out from under her fingertips, cascading over the cliff and down past her. The clatter when it landed below sounded very far away. Beneath the loose stuff, though, was good solid rock. She pressed her fingers into it so hard she thought she would wear grooves in it.

The last step was to get her left hand up there and haul herself over the top. But her left hand was wedged tightly into a crack in the overhang, and she felt like that was the only thing holding her in place. Her right hand was gripping the upper edge, but if it started to slip, or the edge gave way, there would be nothing to hang on to there.

Stuck, she knew she couldn't make any more progress unless she did something. Gingerly, trying to adhere herself to the face, to glue her feet in position, she worked her left hand free and finger-crawled it up, inch by slow, perilous inch. Finally, she was able to reach the lip with that hand as well.

Now it was a simple matter of letting go with her feet so she could hoist herself up to the top.

Sure. Simple.

But before she got a chance, she heard a movement at the top. A footfall, she thought.

"Season?"

No response.

"Season, is that you?" Kerry demanded urgently.

Still no verbal response came. But Kerry gradually became aware of a shadow, a dark form coming over the edge. She hung on to the lip with fingers that trembled from the strain and the anxiety and made herself look up at it.

A tall, sinister man grinned down at her, wearing a long coat that fluttered in the wind at the top of the cliff. His smile looked about as genuine as a ninety-dollar bill.

"Going somewhere?" he asked.

"You want to give me a hand?" Kerry replied, pretty sure she wouldn't accept it if he did. He wasn't one of Mother Blessing's simulacra, she could tell, but that didn't mean he wasn't an ally of some other kind. And she was in about as vulnerable a position as it was possible to find.

"How about a push?" he answered.

Which was all she needed to confirm that he was not exactly a friend. It would be hard to make the right hand gestures while clinging to the edge of the cliff, but she needed to do something to protect herself. So she forced the fingers of her left hand into the appropriate position and spoke one of the ancient words. *"Kalaifa!"*

The man flew from her sight as if swatted away by a giant gust of wind. She knew he had been knocked about twenty feet back, but he was most likely uninjured, unless he'd been speared by a tree branch or something. If he had been just a practical joker, then he'd be fine. If he had more homicidal motives, the immediate threat had been removed and she'd be able to deal with him when she reached the top.

If she hurried. He could still come back and they'd have to do the whole dance all over again. Forcing herself to move faster, she dug in with the fingers of both hands and drew them forward on the top shelf of the cliff, getting some rock and earth under her forearms. The man could already be on his feet, and if he returned all he'd have to do would be to break the grip of one of her hands. Kerry made the decision to finish this now, and kicked free with both feet. She used the momentum to release with her right hand and reach farther out, grabbing ground up to her armpit. Now she could pull her head up over the top. The man was still in the dirt where she had thrown him, glaring at her. She tossed him a quick smile and began hoisting herself up.

A moment later she was safely on the top of the cliff, standing up and dusting herself off.

The man turned indistinct, as if she were looking at him through a wall of Jell-O, and then took on solid form again. This time the form was that of Season Howe, who rubbed her bottom as she smiled at Kerry.

"Ow," she said. "Good job, Kerry."

"Thanks." Kerry touched one of the raw spots on her cheek. "Now maybe you can tell me what that was all about."

"A test," Season said simply. "In the time we have left before the Convocation, there's not a whole lot I can still teach you. But I can test what you've learned, and make sure your reactions are appropriate. So far, so good."

Kerry Profitt's diary, March 12

The ways in which this whole business is like school are numerous. I have always loved reading and writing, but the reading program Season has put me on is almost ridiculous—especially since so many of her magic texts were written back in practically prehistoric times, so the language is all stiff and ancient. Thanks to Season's magic translator (just like with the books Mother Blessing showed me, way back when), I can read the books that look like Latin or Greek or German or whatever. At first glance they're in a foreign language, but when I look at them again, I can make out the words just as if they were written in English. Sometimes bad English, but English just the same. Fortunately I have Daniel's journals, and a few books the Morgans have left around the house, to give me a break.

And then the testing part! Like earlier today, when I had to scale this giant freaking cliff while she stood at the top, casting a glamour to make herself look like some kind of scary bad guy. I never had a midterm like that in high school. Would have reduced class size a bit if we had, I guess. Don't let the PTA know.

I get the idea behind it, of course. We don't know exactly what we're going to be facing, either in more possible battles with Mother Blessing or at the Witches' Convocation. Chances are I won't be forced to climb any cliffs. But I might be put into situations where physical strength and/or bravery are required. So better to know now that I can do it, right? If I had fallen today, ouch. Broken leg, whatever. Or maybe Season had some kind of plan to magically break my fall, although of course she wouldn't have told me that. But if I didn't learn my limits, and then wimped out while facing one of MB's bad things, it could be serious trouble for me and for Season.

So, the testing. And in between, the reading. And in between all of that, the purification rites. Also important, Season says. Not that I've been around any guys with whom to be impure, but she says it's not just that. It's the atmosphere, which is chock-full of pollution and nasty microbes and stuff. It's the gunk we pick up from flies and doorknobs and those buttons you press on the hot air hand dryer in the ladies' room, and also that whole breathing thing. In other words, not just purity of spirit but also of body. Helps make the magic work better, somehow. The impurities in a witch's system act like little blocking agents, she says, impeding the flow of the forces that we channel through ourselves. Like shopping carts and old cars tossed into a riverbed. Take out all the crap and everything moves more smoothly down the correct channels.

The purification rituals take many forms. My favorite is the long, hot baths with lilac petals floating in the tub. Not so great is the standing with arms outstretched and a ten-pound weight in each hand for thirty minutes, while counting backward from a thousand. Season swears both kinds are necessary, along with several others. At least she does them with me (although with the bath one, we go one at a time). By the time we go to the Convocation we will be two pure chicks, I gotta say. And looking just fine in our plain white robes, which is what we wear for this drill.

More later.
K.

By the time they left Adam at Mass General, he had been admitted and sedated. He had tried to give the paramedics and the police his version of events, but Brandy and Scott had been there to intercede with their own translation of his garbled tale.

They had agreed to stick as close to the literal truth as possible. The way they told it, Adam and Brandy had had a fight, and Brandy walked out. But she had second thoughts and went back. By the time she got back, someone had broken into the apartment. Brandy could hear a struggle or heated argument through the door but was afraid to go in, so she called Scott. He came over, and by the time they went inside the assailant had fled. They found Adam, beaten and hysterically raving about a monster—no doubt a really big burglar—and called 911. No, neither of them had seen the assailant—he must have run away while Brandy was waiting outside for Scott. No, she couldn't think of any enemies Adam might have, and she couldn't identify anything that was missing. But she had only known him for a few months, and there might, of course, have been something in his past that she didn't know about.

The police and medical personnel seemed to buy the story. She and Scott told it essentially the same way when they were questioned separately and together, and anyway, it all made so much more sense than Adam's ravings. The fact that Adam's were true didn't enter into it—it was the appearance of truth they were after, not the real thing. Anyway, Brandy reasoned, they weren't under oath, so it wasn't like they were committing perjury.

Lying, yes. But with good cause.

When they were allowed to leave, they sat in Scott's car out in the hospital parking lot, giving themselves some decompression time before he took her home. Brandy looked over at Scott, illuminated by light that washed in from one of the hospital's streetlamps. He looked different than he had before, even at Christmas, somehow—strong, capable, decisive. There was a set to his jaw, a sense of determination expressed by a slight stiffening of his lips, a resolve signaled by a narrowing of his eyes, that she had never seen before.

She liked what she saw.

"You were pretty amazing, Scott," she said quietly.

"What? I had no idea that thing would fall apart. I still wish I knew why."

"I don't mean just that," Brandy said. She didn't want him to think it had been an empty compliment, or worse, a backhanded one. Because that kind of thing had never been beyond her. But it wasn't her intention now. "I mean, that was cool too. But the whole thing. Answering when I called, riding to the rescue like that. A lot of guys wouldn't do that if their ex called up and said her new boyfriend was in trouble."

"What, I'm supposed to just shrug and say, 'whatever'?" Scott answered. "He means a lot to you. You mean a lot to me. That's just the way it is."

"That's exactly what I mean," Brandy said. "You don't even think it's special. You just did it, because that's what a person does. In your world, at least."

Scott shrugged, as if he didn't even get what a big deal it was.

Which was when Brandy realized that the warm spot she held for him in her heart had never completely gone away. Sure, it had cooled. Right down to a frosty chill, for a while. But the embers had still been glowing, she just hadn't seen them. Now, though, she felt as if they were being fanned, fresh air being blown in by one of those big old-fashioned bellows. Heat radiated from her core.

She leaned toward him, touching his arm. "Scott, I—"

"Listen, Brandy," he interrupted, completely oblivious. He stared straight out the windshield as he spoke, not even looking at her. "You'll probably kick me or something for saying this, but it's something I have to get off my chest. I was an idiot."

"You were?"

"Absolutely," Scott insisted. "I mean, I was kind of obsessed with Kerry. You knew that—you probably knew it before I did. But that was just stupid, that grass is always greener stuff.

Kerry's an amazing person, sure. But so are you. You're beautiful, and you're the most insightful, perceptive person I've ever known, and you were right in front of me the whole time. Right in my own apartment, my own bed. So getting all hung up on Kerry like that, and spoiling what we had . . . well, I was a dope. I'm sorry. If there was any way I could undo it, I would."

Brandy could hardly believe what she was hearing. Especially since it was so close to what she was feeling right now. She recognized that it might simply have been a reaction to their mutual brush with death, which often drew people together in an artificial intimacy.

But she didn't think so. Instead, she thought the experience had knocked blinders away from their eyes that they had consciously placed there, not realizing what a mistake it had been.

She placed a hand on his leg and squeezed gently. "I think maybe we can work on it."

His face brightened instantly, and he finally met her gaze. "Do you mean it?"

"Sure," she said without hesitation. "If people can decide to break up, they can certainly decide to un-break up, right?"

"Isn't that usually called making up?"

"Yes," Brandy admitted. "But that sounded too much like a golden oldie. Then again, there's always making out. Which maybe we could talk about too."

"Talking about it seems so . . . I don't know. Counterproductive."

She snuggled a little closer to him. "Well, I guess we don't have to do that much talking."

He started to lean toward her, then suddenly sat upright. "Oh, crap!"

"What?" she asked, startled. She turned in her seat, to see if he had noticed something out her window. *Another attacker?*

"I just remembered, in all the craziness with Adam and everything, we never called Rebecca to tell her we're okay. We should do that, and make sure she lets Kerry know what's happened."

Brandy realized her heart was racing and adrenaline pumping from his sudden motion. "Okay," she said. "Let's give her a call." Rebecca, being Rebecca, would almost certainly be freaking out by now, Brandy knew. She dug her cell from her purse and flipped it open abruptly—glad that Scott had remembered, but upset because she would rather that his attention had been solely focused on her at that moment.

Just the way he is, I guess, she thought. *If I'm going to be with him—and it looks like maybe I am, strange as that seems— I've just got to be able to live with it.* She knew she would have to visit Adam in the hospital. There would be awkward questions. But then, life refused to be as orderly as she wanted.

She dialed Rebecca, and a moment later their friend, breathless and anxious, came on the line.

8

Exactly what she feared had happened. It was all starting up again, and this time a complete non-combatant, the proverbial innocent bystander, had been injured. And Mother Blessing was still after them—this proved it, without a doubt.

Rebecca couldn't reach Kerry and Season on the phone. She rushed about the house, in a near panic. She had to go up to Bolinas, had to find them and let them know what was happening. It would only be a few hours by car. She wanted to wait for Erin to get home from a late class, but as the minutes ticked by she began to worry that Erin wouldn't be coming home—that she was studying late in the library, or had a date, or something. She paced, she tried to sit and gather

her thoughts, but then she squirmed and jumped to her feet again. *Come home, come home, come home,* she silently pleaded. But Erin didn't, and the girl refused to carry a cell phone or pager to class. Something about respecting the lecturer, which Rebecca kind of understood. But then, Erin had never been attacked by a witch.

Since it didn't look like she would show up any time soon, Rebecca settled for leaving her housemate a note. That was probably better anyway, she decided upon reflection, because with a note, Erin couldn't ask any nosy questions. She scrawled, "Erin, I'm out of town for a day or so. I'll call you when I can. Love, Beck," on a sheet of ripped-out notebook paper and pinned it to the kitchen table with a salt shaker.

She didn't, in fact, know if she would even spend a single night away, or if she'd be driving back here much later that night. But if she found Season and Kerry tonight, there was every likelihood that they would insist she stay over. It would be very late by the time she reached the Morgan house. And if she didn't find them at first, she wouldn't be back here until she did, however long that might take.

She tossed some clean underwear, a blouse, and a skirt into her backpack, then put in a toothbrush and toothpaste and a hairbrush. Certain there were things she was forgetting, she decided that nothing else was that important anyway. Outside, a hard, steady rain had been pounding Santa Cruz all evening. Her old VW was parked across the street, and she had almost reached it when she remembered her wallet and cell phone, inside on top of her dresser. She ran back in, fetched those items, stuffed them into the backpack with everything else.

Back in the rain, she dashed toward the car, already wet from her first aborted attempt.

Before she reached it, however, an abrupt movement caught her eye. A dark shape separated from the background, and Rebecca realized it was someone coming toward her. She broke into an all-out sprint, but the shape was much too fast for her. By the time she tried to jam her key into the car's door lock, he was on her.

The man slammed into her, hard, and one of his hands grabbed her wrist, yanking it away from the car door. Only a faint glow filtered from the streetlights through the heavy rain, but that, and the smell, were enough to tell Rebecca that she didn't face a man at all, but one of Mother Blessing's awful simulacra.

She twisted out of its grasp, maybe helped by the rain—its hands seemed slick, and she slid from between them as if she'd been oiled—but she only made it a couple of staggered steps before she tripped over her own feet. The thing came at her again, swatting her as she tried to rise and knocking her sprawling in the wet street. Her face skidded on the pavement, her fingers clutching at it as she tried desperately to right herself. So far the thing had made no sound, and she knew that she should scream but couldn't seem to find her breath.

Instead, she pushed herself to her knees again, and then to her feet, and then it had her, one powerful arm wrapped about her middle. She finally was able to let out a scream, but the creature clamped its other hand over her mouth. Rebecca struggled against it, kicking and squirming, all to no avail. It was far stronger than she was, and she couldn't hurt it. After a moment it moved its hand up to cover her nose as well as her mouth. She gulped for breath but couldn't find it, and seconds after that, the darkness of the night had engulfed her completely.

"A lot of people think witches are inherently evil," Season said. She and Kerry sat in the cramped living room, listening to the wind whistle in the eaves. "That we're in league with the devil. That we're always having unnatural relations with goats. In fact, if there's a devil, I've never met him, and while I enjoy feta cheese on Greek salads, that's the closest I've been to a goat in at least a hundred years."

Kerry laughed at that. It was late and she was in sweats and fuzzy socks, ready for bed. She had been on her way there when Season called her into the living room, apparently in a reflective mood.

"That's why witches have been persecuted so much?" Kerry asked. She had become used to Season's enforcement of the fifteen-questions routine, and it didn't apply after "school hours" were over. "Because of the goats?"

"One of the reasons," Season acknowledged with a nod.

"People often tend to fear what they don't understand. Since our abilities are beyond the scope of most people, beyond what they can possibly ever experience for themselves, they decide that there must be something sinister behind us.

"Of course, witches like Mother Blessing don't help matters any. Whenever people have unreasonable fears and prejudices, if they can point to a specific individual who seems to embody that prejudice, then it's that much easier for them to lump all the rest of that group in the same category. Mother Blessing and the few other witches around who are genuinely evil make good poster children for those who hate witches."

"What if witches made themselves known to the world at large?" Kerry wondered. "If you weren't all hiding all the time, if witches were common knowledge, maybe they'd be accepted better?"

Season hesitated for a moment before answering, looking deep into Kerry's eyes as she did. "How often has that proven not to be true?" she said finally. "Think about African Americans, who were enslaved for hundreds of years, and in some cases are still having a hard time being admitted into parts of American society, a hundred and some years after emancipation. As a group, they still don't have income equity with whites. Think about gay people—we've known about them forever, and look at their struggles with acceptance. I'm not saying that witches are a persecuted minority, exactly. We are, but in a very different way. There are so few of us we'll never have a big voting bloc or anything like that, even if there were issues on which we would want to vote in lockstep. But we aren't lacking for power. It's not political, necessarily, but we have other forms of power."

"Okay, point taken," Kerry admitted. "Maybe coming out as witches isn't the best idea."

"It's never been anything but trouble in the past," Season agreed. "A lot of us still have bad memories of the Inquisition, and Salem, that kind of thing. We seem to be better off staying in the shadows. The whole low-profile bit."

"I guess it's a good thing I have the voice of experience here to guide me," Kerry said, "so I don't shoot my mouth off at the Convocation and say something stupid."

"You're lucky you're so young for your first Convocation," Season pointed out. "By the time you go to your second, you'll be the one with all the experience."

That'll be five hundred years, Kerry thought, blown over by the hugeness of that concept. *Will I even still be alive then?* "That's a pretty big commitment," she said.

Season cocked her head to the right and showed her a surprised face. "I thought you were ready to make it."

Kerry didn't quite know what to say. "I . . . I thought I was too. I mean, I think I am. But . . . you know, I'm young. What if I decide I'd rather be a firefighter or a dentist or something?"

"You're joking."

"About those two particular career choices, yes. Not that there's anything wrong with them. But you know what I mean.

I'm eighteen. How many eighteen-year-olds do you know who figure out what they want to do with the rest of their lives at that age and then stick to it? Most people I've known haven't even stuck to a single college major, much less a career. Much less a career that could last well beyond the usual forty years or so."

Season let out a small sigh. "I know it's asking a lot, Kerry," she said. "Witches live a very long time. It's a serious commitment. Believe me, there have been times that I've regretted the decision too. But not many, and they always pass."

"Well, you're kind of stuck, right? I mean, once you pass a hundred and twenty or so, it must be kind of hard to suddenly decide you didn't mean to be a witch after all."

"It happens," Season admitted. "Just not very often, and the consequences aren't pretty."

"I bet not," Kerry agreed. She tried unsuccessfully to stifle a huge yawn. "I'm totally beat," she said. "I guess I'll see you in the morning."

"Another big day," Season promised. "Almost time to leave for the Convocation."

Another yawn escaped Kerry. "I can't wait."

When Rebecca woke up, she felt sick and sore all over. It took her a minute to realize that some of the soreness was because she hadn't been able to move her arms or legs for what must have been hours—she was tied to a stiff wooden chair in what looked like a long-abandoned kitchen. Light streamed in through warped sheets of plywood nailed over a window, illuminating a stained and faded linoleum floor and gutted cabinets, the sink and appliances long since taken away. There were two other chairs in the room with her, and a wall calendar from 1996, but nothing else except dust, cobwebs, and a black growth on one wall that must have been mold.

Light, she realized. She had been here all night, then. As she tried to turn in the chair to see what was behind her, a wave of nausea passed through her. Her head throbbed, as if someone had been using it to drive nails through concrete.

She remembered the night before—being grabbed on her way to the car. One of Mother Blessing's artificial goons. She couldn't recall anything at all after that, so he must have knocked her out, then brought her—where? Wherever this was, some old empty house. Hours had passed, though, so she could be just about anywhere. Maybe not even in Santa Cruz anymore. She couldn't smell the ocean, but the house's close, musty air overwhelmed any odors that might have leaked in from outside.

The house had a hollow feel, as if it had been vacant for a long time. She was pretty sure she was completely alone. If the thing that had brought her here—or anyone else—was here now, she couldn't see him. She couldn't see much, though. She could try to jerk the whole chair around, but at the moment such a violent motion would probably only succeed in making her vomit or pass out again. *Anyway,* she thought, *the old witch makes those things out of found materials, right? So he could just be a bunch of spiderwebs and mold right now, but ready to pop up as soon as I make a move.*

The most pressing question was the hardest to answer. Why? What good did it do Mother Blessing to have Rebecca locked away in a house? There had been the attack on Brandy's boyfriend, too—was there some new battle going on that they were all going to be sucked into? Had things heated up to this point?

Well, duh, she thought. *I wouldn't be tied to a chair if* something *wasn't going on.*

Through the nausea, she realized two urgent things. She was very hungry, and she really, really had to pee.

Somehow, it didn't look like either need would be satisfied very soon.

From somewhere behind her—somewhere else in the house—a door opened, groaning on its hinges, then closed with a loud bang. Rebecca started, as if the bang had been immediately behind her head. She suddenly felt terribly vulnerable. She was completely immobilized, unable even to turn around to face whoever had entered the house. She could hear floorboards squeaking as if under a ponderous weight. Slowly, the squeaking came nearer.

Rebecca's eyes were wide with fright. Who was it? The simulacrum that had brought her here? Someone else—even a random stranger? Maybe it was someone who could rescue her. That was a pleasant thought, but probably too good to be true. It was far more likely to be someone with a nefarious motive. A few minutes before she had been wishing that there was someone else with her, but now she realized that alone was far safer than trapped here with the wrong kind of company.

"Who's there?" she demanded, trying to sound belligerent, as if she had any control whatsoever over the situation. "Speak up!"

"Now, don't y'all worry 'bout me," a feminine voice said. The Southern accent was so thick it almost sounded cartoonish to Rebecca's ears, accustomed as she was to the way New Yorkers and Californians spoke. "I'm just here to have a little talk, aren't I?"

"How would I know?" Rebecca replied. "Why don't you untie me so we can have a real conversation?"

A soft chuckle. "Well, now, I don't think that'd be very smart, do you? Not very smart at all, Miss Levine. Or can I call y'all Rebecca?"

"Untie me, and you can call me anything you want," Rebecca shot back. The speaker still hadn't shown herself, but Rebecca knew who it was. Who it had to be. Mother Blessing. Daniel's mother. Kerry had described her way of speaking, even imitated her a couple of times. And, of course, Rebecca herself had heard the voice before, only filtered through the voice box of an inhuman being, one of the witch's simulacra. "Are you going to let me see you, Mother Blessing?"

Another laugh met this question. "Well, ain't you just the cleverest little thing?" More moaning floorboards. Rebecca could hear the huffs of the woman's breath as she walked, seemingly with effort, across the kitchen. A moment later, a vast field of powder blue polyester hove into view. Mother Blessing was enormous, one of the biggest women Rebecca had ever seen. If her thighs, wrapped in that tight polyester, were tree trunks, her waist was one of those redwoods that they cut tunnels through to let cars drive under. She smiled a ghastly grin at Rebecca, the Pan-Cake creasing and cracking on her face, the foothills of blue eye shadow leading toward mountains of platinum hair piled on her head in one of the world's biggest beehives.

"No mirror where you live?" Rebecca asked defiantly.

One of Mother Blessing's meaty hands slapped her across the face. *The woman can move fast when she wants to,* Rebecca realized. She had barely seen the slap coming. Even if she had, she wouldn't have been able to dodge it.

"I'm sure y'all are smarter than that," Mother Blessing said. There was no humor in her voice anymore, nothing but anger and an edge of bitterness. "I'm sure y'all don't want to make this any harder on either of us than it has to be."

"That all depends," Rebecca said, her insolent attitude only heightened by the slap. "Just what is 'this' going to be?"

"Just a short little conversation," Mother Blessing assured her. "Y'all are going to tell me where to find Season and Kerry, and then I'll untie you and leave you alone. Now, that sounds fair, doesn't it?"

"Yeah, fair," Rebecca said. "Only, I don't think so. In fact, I think you ought to take yourself a flying—"

Again, Mother Blessing moved faster than Rebecca could have imagined. This time, the slap spun her head around to one side, and she saw flashes of bright light when it connected.

Note to self, Rebecca thought. *No profanities around this freak.*

9

Scott was almost frantic.

Hours had passed since they had called Rebecca to warn her about the attack on Adam, and what that might portend for the rest of them. Rebecca had promised to get in touch with Kerry and let her know about it. Kerry and Season were the only ones who would know what to do, how to respond.

If at all. If there was any reasonable response possible.

But Rebecca had not called back. He and Brandy had taken turns trying her, at home and on her cell, through the night. Neither had slept much. Rebecca's roommate Erin had finally unplugged her phone, apparently, after answering with less and less good humor, then finally insisting that they stop calling. But they hadn't. And they wouldn't, until they talked to Rebecca, or Kerry.

Now the sun had risen, shining down onto New England. It would still be dark in California, Scott knew, but not for long. Daylight would race across the continent, illuminating forests and villages, cities and plains, mountains and rivers, and finally the far coast.

The coast where Rebecca was in some kind of trouble— where Mother Blessing was closing in on them. Scott was certain of it.

"We need to catch a plane," he announced when Brandy came into the room. Her hair was a mess, her eyes puffy and bloodshot from lack of sleep, and she sipped from a Red Bull. They were at her apartment, where they had spent the night. She had tried to grab a few winks from time to time, unsuccessfully. Scott had alternated between pacing, dialing the phone, and staring out the window at the dark city. Once he had taken a shower, just to try to clear the cobwebs from his mind, but then he'd had to put back on the same clothes, reeking with sweat from the fight and everything since. The mood that had come over them before, the definite rekindling of heat between them, hadn't gone away, but it had been overshadowed by other events.

"Do we have a reservation?" Brandy asked, confused.

"No," he said. "So I guess we're paying full fare. Don't worry, I'll take care of it. But we have to get to California. San Jose is closest, I guess, to Santa Cruz. I wish we knew where

Kerry and Season were so we could go straight there, but we need to check in on Rebecca anyway."

"Don't you think that might be a little extreme, Scott?" Brandy wondered. "A cross-country flight because she's been away from her phone for a few hours?"

"Was what that thing did to Adam extreme?"

Brandy nodded, catching on. "I'll get my purse."

Rebecca tried to think about anything except the pain.

Her friends had often called her a retro hippie, and she figured that was why she fit in so well at UC Santa Cruz—even in the twenty-first century, it was the biggest hippie school in the state.

Part of what made her a hippie, she guessed, was her preference for nonviolence, for passive resistance to injustice. It had been the most effective technique for those protesting the Vietnam War or fighting for civil rights in the sixties. Don't fight back, show that you are above violence by refusing to sink to that level. Demonstrate that there's a better way.

She tried to cling to that belief, but it was hard. Her flesh had been burned by at least fifty matches. She'd been pinched, pulled, slapped, punched hard in the abdomen. Her hair had been pulled, twisted, and yanked. If Mother Blessing had had a pair of pliers Rebecca was sure her fingernails would be gone by now, and probably only the lack of plumbing in the house had kept the old water torture thing from happening.

But she had refused to tell the witch anything. Friendship

was more important than physical discomfort, and violence was an insult that could be dealt with only by absolute rejection. Telling Mother Blessing where Kerry was would be disastrous, and Rebecca would withstand any torture rather than reveal her location.

At least she would try.

Kerry was her friend, someone for whom Rebecca would do anything she could. Anything on Earth.

She had stopped trying to reason with the woman. Mother Blessing wanted what she wanted, and there was no getting past that barrier. She had said she wanted to talk, but that wasn't true. She only wanted to listen, and then just to the specific answer that she sought.

Rebecca had tried, early on, to persuade Mother Blessing of the hopelessness of her effort. "Do you know what my last name is?" she had asked, ignoring the fact that the old witch had used it when she first came into the kitchen. "It's Levine. That's my dad's name. My mother was a Yelinsky. Her grandparents lived in Poland in the 1930s. They were Jewish. You know what that means, right? You were around in those days. Of course, you were probably on the other side."

Mother Blessing hadn't responded—verbally, at least. Instead she had struck another match and held the flame in front of Rebecca's eyes. Rebecca had blown it out, and Mother Blessing had quickly jammed the still-burning head into the soft skin right beneath Rebecca's left eye.

Rebecca screamed, and tears that she thought had dried

up started to fall again. "It means they were in a concentration camp," Rebecca said when she could compose herself enough to speak. "They lived through worse torture than you could even imagine with your pitifully small mind. And I'm here, which means they survived it. They survived all that horror, so there is nothing you can do to me—"

Another match struck. "You can make this stop," Mother Blessing whispered, repeating the same chorus she had been singing for a while now. "You can put an end to the whole thing. It's easy. Just tell me what I want to know."

"—nothing you can do to me that is worse than what they went through. There is no way you can make me tell you anything, so just give it up. If you do, I won't tell Season what you've done, and she won't kick your butt for it."

Stories of her family's history had meant nothing to Mother Blessing, so Rebecca stopped speaking them out loud. But they meant a great deal to her. Her great-grandparents were many years gone now, but she had met them as a young girl. She had seen the numbers tattooed on their wrists, had heard the tales they told to adult friends when they thought young Rebecca was sound asleep in her bed. She filled her mind with those tales, the unspeakable things her great-grandparents had seen, had lived through, and with thoughts of Kerry, good, brave Kerry, and she bit the insides of her cheeks until she tasted blood, and she withstood the pain.

She had to.

She *couldn't* give up, *couldn't* turn over Kerry and Season

to the old witch. Mother Blessing was a coward who preferred to let others do her dirty work for her. Rebecca didn't
know much about her, but she knew that. The fact that she
was here, that she was getting her own hands dirty, meant
that things were coming to a head. Some kind of endgame
was in the works.

Well, Rebecca would be happy to see it all end. But on
Kerry's schedule, and Season's. On their terms. Not Mother
Blessing's.

She had never thought of herself as a particularly coura-
geous person, though she had been moved and touched when
Kerry had told her that she was. She still didn't think so. *Stubborn, yes. Intransigent. Not brave.*

She didn't even think she was brave when she finally lost
consciousness.

The girl would *not* give up.

Mother Blessing had thought she was the softest of the
bunch, the weakest link, as it were. A couple of hard tugs on
her shiny red hair and the girl would rat out her friends just
to make it stop.

She was surprised, and, she had to admit, somewhat
impressed, by the girl's fortitude. Annoyed, too. It just made
her work harder than she had hoped to. Sweat filmed her forehead and upper lip, and she was dying for some sweet tea and
a Hershey bar. There was none of that in this house, however.
It was an abandoned place on the edge of town, this awful

Santa Cruz place, with plywood over the windows and a CONDEMNED sign tacked to the front door. Mother Blessing couldn't wait to get out of the house, out of Santa Cruz. If she never had to come back to California again it would be too soon. Her son had died in California, after all. And met Kerry in California.

In some ways, this was where it had all started, this recent cycle of violence and war that led toward the Convocation. *Fitting that it should end here,* she thought.

The girl had lapsed into unconsciousness now, though. Mother Blessing hadn't expected to have to expend this kind of effort on her, but since she had, she was angry with the girl, and therefore less inclined than she might otherwise have been to spare her any unnecessary discomfort.

So since the girl wouldn't talk, she would extract the information she wanted in a different way. A little easier for her, a lot harder on the girl. Mother Blessing offered a halfhearted shrug. Didn't really matter to her, one way or the other.

She looked at Rebecca Levine, her head slumped forward onto her chest, mouth slack, body finally relaxed against the cords that held her in the chair. She was a pretty girl who could have grown into a beautiful woman. Not now, though. Pity she had brought this on herself. Mother Blessing put her right hand on Rebecca's head, feeling the girl's soft hair and the tight, unyielding flesh underneath, close against her skull. She applied more pressure, and at the same time spoke a single word in the ancient language of magic.

Her fingertips dug through the flesh, as if it were no more dense than the thick mud of her home swamp. Pressing harder, they bit into the skull, crumbling bone like stale bread. Beneath the skull there was brain matter, softer still and a little wet beneath her probing hand.

Mother Blessing closed her eyes and concentrated as her fingers rooted around in Rebecca's brain. The girl's thoughts flew into her mind scattershot, as if someone were drumming on the remote control of a TV with a thousand channels. Worries about school and work and Mother Blessing herself, fears, joys, loves, and hates. The simple pleasure of sand between her toes at the beach, and the more recent horror of being attacked in the dark and awakening, bound, all alone in a strange place. A recipe for chocolate chip cookies. A memory of a winter morning in Central Park with her father, trying to ice-skate for the first time. An image of a pelican skimming across the waves, its wingtips dipping into the water.

And finally, a name—Morgan—and a town.

Bolinas.

That's where Kerry and Season were.

Mother Blessing pulled her hand out of Rebecca's skull and shook her fingers as if she had just touched raw sewage.

"There, now, that wasn't so bad, was it?" she asked the lifeless girl.

Rebecca, of course, didn't respond.

That was okay. She had what she needed. She would leave Rebecca's body here. Somebody would find it, one of these days, but probably not soon. Not in this abandoned place. And Mother Blessing would never be connected to it, at any rate.

Anyway, she needed to get to Bolinas, wherever that was. She had a map of California that she'd bought at the airport out in her stolen car.

No simulacra this time. They had helped with Rebecca, to a point. But they wouldn't stand up against Season and Kerry. That had been proven. Still, she needed to keep them pinned down until she could get there herself, needed to make sure they didn't run away yet again.

She had an idea, though. One that would do the job just fine.

She could almost taste victory now, and it was sweet.

10

A steady spring rain had tapped against walls and windows all evening. Kerry was amazed that there had been so much rain in northern California over the winter and in the days leading up toward the Convocation. Season assured her that everything she thought she knew about weather was changing, faster than she could probably imagine.

"Call it global warming, global climate change, whatever you want," Season said. "It's happening. Most people don't live long enough to see the progression firsthand, but I have. Up in the Sierra Nevada mountains, not so far from here, glaciers are receding, and winter's snows melt much sooner than they used to. The Antarctic ice shelf is thinning and weakening. Ocean currents are changing. It's getting worse, and it's happening in a hurry. The snap of a finger in geologic time. It's already reaching the point that people who haven't lived as long as me can observe some of the changes, if they're paying attention."

"Can't you—or we, you know, witches, can't we do something about it?" Kerry asked anxiously.

"You think we aren't?" Season responded. "You should see what things would be like if we weren't butting in as much as we're able. We have a group constantly trying to help mitigate the damage that humans do to one another and to their planet, but there's only so much they can accomplish. As a people, we seem able to create war, famine, environmental catastrophe, and crime no matter what. Against that, witches can only try to hold the line. I told you that we're engaged in a continual struggle between chaos and order. The human tendency supports the chaos side, so it's an uphill climb. But we're still trying, all the time."

Kerry was about to respond when a loud crack sounded outside, and virtually simultaneously the living room window shattered, glass crashing to the floor in great shards. A hot buzz swept through the room and thudded into the far wall, between the two women. Kerry jumped, her heart slamming into her throat. "What—?"

"Get down!" Season commanded. She dove across the space separating them and pushed Kerry to the floor. They both landed hard against the threadbare rug. "Someone's shooting at us," Season explained.

Kerry hadn't known what to expect, but somehow that was worse than anything she would have thought of. She was accustomed to magical attacks, or as close to accustomed to them as she figured one could be. But a bullet . . . that was so brutal, so cold. Witchcraft, magic—these things were part of nature, inextricably tied to it. A few ounces of lead formed into a killing instrument was decidedly unnatural and filled Kerry with revulsion.

"Who . . . ?" she began. She didn't bother to finish. *Who else?* Somehow Mother Blessing had found them.

She didn't usually use bullets, though. She had seen for herself how useless they were against Season.

Against Season . . . but not against Kerry. Had that shot been meant just for her? Take out Season's ally, and then go up against Season one-on-one? Kerry shivered, and not just from the cold air that streamed in through the broken window.

"We should find out who," Season suggested. Staying low, she crawled to the wall beneath the large window. She motioned to Kerry to keep down, even as she lifted her own head to the windowsill and peered out.

"Who's out there?" Kerry inquired urgently. Her terror was quickly moving toward rage. She felt violated by the attack and wanted to take some kind of action.

"It's—down!" Season dropped her own head below the edge of the window again, just as another bullet whipped through some of the remaining glass. Shards showered onto her head.

"There are a few of them," Season told her.

"But who are they?"

"I don't know," Season answered. "They just look like regular guys. Like hunters, I guess. A couple in camouflage clothing, others in normal street clothes. They're all carrying guns, and they're spreading out—it looks like they're trying to surround the house."

"But . . . they can't do that! Why?"

"I have to think Mother Blessing is behind it somehow," Season replied.

"I got that much."

"Then you know as much as me," Season snapped. "Sorry," she said a second later. "I'm just trying to figure this out. It's a new tactic, but it's still part of the same war, I'm sure."

Kerry was quiet for a moment, listening hard. Outside she could hear soft voices and the occasional snap of a twig or rustle of leaves, but for the most part the movements of their hunters were masked by the patter of the rain, which now blew inside through the shattered window. They could have been closing on the house, for all she could tell—about to burst in at any moment.

"She's controlling them," Season ventured. "I don't know where she found them, maybe just around the community. They don't look like men who know they're engaged in a life-or-death task—their faces are kind of blank, so I'm sure she's taken them over. But still, they won't be as easy to deal with as simulacra."

"Why not?" Kerry wondered out loud. "They're just humans, right? And if they're not altogether there, they should be—"

"That's exactly why," Season explained. "Their humanity. They can think, they can reason, and they can communicate. Mother Blessing may be behind them, controlling them, but she left them enough of their own personalities to allow them to become an effective unit."

"Great," Kerry said. "Then what do we do?" A horrible thought struck her. "Do we have to kill them?"

"I'm thinking," Season said, her tone bordering on impatience again. "If they were simulacra, I wouldn't hesitate to blast them. But they're human—we can't just kill them. Not only would it be wrong, but it would negate all the purification rituals we've just put ourselves through. We'd have to start over, and there's no way we'd be ready for the Convocation."

Another sound from outside, a footstep on gravel. The men were closer now. Neither Season nor Kerry had shown themselves at the window, so no more shots had been fired, but Kerry was convinced that wouldn't last long. As soon as the men were inside, she and Season would be the proverbial sitting ducks.

"Can we disable them in some way?" Kerry asked. "Immobilize them, paralyze them, something?"

"If they were acting of their own volition, we could," Season said. "Since they're not, it would mean trying to counter Mother Blessing's influence. I don't know if it'll work."

"It's worth a try, though, right?"

"At this point, anything's worth a try," Season said. She started to add something, but was interrupted by the sound of breaking glass from elsewhere in the house.

"They're coming in!" Kerry breathed.

"Then we have to get out," Season replied. "Kitchen!"

Both women scrambled on hands and knees toward the kitchen entry. From the back door there, a couple of steps led to the small yard, which was overrun by thick shrubbery and low-hanging tree branches. More noise inside the house told Kerry that someone had entered through the bedroom Season slept in, which also had a door facing off to the side of the house. They had no doubt broken one of the panes out of the door and reached in to open it. If they hadn't completely surrounded the house yet, the kitchen door might still be safe.

That was, as Kerry's mother used to say, a pretty big if.

In the kitchen at last, Season once again took the lead. While Kerry hugged the floor, Season looked outside. Not seeing any of the men from her vantage point, she laid out her plan. "I'm going to open this door," she said. "And then I'm going to run like hell for the trees. You give me a couple of seconds, to draw their fire if they're watching, and then follow. We'll meet up at that cliff you climbed."

"All I heard was the run like hell part," Kerry admitted. "And don't worry, that's exactly what I had in mind."

"If they hit me—"

Kerry cut her off. "They won't. Don't even go there."

"I'm just saying—"

The scuff of a foot on the floorboards. "Would you just go, already?" Kerry was afraid she'd have to shove Season out the door.

But Season was already in motion. With a single smooth move, she swung the door open and launched herself into the darkness outside. Kerry held her breath, expecting the roar of gunfire. Instead she heard the crash of underbrush, and then silence. Fearing the worst—that Season's exit would have alerted the hunters to this way out, even though they had previously been unaware of it—she swallowed once and charged out the door. A patch of light from inside the house floated between her and welcoming darkness, like a wall she would have to penetrate, but she was through it quickly enough and embraced by shadows. Behind her, she heard voices calling out, and then the report of a gun. Leaves not far from her flew as a bullet tore through them, but she kept her head down and ran.

The ground was wet and slick, and branches whipped against Kerry's face and limbs as she ran, snagging fabric and ripping flesh. Not as bad as bullets would, though. She kept running, full out, trying to breathe easily. She knew she was in the best shape of her life—her legs pumped beneath her, each long stride carrying her away from the hunters and the death-trap their borrowed house had become. As long as she didn't slam herself into a tree trunk in the dark, she would be okay.

Fifteen minutes later she had reached the end of the world.

It might as well have been, at any rate. Of the black Pacific she could see nothing. There were no stars, no moon to be reflected in the water—the clouds overhead blotted out all light. All she could see on the cliff's edge was Season, trying to keep her balance on the rain-slick rocks. Kerry joined her friend there and found cover behind an upthrust boulder, so she couldn't be observed from inland.

Season sat down beside her. Both of them were soaked to the skin, but alive and unhurt. Pneumonia was far easier to fight off than bullets, at least for Kerry.

"Now what?" Kerry asked.

"I hadn't thought that far ahead," Season said. "I just wanted us out of there. Now I guess we hope they give up when they find out the house is empty."

"But they know we were in there," Kerry countered. "They saw us through the window. One of them shot at me when I was running away."

Season shrugged. "I didn't say it was a good plan. Just the best I could come up with at the moment."

"You really think they'll give up?"

"I wouldn't want to count on it," Season admitted, wiping back the hair plastered to her face by the rain. "I guess it depends on how determined Mother Blessing is, and how much control she has over them."

"I have a feeling she's pretty determined."

"I put more hope in the second part, myself," Season said. "If her control over them slips, they'll probably wonder what on Earth they were ever doing out here and head for home."

"That would be good," Kerry said. She allowed herself a flash of optimism, but it didn't last long. "But what if they don't go home? Then we're pretty much trapped here on the cliff."

"Except for one thing," Season pointed out. "We know we can climb down. In this rain they probably can't—especially since they don't have complete control of their own bodies. I'm not saying it would be easy, in this weather, but we could do it. They'll fall for sure."

"And then we'd be killing them anyway," Kerry observed. "Not directly, maybe, but just as dead."

Season contemplated that for a moment. "Yes, that's true. We would be killing them, if you look at it like that."

"So it's not a very good option, is it?"

"I guess not."

They both fell silent then. Kerry tried to think of some other plan, some way to get out of this position. Nothing came to her. They were stuck on a cliff's edge in a driving rain, and armed men were looking for them. Even if they stayed out here all night, there was no guarantee the men would give up. Maybe they'd never give up.

"Kerry . . . ," Season whispered after a time. "I see one of them."

She was peeking around the edge of the sheltering boulder, looking back in the direction of the house.

"Has he seen us?" Kerry asked quietly.

"Not yet," Season answered. "And so far, it's just one of them."

Kerry hazarded a glance of her own. The hunter had broken out of the tree line and was walking toward the cliff, cradling his rifle in his arms and scanning the horizon with every step. Safe behind their boulder, they would be hidden until he was right on top of them. But then it would be a matter of kill or be killed, Kerry was convinced.

"We've got to try something before any more come," she suggested. "Maybe if we pick them off one by one—"

"That's what I was thinking," Season interrupted. "Wait here." She broke from cover and ran toward the man. He reacted to her charge, shouldering the rifle and sighting down it. He moved more slowly than Kerry expected—she guessed that Mother Blessing's remote automation included a built-in time delay, as if some electronic signal had to travel back to her, wherever she was, so she could give the appropriate order.

But Season moved fast, weaving as she ran to make it harder for the sluggish man to draw a bead on her. As he tried, she threw up her hands and shouted, *"Takilata!"*

The man stopped dead, as if he'd been struck by a hammer or walked into a brick wall. A look of confusion swept across his face. Season's spell was working!

Kerry's celebration was short-lived, however. The man lowered his gun for a moment, shook off the spell like a man stepping out of a shower, and then raised his weapon again, aiming it right at Season. Kerry stifled a scream as he pulled the trigger. Season hurled herself to the ground, and the bullet whizzed over her head and off to sea.

Hardly losing a moment, Season lunged to her feet and closed the remaining distance between her and the gunman with a fast, zigzag dash. He brought the gun around again, trying to get her in his sights, but his reaction time was too slow. Before he could get off another shot, Season was there. She ducked under the rifle's barrel and slammed it toward the sky with one hand. He managed to squeeze the trigger, but his shot sailed harmlessly toward the clouds. Season braced herself on her left foot and kicked out with her right, catching the man in the gut. He doubled over, and she twisted the rifle from his hands, swinging it around as she did. The rifle's wooden stock collided with the man's jaw, and he crumpled like an empty paper bag.

Season motioned for Kerry to leave cover and join her. Nervously, afraid to abandon the sheltering rocks, she did so. The man on the ground hadn't moved, and as she approached him, Kerry could see the gleam of dark liquid around his nose and mouth. Blood.

"He's . . . ?"

"He's alive," Season assured her. "But it'll be a little while before he's a problem again. He's just one of them, though, and those two shots will have alerted the others. I think we need to get out of here. This is going to be tougher than I had hoped."

11

Season led Kerry back toward the house by a different, and more roundabout, route than they had taken going out. This was a path Kerry had never seen—didn't even know was here—and it seemed to confirm her guess that while she had been holed up in the house reading, Season had been out scouting something. She should have known it would be escape routes, since they were one of Season's specialties.

"The spell I tried should have paralyzed him," Season whispered as they hurried through the trees. "But it barely slowed him down. Mother Blessing's spell is too deeply embedded for me to break. Our best bet is to deal with them one by one, if they're spread out enough, and make our way to the car. Chances are she's already overextending herself, so they probably won't be able to follow us any great distance."

"That's encouraging," Kerry replied softly.

"We do the best we can." Season tossed her a wry smile and kept going through the woods.

They met the second of the hunters as they rounded a bend on the trail. He was coming in their direction, shuffling along like a sleepwalker. When he saw the women, though, he seemed to wake up a little. "Over here!" he shouted, bringing his gun up at the same time.

"*Takilata!*" Season tried, making the appropriate hand gestures.

Once again, the man was affected only momentarily. He was so close, however, that Season was able to reach him before he recovered. She cupped both hands over his ears and brought them together hard. The sensation seemed to stun him for another moment, and she followed up with a precisely aimed elbow to his windpipe. He dropped to his knees, choking. Season pushed him over and he fell on the ground, writhing and gasping for breath. She knelt beside him, touching his neck. She looked up at Kerry as she did. "Dislocated his windpipe for a second," she said. "I've fixed it. He'll be fine. But he won't be shouting again soon."

"How did you learn all this stuff?" Kerry inquired.

"Here and there," Season said vaguely. Kerry took the hint and let it drop.

Leaving him moaning softly on the wet path, they continued toward the house. Rustling nearby indicated that the man's initial cry had not gone unheard. Season gestured to Kerry and they both left the path, taking to the trees and waiting, as still as possible, a couple of feet back.

Less than a minute later, two of the hunters came down the path, stiff-legged and awkward. Their guns were at the ready, but their eyes were only on the trail. They walked right past Season and Kerry without ever noticing them standing among the trees. The women waited another couple of minutes, until they could no longer hear the two men, and then took to the path again.

They were almost back to the house when they encountered yet another of the hunters. Season braced herself for action, but Kerry put a restraining hand on her arm. "Let me try something," she said.

Season looked surprised, but then smiled. "Be my guest."

Kerry waited until the guy had spotted them and prepared to sound the alarm, and then she folded the fingers of her right hand until the fingertips touched the palm, and extended her thumb. With her left hand, she made a lifting motion. *"Kenesep!"* she exclaimed.

The man's cry died in his throat as a plume of earth rose up and hurled itself into his face. He backpedaled away from it, but his impaired control over his own limbs got in the way and he fell over backward, smacking his head against a tree stump with an audible crack. He rolled to the ground and lay still.

"You don't think I broke anything, do you?" Kerry asked, suddenly worried that she'd taken it too far.

"I doubt it," Season answered. Dropping to one knee beside the man, she examined the back of his head briefly. "I think he just got knocked out. Come on."

The 4x4 they had bought in San Francisco was parked within view, and there were no hunters readily apparent. They broke into a sprint. Kerry knew they'd left their purses, driver's licenses and all, back in the house, and probably their keys as well.

She also knew that wouldn't matter—such inconveniences were easily fixed with the help of a little witchcraft.

Season hit the driver's side door and yanked it open. Kerry ran around to the passenger side, and by the time she was in her seat, Season was already backing out of the gravel drive-way. Kerry buckled in just as Season straightened out on the dirt road and stomped on the gas.

Some of the hunters heard the sounds of the vehicle and came running—running, at least, to the extent that their slow-moving bodies would allow. A couple of them raised their rifles, and Kerry heard shots fired behind them. No bullets impacted the Raider, however. Within minutes she and Season had left them far behind, cutting through the rain toward the highway out of Bolinas.

Mother Blessing knew when her targets were out of range. During the search and battle, she had taken refuge in a cheap motel room on the San Francisco peninsula, directing the action from there since she couldn't both drive and participate. Trucks rumbling past threatened to disturb her concentration, but she tuned the room's TV to a channel it didn't receive and cranked the volume, letting the white noise drown out traffic sounds from outside. Watching through multiple pairs of eyes—and eyes she had not manufactured, but only enchanted—was a strain in itself; doing that and controlling muscles, planning and executing strategy, took a lot out of a person. And now she knew that Season and Kerry were headed north—toward the Convocation site, no doubt—and that her plan had not worked.

Still, she'd had to try. The Convocation was upon them. Season could have decided to leave at any minute. Since she couldn't make it to Bolinas herself in a timely enough fashion, she had stopped in this motel and used its telephone book to locate a gun shop in Marin County, not too far from Bolinas. She then constructed a simulacrum and sent it into the shop, watching through its eyes to see who was inside. There were half a dozen men, some dressed like they were ready for the hunt, others engaged in conversation, shopping, or just browsing.

She didn't care why they had gone in, only that they were there.

It was brutally difficult—almost impossible, really—to cast spells over long distances. But the distance in this case wasn't too extreme, less than fifty miles, and she had the help of the simulacrum, whose hands could be sculpted into the precise necessary shapes for limited durations. She cast an overall spell on the men in the shop, freezing them where they stood, and then spent more time enchanting each one individually. She drilled the address of Rebecca's friends, the Morgans, into them, showed them their targets, and sent them on their way.

If that first shot had hit Kerry, she'd have had them both. Season wouldn't have abandoned the girl. She would have been so angry that she would have waited for Mother Blessing to arrive, just so she could have it out with her. Mother Blessing chuckled dryly. Human emotion could be so counterproductive, and Season had never been able to completely shake that handicap.

As it turned out, though the man she had used for the first attack had been the most seasoned hunter of the lot, her own manipulation of him had affected his ability to aim cleanly and to squeeze off a good shot.

Not for the first time, she wished she could have been there in person. All the distance Season kept between them had kept her alive too many times. Mother Blessing was grimly aware that she had not been able to best Season the last time they'd been face-to-face, but that was then.

This was now. She was ready this time. She was primed. She had been preparing, training, learning.

All she needed was to meet up with Season Howe, one-on-one.

It peeved her royally to realize that it probably wasn't going to happen. Season had too much of a start. She was already racing toward the Convocation, while Mother Blessing tried to recover from a difficult, and ultimately futile, exercise. Perhaps she had, in fact, compounded her earlier mistake by going with surrogates yet again. If she had just driven straight to Bolinas, it was possible that Season and Kerry would have still been there, would have waited until morning to make the drive north.

But now she had flushed them out, and they were on the wing again. Even if Mother Blessing got on the road right now, Season had a couple of hours' head start. Mother Blessing's only hope was to drive through San Francisco, over the Golden Gate Bridge, and onto Interstate 80. From where Season was, she'd have a long haul to get to the Interstate, looping over the north end of the San Francisco Bay. Their way would be slow. It was remotely possible that Mother Blessing would be able to intercept them before they reached the Convocation, if she hurried. Maybe in Sacramento.

Leaving the TV blaring its noisy signal, Mother Blessing dragged herself wearily to her car.

Season pulled the car to a stop outside a twenty-four-hour family restaurant near Richmond. She had watched the mirror constantly since leaving Bolinas, and there had been no pursuit. She and Kerry were both hungry, and if they were going to drive all night they'd need some nourishment, and probably caffeine.

This place would be quiet at this time of night, she explained. They'd be able to scrutinize all the diners at a glance as soon as they went in, and if anyone looked suspicious or made a move against them, they could immediately retreat or fight back.

Before they went in, Kerry pulled her cell phone from the purse that Season had magically arranged to be inside the car. *Either that,* Kerry thought, *or the purse is an exact duplicate of my old one, right down to the last stick of gum in its wrapper and the programming on the phone.* Only the names on her driver's license and credit cards were changed—now, as far as the public was concerned, she was Brenda Peterson, and Season was Amanda Cowles.

"I need to call Beck," she said. "I've been really worried about her."

"That's fine," Season said. "I think we're safe for the moment."

Season punched up Rebecca's home number. The phone rang only once before someone snatched it from the cradle on the other end. "Hello?" the voice asked breathlessly. Kerry recognized it at once, but it wasn't who she wanted to talk to.

"Erin?" Kerry said. "It's Kerry. Is Rebecca there?"

"God, no," Erin said. She sounded distraught. "I was hoping you were her."

"No, sorry. Where is she?"

"That's the thing, Kerry. I don't know. Scott and, what's her name, Brandy, were calling and calling, like, all night last night. They stopped for a while this morning, but they've been back at it now and then. I'm really worried about her. She left me a note saying she was leaving for a day or so, and that's the last anyone seems to have heard from her."

Kerry's heart sank. The bad feeling she'd had about Rebecca was accurate, and then some. Unfortunately, it didn't take an advanced degree in mathematics to put the puzzle pieces together. *Rebecca knew where we were,* she thought. *Rebecca vanishes, Mother Blessing turns up. Not a complicated pattern.*

"Okay, Erin," she said. "If you hear from her, please have her call me right away. I'll have her check in with you if I can reach her."

"Thanks, Kerry," Erin said. She sniffled, and Kerry guessed that she had started to weep. Sometimes the two housemates seemed barely aware of one another's existence, but that arrangement had worked for them. Rebecca even seemed to prefer it, since it made it easier to keep important aspects of her life private. But Erin genuinely liked Rebecca, in her own way. Of course she'd be worried and upset.

Kerry ended the call and turned to Season. "Rebecca's missing," she said. "Since last night sometime."

"Plenty of time for Mother Blessing to have found us," Season said, catching on instantly.

The ease with which Season jumped to the same conclusion that she had chilled Kerry to the bone. "That's what I was thinking."

"Try the others," Season urged. "Make sure they're okay."

Kerry was already scrolling for Scott's number. She prepared to call it, but at the last second changed her mind and chose Brandy's instead. She knew those two had had their troubles, and she knew that she was at the root of at least some of it. Why make things worse by always calling Scott first, instead of Brandy?

"Kerry?" Brandy answered a moment later.

"Hi, Brandy." Kerry didn't have time for pleasantries. "Have you heard from Rebecca?"

"No, we haven't been able to reach her all day," Brandy said. "Have you?"

"I just now talked to Erin and found out she was missing. I didn't know. Erin said she was going out of town for a while but didn't seem to know much more than that."

"It gets worse," Brandy told her. Kerry almost pulled the phone away from her head, afraid to hear what Brandy might have to say now.

"What?" she asked, almost against her own will.

"Adam was attacked," Brandy said. "By a simulacrum. Scott and I managed to fight it off—well, Scott did really. It was like some kind of miracle, Kerry—the thing just fell apart in his hands. But that was yesterday. We wanted to let you know Mother Blessing was on the move again, so we tried to call you. But when we couldn't get you, we called Rebecca. She said she would go to wherever you are and find you, warn you that something was up."

"Oh, no," Kerry said, as the weight of Brandy's words sank in.

"Yeah."

"Brandy, Rebecca never showed up, but some goons under Mother Blessing's control did."

"And Rebecca's the only one who knew where you were."

"Yeah," Kerry echoed Brandy. "I didn't want to tell Erin, but I'm really worried about her."

"Sounds like you have reason to be," Brandy said. "I kept hoping maybe she was with you, and you were all out of cell range or something."

"No such luck," Kerry said. "I wish."

"Me too."

Both were silent for a moment. Kerry thought she was going to cry, like Erin had. Only with more reason.

"I should tell Scott," Brandy said.

"Is he with you?"

"Yeah," Brandy said. "We're in a rental car, on our way to Santa Cruz. We landed at the airport in San Jose about a half hour ago—first flight out of Boston we were able to get."

"You guys be careful," Kerry urged, surprised to learn that they were already in California. "Chances are Mother Blessing is on her way up here, heading for the Convocation. But if she is still in Santa Cruz, I don't need to tell you she's very dangerous."

"I know, Kerry," Brandy said. "We won't take any stupid chances. But what if Rebecca is, I don't know, trapped some-place and needs our help? We have to look for her."

"You do that. I'll see if Season knows a way to search for

her remotely. When you've found her, or . . . or when you're ready, head north, to Oregon." She drew the phone away from her mouth. "Where should they meet us, Season? After?"

"Have them wait in Klamath Falls," Season said. "That's not too far, and there are motels they can stay at."

"Klamath Falls, Season says," Kerry spoke into the phone. "I'll call you when I can to find out where you are. The Witches' Convocation is about to start, but we'll hook up with you after that. And everything will be different then, I can guarantee it."

"Everything's already different," Brandy said. "That doesn't mean I have to like it."

"Yeah," Kerry agreed. "That's a really good point."

12

I t felt to Kerry as if they'd left the world behind.

    She had never been anywhere so desolate, so isolated. Even the Great Dismal Swamp had been teeming with life, and there had been people around, towns all around it.

    Not here, though. None of that.

    She and Season had traded off at the wheel of the Dodge Raider through the night. They had bisected California on Interstate 80, leaving city and suburbs behind, entering agricultural areas, then the soupy region of the Sacramento Delta. Sacramento came and went in the dark, and once again they could smell rich and fertile farmlands surrounding them. Then the road started to climb. Flat fields turned to foothills, alfalfa and sugar beets to pines and firs and towering redwoods that blotted out the stars.

They had stopped for a few hours in Truckee, checking into a motel and grabbing some much-needed sleep on top of matching twin beds without even bothering to pull down the bedding. Breakfast was had at lunchtime in a nearby café, and then they were back in the car. The highway left California behind as it wove down from the mountains—the same Sierra Nevadas, Kerry reflected, that Season had mentioned earlier in her diatribe about global warming. That had been an eon ago, though, another age, before people had started shooting at them.

Coming down out of the mountains, they drove into Reno, which jutted up from the relative flatland like a child's toy forgotten on a lawn. Soon enough, even Reno vanished in the rearview mirror, and with it anything that smacked of population. The highway turned to the north and sliced through a state that seemed utterly abandoned. Every now and then there would be a roadside gas station/store/restaurant, or the buildings of some distant ranch, and then nothing again but mile after mile of rolling plains of sagebrush.

Then Winnemucca, a blink of the eye, and Season, who refused to reveal their destination except as the site of the Convocation, surprised Kerry by turning off Interstate 80 altogether.

Now she drove due north on Highway 95, a narrow strip of roadway that barely deserved the dignity of being numbered. It was paved, Kerry reflected, but that was about all it had going for it. With the setting sun on Season's side of the car, they drove up and up. There were mountains looming in the distance—this was basin and range country, Season had explained, which meant relatively parallel mountain ranges separated by deep valleys, like the wales of corduroy, cutting across the landscape. They followed the roadway through one of the valleys. Then the sun dropped behind the mountains to the west, and Season pulled over to let Kerry take the wheel for a stretch.

"Where are we?" Kerry wanted to know.

"Right here." This was about the extent that Season had been willing to reveal for hours.

"And where are we going?"

Season ticked her head north, on up the road. "That way."

Kerry blew out a frustrated sigh. "Okay. Will I know when we get there?"

"You'll know," Season promised her. "You will definitely know."

Kerry drove on, into the gathering dusk. There were no lights to be seen anywhere. If anyone actually lived out here, she couldn't tell. The idea suddenly struck her that this would be an awfully remote place to run out of gas, but then she smiled at her own naïveté—they hadn't stopped for gas since they'd bought the vehicle, and they wouldn't have to.

Finally, as stars began to wink into sight in the darkening sky, Season touched her right arm.

"Slow down," she said.

"Okay." Kerry complied. "Are we looking for something?"

"We are," Season confirmed. Kerry continued up the road for a couple of miles, with Season eyeing the left shoulder. Finally, she touched Kerry's arm once again. "We're looking for that."

Kerry followed her pointing hand. Season seemed to be pointing to a narrow, rutted track that led away from the highway. "That . . . that little path?"

"That's right," Season said. "Take that."

"This thing will be okay on that road? Is that really a road?"

Season showed her how to shift the Raider into its four-wheel drive mode. "This thing can go anywhere," she promised. "Just don't go too fast if you don't have to. Slow and easy."

Kerry almost asked why she might have to go fast, if slow was preferred, but then decided she'd rather not know. With Rebecca missing and Mother Blessing on the warpath, she had enough troubles weighing on her mind as it was. She turned onto the little track. The Raider chewed up the road easily, and she increased its pace a little, learning to slow down when approaching bumps or hollows. The headlights illuminated bugs flitting past, occasional clumps of sagebrush, dirt, and not much else. Once a pair of pronghorns dashed across a hill, limned against the rising moon.

A couple of hours later, Kerry yawned and stretched, gripping the wheel with one hand while she pushed the other against the ceiling, then trading off. "We're almost there," Season assured her. "Not much farther."

Kerry looked out into the distance and realized that beyond the headlights she couldn't see anything at all. The moon seemed to shine down on absolute nothingness.

"Are we still in Nevada?" she asked. "Are we still on Earth?"

"We may have passed into Oregon," Season told her. "I'm not a hundred percent sure about that. But don't worry, we're just about there."

Kerry brought the 4X4 to a shuddering stop and stared at Season as if the woman had gone insane. "Almost where? We're nowhere! There's nothing here. No one. Nada." She shut off the headlights and got out of the vehicle. She hadn't realized it, so focused was she on the narrow cone that the headlights illuminated, but they had been driving for some time on a perfectly flat, perfectly empty stretch of land. Beneath her feet, the hardpan was baked solid, the dirt cracked in hexagonal shapes. It looked like brownies left in the oven too long. She spun around, indicating the field of nothingness with her hands.

With the headlights gone, the moon shone down on the vast, empty space, which seemed to glow whitely of its own volition. Overhead, against the black backdrop of night, Kerry thought she could see every star there had ever been. The white sweep of the Milky Way had never been so distinct.

Season walked over to her, her boots crunching on the crusted earth. "Feel better?" she asked sympathetically.

"I'll feel better when I know where we are," Kerry groused.

"We're in the Owyhee Desert," Season told her. "It crosses

between northern Nevada and southern Oregon. A lot of maps don't bother to name it, because what's the point? There's nothing here."

"A whole lot of nothing," Kerry said. "I can see that much."

"I mean, real nothing," Season said. "This is one of the emptiest spots in the United States. The population density of Humboldt County, Nevada, which we just passed through, is somewhere less than two people per square mile, and most of those live back down in Winnemucca. Here it's probably figured in negative numbers."

"Meaning what?"

"Meaning there are more dead people than living, around here."

"That's a comforting thought," Kerry said.

"It's just empty," Season said. "Nothing wrong with that. It's what we're looking for."

"It is?"

"I'll show you," Season offered. "Get back in."

Kerry grudgingly complied. She had come to trust Season, but she didn't like how secretive her mentor had been about this whole thing. She could probably backtrack and return to civilization if she needed to, but only because there were so few roads that it would be hard to get genuinely lost.

But she got in and buckled up, with Season taking the wheel again. The older witch started the engine, flicked on the headlights, and began driving up the dirt trail, faster than Kerry had done.

"We're really someplace?" Kerry asked. "This is like some kind of weird hallucination."

Season chuckled. "That's it exactly," she said. "Don't see what your eyes tell you to see."

"Sometimes you are so opaque," Kerry commented. "Why don't you just say what you mean?"

"Don't see dark, flat, empty land," Season pressed. "Close your eyes and see the Convocation."

"How can I? I don't even know what it looks like. But if it looks like this, I'm going to be seriously bummed."

"It looks like a carnival," Season told her. "Not a modern one. Maybe a medieval one. Look at the peaked tents—blue, white, red, yellow, green. Look at the banners and pennants fluttering from their points, at the bright piping wrapped around their guy lines, like garlands around the staircase at Christmas. Look at the little wooden buildings where people serve food and drink, and the fires roaring in the wind, sprays of sparks dancing up into the sky, where they cook the beef and ham and turkey, and the smaller fires where they grill the vegetables. Smell the aromatic smoke that funnels up like dust devils. Look at the people walking between the tents and the buildings, chatting and laughing and enjoying being in one another's company again, safe and at home. See the dance floor, encircled by glowing paper lanterns, where couples in their most elegant finery twirl to the music provided by the band in the little frame gazebo."

Kerry realized that she *could* see the things Season described as the Raider bounced its way across the blank lunar landscape. It was just because her eyes were shut, and Season's words were so hypnotic, so evocative, she knew.

But no! Her eyes were wide open. Somehow, as if they had passed through an invisible curtain, they were now driving toward something, instead of toward more of the same nothing. It was just as Season had described it—she hadn't been imagining it after all, she had been stating what she was seeing, right in front of her. The tall tents with fluttering flags, the fires, the crowded dance floor.

And most of all, the people.

The witches.

Kerry Profitt's diary, March 21

I'm home.

I've never been home before. Not really. Well, okay, maybe when I was a little kid and both of my parents were alive, back in Cairo where I was born and bred. But not since then. Certainly not since Mom passed on and I had to move in with my aunt and uncle.

But I'm home now. I felt it as soon as I could truly see the Convocation, as soon as Season's words turned into reality for me.

If you weren't meant to be here, you would never see it. If for some bizarre reason you were driving on that goddess-awful dirt road and you weren't a witch, you'd just keep driving right through, never realizing that you had just missed the greatest celebration you could ever have imagined.

I'm meant to be here, then, because I can see it, and smell it, and hear it. Season and I are staying inside one of the little wooden caravans, like an old-time gypsy's, or a carny's, and every now and then I just have to get up and go to the door and stare outside at everyone and everything. Kind of like pinching myself to make sure I'm not dreaming, only without the pinch part.

It's amazing. Everyone is so happy, so friendly. Smiling. Laughing. Shouting to people they haven't seen in . . . well, in five hundred years. Calling to each other, running together, hugging. Lots of hugging.

And the sounds are so musical, so enchanting. The smells are heavenly. The clothes are . . . everything. Outfits from every time period in the last five centuries, and from every part of the world, but they all mesh together, they all blend perfectly, and they are all beautiful—the finest fabrics, the most skilled workmanship. I felt like a grunge in my dirty T-shirt and jeans and red-checked tennies, but then I looked down at myself, and my clothes seemed to have a glow to them. Same clothes, but somehow they had become fitting and appropriate and perfect, just like everyone else's. Every skin color on Earth is represented, too, and just like the clothes, it all makes a glorious visual display.

It's the world's biggest, best party. That's the only real way to describe it. A party where everybody likes each

other, and no one is obnoxiously drunk or hitting on someone who doesn't want to be hit on.

It's a celebration of witchiness. It's a gala. It's a convention. It's a business meeting. It's a dream.

It's the Convocation.

It's home.

Somebody pinch me after all. Or don't, on second
thought, because I don't want to wake up from this.

More later.

K.

13

When Brandy and Scott got to Rebecca's house in Santa Cruz, the place was crawling with police. Rebecca's VW was parked across the street, with yellow police tape surrounding it and the area immediately around it. Arc lights on tall stanchions gave a surreally bright glow to jumpsuited officers with cameras and evidence kits. It looked like a CSI episode come horribly to life, since it brought home with cruel bluntness the fact that Rebecca was truly missing.

At the door to the house, they had to introduce themselves to a sympathetic but terse female officer, who then announced them to Erin. Erin immediately rushed to the door to let them in. They had never met her, but Brandy recognized her from Rebecca's descriptions and a couple of photos. She was the archetypal California blonde—petite, button-cute, hair pulled back into a bouncy ponytail. But her red nose and the dark circles around her puffy eyes showed that she was not always the epitome of perky.

She led them into the kitchen. Brandy could hear cops moving in other parts of the house, and the static and buzz of their two-way radios. The kitchen was mercifully empty of them, and Erin sat down at a vintage Formica-topped table, in front of a cup of tea that looked like it had been there awhile.

"I'm so sorry I, you know, hung up on you guys," she said sadly. "I . . . you know, I thought she was just out or whatever, and you were just getting on my nerves. But if I had known . . ."

"How could you?" Brandy asked, pulling out a chair of her own and joining Erin at the table. "Her note said that she was going away for some indefinite period of time. So when she did just that, you had no reason to think there was anything wrong."

"Yeah, I guess so," Erin agreed as tears began to roll down her cheeks. "But still . . . there must have been something I missed. Some clue. I should have noticed sooner that her car was still there."

"You can't beat yourself up too much," Scott told her. He had remained standing, scanning the kitchen as if there might be a clue everyone else had missed. "Whatever happened to her is not your fault, I know that."

Brandy reflected that he couldn't tell Erin why he knew it.

Erin had no inkling, she was certain, of the existence of Season Howe and Mother Blessing and the whole long war between them. Rebecca had sworn that she would never tell anyone outside of their circle—those who had been living in the La Jolla house the night they found Daniel Blessing, half dead, in the shrubbery outside. The night it all began. Brandy had never had occasion to think Rebecca anything less than scrupulously honest—if she made a promise, she kept it.

She almost wished she could say something now. If Erin could know what her housemate was really caught up in, it would lessen any feelings of guilt she might have over Rebecca's disappearance. But Brandy held her tongue. Erin was so emotionally vulnerable right now, so close to the edge, that she would either think Brandy was a complete, unabashed liar, or she would believe the story, realize that the entire framework of knowledge she had about the world was wrong, and go totally insane.

The La Jolla housemates had at least had some time to get used to the existence of witches, and the knowledge had been thrust on them at a time when they were relatively happy, secure, and comfortable with each other. Erin had no such advantages. She would be knocked over at her weakest point, and her grip on reality might not survive it.

So instead of telling her the only thing that might really ease her pain, Brandy took Erin's hand and gently rubbed the back of it. "He's right," she said. "It's not your fault, Erin. We'll look for her. She's probably fine."

Only, of course, she probably wasn't. Mother Blessing had located Kerry and Season. Only Rebecca could have told her where to look. Unless she had come across the information some other way, Rebecca was certainly in serious trouble.

Behind her, Brandy heard Scott walking around, and then he left the kitchen altogether. She glanced at Erin and they both fell silent, listening as he addressed a police officer they couldn't see.

"Can you tell me anything about the investigation?" he asked. "We're close friends of Rebecca's—we actually just flew in from Boston to see her, and if there's anything we can do to help we'd really like to know."

"The best I can tell you is to keep out of the way and let us handle it," the police officer replied, his tone sympathetic but firm. "We can do our jobs."

"I know," Scott pressed. "But have you, you know, checked the hospitals and stuff? In case she's been in an accident or something?"

"We're working on it, son," the officer said. "Like I said—"

"I didn't mean to imply that you weren't," Scott said, cutting him off. "I just figured, if there was something we could do that would take some of the pressure off you, we'd be happy to."

"If I think of anything, I'll let you know," the officer said. Brandy heard the jangle of equipment on his belt as he walked away, and then Scott came back into the kitchen.

"They've got nothing," he said. "They're never going to find her."

The cops had nothing, but Brandy and Scott had no clue where to look for her either. The reality of it loomed over Brandy like a falling piano. Soon enough, the piano would hit.

"I've been missin' y'all."

Kerry was not surprised to hear Mother Blessing's voice, or to see her when she spun around at the sound of it. Season had assured her that their enemy would be in attendance. She also swore that Mother Blessing would be polite, even friendly, on the grounds of the Convocation, but Kerry tensed just the same, ready to run or fight.

Mother Blessing stood a dozen feet behind them, supporting her weight on a black metal cane. Even her usual polyester stretch pants and tentlike top seemed enhanced by their presence here, looking more like the garb of some weird kind of royalty than like the discount store specials they usually resembled.

"*Barely* missing," Season added.

Mother Blessing's smile broadened. "Well, a lady has to try, right? I thought maybe I'd run into y'all in Sacramento, but somehow you got past me."

"Imagine that," Season replied, returning the woman's ghastly grin. "I hope you didn't injure any innocent civilians while you were looking for us."

Mother Blessing laughed uproariously, as if Season had just told the best joke ever. Kerry couldn't quite get over these mortal enemies acting like old friends. She was reminded of politicians shaking hands before a debate, calling each other liars and cheats for an hour, and then shaking again when it was all over.

Then the old witch focused her gaze on Kerry, who twitched uncertainly beneath it. "Hope y'all are well, Kerry," she said. "It's been awful lonely at home since you left."

"Yeah, I bet you really wish I was back there," Kerry said, not bothering to hide the sarcastic edge. She was no politician, and she didn't intend to behave like one.

Season poked Kerry in the ribs, covering the action by laughing and grabbing Kerry's arm. "Kerry's told me all about how much she's learned from you, daughter," she said. It freaked Kerry out to be reminded that the youthful Season Howe was, in fact, Mother Blessing's mother. "I'm surprised that you turned out to be such a good teacher."

"Kerry's a good pupil," Mother Blessing answered. "A natural."

"That's true," Season said. "I guess you have an eye for them."

"I like to think so."

"We were just on our way to get some breakfast," Season said, bringing the uncomfortable conversation to a diplomatic close. "Would you like to join us?"

Kerry wanted to poke Season this time, but her friend had moved out of reach. Fortunately, Mother Blessing politely declined the offer.

Walking through the golden sunshine toward a tent from which wafted a glorious assortment of aromas, Kerry fixed

Season with a curious glare. "What was all that about?"

"It won't do us any good to get into a brawl here," Season answered reasonably. "We're at the Convocation. No one's getting hurt now. Nothing's going to happen until Witches' Tribunal, and then it'll be under the procedures that have been in place for centuries. If she was going to kill us, she needed to do it before we got here. Now we're perfectly safe from her."

Kerry couldn't quite wrap her mind around that idea. Perfectly safe? There had been a time in her life when she had felt safe, but not in the last year or so. She had been on edge virtually every minute, starting at every unusual noise, eyeing strangers with suspicion. She supposed that maybe she would be able to fully relax again someday.

It would take a while, though.

Regardless of Season's assurances, she would not trust Mother Blessing until after the Witches' Tribunal had dealt out its justice.

The breakfast offered in the tent was every bit as delicious as its odors promised. A crew of chefs in restaurant whites with tall hats—but all decorated with a wide assortment of cheerful buttons, braids, tassels, patches, and other additions, and all working with uniform good cheer—turned out an equally wide assortment of dishes. There were omelets and eggs of every style, various meats and sausages, pancakes and waffles, cereals, pastries, fruits. . . . Kerry could barely bring herself to pick anything, because it all looked so good.

"No wonder you cook so well," she said to Season as they

examined their options. "Do witches always eat like this?"

"Sometimes its gruel and hardtack," Season teased. "But what's the point of having a party if you can't indulge yourself?"

They filled plates and then sat down at long tables. The benches were filled with witches chatting, laughing, and seeming to have a good time. There were more women than men, but not by a huge margin. Kerry and Season squeezed in at the end of one of the benches, where a couple of people moved over to make space for them. Season hugged them both, a man and a woman.

"It's so good to see you," she gushed. "Kerry, this is Horace and Mae. They're witches from—Wisconsin, is it?"

"Madison," Horace said, beaming at Kerry like they were long-lost pals. He was as lean as a greyhound, with thinning silver hair combed over a bald spot, and small-lensed wire-rim glasses perched on a prominent nose. He could have been sixty or, Kerry knew, six hundred. Mae was rounder, more heavyset, with grandmotherly gray curls and a pearl chain attached to her horn-rims. Both were dressed like the grandparents in one of those black-and-white TV sitcoms from the fifties that ran on TV late at night.

"I've been to Madison!" Kerry said excitedly. The giddy mood of the other diners was infecting her. "Last fall, on my way down . . . down south."

"You've got to be pretty far north for Madison to be on the way south," Mae observed with a giggle.

"I figured that out," Kerry replied. She had realized that

she didn't want to get carried away and reveal that she'd been on her way to stay with Mother Blessing. Everybody acted friendly here, but that didn't mean there weren't factions, and she wanted to be cautious about saying too much to the wrong person. At least until she could get the lay of the land, or find out from Season who to trust. "I didn't exactly take the most direct route."

"Did you like it, Kerry?" Horace asked.

"I really didn't stay long," Kerry admitted. "It was cold, mostly. That's what I remember."

"Well, you should come back this time of year. Between now and early summer. It's a real nice place."

"It looked like it," Kerry said. "I'd like to go back sometime."

"I met Horace and Mae in . . . what was it, 1890?" Season asked.

"Ninety-one, I think," Mae corrected. "That winter."

"They helped me out of a tight spot," Season continued. "They're good folks." Kerry waited for her to elaborate further, but she didn't. Instead she dug into her breakfast with gusto. Kerry followed her lead and did the same, not wanting to let it get cold.

After breakfast Season introduced her to another dozen or so old friends as they wandered through the lanes between tents, pavilions, and small wooden buildings. In these, every kind of witchy activity Kerry could imagine took place. Some held demonstrations of spells or potions. Some were shops where magical implements—swords, daggers, wands, cauldrons, herbs, censers, brooms, crystals, and more—were displayed and traded. Everything within the Convocation grounds seemed to be bathed in a soft, gentle glow. Kerry had thought at first it was just early morning light slanting down on things, but as the day wore on, it didn't dissipate or change. Finally, she asked Season about it.

"It's the light of magic," Season said. "Sometimes you'll hear late afternoon, just a little before sunset, when the sun is at an angle and the light has a golden tinge, referred to as the 'magic hour.' And that's by civilians. They don't know how close they are to the truth, but somehow the truth has filtered down to them."

Kerry didn't understand. "But . . ." She couldn't even come up with the question.

Season got it, though. "It's all around us. This whole thing, the Convocation. Remember the desert outside here? Flat, dry, hot, empty? We are here, we're not an illusion. But to an outsider, we wouldn't be. It's magic. We are bathed in it here, suffused in it. Those pavilions, those chairs, those trailers . . . they weren't here two days ago, and they won't be here next week. Not in the sense that one typically thinks of as 'here.' The molecules that make them up will be returned to where they came from—around here, pretty much dirt, and maybe a few scrubby sagebrush bushes for texture."

"But I don't see a glow like that when I cast a spell," Kerry pressed.

"Because a spell is an isolated instance of magic," Season explained. "Transitory, only there for the moment. Here there's nothing isolated about it. It's as much a part of our environment as the air itself. It would be strange if there *wasn't* an optical manifestation of it."

Good enough for me, Kerry thought. *That explains why my cruddy jeans and T-shirts look so spiff, and Mother Blessing's nightmare wardrobe too. Probably why everyone's in such a good mood, too.* For her part, Kerry felt better than she had in ages—years, maybe. Not just physically, but emotionally. She felt like she was in the bosom of a large, extended family, surrounded by people who cared about her, even though in fact most of them had never met or heard about her. But everyone Season introduced her to greeted her happily. She had never been made so welcome anywhere in her life.

For the morning, she and Season had no particular schedule, no appointments to keep. They just wandered, taking in the sights and sounds. Kerry tried to estimate the size of the Convocation, or the attendance, but found that it was impossible. Sometimes she thought they were almost at the end of a row, but then they would go into a tent or a shop, and when they emerged the row would stretch out toward the horizon, the empty desert she thought she had glimpsed totally eclipsed by light and color and activity. Every now and then she got the feeling that things were changing right behind them—like if they went into one stall, the one they had just left would metamorphose into something entirely different, so that one could never experience the whole array.

An astonishing variety of blooming flowers edged the paths and filled in spaces between the tents and buildings, a carpet of reds, whites, oranges, pinks, yellows, violets, and greens. Considering what she knew the "real" landscape around her looked like, Kerry was especially delighted to see the displays of poppies and daisies, lupines and lilacs, sunflowers and sacred datura.

Only one thing nagged at her, keeping her happiness from being complete. She remembered how much Daniel had looked forward to his first Convocation. He had told her stories of past ones—like Season and her daughter, he'd never been but he was full of the tales that witches handed down to one another. She couldn't help wishing it was Daniel walking beside her now. Maybe even him and Season, both having learned that they weren't one another's real enemy. Daniel's large, warm hand enveloping hers, his ready smile, his clear gray eyes crinkling in the golden magic-light. That would have made this experience perfect.

That afternoon she and Season took part in a ritual with about a thousand other witches.

With no verbal communication of which Kerry was aware, no printed schedule or loudspeaker announcement or anything like that, everyone seemed to just filter toward a vast, empty, grassy meadow that she would have sworn hadn't been there before.

Kerry wore a simple white shift that she'd picked up in one of the shops, which she learned were "shops" only in name, since they accepted no payment for the merchandise they provided. Her feet were bare. On her head was a wreath of fresh spring flowers: greens, whites, pale yellows. Ribbons streamed down her back, entwining with her long, silken black hair. She had no makeup on, but she felt beautiful without it. Not that she had done more than glance into a mirror to make sure the wreath was on straight since she had arrived at the Convocation—the beauty she felt was of the spirit, not the flesh. It was a sense of peace, of belonging.

With Season at her side, and with hundreds of other witches joining them, she walked down a gentle slope toward the meadow, as if she just knew it was where she was supposed to be. Some of the witches spoke in hushed, almost reverent tones, but here the mood seemed different than it had up on the hill. This was a special place, a sacred place, and the sometimes rowdy, raucous good humor of the Convocation's public spaces was left behind. In its place was a more spiritual, but equally comfortable, atmosphere.

In the meadow, the witches formed naturally into a great circle. Three witches, two women and a man, stood at the center of the circle, gathered about an altar of upthrust stones that looked like it had been there for a thousand years. On the ancient altar were a spray of flowers and branches, a cauldron also filled with flowers, a fat red candle, a knife, and a censer. When all the witches were gathered—and Kerry didn't know how the ones at the center knew that no more were coming, but they seemed to—one of them lit incense in the censer, and then lit the candle. Flame leaped up from each, then settled to a steady glow.

One of the women at the front lifted the knife and held it in the smoke from the censer for a second. Her hair was waist length and silver, hanging in thick braids around her, and her skin, though lined, looked as fresh as a child's. She smiled out at the gathering, turning in a slow circle so everyone could see the knife. Then she put its point down into the cauldron and said, "I consecrate and cleanse this water, that it may be purified and fit to dwell within this circle of our love. In the name of the Goddess and the God, the Mother and the Father, I consecrate this water."

That said, she lifted the knife from the cauldron, and Kerry saw that its blade was wet. There was water in the cauldron, then, with the flowers inside it sticking out as if from a vase. The man, tall and dark, with a heavy brow and huge hands, stepped to the cauldron next, and dipped his fingers into the water. He turned to the north and dribbled some of the water in that direction. Then he dipped his hand again, and repeated the process to the east, south, and west.

Preparations finished, the third witch took her place at the altar. This one was younger than the others, her blond hair almost white in the sunshine. She put her hands in the flowers, both the ones laying across the altar and the ones in the cauldron, and said, "O great Goddess, you have thrown off the icy grip of winter and embraced the warmth of spring. Now is the greening, the rebirth, the renewal. All things begin again, life takes root in all ways, in the germination and sprouting of every seed, in each breeze that bears warmth on its shoulders, in each ray of sunlight that falls upon your earth."

All three of the witches at the altar joined hands, and as one, the witches in attendance did as well. Everyone in the crowd, at least a thousand strong, was connected to everyone else. The witches at the altar began to speak, and the ones in the audience said the words along with them. Even Kerry knew what to say, as if reading from an invisible script.

"We walk the earth in kinship, in friendship, not in dominance. We are one with the trees and flowers in the field, one with the rocks and hills and mountains, one with each drop of water in the oceans and each grain of sand in the deserts. We are one with all the creatures on, beneath, and above the earth and her oceans. We ask not permission to use the earth but to exist with the earth, in harmony and cooperation with the Goddess and all she represents. We pledge in return to adore and appreciate her clean skies, her fresh rivers, the green and abundant bounty of her skin."

Even as she spoke the words, holding Season's hand in her left and a stranger's in her right, feeling the power of the thousand flowing through her like an electric charge, Kerry thought she could see minuscule green sparks rising up from the candle like motes of pollen. They rose until they were above the crowd, above the depression of the meadow, above the level of the rest of the Convocation, up the short slope, and then they spread in every direction.

That's magic, she thought with a growing sense of awe. *That's our magic, going out to touch every spot on the Earth. Spreading out to protect the air and water, to cleanse, to purify.*

A few moments later, the candle's flame changed, and the greenish dust was dissipating. The witches released hands, and the ones at the altar spoke the words that broke the circle. Season gave Kerry's hand an extra squeeze, and the beatific smile on her face, Kerry guessed, probably matched her own. She could barely believe that she had been part of something like that, something that gave back to the planet from which she had taken so much. They had celebrated nature, and spring, and themselves, all at once. But their celebration had not been an empty gesture, simple praise or lip service. It had included specific and concrete action designed to improve the world they lived in, or at least to help it withstand the ravages of their own kind.

As she walked back up the hill in the company of her fellows, the glow of witch-light was accompanied by the inner glow of deep, lasting satisfaction.

This, she thought happily, *completely rules!*

14

That first full day ended in one of the many tents set up for dinner. If anything, the mood at the evening meal was even rowdier than the earlier ones—the tables were full, and someone at any given table seemed to know people at one of the others. The laughter was loud and long, the stories told hilarious and often bawdy. After the dishes were cleared away, people stayed in the tent, although not necessarily in their seats. Old friendships were re-established and new ones struck. Kerry was treated like one of the gang. In general, the atmosphere was of a holiday meal with close family members, except that it was the biggest family Kerry had ever dreamed of.

The second day was much like the first. This time she felt

more at ease, more familiar with her surroundings—ever-changing as they were—and a few times, she and Season split up to do different things. There was a lecture on growing herbs that Kerry wanted to attend, for instance, but Season wasn't that interested and said she had a business meeting that overlapped it. The Convocation wasn't just a fair and a cele-bration, it was a time of examining the past and planning for the future. This was the only area Kerry felt shut out of, but she figured that she was so new at the whole witch game that she wouldn't have much to offer that would be useful.

The whole thing was eye-opening. She had never imag-ined that witches came in such a vast assortment of shapes, sizes, colors, nationalities, and temperaments. Given her expe-rience with Season and Mother Blessing, she had assumed that there would be a lot more infighting and treachery than what she had encountered here so far. Her perception, born of hard experience, was that witches were constantly at war with each other, which didn't seem to be the case at all.

The infighting didn't happen until the third day.

When that morning broke, it felt just like the one before. The golden light of magic filled the air, and Kerry's spirits felt lighter than ever, as if her very soul had been tethered to the earth but had now been set free. She woke up soaring.

Season's demeanor that day was different, however.

From the minute she got up, it seemed there was a weight on her. Her smiles were forced and artificial. Even her pos-ture was a little slumped. She wore a conservative white blouse with black pants and boots and tied her hair back in a tight ponytail, a look that was a little formal and severe for her.

Kerry knew what the problem was, of course. Today was the Witches' Tribunal. Her case against Mother Blessing—or Mother Blessing's against Season—would be heard. She wasn't clear on which was the defendant and which the plaintiff. Then again, if it hadn't been for courtroom shows on TV, she wouldn't have known the difference anyway, her own life having been mercifully trial-free. She guessed it didn't much matter. The important thing was that Season would have her say, and justice would be meted out.

After breakfast she accompanied Season to the Tribunal— a vast open-air pavilion with several hundred seats set up in a configuration not unlike a TV courtroom's. They sat about halfway back and observed while several other cases came up on the docket. The Tribunal itself consisted of five witches, dour-faced, gray-haired eminences one and all, as opposed to the jovial group outside this pavilion. Season explained in hushed tones that it was deliberate—to sit on the Tribunal, one had to be a witch of considerable experience and wisdom, having attended at least three previous Convocations. Away from the Tribunal grounds, these justices might be as carefree as any other witch, but while they worked they kept serious demeanors to indicate the care with which they did the job and the respect they held for accusers and accused alike.

In this crowd, however, no one wore black robes, and that included the jurists of the Tribunal. They wore long, flowing robes, but two were of a deep forest green, one of darkest midnight blue, and two a rich wine color. The robe colors might have had some significance, but if so, Kerry wasn't told what it was.

The cases mostly involved matters that seemed minor to Kerry—the equivalent of small claims court or disputes over whose dog was using whose yard as a restroom. One male witch was accused of having counteracted the spell of a female for no reason except that he was angry because her dog had beat up his at a picnic. He claimed that her dog had been a vicious brute who should have been put down, but even so, that was not the reason he had counteracted her spell—it was because he had been asked to by the person her spell was directed at. Doing so, he declared, was perfectly legal under the witches' code of justice.

The judges agreed with his argument, but they still faulted him for not having communicated with her directly before countering her spell. Both witches were directed to do volunteer work in their community—nothing witchy about it, simply labor in the service of the people among whom they lived. All in all, Kerry decided, it was a lot like watching an extended episode of *Judge Judy*, except that the justices were less annoying and there were no commercial breaks.

By the time Season's case came up, however, she was having to stifle her yawns. Everything had been so orderly, so composed, that it was all a little dull. She knew that the dispute between Season and Mother Blessing was made of juicier stuff, and she guessed that many of the other spectators in the place were there to watch it unfold.

The justice at the far left of the bench, one of the two men, called Season Howe and Myrtle Blessing—one of the few times Kerry had ever heard her referred to as anything but Mother Blessing—to the front. Both women rose and advanced, though Mother Blessing's legs seemed to have gotten worse—she relied more heavily on the cane, and she had a noticeable limp, accompanied by several winces and even a groan or two. Kerry thought the whole thing way over-the-top theatrical, and couldn't believe she was laying it on so thick. Surely the justices would see through it.

But instead, the one in the center—the oldest, judging from normal, non-witchy standards, which Kerry understood to be meaningless in this instance—tossed her a look of profound and genuine sympathy. "I'm sorry to put you through this, Mother Blessing," she said. "And I trust we will resolve this matter swiftly and to everyone's satisfaction."

"That's all I'm hopin' for too," Mother Blessing said. Even the cornpone Southern accent had been intensified for the occasion. Mother Blessing was obviously going to play every card at her disposal, and then some.

"I'm sure that's the result all of us will work toward," Season said. She sounded intelligent and articulate. Kerry hoped that didn't work against her—the city slicker trying to take advantage of the down-home gal. Both parties to the action were directed to sit at the front of the gallery, between the bench and the spectators. Season took her seat primly, with her legs crossed and her hands folded in her lap, while Mother Blessing practically sprawled into hers.

The center jurist, the one wearing the dark blue robe, glanced at a piece of paper, as if reminding herself of the nature of the case, and then addressed Mother Blessing. *Or Myrtle,* Kerry thought with a private smile.

"Mother Blessing, we are here to consider an event that occurred in the year 1704, in the place known as Slocumb, Virginia. Were you present at that event?"

"Durn tootin'," Mother Blessing said, provoking a raucous laugh from the audience, if not from the justices.

"And would you tell us what you remember about that event, including specifically the role that Season Howe played in it?"

"Yes," Mother Blessing said, more sober now. "I will."

She spent the next half hour telling the Tribunal pretty much the same story Kerry had read in Daniel's journals, adding some of the details that Daniel had apparently not known but that she had mentioned to Kerry. There were even a couple that Kerry hadn't heard before. For instance, when she described how Season had gone berserk and started magically blasting townsfolk, including her husband, Winthrop Blessing, she mentioned that Season had specifically singled Winthrop out, shouting, "You'll never live to spread your lies about me!" at him as she reversed his own musket ball into his brain.

With the exception of those embellishments, however, it was the same story Kerry had heard before. When witchcraft was determined to be the cause of the deaths of the Flinders children, both of the town's witches were suspected. Mother Blessing cooperated with the investigation, while Season Howe flew into an unreasonable fury, answering even the most innocuous questions with violence and death. The more she raged, the more furious she became, feeding on her own anger in some sort of escalating feedback loop. Finally, Mother Blessing, to save her own life and the lives of her unborn sons, had taken refuge deep in the Swamp. Season had continued her rampage even after everyone in town was dead, burning each house and starting a fire that burned for months, feeding off the peat that grew in the Swamp.

By the time she had finished her tale, tears streamed down Mother Blessing's face, smearing her eyeliner into twin black rivers. "I didn't dare come out of the Swamp for a month, maybe more, your honors," she declared. "When I finally did, and went to look at the town where I had lived, where my husband had died, where my sons had been conceived, the ground was still hot to the touch. Nothin' grows on that soil to this day, and you'll never convince me that anything will. It's cursed land, blasted and scorched by the explosive temper of . . ."—here she lowered her gaze, as if she was afraid to look directly at Season, and ticked her head toward her foe instead—". . . of Season Howe."

Kerry glanced around the pavilion. Faces were serious,

reflective. Mother Blessing had told her story well, tossing in whatever theatrics she could to make sure it played to the room. People seemed to believe her. Kerry noticed a few spectators eyeing Season carefully, as if she might throw a murderous fit right here before the Tribunal.

"Is there anything else you would like to add?" one of the justices asked Mother Blessing.

"Only that both of my sons, blessed be their spirits, were later murdered by Season Howe for the crime of tryin' to find her and bring her to some kind of justice."

"Justice is why the Tribunal exists," another jurist pointed out. "It is not yours to deliver."

Mother Blessing sniffled and dabbed at her eyes with a formerly white handkerchief that had turned ash gray. "It's not so easy to tell a pair of grievin' boys that, your honor. Ones who never got the chance to know their daddy in this life."

"I'm sure that's true," the jurist replied.

"Season Howe," the justice in the center intoned. "You stand accused. How plead you?"

Season had sat quietly through Mother Blessing's entire monologue. Kerry thought it must have been difficult to resist rolling her eyes at some of the more obvious whoppers, or laughing out loud from time to time, but Season had managed. She maintained an air of dignity even as she turned in her seat to face the bench.

"I plead not guilty, your honor, and request the Tribunal's permission to state my case."

The justice nodded. "By all means," she said.

Season cleared her throat and began. "My daughter speaks the truth, up to a point," she said. "We did both live in Slocumb at that time. She did reside with her husband, Winthrop Blessing. What she didn't mention—what she apparently never mentions when she tells this tale—was that they had a first son, whom she named Darius. I had followed the tradition of giving my daughter a name from nature, but as you can see, that is but one of the many ways in which she chose to differentiate herself from me. When my former husband, Forest, heard about Darius, he came to Slocumb to meet his first grandchild. Forest was an evil witch, as I'm sure many of you will remember. Cruel, heartless, cold, and dedicated to dark pursuits."

There was a murmur of recognition and assent from the crowd—apparently Forest Howe's unpleasant reputation had not been forgotten.

"In Slocumb," Season continued, "Forest's influence over Myrtle grew quickly. I had tried to keep them separated from the time I first learned of Forest's true nature—sadly, only after Myrtle was born—but they were both adults now and I couldn't prevent them from being together. Myrtle, it turned out, was her father's daughter, much more than mine.

"Mother Blessing's version of events that followed is true again, up to a point. The widow Flinders did awaken to find her children brutally murdered. The townspeople did rouse the two of us, the two prominent witches in town—but not to question us. Instead, they wanted us both dead, right then and there, no questions asked. There had been earlier incidents, no doubt games Forest and Myrtle played, and the town had had enough.

"Both of us fought back," Season went on. "The townsfolk were prepared for resistance, and battle was joined. In the fight, the townspeople killed Forest and young Darius, and Myrtle simply became unhinged. From that point, everything she attributes to me was, in fact, her doing. She killed every living soul in town. She blasted the houses, ruined the land, started the fires. People from nearby towns saw the smoke and came to help, and Myrtle accused me, told them I was a witch—in itself, one of the most serious crimes with which this Tribunal has to contend. I ran, to save myself. Ran and hid. I had been injured in the battle, could barely escape with my life. But I left only after the town was razed by her magic. She claims to have run before the town was destroyed, yet she knows precisely the progression of events. How would she know? She never told a soul, including her other sons, Daniel and Abraham, about Darius and Forest. She didn't tell this Tribunal. But you all remember Forest. Do you recall any instance of him appearing after 1704? Do you know how he died, unless you've heard it from me? You certainly have never heard it from Myrtle, who has conveniently forgotten that she ever had a father."

She stopped then, regarded the audience impassively, and even let her gaze sweep across her daughter.

After a respectful period, the center justice spoke again. "Mother Blessing," she said. "You have now heard Season

Howe's rebuttal to your testimony. Do you have anything you wish to add?"

"Durn—I mean, I sure do, your honor," Mother Blessing replied, garnering another laugh. Not as big as the first one, though. By now, the crowd was caught up in the drama of the moment. "No, I did not mention the fact that Season Howe is my mother—a fact I try hard to forget every day of my life. I didn't mention my father, either, because he wasn't there when all this happened. I don't have the first clue how he died— she made sure that I never really got to know him. Just like my boys never got to know Winthrop. Almost seems like she has somethin' against fathers and sons, doesn't it? As for this 'Darius,' I reckon she made him up out of whole cloth. Go ahead and examine the records—you won't find the birth of any Darius Blessing ever reported."

"We have inspected the records, in consideration of this account," one of the jurists who hadn't yet spoken announced. "And it is true, there has never been any report of the birth or death of Darius Blessing."

Mother Blessing gave a satisfied nod at that pronouncement, and a ripple of talk rushed through the pavilion.

"Season Howe?" the middle justice asked, raising her voice to be heard over the crowd.

"I'm sure the lack of responsibility Myrtle demonstrates by not having properly reported the birth and death of her first son will not be construed as evidence of anything but that simple fact," Season said.

"Very well," the center jurist said. "We will deliberate."

They left Season and Mother Blessing sitting in the front of the room while the justices put their heads together and spoke in low tones. They had done the same with the day's other cases, but Kerry thought this one probably deserved a more careful and spirited debate than those simple ones.

After only a few minutes, however, they broke their huddle and addressed the crowd. "We have been unable to arrive at a conclusion," the eldest announced. "Both stories have the ring of truth to them, although clearly both cannot be true. If there is more evidence to be presented, the Tribunal would be willing to hear it."

Mother Blessing spoke up first. "I really don't know what more y'all could possibly need," she said. "It's plain as day that she's lyin'. Just look at her."

The audience reacted with a surprised chuckle at her audacity. Horrifyingly, Kerry was afraid her pronouncement might have the desired effect. She saw some of the audience, as well as the Tribunal, examining Season as if looking for a big red L to appear on her forehead.

When the laughter faded, Season took her turn to address the Tribunal. "Myrtle's argument doesn't seem particularly compelling to me," she said. "I'd like to suggest a more definitive approach. I hereby request a Viewing."

Kerry didn't know what a Viewing was, but she could tell by the universal gasp of astonishment that it was not standard everyday Tribunal procedure.

"That's highly irregular, Season," the center justice declared. "Not without precedent, but unusual to say the least."

"I appreciate that," Season said.

"Not only is it unusual," the justice went on, "but I'm not certain we can accommodate the request. You are aware of the level of power and proficiency required for a Viewing?"

"I am," Season affirmed.

"You could not possibly accomplish it on your own," the justice said. "Mother Blessing could legitimately be a party to it, but the Tribunal can't force her to merge her power with yours, and given the circumstances—"

"Uh-uh. No way," Mother Blessing interrupted. "I ain't lettin' her get inside of me."

"As I suspected," the justice said. "The Tribunal itself cannot be a party to such an action, since we have to be free to see and interpret for ourselves. Unless you have some other suggestion—"

"I do," Season said, also interrupting. She turned her head, and her gaze caught Kerry's, bored into her. "I request that the Tribunal allow Kerry Profitt to participate."

15

Kerry felt her cheeks crimson as every eye in the pavilion fell on her. "Me?" she asked, fully aware that it was a cliché even as she said it. Surely there was no other Kerry Profitt around. And if there had been, just as surely Season would have mentioned the coincidence to her.

So the only out was if she had misheard altogether.

Since Season's gaze was fixed on her, and a slight smile curved her red lips, she didn't think that was the case. Kerry couldn't hear her voice over the buzz in the pavilion, but the word on her mouth was unmistakable. "You."

Kerry realized that her left hand was stupidly pointing at her own chest. "But—but I—" she stammered.

"Kerry Profitt," the center justice said, looking at Kerry as if she had only just crawled out from under something unsavory. The audience fell silent as she spoke. "She is . . . quite inexperienced, isn't she?"

"Maybe not as inexperienced as you might think," Season said.

"She does look very young," the male jurist on the end observed.

"She is young," Season admitted. "So were we all, once."

"A very good point."

Finally, Mother Blessing was able to do something with her mouth other than sit there with it hanging open. "I don't . . . I don't think that girl ought to be allowed to have anything to do with this," she declared.

"And why not, Mother Blessing?" one of the justices inquired.

"Because . . ." Kerry could see her trying to come up with some legitimate objection. "Because I taught her. I knew her before Season ever did."

"Well, then," the center justice noted, "you should be assured of her objectivity, isn't that right?"

Mother Blessing had opened her mouth and set her own trap. Kerry knew her well enough to recognize the look that crossed her face—the realization that she wasn't going to get her own way this time.

"All right," she said finally. "Let her try. We'll see if she has the stuff to pull it off."

The justices seemed satisfied by that. "Kerry Profitt," the

eldest said, looking right at her. "Please approach the Tribunal."

As Kerry stood and made her way down her row of seats, various witches—some she had met over the past couple of days, others she had not—offered whispered encouragement. She was glad. Their confidence in her helped fight off the rubber knees, the dry throat, the quavering hands, as she stood before the bench.

"I'm Kerry Profitt."

"Do you know Season Howe?" the middle justice asked.

"I do."

"And do you know Mother Blessing?"

"Yes, I do."

"And do you have reason to believe one of them more than the other, in this case?"

"Definitely," Kerry said.

"Season Howe has asked for your assistance with a Viewing. It won't be easy. It will be a strain on you, physically, mentally, and emotionally. Your power will be linked with Season's. The two of you will be allied, for the duration of the Viewing, more closely than most people ever are with anyone—right down to the center of your being. This is necessary, however, because no witch lives who can manifest a Viewing by herself. Two very powerful witches can do it, three or more is better. Are you willing to participate in the way that I've described?"

Kerry swallowed. She still couldn't quite believe that Season had selected her for this. There must have been dozens of witches in this pavilion alone who were better suited for it.

But she asked for me.

"I am."

"And are you prepared to let this Tribunal see whatever there is to see, without trying to warp or alter the reality we are being shown?"

She hadn't even known she could alter any reality at all. But then, she still wasn't really clear on what the Viewing entailed. "I am."

"Very well," the jurist said. "This Tribunal calls for a Viewing."

Another buzz from the audience. Apparently a Viewing was a big deal, not something they experienced every day, or maybe even every Convocation. Kerry had the sense of having been swept up in something huge.

Season held out her hand to Kerry, who took it. Season gave hers a squeeze. "You'll be fine," she said quietly. "Don't worry about a thing."

"Just let me know what to do," Kerry said. "I'll give it my best shot."

"Just follow my lead," Season said. "We won't be alone for long."

Kerry wondered what she meant by that but didn't get a chance to ask her. Season took Kerry's other hand and held both tightly. She closed her eyes. Kerry did the same, but not before catching a glimpse of Mother Blessing watching them with a scowl, arms crossed over her expansive bosom. She looked like she wished they were both dead, which she no doubt did, having tried numerous times to achieve exactly that result.

As soon as Kerry's eyes were closed, though, she felt something like a powerful electrical current running through her hands and up her arms. The charge traveled into her shoulders, across her back, then down her spine, through her body, down her legs. She was aware of the fine hairs on her arms and legs standing on end, aware of the air brushing against her skin, aware of every inch of fabric that covered her and the weight of her hair against her back. The smells of the pavilion—the odors of people, flowers, soaps, perfumes, sweat, dirt, even the wood of the chairs—filled her senses. She thought she could hear the breathing and the beating heart of everyone in the place.

But then all those things fell away, as if she had shot up into the air and left everything behind. The sounds were replaced by a rushing noise, the smells by a coppery, electrical scent, and the sensations against her skin vanished completely, as if she had stepped out of her own body.

She was tempted to open her eyes and see what was going on. But Season had said to follow her lead, so she would not open her eyes until she was told to.

As it turned out, she didn't have to. Another moment of darkness passed. A dizzying feeling of vertigo struck her, a wave of nausea that was gone as quickly as it had come. Then her eyes were open of their own volition, and her vision filled with greens, every shade of green: the pale, almost yellow color of new leaves; the dark bluish tinge of fir trees by moonlight;

the rich velvet of freshly cut grass, and everything in between. Gradually, shapes delineated themselves in the field of greens, and she realized she was looking at the Great Dismal Swamp, with its tall trees, its thick, almost impenetrable layers of underbrush, its stagnant pools, its hanging mosses.

More disconcerting still was the fact that *through* the Swamp she could see the Tribunal pavilion. It was as if she was looking into a window at night, with the light on the other side— one level of view showed the Swamp, but another one showed where her body stood, hands clasped with Season's. She could even turn her head and take in the bench, Mother Blessing, the audience, without affecting her view of the Swamp. The whole thing made her dizzy again.

When the eldest justice spoke, her voice was muffled as if by distance, but Kerry could still make out the words. For the first time she realized that the people attending the Tribunal could see what she was seeing—at least they could see the Swamp part of it. This, then, was the Viewing—somehow, she and Season were projecting an image of the Swamp for them.

"You are showing us Slocumb, Virginia, on October twentieth of the year 1704?"

"We are." Season's voice, sounding closer than the justice's.

The image seemed still, static, and Kerry wondered how it could possibly be of any use to the Tribunal. But almost as soon as she thought it, as if in response, there was motion—a figure breaking through the trees, approaching them. A man. He was dressed in modern clothing, not the garb of the eighteenth century. A clean white shirt, sleeves rolled up over tanned forearms. Faded jeans. Brown hair swept away from his forehead. Gray eyes that twinkled as if he had just thought of a private joke. A smile that carved crags in his cheeks.

Daniel!

"Hello, Kerry," he said as he neared them. "It's so good to see you, even . . . even this way."

"I—I don't quite know what to say," Kerry confessed, her heart fluttering against her ribs like a bird in a delicate cage. "You're . . ."

He chuckled. "A sight for sore eyes? Dead? Both?"

In the pavilion, Season released Kerry's hands.

In the Swamp, Daniel took them, lifted one to his lips, pressed it there. Then he let it go and encircled Kerry with his arms. She moved into the hug, and she felt—really felt!—his body, the familiar solidity of his muscular form, the warmth. She could see Season standing beside her, watching with a happy smile.

"This is . . . kind of overwhelming, Daniel," she said. "I mean, I'm thrilled to see you, but . . ."

"I understand," Daniel said sympathetically. "It's not what you were expecting. The Viewing requires a Guide, and Season asked me if I would fill that role. Knowing I would get to see you, I happily agreed. And since my passing, I've come to learn the truth about Slocumb, so I'm happy to share that truth here."

Kerry risked a glance around the pavilion. Daniel wasn't there, so he existed only in the reality represented by the Swamp.

"I guess I just don't get how all this stuff works," she admitted.

"No one expects you to yet. You will, in time. Just remember, death is a passage, not a destination."

"So you've told me," she said with a cheerful giggle. The realization that she was genuinely talking to Daniel filled her with a joy she could barely contain.

It took Season to remind her of the serious nature of their activity. "We should get to work," she said firmly.

"Right," Daniel agreed. He gestured behind Kerry, and she turned around.

As she did, the view shifted, and she knew the whole Tribunal audience was seeing what she did. Behind her stood the village of Slocumb as it had on that cold October day. A bitter wind rustled the trees and a rare dusting of snow powdered the ground and the rooftops. The houses were mostly wood-framed, although a few were built of stone or brick. Every one had a prominent chimney, and smoke leaked from most of those. Roofs were steeply pitched and interrupted by gables. Most of the houses were shallow, Kerry guessed only a single room deep.

Daniel led the way toward the village, Kerry and Season following right behind. None of them spoke now, and though Kerry thought she should be able to hear the sound of their feet crunching the frozen earth, their progress was silent. All she heard was the rush of the wind in the trees.

And then the quiet was split by a shattering scream from an open window of the nearest house.

The scene shifted, and they were inside that house. A woman—Kerry knew her at once as the widow Flinders—stared into her children's room, her hands clutching her cheeks in horror. Inside the room was a scene that Kerry didn't want to see. She knew what was there, had already caught a glimpse of blood, shockingly red on the hardwood floor. Kerry tried to keep her gaze riveted on the widow. As awful as the woman's horrified pose was, it wasn't as bad as what was inside the room. Her three children brutally savaged, torn apart with animal fury. The widow Flinders screamed again and ran through the room to the open window, as if whoever was responsible might still be standing outside.

The widow screamed again, louder. In the snow outside were the tracks of a large canine. A wolf, Kerry thought. But the children's room was on the second floor of the house, the window a gabled one set into the roof. How could a wolf have climbed up to that room to do this work?

The widow's screams roused the town. Soon people came running from every direction. Mostly men, many carrying weapons or tools that could be pressed into such service—axes, hoes, muskets. They called to her, and when she couldn't answer, having succumbed to great, wracking sobs and fallen into a heap on her floor, some of them rushed into her house.

Before Kerry had to look at the carnage again, the scene shifted once more. She had the sense that this was Daniel's doing, that his role as Guide was to lead them around, highlighting the most significant events for the benefit of the

Tribunal. Now they were outside a house that Kerry knew was Mother Blessing's. Some of the townsfolk, led by a man who had to be Parson Coopersmith, rapped on the door of that house. They looked apprehensive, their weapons bristling toward the door as if they could hide behind them.

Mother Blessing opened the door, looking much as Kerry knew her. The wind fluttered her white cotton nightdress around her. She was a little younger, a little smaller than she was now, but still she dwarfed the man—Winthrop Blessing, no doubt—who tried to crowd into the doorway beside her. There was a brief, clearly antagonistic exchange between the Blessings and the parson, following which she closed the door. Barely a second later—Kerry understood that Daniel was compressing events to a certain degree—she reappeared at the door, this time dressed in a dark, high-collared dress and heavy black shoes. As soon as she stepped out, Parson Coopersmith grabbed one of her arms, and a burly man took hold of the other. Weapons were pointed at her. Winthrop looked on in horror as his wife was led away. Another man shoved Winthrop aside—a man with a ragged, wild look, an unkempt beard, and an infant in his arms. That was Forest Howe, Kerry knew. With young Darius. Forest stalked behind the group taking Mother Blessing away, shouting at them. Kerry was glad she couldn't hear the words.

Another whirlwind shift, and a similar scene played out at Season Howe's house. Season came out fully dressed, with a cap over her blond hair and a brown dress belted around her slender waist. As with Mother Blessing, she was taken captive immediately upon her emergence.

Shift again. Slocumb's town square. Witches being hauled in from two directions. Mother Blessing scowling, tugging, trying to free herself, while Season cooperated, chatting almost casually with those who led her.

Mother Blessing tore an arm free from her captors and pointed accusingly at Season. Parson Coopersmith flinched from her, and apparently that simple action ignited her fury. Now Daniel let them hear her words, screamed in rage. "So you believe that I am a witch, Parson? I'll show you what a witch can do! You should be glad I have suffered you for so long!"

Parson Coopersmith was almost blubbering as he replied. "M—Mother Blessing, there is no need f—for—"

But she cut him off with a simple gesture and a magical blast that Kerry had seen before. *"Hastamel!"* Mother Blessing shouted. A burst of energy expelled from her hands and struck Parson Coopersmith in the center of the chest, rolling through him like a cannonball.

The square was still for a moment, as bits of the parson pattered down on the cobblestones like a heavy rain. Then the townspeople turned on both Season and Mother Blessing, as if they had been equally responsible for the clergyman's demise. A pitchfork's tines drove into Season's ribs before she could even react. Musket balls flew. Axes were swung. Season defended herself magically, even as blood gushed from her initial wound. She drew back to a more defensible position, with the chimney of a nearby house at her back.

Mother Blessing, meanwhile, stood her ground in the center of the square, hurling spells in every direction. Bits of the parson still clung to her cheeks and dress. The townsfolk reacted in kind—trying to shoot her from a distance, prying cobblestones up from the square and throwing them at her. Forest and Darius were spotted at the edge of things, Forest tossing out spells of his own, and the attack was expanded to include him. A musket ball slammed into his shoulder, a cobblestone tore a gash in his forehead, and then he and the child both went down under a mob of townspeople wielding flashing blades and heavy objects. Mother Blessing saw this happen, and her fury visibly grew, her cheeks purpling, her mouth working in incoherent rage.

Season abandoned her position by the chimney and tried to approach Mother Blessing. Her posture and expression were consoling, as if she were trying to calm the other witch. But Mother Blessing wanted none of it, and she drove Season back with wave after wave of magical attacks that Season, injured and weakened, could barely withstand.

Kerry could see the intensity of Mother Blessing's frenzy spiraling out of control. She no longer cared where she aimed her attacks—Kerry wasn't sure she could even see anymore, or if she had been blinded by her own furor. Magical energy swirled around her in a kind of tornado that echoed what must have been going through her twisted mind. The power of her assault tore bricks from houses, ripped boards from their walls and sent them sailing into the Swamp, yanked shingles from their roofs. The dead in the square outnumbered the living now, and not even the people hiding in their own homes were safe from the onslaught.

Kerry looked away from the incredible scene and toward the Tribunal, where she saw faces in shock, aghast at what they were observing. It was obvious to everyone now, Kerry was sure, whose version of the day's events was more accurate.

And while she watched, unable to move or speak on that plane of reality, unable to do anything to intercede, she saw Mother Blessing leave her seat. Arms reached out to stop her but she deftly evaded them. She held something in her right hand—it took Kerry a moment to recognize it as a knife—and she raised it high as she lunged at Season.

Kerry felt the cold steel slicing into Season's breast as surely as if it had been her Mother Blessing had stabbed, felt the shock and pain as the knife's keen blade drove into Season's heart.

Connected to Season, she knew every bit of Season's agony as the life ebbed out of her.

16

In Slocumb the Season who stood with Kerry and Daniel opened her mouth in a surprised-looking O shape. A red spot blossomed on her white blouse, spreading like a rose opening its petals, and then a single drop trailed down the outside of the blouse.

In the Tribunal pavilion, Season made a small whimpering sound. Her eyes rolled back in her head and she collapsed to the floor as if all her muscles had failed her at once.

Kerry couldn't catch her breath. "She stabbed you," she said, but it came out as little more than a squeak.

"I know," Slocumb's Season said, more calmly but still with an edge of worry. She raised a hand to her blouse, touched her chest. The hand came away bloody.

"Season," Daniel said urgently, reaching for her.

"It's okay, Daniel," she assured him.

Kerry had been astonished by many things over the past few days—*make that several months,* she mentally amended—but few things surprised her like the sight of Daniel embracing Season and then drawing away with her blood staining his own crisp shirt. "I am sorry," he said. "For so much."

"You did what you believed was right," she assured him. "No one could expect more than that."

He glanced toward his mother, who in Slocumb was directing her power against what was left of the small town. Houses had been torn apart as if by hurricane winds. Most of the buildings were ablaze now. Nothing living still moved, as far as Kerry could see. "I was . . . I was wrong. We all were."

Season winced—she was still upright in this reality, but the pain she felt was evident. "Now you know. Now everybody does."

Kerry's own discomfort had lessened, becoming a deep, persistent ache instead of the sharp pain it had been at first. She guessed that she had felt it because she and Season were linked, but then as Season faded in the real world—at least, what she perceived as the real world—that connection was broken and the agony became less distinct.

But was Season dead, in that world? And if so, what did that mean for Kerry? Would she be able to get back there?

In that world Kerry could see that the other witches in the audience at the Tribunal had restrained Mother Blessing, wrenching the knife from her grasp and hauling her away from Season's fallen body. On that plane Kerry could only stand there watching Season bleed on the ground. Some witches had gathered around her body and were performing healing spells, and one of them helped move Kerry out of the way.

"Are you . . . are you dying, Season? That knife couldn't really hurt you, could it?" Kerry remembered Mother Blessing firing four bullets into Season's chest, and Season spitting them out into her hand.

"It's within the grounds of the Convocation," Season explained. "It's as infused with magic as everything else there. I'm afraid it was a very effective attack."

"But . . . how effective?" Kerry demanded. "You can't . . ."

Even as she spoke she could see the witches in the pavilion pulling back away from Season's lifeless form. One of them brought out a length of white linen from somewhere and laid it reverently over Season's body.

Once again Kerry's moorings had been yanked away from her. The deaths of her parents, then Daniel, now Season—it seemed that every time she became attached to someone, that someone was taken away. She didn't want to make Season's death be all about her, but it was a disturbing reality just the same.

Then she felt Daniel's comforting hand on her shoulders. "A passage, Kerry," he reminded her. "Not a destination."

"I'm standing here talking to you, right?" Season said.

"Yes, but . . . I'm confused," Kerry complained. Behind

them Mother Blessing's Slocumb rampage continued, but no one was watching it—the witch was just as alone now as she had been on that fateful day.

"And you have every right to be." Season rubbed her arm, and with her and Daniel consoling Kerry, she realized she felt almost okay about it. "Life is a wonderful thing, Kerry," Season went on. "And you should embrace it every day. You should look at each new dawn as another opportunity, another promise of hope and love and miracles, and you should look at the stars at night the same way. But life—the kind of life you're thinking about—doesn't last forever. For anyone. Not even witches."

"She's right," Daniel added. "Which is why you need to make the most of every minute you do have."

"Do you understand how incredibly powerful you are, Kerry?" Season asked her. "Not one witch in a hundred could have worked with me to pull off a Viewing. But I had every faith in you, and you pulled it off. You've accomplished every task I've ever put before you. Now I'm asking you to do one more thing."

"What?"

"Go back into your world. Be the best witch you can be, and the best person you can be. Put your abilities to work in the service of something good, something lasting and true. I don't know what that should be, but you'll find it if you look."

"That's all?"

Season and Daniel both laughed. "A lot of people don't

seem to be able to do that much," Daniel said. "If you can, you're ahead of the game. But I know you will."

"But . . . but I'll miss you guys so much," Kerry said. "Both of you are the most—"

"We'll be there when you need us, Kerry," Season interrupted.

"And you've been to this plane now," Daniel put in. "You can come back, you know. Drop in from time to time. We'd love to see you, and I know Rebecca, Josh, and Mace would as well. Your parents, too."

The awful reality of Rebecca's death struck Kerry with sickening certainty. Her head spun with the ideas and possibilities they were laying before her. "I guess I still have a whole lot to learn about this stuff."

"You do indeed," Season agreed. "And you can't do that here. You need to go back now."

Kerry glanced into the Tribunal pavilion. Season's body was being taken out, elevated over the shoulders of those carrying her. She could see tears there, but also smiles and laughter. She thought they were remembering Season as she had been, sparkling, full of life and good cheer.

"Go," Daniel urged. "Everything will be fine."

Kerry looked at them both, not wanting to leave them behind, but knowing she had to.

She closed her eyes and centered herself. Willed herself to feel the power that surged inside her.

A sharp drop, a moment's vertigo . . .

And then she was back in the pavilion, with its million aromas, its crush of people, its voices.

Its life.

"Welcome back, Kerry Profitt." That was the center jurist, the eldest one, smiling at her from the bench. "You performed admirably."

"But . . . Season . . ."

"Has moved on," the jurist confirmed, nodding.

Kerry looked around for Mother Blessing. As if guessing who she sought, the male justice on the end said, "She has been taken into custody. Thanks to you, Season, and Daniel, this Tribunal now knows the truth about what happened in Slocumb, and that the blame for all those deaths, all that destruction, rests with Myrtle Blessing. Further, we know of the crimes Myrtle Blessing has committed to cover that one up—the sacrifices of her sons and the many more deaths, over the intervening years, for which she is responsible. And, of course, her murder of Season Howe, right here in our own presence. She will be held accountable for all these crimes."

"What's going to happen to her?" Kerry wanted to know.

The justices looked at each other, as if not sure they wanted to tell her. Finally, the eldest spoke up. "She has committed crimes of the most grievous nature. She has shown no remorse, given no indication that she is willing to stop her criminal actions. She will be stripped of her power." The jurist paused for a second, then added, "All of it."

Kerry considered that for a moment, tried to imagine what

it would mean. Mother Blessing unable to manipulate others, manipulate the very earth to do her bidding? She would be—

Wait a minute, Kerry thought, the true meaning of the justice's words becoming clear to her. "But she's hundreds of years old!"

The senior jurist nodded. Kerry thought maybe there was the briefest glimmer of a smile on her face. Just for a split second. "No one said she would enjoy the process."

Kerry stood before the bench, speechless for a moment, horrified at the possibility. Before she could fully compose her thoughts, the justice banged three times on the bench with the palm of her hand. "I declare this Witches' Tribunal adjourned until tomorrow!" she shouted. "And I further declare that it's time for dinner!"

This declaration was greeted by a loud whoop of approval from the crowd. Kerry started for the nearest exit but was caught by a few of the audience members, who offered congratulations and support. Each one held her hands or hugged her, and then more came over, and still more, and then there was a mob around her, and more hugs, and more, and more, and more.

And that was just the beginning of the fun.

17

Kerry had gone inside the little caravan to change clothes for dinner and the evening's celebration, and to grab a few quiet moments to herself after the drama of the Tribunal and its raucous aftermath. At one point she caught a glimpse of Season's bed and then looked around expectantly, remembering even as she did that the trailer would be empty. She didn't quite know how to react for a minute. She had been with Season every day since Christmas Eve, and even before that she couldn't recall a day in which Season hadn't been on her mind from waking until sleep finally captured her again. Suddenly all that was over, and Season wouldn't be greeting her as faithfully as the sun and stars did anymore.

Not only that, but the sun would never set again on Daniel

Blessing, or Rebecca Levine, or Mace Winston, or Josh Quinn. She had lost so much—they all had, really. Kerry was becoming convinced that what Daniel and Season had insisted was true: Death was just a passage to another level of existence, and not necessarily something to be mourned. But that didn't keep her from mourning her friends just the same. She figured that ultimately none of them would regret the price they had paid, since the end result was keeping Mother Blessing from continuing her destructive rampage across the land. Certainly plenty of innocents had already fallen victim to her misguided quest, but now at least no more would have to worry about that.

So Kerry tried to smile and greet the evening with the cheerful outlook Season would have wanted her to have. She put on a fresh, pale green frock, slipped sandals on her feet—both things one of the "shopkeepers" had insisted on giving her after the Tribunal was over—and went outside to dinner.

The first morning she had entered the meal tent feeling like a stranger, grateful that she had Season to cling to.

This time, though, she was hailed by at least a dozen people as soon as she had filled her tray. Hands full, she smiled and nodded to several and then sat down next to Tamsinn, a young woman from Pensacola she had met the evening before. Tamsinn was blithesome, with close-cropped purple hair and a ready smile. She greeted Kerry with a grin and a squeeze.

"Are you okay?" she asked. "I know this afternoon was rough on you."

"I think so," Kerry answered, as honestly as she could. "I mean, I'm sure I have a way to go before I'm really back to normal, whatever that is. But I'm not as wrecked as I would have thought either."

"That's good," Tamsinn said. She took a sip of her herbal tea and squinted at Kerry through the steam. "I know this whole deal can seem all huge and complicated when it's new."

"Yeah," Kerry agreed. "I'm definitely still at that stage."

"It'll go by fast," Tamsinn assured her. "Seems like I was there just the other day."

"How long has it been for you?"

Tamsinn scrunched her face up while she did the math in her head. "I guess sixty-two years," she said finally.

Kerry was stunned, although she knew she shouldn't have been. She would have sworn Tamsinn was no more than a year or two older than her, if that. She had learned plenty of times that among the community of witches one couldn't guess age based on appearance. But she wondered, not for the first time, when she would reach the peak of her power, and where she would "freeze," in terms of appearance, as witches did.

"If there's anything you need, Kerry, any questions you have or anything like that, you just let me know, okay? I'll be happy to help. Me and about a thousand other witches, or more. We're here to help guide you, to teach you what we can, and to help you figure out what you're about."

"Thanks, Tamsinn," Kerry said. "That means a lot to me."

Both women resumed eating then, unable to resist the

allure of the excellent meal. After dinner there would be a celebration, and then tomorrow, one more day of Convocation. There would be another day of Tribunal tomorrow as well, but she couldn't bring herself to go through that again. She had a feeling that she would cut out early tomorrow, go looking for Brandy and Scott. She needed to tell them about Rebecca, in case they didn't already know. And she found that she missed them a lot.

But before that, she had to finish her dinner.

And then there would be a party to remember.

Kerry lifted a forkful of fresh vegetables and tried to look at every spot in the tent, every face, every outfit, burning it all into her mind.

After all, five hundred years was a long time to wait until the next time.

She found Brandy and Scott at the While-a-Way Motel in Klamath Falls, Oregon, in a room on the second floor. A Harley Davidson convention seemed to have taken over the first, or at least the parking lot and swimming pool area. That didn't matter to Kerry—it wasn't hot enough for swimming yet anyway. The parking lot thing was a little more problematic, but she found street parking for the Raider and hiked in.

Scott threw the door open at her knock and dragged her inside, wrapped in his arms. Brandy joined him, and the three of them held each other for minutes before anyone was willing to break the hug. Kerry had always loved hugging, but her ribs were still a little sore after the lovefest that the last day and night of the Convocation had turned out to be. She had skipped the second day of the Tribunal in favor of trying to get acquainted with as many of her fellow witches as possible.

Finally, she was able to sit down on one of the beds. Brandy claimed the other, and Scott rolled over a wheeled chair from the little dining table. The room was motel basic, adequate for their needs but not much more than that. Kerry noted with a private grin that only one bed seemed to have been slept in. "So?" Scott began while she looked around. "We want to hear everything."

"So do I," Kerry replied. "But first, I should tell you about Rebecca. She's gone—Mother Blessing got her, as we feared. I don't suppose you found her body?"

Their faces fell instantly, so dramatically that they really didn't need to say any more. Brandy did anyway. "We looked all over Santa Cruz for two days, called every hospital up and down the coast, called the morgues, bugged the cops until I thought they'd arrest us. She never turned up. At this point, I have to say I don't think she's going to."

"I'm sorry, Kerry," Scott added. "I know what she meant to you. To all of us, really."

Even though she had already known, talking about their friend felt like a shaft in the heart for Kerry, but she remembered what Daniel and Season had told her. *Just a passage.* She would have to explain that to Brandy and Scott if she could, and she hoped they would understand it without the visual aid that she'd had.

"I'm sorry too," Kerry said, leaving it there for the moment. "Season's dead, too. Mother Blessing killed her at the Convocation. It was awful. But Mother Blessing is being . . . held accountable, finally. For everything she's done. Slocumb, Daniel and Abraham, us. Everything."

"So . . . it's all over?" Scott asked, his voice tinged with excitement. Kerry couldn't tell if he was pleased, or maybe a little disappointed, that their long adventure was coming to a close.

"That part of it's over," she confirmed. "There's no more struggle between Season and Mother Blessing. No more looking over our shoulders, wondering who's coming for us next. We can finally relax, I guess."

"There's another part?" Brandy pressed. "What's left?"

"The part where I really am a witch now," Kerry said. "And remaining one, and working to develop my abilities."

She watched their faces carefully when she told them. Brandy's looked tentative, as if she was withholding judgment on Kerry's future plans. But Scott grinned like some kind of madman. "That's great!" he enthused. "I think you'll be such a good witch. Does that sound stupid? Kerry the good witch?"

"A little," Kerry said. "But I get what you mean, and thanks."

"I guess we should tell her our plans, too," Brandy said, leaning over to tap Scott's shoulder.

"I guess so," he agreed.

"'Our'? You guys have 'our' plans?"

"Well, we still have plenty of school to get through," Scott said. "Maybe even grad school, who knows? But the tentative plan is, as soon as we graduate, we get married. And then, as soon as we can, we start working on a family."

"I guess we're kind of used to having a lot of people around," Brandy said. "And a lot of excitement."

"And of course, Aunt Kerry is definitely a part of whatever family plans we make," Scott added.

Kerry laughed. "I'm an aunt already? The graduating part hasn't even happened yet."

"Well, when it does," Brandy clarified with a laugh. Kerry was thrilled to see the two of them looking so happy. Every time they glanced at each other, their gazes held. *They are definitely in love,* she thought.

Nothing wrong with that.

Kerry Profitt's diary, March 24

They kept telling me that death is a passage, and okay, I can buy that.

What they didn't say is that there are plenty of other passages too. Scott and Brandy, starting a family? Scott and Brandy sitting in one room speaking civilly to each other would have been a lot to ask four months ago. I don't know if they'll really do it—who ever knows what's going to happen next week or next month, let alone two years from now? There are a lot of passages ahead for them, and maybe they'll weather them together. Maybe not. They'll be okay either way.

Maybe that's what Daniel and Season have left me with. I'm going to be fine. Scott and Brandy too. Things work out if you let them, if you work at them, if you help them along. And if you open your eyes and your mind and your heart to whatever each day brings. Sounds like something out of one of Brandy's pop psychology books, but there it is.

Anyway, I hope they do start a family, because it's been a while since I've really had one I could call my own. Now I'll have two—theirs, and the family of witches. The members of the Convocation took me in, embraced me, really made me feel that I was welcome there, wanted there even without being under Season's wing.

Of course, it's a long time until the next Convocation. There's a movement under way to hold them more often, maybe every hundred years instead of every five hundred. Easier to keep track of old friends, and new ones, that way. I'm voting in favor of it.

After the Tribunal, and the celebration that followed, I made my way back to our trailer, a little sad that Season wasn't in it with me but also happy, happier than I can remember being, oh, pretty much ever. Because there was a new sensation I was carrying around with me, and it wasn't the love of any particular individual, I realized, and it wasn't even my new understanding of my own power.

It was peace.

That's all. That simple.

I don't know what Scott and Brandy's future holds, and

I don't know what mine does. I'm the new witch on the block, the new pawn in a very, very old game. Chaos and entropy on one side, order on the other.

But that's the future. That's tomorrow, and all the tomorrows after that.

For now, for tonight, I cling to peace.

And that's all I really need.

More later.

K.

Read how it all began for Kerry in

VOL. 1

Kerry Profitt's diary, August 11

Once again I woke up screaming. Drenched in sweat, wet sheets tangled around my legs as if I'd been flailing them for hours. Brandy even came into our room and told me she could tell the instant I snapped out of it. My mouth was open like a gasping fish, she said, and then it closed, and my eyes opened. And I had let out a real ear-piercer, because, after all, there was this face in front of me, looking at me like I was some kind of sideshow freak.

Which, you know, if the shoe fits . . .

When my heart stopped trying to tear through my rib cage, and I could breathe again, she asked me what I'd been dreaming about. Hell if I know, I told her. Whenever I wake up, I can never remember anything more than an overpowering sense of dread. Doom on wheels.

Maybe it's the weird hours I've been keeping. I worked till eleven last night, same as the night before, but had the breakfast-and-lunch shift for three days before that. Today it's the late shift again, so I slept in probably longer than I should have. My head is throbbing so hard I can barely see the computer screen, and who knows if I'll be able to read this later?

But that's why Einstein invented ibuprofen, right? And spell check. And Scott's brewing fresh coffee. Nectar of the gods.

More later.

K.

*S*he couldn't see the ocean from where she stood on a grease-caked cement step just outside the kitchen's back door. A row of bungalows—identical dark boxes, some with glowing windows—blocked her view. She could hear the water, though—the steady, dull thunder of the surf reminding her that it was close, at the edge of both the Seaside Resort and the continent. And she could smell it, a sharp tang that battled for supremacy over the smells of steak, seafood, and smoke that blew out from the kitchen. Towering above the bungalows, underlit by the resort's floodlights, incredibly tall palm trees swayed on their skinny trunks in the evening breeze, looking like skyrocket bursts frozen in time at the ends of their own contrails. A sliver of crescent moon dangled above them, high and distant.

Kerry Profitt was a daughter of the Great Plains, born and raised near the confluence of two great rivers in Cairo, Illinois. But the Mississippi and Ohio, powerful as they were, had nothing on the Pacific Ocean. The ocean was magical to her, its depths and mysteries were boundless, its call irresistible. She had made a point, since hitting La Jolla, California, for her summer job, of keeping it in sight whenever possible. Bad for the skin, all that sun and salt air, and she, with her complexion like fresh snow ("whitest white girl I've ever seen" was what Brandy said) knew better. But she couldn't deny the ocean's magnetic pull.

Lost in thought, she didn't see the shadowed figure slip into the alley, didn't know she wasn't alone until the voice startled her. "Hey, Kerr, where is it the swallows go back to?"

Startled, she managed to keep her cool, and she smiled when she recognized the voice. She knew it belonged to Josh Quinn, one of her housemates, but it took her a moment to refocus her gaze and pick him out in the dark alley. His skin was every bit as pale as hers, but by choice, not genetics, and the black of his hair came from a bottle, unlike hers. He looked as out-of-place in the valet's uniform—white shirt, maroon vest, black pants—as a lion on a kindergarten playground.

"Umm . . . Capistrano, I think," Kerry replied after a moment's consideration. She was used to this kind of thing from Josh, king of the nonsequitur. *If his middle name isn't Random, it should be.*

"Yeah, that's right," he agreed.

Since it didn't seem like he was going to take the discussion any further, she decided to press the point. "Why?"

He struck a match in the darkness and shielded it with cupped hands to a cigarette held between his lips. "These tourists, man," he said around the butt. Then, blowing out a plume of smoke—away from Kerry, because she would have killed him if he hadn't—he continued with an exasperated tone. "They're like those swallows."

"The ones in Capistrano?"

"Yeah, those."

"In what way?" *You had to ask,* she immediately chastised herself, bracing for the answer.

"Some of them seem to come here every summer, like clockwork."

She had noticed the same thing, though without the bird metaphor. "Good for business, I guess," she pointed out.

"I guess. But this one guy—you know the kind, enormous gut, Texas accent, gold watch that cost more than everything I've owned in my life put together—yelled at me just now because I didn't turn on the heat in his Mercedes."

"The heat?" Kerry asked with surprise. It was a fairly cool night. They all were here, close to the water, and balmy eves, she had learned, were not so much a southern California thing. Once the sun went down, the day's heat fled fast. But even so, far from wintry cold.

"That's what I said. Only it was more like, 'Dude, are you

freaking crazy? It's August!' And he was like, 'I told you last year, if it's after dark, I like the heat on when you bring the car around. It takes time to warm up.'"

"But you didn't work here last year," Kerry pointed out.

Josh jabbed the glowing end of his cigarette at her to emphasize his point. "Exactly," he said. "But you think reality matters to this guy? Like I'm the first Goth valet in California history or something, so it couldn't have been someone else he told last year. He's so convinced it was me, he stiffed me on the tip."

Kerry pushed aside the hand that held the cigarette. She had made clear, plenty of times, what she thought of that habit and couldn't understand how he managed to reconcile it with his vegan lifestyle. "Hey," he had said when she'd raised the question once, "who said life was free of contradiction? Anyway, it's a vegetable. If tobacco had a face, I wouldn't smoke it." Sympathetically, in spite of the noxious weed, she rubbed Josh's bony shoulder. "There are always a few pains," she said. "But most of the guests are pretty nice."

"Maybe to you," Josh countered. "You can spit in their food. All I can do is adjust their seat backs wrong, and the potential threat level just isn't the same."

Kerry laughed then and punched the shoulder she had just been rubbing. "I'll tell you what," she offered. "I'll trade places with you for a day. You deal with complaints about food being too hot or too cold or too spicy or too bland, and guys grabbing your ass and winking at you like you're going to go, 'Oh, you're just so handsome. I'll put this tray of food down and meet you in the alley.'"

"I guess it depends on the guy," Josh suggested with a smile she could see in the glow of his cigarette embers as he inhaled. "Hey, my principles are nothing if not situational. And believe me, I'm not under any illusions that you have an easy job either."

"Summer jobs aren't supposed to be easy," Kerry replied, ignoring his jokes. "They're supposed to be brutal and demeaning and ill-paying. Toughens you up for the rest of your life."

Josh nodded. "I guess you're right." He flipped his smoke to the sidewalk and crushed it out with his shoe. "So, you ready to jet? Waiting on Mace?"

"Waiting on Mace," Kerry confirmed. It had become a house motto over the summer. Mace Winston was never ready on time for anything—he was the only person she had ever known who was perpetually late *leaving* work. She was more than ready to go—her headache from that morning had never really gone away, and working in the noise of the crowded dining room had just made it worse.

Before Josh could reply, Mace came through the kitchen door. He was a dishwasher, and the hairs on his muscular forearms were plastered to his skin by the water that had leaked into his rubber gloves. Even the sleeves of his T-shirt were wet. His broad, handsome face was flushed from the hot water he'd been working in, a line of sweat sitting on his upper lip.

He tossed Kerry a lopsided grin, as if something hurt

in a place too embarrassing to mention. "You've got to start encouraging those folks to eat less," he told her. "Fewer side dishes. Better for their hearts, and better for me."

"I'll see what I can do," she said with a laugh. Neither of these guys were people she'd have been likely to hang out with under other circumstances, but over the course of the summer, they'd become close friends. Whenever she was talking with them, Kerry felt an easy, pleasant sense of comfort envelop her like a warm blanket on a cold night. It almost—but not quite—overwhelmed the sense of impending disaster her dreams had left her with and the headache that accompanied them. "Now can we go home?"

The others offered consent, as if either of them would be likely to argue in favor of staying and working awhile longer. Kerry took one last glimpse toward the water she couldn't see, breathed in a final lungful of ocean air, and headed for the parking lot with the others.

The Seaside Resort at La Jolla, to use its full name, was as soulless and impersonal as most large corporations. But it was also a corporation that recognized the fact that its business was largely seasonal, and to help it through the busy summer season, it hired a lot of temporary workers. Summer help came from all over the world—Prague, Sydney, Heidelberg, Minsk, and even the exotic climes of King of Prussia, Pennsylvania. So the resort offered, as one of its worker-friendly perks, a roommate-matching service. Kerry had signed up, filling out the requisite forms and answering a slew of questions about things she wouldn't even have talked about with the aunt and uncle she lived with. She was slotted into a house in nearby Bird Rock with five people with whom she had in common only the fact that they all worked for Seaside.

After a few weeks of initial discomfort, though, everyone fell into a kind of casual routine. Kerry, Josh, and Mace shared the house with Scott Banner and Brandy Pearson, who had come out from Harvard as a couple, and Rebecca Levine. The couple didn't get to share a room since there were only two bedrooms in the small cottage, and nobody was willing to cram four into one room so that two could have the other. But Brandy and Scott still managed plenty of alone time in the house, and they'd both had tonight off. They had said they were going to a movie, and as Mace pulled his massive baby blue Lincoln Continental onto the narrow driveway, Kerry noticed that Scott's RAV4 was still gone.

"Guess the lovebirds are still out on the town," Josh pointed out, echoing Kerry's observation.

"Too bad for them," Mace said, without a hint of sympathy. The driveway ran alongside the house, crowded on one side by the neighboring house's oleander bushes and on the other by the cottage itself. There was room for both cars if the RAV4 got tucked in first, but when Mace's monstrosity had pulled in as far as it could, the RAV4's rear end wouldn't clear the sidewalk. Which meant he had to park on the street. Mace had urged him just to block the sidewalk a little, but Scott was full of Harvard-induced social activism and refused to in case someone came by in a wheelchair. Kerry admired the stand he took, but couldn't have said for sure if she would be as noble if she had to be the one looking for street parking late at night.

The cottage was dark, as if Brandy and Scott had left during the day and had forgotten that no one would be home until after eleven. Rebecca had been working early shifts, and was no doubt already sound asleep—the girl could sleep anywhere, through anything, Kerry had decided.

The nearest streetlight was half a block away, largely obstructed by a big willow tree that overhung most of the miniscule front yard. A low hedge ringed the front of the house, bisected by a flagstone walkway that led from the sidewalk to the front steps. Their landlord paid for landscaping. If it'd been left up to the six of them, Kerry was sure everything would have died by July.

"Somebody could've left a light on," Josh complained, fumbling in his pocket for keys. "I can't even see the front door."

"Like they're gonna think of that," Mace replied quickly. "Probably too heavy into lip-lock mode when they walked out. And Sleeping Beauty was most likely out before the sun went down."

Having no flashlight handy, Kerry, who was not yet out of the Lincoln, hung back to hold the door open in case its dome light could cast a little illumination to help Josh. With considerable and fluent cursing, Josh managed to jam his key into the lock and got the door open. Inside, he flipped switches, and light blasted out from the coach lamp by the door, the windows, and the gaping doorway.

Light that etched, among other things, a pair of legs sticking out of the hedge. Male legs, it looked like, clad in dark pants, feet in what Kerry guessed were expensive leather ankle-high boots. She realized that a far more appropriate response to noticing the legs would have been to scream rather than, well, *noticing* them.

But the scream, practiced so often recently in dreams, wouldn't come. It caught in her throat like a chicken bone. Instead she barely rasped out Mace's name, since his back was still visible in the doorway.

"*Mace . . .*"

He turned, gave her a questioning look.

"Mace," she said again, a little more forcefully.

"What's up, Kerry?"

She pointed toward the hedge. Taking a step closer, she could see that the man, whoever he was, had crashed through the brush and was lying mostly covered by its greenery. "Umm . . . he doesn't belong there."

Finally Mace noticed him. "Oh, Jesus, Kerry. Get inside, I'll call the cops."

"I don't know if he needs cops," Kerry said, inching closer. "An ambulance, maybe."

"He's just some drunk, Kerry," Mace argued. "Fell down there and couldn't wake up."

But Kerry didn't think so. She'd been around enough drunks—held the hair away from friends' faces when they got sick, dodged clumsily groping hands at parties, even tucked her own uncle Marsh into bed a time or two or ten—to know the stink that wafted around them like a foul cloud. The closer she got to this man, though, the more she knew the smell was all wrong. Instead of the miasma of alcohol, there was a familiar metallic tang. The man in the hedge was very still and silent, and she moved closer still, as Mace watched, frozen, from the doorway.

The smell was blood, and it was thick in the air around the man.

Crap, she thought. *He's been stabbed. Or shot.*

She knew there was no way he hurt himself that much falling through the hedge. He'd have been scratched up—*could even have put out an eye on a branch*—but he wouldn't have opened enough veins to kick up a stench like a blood bank on two-for-one day. Kerry had nursemaided her mom for years while cancer had spread throughout her body, finally taking the older woman. Kerry was no trained doctor, but she'd learned a little something about emergency medical care during the ordeal, and she had a feeling that this guy was going to need everything she could offer and then some.

Another smell, underlying the one of blood, nagged at her, and Kerry suddenly realized that it was a faint electrical stink of ozone, as if lightning had struck close by.

"I don't think he needs the police," she repeated, leaning

forward to find the man's wrist in hopes of checking his pulse. By now, she noticed, Josh's lean form had appeared in the doorway, silhouetted behind Mace. "At least not first thing. He needs a paramedic."

The hand she had been groping for clamped around her forearm with surprising strength. "No," the man said, his voice an anxious rasp almost indistinguishable from the rustling sound his motion made in the hedge. "No doctors."

Her heart jumped to her throat, and she tried to yank her arm free. But the man held fast to it, even raising his head a little to look at her. A stray beam from the streetlight shone through the leaves onto his right eye, making it gleam like something from a Poe story. "Promise me, no doctors," he insisted. "Take me in and give me shelter or leave me here, but let me live or die on my own terms."

Mace and Josh had both come down from the doorway and hovered over Kerry and the wounded man like anxious seagulls at the beach, looking for handouts. "Dude, let her go," Mace ordered, snarling. "Or I'll really put a hurtin' on you."

She heard Mace shift as if he really did intend to attack the wounded man, and then she did something that surprised even her. She spread her one free arm—the man on the ground continued to clutch her right arm with a grip so powerful she didn't think she could have shaken it—over the man, as if to protect him from whatever Mace might have in mind. "No!" she shouted. "He's hurt bad enough. Leave him alone or help me bring him inside, but don't be stupid."

"I've got to wonder about your definition of stupid," Mace said, sounding petulant.

"He's right, Kerr," Josh added. "You want to bring some bloody stranger into our house?"

"You guys both missed Sunday school the day they talked about the good Samaritan?" Kerry shot back over her shoulder. "If you don't want to help me, just get out of the way. He's losing blood and he can't stay out here overnight." She pushed her way deeper into the thick hedge, feeling the branches scratch and tear at her skin like a hundred cats' claws, snagging her long, fine black hair and the fabric of the white cotton dress shirt that, with snug black pants, was her restaurant uniform.

She reached around the stranger's head with her left hand, hoping she could ease him up out of the hedge. Holding back the worst of the branches with her own body so he wouldn't suffer any further injury, she found the back of his head and slipped her hand down to support his neck. His hair was long in back, and matted with sticky blood. Never mind the tears, the bloodstains would make her uniform shirt unwearable.

"That's crazy talk," Mace complained behind her. She ignored him and drew the man slowly forward.

Josh unleashed another string of colorful profanities, but he knelt beside Kerry and shoved branches out of the way, helping to bring the wounded man out of the hedge. "I guess we need to get the mug out of our bushes anyway."

"You're both crazy, then," Mace opined. Kerry couldn't see Mace, but from the sound of it, she gathered that he had given up on them both and was on his way back inside. She found herself hoping that it wasn't to get a baseball bat or to call 911.

What do I care? she wondered. The good Samaritan thing had been a flip response to Mace and Josh's moaning, but it wasn't any kind of lifestyle choice she had made. She guessed that, as Josh might say, it meant the reaction she was having in this case was situational. Something about this battered, broken man in their bushes played on her sympathy, and she was unwilling to leave him there or to go against his stated wishes by calling the authorities.

With Josh's assistance she was able to disentangle the man from the hedge. In the light, the blood on his face was shocking—dark and glistening and obviously fresh. He might have been handsome once, but age and the damage caused by whatever had done this to him had taken care of that. She felt, more than ever, an urgency about getting him inside, getting his bleeding stopped, and trying to prevent shock.

"Can you stand up?" she asked him, not sure if he was even still conscious. But he forced his eyes open again, raised his head, and looked at her with something like kindness. His mouth curled into an agonized smile.

"Not a chance," he whispered. Then his head drooped, his eyes closed, his muscles went limp. For the first time, his grip on her forearm eased. She touched his neck, felt the pulse there.

"He's still alive," she declared.

"But he's deadweight," Josh said. Josh was, well . . . "lean" was a polite way to put it. "Scrawny" was more the truth. And the stranger was a big man, probably a little more than six feet tall, weighing a couple hundred pounds. "You think we can carry him?"

Kerry spoke without hesitation, without doubt. "We can carry him. You take his feet."

"Oh, I almost forgot," Josh said. He used the name that the housemates had applied to Kerry ever since they'd become familiar with her stubborn streak, "Bulldog."

Hoisting the stranger's shoulders, she grinned at Josh way down at the other end. "Woof."

Kerry Profitt's diary, August 11–12

Just for fun I looked back to see my first impressions of my housemates. Thinking to compare them, I guess, to current impressions.

Just goes to show how wrong you can be sometimes.

"Can you say insufferable?" I had typed about Josh Quinn. "Gay, Goth, vegan, and obnoxiously adamant about all three. If he keeps it up, I'll be surprised if he survives the summer. Not that he could be 'voted out' or whatever. Not that, to push the metaphor to the breaking point and beyond, this is a reality TV show or anything. *The Real World*, *Big Brother*, *Survivor*—they have nothing on the trials and tribs of six genuine strangers trying to get along in a house without cameras, supercool furniture, and a cash prize on the other end."

There was more, but why cut-and-paste all night when

I can simply scan the folder menu and look it up? Suffice to say, his first impression was the kind that almost makes you hope it'll also be a last impression.

Mace Winston, on the other hand. Then, I wrote: "Hmm . . . he's got a body like Michelangelo's David—not that I've seen under the fig leaf, figuratively speaking. But handsome, buff, and he tooled up in this sky blue Lincoln Continental—except for the left rear, I think he said quarter-panel, which is kind of rust colored and clearly taken from a different car. He said he found the whole thing in a desert canyon somewhere in New Mexico, full of bullet holes and snakes, but he cleaned it up and fixed it up and here he is. He really does wear the boots and one of those straw hats and he has squinty, twinkly eyes like some movie cowboy and somehow it all works for him. I don't know if there's a brain in his head. Ask me later if I care."

But tonight, when the chips, as they say, were down, Mace turned away and Josh came through. Although the heaving and ho-ing would have gone better had it been the other way around, I'm sure.

Okay.

Ms. Harrington, in eleventh-grade speech, used to give us holy hell when we started with "okay" or "umm." She said it was just a verbal time waster, a way of saying that our thoughts obviously weren't well enough organized to begin with because if they were, we'd start out by saying what we really wanted to say.

Boy, was she right.

So . . . okay. Umm . . .

There's a man in our living room, passed out on that butt-sprung lump of fabric and wood that passes for a sofa. We managed to stop most of the bleeding, put bandages on the worst cuts, got a couple of blankets (mine, since no one else would volunteer theirs) over him, elevated his feet higher than his head. Near his head there's a glass of water, in case he wakes up and is thirsty, and he seems to be breathing okay.

He looks like he lost an argument with a wood chipper. I can't even imagine what happened to him. Hit by a truck that hurled him all the way across our lawn? Picked up by a stray tornado and dropped there?

But he said no doctors, and that's exactly how many he's getting. Why? And why did I argue against calling the police? Rebecca woke up just before Scott and Brandy finally came home. I had the same argument with them that I'd had with Mace, although Scott came over to my side pretty quickly and Rebecca, bless her huge hippie heart, lit a candle and dug right in to help with the bandaging. With Josh already allied, that made four against two—Mace and Brandy. Brandy did a lot of huffing noises and is now either sound asleep, or pretending to be, as I laptop this. Is that a verb yet? If not, how soon?

Other good verbs: To delay. To procrastinate. To put off.

Okay.

Of course, what I wanted to do with my summer was to lead a life that might, by some reasonable definition, be normal. As opposed to the life I've led for the past, well, lifetime. Summer job, summer friends, maybe a summer boyfriend, even. Just, y'know, normal stuff.

I don't think this qualifies.

And to be fair, they're entirely correct (and "they" know who they are). We don't know who he is—he could be dangerous, a felon, a crazy person. Or even, you know, someone from Katy Perry's band, although maybe a little senior for that. But, to continue being fair, he's not the one who said "no cops." That was, not to put too fine a point on it, me. He just said "no doctors," and maybe he's a Christian Scientist or whatever. I was the one who said "no cops," and I'm still not sure why I did that. But it was the right thing to do.

I hope.

Journaling is supposed to help one figure out one's own emotions, right? Tap into the unconscious, puzzle out the mysteries therein? Not tonight, Dr. Freud. I don't know why I trust the old road-kill guy snoozing on the couch. But I do.

Go figure. Go to sleep. Go to hell. Just go. See you tomorrow, if we're not all murdered in our sleep. Or lack thereof.

More later, I hope.

K.

JEFF MARIOTTE has written more than forty-five novels, including the original supernatural thrillers *Cold Black Hearts*, *River Runs Red*, and *Missing White Girl*; the horror epic *The Slab*; and books set in the universes of *Buffy the Vampire Slayer*, *Angel*, *CSI*, *Supernatural*, *Dark Sun*, and others. Two of his novels have won the Scribe Award for Best Original Novel, presented by the International Association of Media Tie-In Writers. His nonfiction work includes the true crime book *Criminal Minds: Sociopaths, Serial Killers, and Other Deviants*, as well as official series companions to *Buffy the Vampire Slayer* and *Angel*. He is also the author of many comic books, including the original Western/horror series Desperadoes, some of which have been nominated for Stoker and International Horror Guild awards. Other comics work includes the horror series Fade to Black, the action-adventure series Garrison, the best-selling *Presidential Material: Barack Obama*, and the original graphic novel *Zombie Cop*. He is a member of the International Thriller Writers, the Western Writers of America, and the International Association of Media Tie-In Writers. With his wife, Maryelizabeth Hart, and partner, Terry Gilman, he co-owns Mysterious Galaxy, a bookstore specializing in science fiction, fantasy, mystery, and horror. He lives on the Flying M Ranch in the American southwest with his family and pets in a home filled with books, music, toys, and other examples of American pop culture. More information than you would ever want to know about him is at www.jeffmariotte.com.

Bury Yourself in These Eerily Good Reads

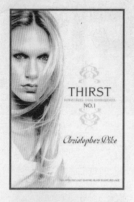

SimonTEEN

Simon & Schuster's **Simon Teen**
e-newsletter delivers current updates on
the hottest titles, exciting sweepstakes, and
exclusive content from your favorite authors.

Visit **TEEN.SimonandSchuster.com** to
sign up, post your thoughts, and find out what
every avid reader is talking about!

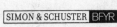